NMC/EXP

THE COLD MILLIONS

'A great tapestry of busyness . . . Walter's descriptive
passages are marvellous'
Sunday Telegraph

'A layered, multi-character panoramic'
Vogue

'It's often said that a novel contains the world; Walter brings new
meaning to this phrase . . . Warm and deeply humane, this transporting
novel is a staggering achievement from a landmark writer'
Esquire

'Colourful and punchy'
The Times

'Expansive, beguiling . . . A thrilling yarn that simultaneously
underscores the cost of progress and celebrates the American spirit'
O, The Oprah Magazine

'It's a tremendous work; a vivid, propulsive, historical novel
with a politically explosive backdrop that reverberates through our own'
USA Today

'Superb . . . a splendid postmodern rendition of the social realist
novels of the 1930s by Henry Roth, John Steinbeck and
John Dos Passos, updated with strong female characters and executed
with pristine prose. This could well be Walter's best work yet'
Publishers Weekly, starred review

'A timely and poetic read that vividly depicts the American
melting pot at its most unequal and volatile . . . a compelling portrait
of America at the dawn of th

D1514366

'Jess Walter is a superb storyteller. As polished and hard as
a diamond, *The Cold Millions* reminds us of America's tempestuous
past and suggests that all this is anything but past'
Boston Globe

'This latest tour de force is testimony to Walter's protean storytelling
power and astounding ability to set a scene, any scene'
Kirkus Reviews

'Walter marshals a motley, fascinating cast of characters
so finely drawn that they lift from the page. I haven't
encountered a more satisfying and moving novel about
the struggle for workers' rights in America'
San Francisco Chronicle

ABOUT THE AUTHOR

Jess Walter is the author of six other novels, including the number-one
New York Times bestseller *Beautiful Ruins*, *The Financial Lives of Poets*,
The Zero and the short-story collection *We Live in Water*. He lives in
Spokane, Washington, with his family.

THE COLD MILLIONS

A NOVEL

JESS WALTER

PENGUIN BOOKS

PENGUIN BOOKS

UK | USA | Canada | Ireland | Australia
India | New Zealand | South Africa

Penguin Books is part of the Penguin Random House group of companies
whose addresses can be found at global.penguinrandomhouse.com.

First published in the United States of America by Harper Books 2020
First published in Great Britain by Viking 2020
Published in Penguin Books 2022

001

Text copyright © Big Text, Inc., 2020
Map copyright © Springer Cartographics, 2020

The moral right of the author has been asserted

"The Kid" was originally published in a slightly altered form
in *Harper's Magazine* under the title "Plante's Ferry".

This is a work of fiction. Names, characters, places and incidents
are products of the author's imagination or are used fictitiously
and are not to be construed as real. Any resemblance to actual
events, locales, organizations or persons, living or dead,
is entirely coincidental.

Printed and bound in Great Britain by Clays Ltd, Elcograf S.p.A.

The authorized representative in the EEA is Penguin Random House Ireland,
Morrison Chambers, 32 Nassau Street, Dublin D02 YH68

A CIP catalogue record for this book is available from the British Library

ISBN: 978–0–241–98552–6

www.greenpenguin.co.uk

Penguin Random House is committed to a
sustainable future for our business, our readers
and our planet. This book is made from Forest
Stewardship Council® certified paper.

To my father, Bruce, and my brother, Ralph

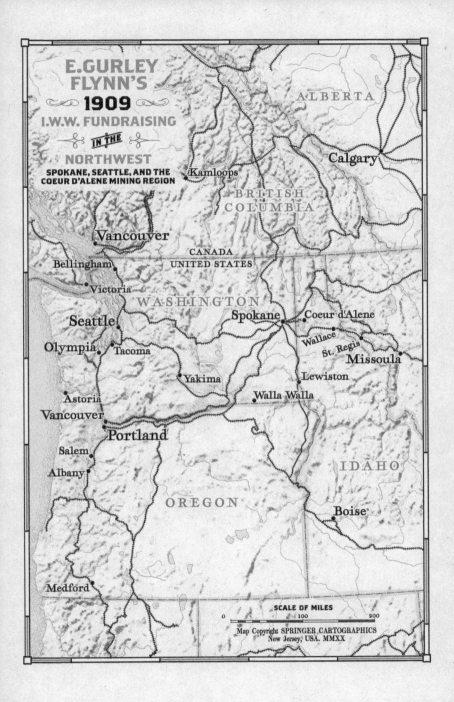

Waterbury, 1909

DARKNESS CAME on that town like a candle being snuffed. This was my wife's primary complaint about Spokane after two years of me copping there, what Rebecca called the "drastic dark" of autumn. We'd come from Sioux City, a town she still called home, and where I'd walked an easier beat. I found Spokane in a land-spec ad, but the piece I bought turned out to be cliff-face basalt and not arable, so we took four rooms in a brick apartment north of the river, and I got on with that roughneck police force. These were hard years, '08 and '09, everything about Spokane hard, bringing to mind Rebecca's word, *drastic*. Steep hills, deep canyons, cold winters, hot summers, and those dark autumn evenings that made her so melancholy, when five felt like midnight.

It was one of those nights Chief Sullivan pulled me aside. A burglar was prowling the big houses on Cannon Hill, and he needed good, sober cops on it. Nothing got up the mayor's ass like someone prying south-side windows, stealing candlesticks from the Victorians on the hill, the mayor quick to remind Sullivan that he was acting police chief and his act was to make the moneyed wives of those mining millionaires feel safe. Sullivan assigned me and two other cops to patrol the lower South Hill and catch this master burglar.

It was vagrant season. "So all's you'll miss is bum harvest," Chief
Sullivan said. Good by me, as I preferred real police work to the endless roust-and-run of tramps anyway.

Sullivan talked up this South Hill window-crawler like he was the
dastardly demon of hell himself. One of the silver barons had threatened to bring in a Pinkerton, and nothing ate at Sullivan like someone
hiring private. There were six detective agencies in Spokane, three
nationals—Pinkerton, Thiel, and Allied—and three local thug shops
used by the mining companies for union busting. The national detectives treated us city cops like horse clods, fine for running bums
and whores but about as helpful solving crime as a blind ranch dog. I
thought this perception not entirely unfair, and had complained more
than once about the laziness and graft of the old brute cops. I'd even
considered putting in papers with the privates myself.

If I stayed a cop, it would be for John Sullivan, for I admired the
man. Sully was honest and affable, off-the-boat County Kerry, six-
four and 220, five of those pounds brush mustache. He'd come on the
force just after the Great Fire of '89, with brutes like Shannon and
Clegg, and to hear them tell it, those three had singlehandedly driven
out the last of the Indians and tamed the whole frontier town.

But unlike those others, Sullivan wasn't only brute. He was brave.
Savvy. In '01 two holdup men set up shop on the north end of Howard
Bridge, like fairy tale ogres, robbing every wagon that crossed. When
Sullivan came to arrest them, one man pulled a pistol and squeezed off
a couple before big John could knock the gun from his hand. As he
was beating the robbers, Sully realized his boot was filling with blood.
The ogre had shot him in the leg, below the groin. He dragged both
outlaws to jail, then rode his horse to the hospital, where he promptly
underwent surgery, met a nurse half his age, and married her.

How could you not want to work for such a man?

Sully could grow nostalgic for the rough old days, but he was also
clear: the old Klondike town had grown into a proper city and the time
was up for a brute like Clegg, who saw his job as hassling tramps and

whores into paying him for protection, and was not above running a girl himself if she came up short. "Nah, it's the last shift for them old boys," Sullivan said when I complained about Clegg taking booze from the evidence room.

He made a point of promoting cops like Hage and Roff and me, for our brains and our rectitude, I guess, but also because we didn't care ·if Bill Shannon could throw a keg through a window, or that Hub Clegg once rode a patrol horse through a burning tavern to rescue a favored sporting girl.

That's why he put us three on the Cannon Hill burglar. But three men was a big commitment during vagrant season, with the east end full of floaters and union men coming from all over to agitate the Stevens Street job agencies. I was not unsympathetic to their cause, for there was no denying the corruption of those employment agents, who charged the poorest men a dollar for suspect job leads. But the IWW protested by filling the town with stinking foreign rabble, and this brought out the tavern girls, opium and faro boys, mystics, seers, and pickpockets, a cloud of vice that swarmed the tenderloin like mayflies over a putrid stream.

"Take this window thief down fast, boys," Sullivan told us, "for we'll need your batons the other side of it."

And so, Hage and Roff and I ventured out into that cold dark evening. We took an empty trolley up the South Hill, got off at the first stop. We were in plainclothes and overcoats, with fur hats for warmth and so my bald head wouldn't reflect the streetlights. The plan was for Hage to amble the alleys while I walked the street in front and Roff the street behind. We'd square each block this way, work our way up the hill starting at Seventh. There was a low ceiling of chimney smoke, and the streetlights cast shadows long and eerie. As I walked, I peered past split curtains into grand houses that burned gold with wood fire and candlelight, and I missed my own home fire, Rebecca and the kids, the night so cold and quiet I doubted our thief could be afoot.

After Seventh, Hage and I met on Adams, at the alley entrance, where Roff had stopped to piss on the knuckled root of a maple.

"I don't like it," Hage said.

"Roff pissing on trees?"

"I don't like that, either, but I mean walking up this hill hoping to bump into some ace burglar on the job."

"Well, we won't find him rousting bums downtown with Clegg."

"We will if he's a bum."

"Fancy work for a bum."

"I suppose so."

Roff had finished pissing. We turned the next block and split up again at Ninth, where I was admiring the pillared porches of the big houses and paused to light my pipe. I wondered then if Rebecca's feelings about Spokane might change if I could ever get us off poverty flats and into one of these grand houses on the hillside.

Wasn't likely on a cop's salary; Chief Sullivan himself lived in the flats. Anyway, I didn't think even these grand houses could make my wife happy. Not anymore. Not here. What was it about these steep, western, water-locked cities—Seattle, Spokane, San Francisco? All three I'd visited, and in all three, the money flowed straight uphill. It made me think of something I'd heard about the Orient, that water drained the opposite way there. Who wanted to live in a place where water spun backward or money flowed uphill? These towns that had no business being towns, straddling islands and bays and cliffs and canyons and waterfalls.

I fell deeper into this somber mood and was thinking Rebecca's word, *drastic*, when Roff stepped from the shadows.

"You got something?" I asked. "Or—"

I couldn't say what came next: the crack, me yelling, "Stop," or the flash, or realizing this wasn't Roff. As to what came last, I have no doubts, for I doubled over and held my flaming, open guts. There was another order that made sense (*not Roff, "Stop," flash, crack, doubled over, flaming guts*), but I couldn't place it—

The man who was not Roff was running away, his long black coat flapping, his shoes clicking on cobblestone, and I thought of Sullivan taking a gunshot to the leg and still bringing in his man, and I managed to get my revolver and squeeze four off, but I fired wildly and the man ducked between two houses down the block.

I was folded in half, pitched forward on my knees in gravel, my guts a sinkhole, and I cried out, to my shame—

Hage was first to me, saying my name over and over, "Alfred, Alfred, Alfred."

"He shot me!" What grave disappointment, my lack of imagination. When I think of all the things a man could say. Shakespeare or Greek or even the Bible. Proper last words. But all I could manage was "He shot me."

"I know, Alfred," Hage said. "I'm sorry."

Hage reached into my coat, around to my back. "Roff!" he yelled. I could hear in his voice that there was no exit hole. The bullet was inside. They would have to go for it.

I'd heard from the old cops that a mortal wound did not hurt as much, but this, like everything about the brutes, every word out of their fat mouths, was a fairy tale, a justification, a pernicious lie.

"Roff!" Hage yelled. "Waterbury's shot!"

"How could they know?" I said.

"What?"

"How could they know what a mortal wound feels like?" Even to my ear the words were garbled, like I was talking underwater. My thoughts, too, leaked out: A gut shot could take hours, days, but the result was the same: agony and—

Other thoughts crowded: Had I eaten dinner? Was that to be my last meal? Who would tell Rebecca? Would she mend this shirt? Maybe she could sell my clothes and make a little money. I reached down to feel if the bullet had gone through my coat.

"Coat's fine," I said, but my voice sounded far off.

"Roff!" Hage yelled again. "He shot Alfred!"

"Lay me down," I said, and Hage helped me onto my side.

"Roff!" Hage yelled again.

"Rebecca," I said, but it was bubbles in water. I wanted to make sure that she knew—what? I could not think. "Rebecca," I said again, clearer this time. And even if I had memorized all of Shakespeare and the Bible, I suppose this is what I would have wanted to say at the end, *Rebecca* on my lips, *Rebecca*, *Rebecca*, over and over, into the dark.

PART I

. . . we love most what we must have but can never have;
and so on we go, west and then west.

—Brian Doyle, *The Plover*

1

They woke on a ball field—bums, tramps, hobos, stiffs. Two dozen of them spread out on bedrolls and blankets in a narrow floodplain just below the skid, past taverns, tanners, and tents, shotgun shacks hung like hounds' tongues over the Spokane River. Seasonal work over, they floated in from mines and farms and log camps, filled every flop and boardinghouse, slept in parks and alleys and the pavilions of traveling preachers and, on the night just past, this abandoned ball field, its infield littered with itinerants, vagrants, floaters, Americans.

The sun was just beginning to edge the mountains when Rye Dolan sat up, halfway down the first-base line. He looked across a field of sleeping humps, his older brother, Gig, beside him, curled a few feet from the pitcher's mound.

Rye turned back to watch the sunrise over the Selkirks—a smoky red gash where someone had set a fire to get a job fighting it. Last year, Rye might have paid to get a shovel on that blaze, but Gig had gone and joined the IWW, the union fighting the corrupt employment agents who charged a buck for job leads.

Left untended, that same dollar could bring his older brother plenty of trouble. Like last night.

Pay in pocket, Gig Dolan liked to bounce from Dutch Jake's to Jimmy Durkin's until the money ran out. And while caring for Rye the past year had half tamed him, they were coming off three weeks apart—Rye picking up a late harvest near Rockford, Gig getting on a skid crew at a Springdale log camp. Fired for union agitating, Gig came back to booze it up with his east-end labor pals and hawk daywork at the city's vaudeville theaters, and it was there, among the freaks and jugglers, the variety houses and leg shows, that he happened to meet an actress, name of Ursula—Rye back in Spokane less than an hour before his brother was showing him a newspaper review of her show. "And therein," Gig said.

"I'm at the Comique Theater last week hauling lumber for the carpenter when this red-haired vision emerges from her dressing room and says, 'Well, who are you?' and I say, 'Why, the hero, of course,' and she says, 'Then you must get the damsel,' and I say, 'Every night. Twice on Saturdays.' And she says, 'I'll bet that second performance really suffers.' And I smile back and say, 'Oh, I don't know. Goes on longer, but what's lost in zeal gets made up in familiarity.'"

She went by the name Ursula the Great, the *Spokesman-Review* referring to her as "a spectacle of indecency" and "the last of four acts of increasing depravity." Gig talked Rye into using their sock money on a shared public bath—older brother taking the suitor's hot, Rye settling for warm flotsam—and they got haircuts and nickel shaves, though a scrape was hardly needed on Rye's baby face, and instead of boiling clothes over a cook fire, they paid for proper clean-and-folds in the Chinese Quarter. All gentlemanned up, they got fifty-cent seats at the Comique and settled in for some mild depravity—blind accordion player, Bavarian juggler, wrestling match between armless and legless men (always bet legs)—until the curtain split for the finale, depravity number four, and the smoky stage lights revealed the source of Gig's infatuation, Rye wondering what pinch-hearted critic came up with a word like *depraved* upon first glimpsing the flame-haired beauty who strode into the lights in front of a big iron cage—

For inside was a full-grown cougar! Pacing and snarling while the band played a hurdy-gurdy and the big cat stalked and Ursula danced around it singing a few numbers and slow-stripping to nothing but corset and stockings, kicking those long legs higher and higher, leaning her backside against the cage until all went black and the spotlight came up and the whole theater held its breath as Ursula unlatched the cage door and the big cat lowered its head, hissed, and spat—and brave Ursula ambled in as if going to her pantry for butter, closed the cage door behind her, and serenaded the beast, holding an ungodly high note as she ripped off the corset, and oh! the flash of flesh, of narrow waist and pale back, and the fury of that mountain lion as it made to pounce at her bare breasts—which Rye could only imagine, as she was facing away—and that was when Ursula tossed the corset at the cat, who tore into it in lieu of her fair skin, and drowned out by cheers and whistles, she took a silk robe from the back of the cage, slipped it on, tied the belt, and, still singing over the roar of cat and crowd, Ursula the Great walked out of that cage in one lovely piece.

Rye had to agree: This Ursula was the real thing. Made the blind accordion player seem like . . . a blind accordion player. Afterward, Rye ran the aisles for leftover food, but Gig was smitten, and when Gig was smitten, by cause or by woman, there was no sense in him, and he dragged them out of that warm theater and down the alley to the stage door.

A thick doorman was manning that post, and even with the brothers' freshly shaved faces and laundered shirts, he wasn't about to let such worn boots in to see the talent. Gig pleaded, but the doorman explained: Ursula was otherwise engaged, and for two bits he said how, entertaining a gentleman, and for two bits more, who, a wealthy mining man named Lemuel Brand. The Dolans had been sharked by enough of Lem Brand's operations to know it didn't matter how charming and handsome Gig was, a skid-rower like him was no match for a man of means like Brand, so they started back up the alley, Rye saying, "I hope the cougar wins next time," when a call came from the stage door—"Gregory!"—and Ursula, still in the robe, emerged into flickering gaslight. "Gregory," she called again, like she hadn't hit the note the first time, and he ran down the alley to her. Gig listened as Miss Great explained, shoving his hands in his trouser pockets at the bad news, Ursula touching his chest, Gig nodding, turning and leaving her at the stage door, returning to Rye at the end of the alley. She watched him go, hand on heart, Gig refusing her the satisfaction of looking back.

"Well?"

"She swears she won't bed the man," said Gig, "but he owns the theater, so—"

And with no words on the other side of that so, they ventured back onto the street to salve Gig's wounded soul.

Two hundred fifty taverns in Spokane and last night every one of them hummed on high, like a pot before boil, street cops looking for drunks to rake and the tenderloin packed with the end of harvest, the closing of log camps and the coming union action, downtown whipped up like a wind-fed blaze. A week earlier, a union speaker had gotten arrested and word went out in the *Industrial Worker* newspaper for floaters to come for the Spokane Free Speech Fight, bums dropping like apples from boxcars and rail trusses—humps from Chicago, Denver, Seattle: white, black, Indian, Chinese, Cossack, Irish, Italian, Finn—barstools and benches bent with their backs, Rye marveling at the endless babble of Celestial-Russo-Flemy-Serb-Salish-Spanish.

The Dolans ran into a couple of Gig's labor friends coming from the big IWW hall on Front Street—gregarious James Walsh, sent from Chicago to run the Spokane labor action, and an intense Montanan named Frank Little, who Walsh introduced as "part Indian and the rest trouble."

Rye didn't like it when Gig ran with these union types; he thought their revolutionary banter half foolish and half dangerous and was never quite sure which was which. He couldn't keep up with the boozing and sporting and jawing about wage slavery, and all things equal, he preferred the peace of Mrs. Ricci's boardinghouse across the river in Little Italy. A warm soup, a hard cot, an early rise to get first crack at a good job.

But last night, in sympathy with Gig's heartache, Rye let himself get pulled in the wake of the union men, who sneaked Rye into Jimmy Durkin's big beer hall under a sign that read, "IF YOUR CHILDREN NEED

SHOES, DON'T BUY BOOZE." They toasted Rye's hand-me-down boots and told rich stories of sharks and foremen, and soon Rye was nodding, laughing, singing along.

It's quite a thing when the world is upside down to hear someone say it don't have to be—that a man could be paid enough to feed and house himself. Two beers in, Rye felt lifted by a sense of hope.

James Walsh was a musician and mining man who had once rounded up twenty toughs, dressed them in red, and taken them cross-country on cattle cars to shake up the 1906 IWW convention in Chicago, stopping to sing in work camps along the way. He called it the Overalls Brigade and said it was "to remind the dandies in suits and spectacles arguing over amendments and articles that this is about the goddamn rights of goddamn men." That night in a packed Durkin's, he opened the taps on his charm, calling Rye "boyo" and Gig "the esteemed Senator Dolan," buying round after round until Rye was drunk for the first time in his life, arm over shoulder with the labor men, warbling along to Frank Little's IWW songbook:

> Oh, why don't you work like the other men do?
> How in hell can I work when there's no work to do?
> Hallelujah, I'm a bum
> Hallelujah, bum again—

Then the beer ran out, as beer will do, and whiskey, clocks, and nickels, too, and the union men left and it was just Gig and Rye, on a full-blown now, ducking the vagrant patrols and singing their ire in the street, a bitter tune their father taught them—*Here's a memory to all the boys, that are gone, boys—gone!*—too bent for Mrs. Ricci, the boardinghouse widow who did not abide Gig's drinking, and that was when older brother told younger about this overgrown ball field, and the big cook fire on the pitcher's mound, although by the time they staggered down the hill into Peaceful Valley the fire was dying, the diamond dotted with bedrolls. Their own packs back on Mrs. Ricci's porch, Rye and Gig curled on their coats on the dirt infield, not for lack of outfield ambitions but because if you were tempted by that soft center-field grass, you might wake in dew and catch your death—

Catch your death. Now, there was a thought. As he watched the smoke-red sun rise in the sky, Ryan Dolan recalled his mother saying it when he was a boy and used to wander outside without coat and shoes. Well, he'd got to know death pretty well in the interim, was practically on a first-name basis, and from what he could see, it was death generally did the catching.

Rye nudged his brother: "Hey Gig, let's see if that doorman at the Empire will pay us two bits to carry his trash to the river."

Gig sat up and yawned. He patted himself for paper and tobacco, neither of which he had. "You go on, Rye-boy," he said. "I'm going to the hall today."

Here was Rye's chief complaint about Gig's involvement with the Industrial Workers of the World, the one big union that took anyone as a member: Finnish logger, Negro seamstress, Indian ranch hand, even floater like them. What good was a union meant to help them find work if Gig spent so much time there that he couldn't work?

Gregory Dolan was a man of squares—shoulders, jaw, thick brown hair over arch blue eyes. Smart, too, about books, though less about work, which was more Rye's area. Gig had made it to grade eleven, three years beyond any other Dolan, and was his own schooling after that. He always carried a book in his bindle and read as if he expected an exam. Rye could read fine, well enough to make out a pay sheet or a flyer for a brush job, but he never much saw the point in studying economics to hoe a field for sixty cents a day.

The other difference between them had to do with the fairer sex. Rye Dolan was tall enough to fool a job agent, but up close he was boy-faced and pin-shouldered, with ears like the handles of a vase. But even ladies in automobiles cast long glances when Gig strolled the street. And among variety girls, sport ladies, tavern hags, and soiled doves, no vagrant in history got more half-offs and free rolls than his big sweet brother, Rye suspected.

"Just come with me to the Empire," Rye said. "We'll go to the hall after."

"Nah." Gig's smile spread to a yawn. "I think I'll lie here and reflect some more on the nature of man."

"Well, I ain't going without you," said Rye. His whole world was on that ball field: Gig and Rye Dolan, last of the Whitehall Dolans—sister Lace dead at sixteen bringing forth a cold baby in a Butte hospital, brother Danny a pond monkey in an Oregon timber camp until he side-spiked a rain-slick log boom, lost his balance, and drowned in a river of trees. Then there was their father-who-aren't-in-heaven, that cursed old mine muck Dan Senior, so long to the dirt that the brothers could barely conjure his face, though they could recall his sadder songs and every inch of the back of his hand.

Their ma was the last to go, from TB. The only kid still at home, Rye helped her to Mass and picked up enough work for a pasty-and-turnip dinner. He wetted scarves for her to breathe through and whispered a thousand lies to the woman, promised to write her sister in Galway and said Da was waiting in heaven with Lace and Danny, and, oh yeah, Gregory was on his way home with a sweet Catholic girl—so many lies Rye told in that room he was surprised Christ Himself didn't appear to smite his bony back. Ma died feverish, unable to afford a hospital, coughing knots of blood, bruises rising from nothing but the idea of them, joints swollen with tumor, moaning and yelling and praying and wailing, and, alone at fifteen, Rye thought the devil had come into her until the parish priest came to last-rite the poor woman and said, "That's just dying, Ryan." Christ forgive him, Rye felt delivered when she finally stopped gurgling and left her wretched banty body, the undertaker carting her off like rubbish. A day later, Rye pawned his parents' wedding rings and, dirt still wet above his mother's moldering corpse, he became the last Dolan to walk out of Whitehall, Montana—off to find his long-lost brother, Gregory.

And find him Rye did, two weeks later, sacked in a crib this side of Spokane with a hard piece of trouble. He stepped into that room with its dusky-whiskey-smoky smells and said, "Gig, our ma's dead," his big brother staring as if he didn't recognize this long-armed kid. Then Gig made a noise like the air was pressed out of him, and turned and wept into his girl's rashy bosom. This made Rye cry, too, the only tears he shed during the matter, standing in a dank flop watching his big brother sob on this girl's chest. Next day Gig sent the girl back to the house of trouble where he'd found her, and the brothers lit out—

For a year they moved, barely pausing for breath. They walked twenty miles some days, and ran down freight on the slow edges of towns, hopped boxcars and crouched on the blinds between mail cars. Gig showed Rye his favorite way to travel—in the open, on flat cars and lumber racks: "flying," he called it, wind in his face, sun on his arms. They flew and floated this way, job to job, week to week, farm to farm, Washington to Oregon to Idaho, until they landed a gyppo logging crew on the St. Joe River, Gig talking his way onto one end of a two-man misery whip, Rye ladling water and pounding wedges in the kerfs to keep the saws from binding. But they got run from that job, too, replaced by the foreman's nephews. They followed rumors to interior farms and staggered harvests, bushed wheat and picked huckleberries. The Panic of '07 had run the banks, and it was rare to find a boxcar or a barn without a vagrant in it. Most days they'd wait hours in line at the job sharks' only to be told there was nothing for them. They huddled under burlap on boxcars, drank from streams, and ate squirrel meat over jungle cook fires, boiled up their clothes and slept beneath stars, ducked train gangs and rail bulls, and if it wasn't an easy life, Rye would be lying if he didn't admit some adventure in it.

Spokane was base for five thousand floating workers, and the brothers put on their best shirts and queued at some of the thirty employment agencies lining Stevens Street, beneath bunk signs promising work for GOOD MEN! $1! JOBS FOR ALL! INQUIRE WITHIN!

A hard season for men, but lying was having a banner year.

Rye acted older, Gig sober, and they forked a dollar for the pleasure of a twelve-hour workday, knowing full well the shark was likely to split their buck with the straw boss and pull the job after two weeks for another crew (at a dollar-a-man), churning them like water in a paddle wheel, so no man could get a foothold. The Bunker Hill Mine rotated three thousand hungry muckers through fifty jobs that summer—three grand in fees split with the bosses, the sharks bleeding them other ways, too, subtracting two bits for doctoring, for stale bread, for a straw mattress. Then, harvest over, they recast the migrants as worthless bums and had security men knock their heads and drive them from town.

This was the call of the IWW, the Wobblies, whose nickname came from a Chinese rail hump asking for the "Eye-Wobble-Wobble." The whole operation had started in Chicago in 1905, and it landed hard in Spokane, where seven freight and passenger lines converged in the busiest terminal west of Chicago, a kind of Tramp Central Station. A thousand signed up in Spokane for IWW red cards, one of them Gregory Dolan, who dragged Rye downtown to hear Walsh call for nonviolent action, to peaceably gather in the streets to protest the sharks. And if the cops wanted to arrest them for speaking out, fine: they'd pack the jails, clog the courts. The union action cooled that spring of '09, when the floaters went back to work, and Gig and Rye caught on at an apple orchard, made enough to sock-bank twelve bucks each to give to the widow Mrs. Ricci, so they might winter at her house in Little Italy.

It was Gig's favorite place on earth, Spokane, "theater capital of the west," he always said, by which he meant "actress capital," since every brothel and crib girl listed herself in the city directory as "actress." And while Rye didn't share his brother's affection for Spokane's unrulier side, the city had begun to feel like *his* home, too, after Mrs. Ricci rented them her enclosed porch for half what a proper boardinghouse charged, and even offered to sell the brothers the orchard behind her house, where they might build their own place. "Our porch should have posts like that," Rye would say as they walked through a neighborhood, or: "What about a rainwater cistern, Gig?"

Rye could see them settling in Spokane for good—so long as they found regular work and Gig went easy on the booze, so long as they camped outside on warmer and drunker nights, so long as a saw didn't slip, or a hay pile fall, so long as they didn't fall from a train or get killed by company thugs or rail bulls. So long so long so long—so long as Gregory and Ryan Dolan continued to draw breath—that cool fall day in the Year of the Lord nineteen hundred and nine.

Gig was twenty-three and Rye not quite seventeen.

And lying there, Rye had an insight that felt like a reverie, that, man or woman, Catholic or Prod, Chinese, Irish, or African, Finn or Indian, rich or poor or poor or poor, the world is built to eat you alive, but before you go down the gullet, the bastards can't stop you from looking around. And he doubted that any magnate in a San Francisco mansion ever woke to a better view than he and his brother had that morning, staring at a red slash of sky from the crisp dirt infield of a weedy baseball diamond.

"Sorry about Ursula," Rye said.

Gig leaned over, his wide, open face spreading into a grin. He shrugged. "Ah, nothing to do about that," he said, "but play ball."

Rye laughed and was about to make a joke about forming tramp teams and going nine when a commotion rose on the road behind them.

This was no smoke on the horizon, no reverie, but a gang of men descending the hill above the quiet diamond. Around them, stiffs leaped up, packed bindles and pulled on boots, grabbed pans and worn spoons, but there was no time. The mob bled onto the field and, as easily as if they were threshing wheat, began swinging at men's heads.

2

They were off-clock cops and mining agents, security guards and private citizens, coats off, shirtsleeves rolled, boots kicking up dust. They swung billies and bats and the handles of axes, hoes, and shovels. They were on their third hobo nest of the morning, having given up all pretense of finding the murdered cop Waterbury's killer.

Gig and Rye were up and running toward left field when they passed a boy wiggling into his boots, and Rye recalled the boy's name—Diego—and that he'd been turned down by the job agents after his left foot got mangled in a baler. Just as Rye remembered that, Diego took a rake handle to the back.

"Goddamn tramps!" someone yelled, and "Move on, bums!" They'd been rousted and run from jungles before, but this felt different to Rye. These men wanted to bury them.

The brothers jumped the low left-field fence and skidded down an embankment toward the river, the more zealous of the stick-wielders following. A row of two-post houses lined the river road, and from a wood-piled porch, a woman in a yellow dress sipped from a tin coffee cup and watched the chase like it was a play at the Pantages.

Only then did Rye see that two other tramps were running with them. One was his friend Jules, an old Spokane and Palus Indian he'd met at Billy Sunday's tent revival. Jules had been on his crew in Rockford, and was a tireless worker despite being sixty, a former cowhand with a bent back and weathered face, black hair like spilt oil. He was a tireless talker, too, a cook-fire storyteller who switched midtale from English to French, and whose booming laugh was, he said, "the only Salish I still speak."

Rye didn't know the other man running with them. He was thin and pale, in a worn coat and a hat that retained little of its original form. His mustache was graying, but otherwise the man's age was a complete mystery: he could be thirty as easily as he could be fifty.

The four of them scrabbled to a ledge just over the rushing river, but here they ran out of path and had to turn back—four tramps faced up with six armed men on a narrow slab of dirt.

The mob leader stepped forward: "Looks like you're at a cross-roads." He was tall and thick, with slate hair like a fresh-tarred road. Rye figured him for an off-clock cop and imagined his police mack on a doorknob back at one of those Spokane clapboards, bread cook-ing, wife tending babies while he went to take tramps' teeth.

Gig stepped forward, too—he and the cop out like chess pieces. "What's this about?" Gig asked in his citizen voice.

Rye had seen Gig do this before with the police: play it casual, like he'd sat up suddenly in a barber chair. Once they were camped in a rail yard when two cops came through to clear the line for Taft's traveling train. Gig started in over whether Taft had the votes to pass the Payne-Aldrich Tariff Act, and by the time the train car rumbled past, draped in bunting and flags, Gig had one of the cops believing William Jennings Bryan would've made a better president.

But this one wanted no part of Gig's charm: "You anarchist Wobs ain't welcome here," he said.

"Well, then it's your lucky day," Gig said, "for there are no anar-chists here. And while I am a member of the Industrial Workers of the World, I don't believe that to be against the law."

"It is to me," the slate-haired man said. He smacked his hand with his baton. "So what do you stinking bums want first? A beating or a bath?"

Rye made eye contact with Jules, and they both looked over their shoulder. The river, then? But the Spokane was no bath, no gentle dip or quaint Montana fish stream. This was a Pacific-bound rager, a drowner, a freezer, a cold, rocky white-water deluge draining the whole of the Coeur d'Alenes from the big lake to the massive Co-lumbia.

Gig was still playing lawyer. "Why don't you tell us first what law we've broke."

"The anti-agitating law," Slate Hair said. "No more than three men can gather for public speaking or organizing."

"And what were we organizing?" Gig asked. "A union of sleepy ballplayers?"

Even the civilians grinned at this, and Jules gave one of his big-throated laughs. Their fourth, the thin man in the worn suit, stayed quiet, hands in his pockets, head forward, Sunday slant to his hat.

"A policeman got shot two nights ago," said Slate Hair.

This quieted even Gig, who cleared his throat. "You don't think one of us had something to do with that."

"No," Slate Hair admitted. "I don't. But if it gives me reason to roust a hobo camp, I'll take it." He took another step forward with his nightstick.

That was when the fourth man did the strangest thing. Without a word, he walked to the other side like he'd just remembered an appointment. Maybe it was his thin, hunched shoulders or his sad-sack face, but the civilians didn't seem concerned in the least when he strolled up, calm as a man approaching a bank window, toward a young man to the right of Old Slate Hair, standing with his own smaller blackjack, a junior version of the mob leader's club.

The thin tramp was relaxed, smiling, leaning forward, hands in his trouser pockets, so the civilian didn't even flinch when he reached out and yanked the man's club away—like a parent taking a stick from a child. He must have planned the move while Gig talked, because he didn't hit the smaller man; instead, he stepped once to his left and swung the club matter-of-factly at the pumpkin head of Slate Hair, as if he were still at that bank window—*I would like to deposit . . . your skull.*

The blow caught the big man with a sideways stroke across his thick jowl, Slate Hair's jaw cracking like dry sticks under boots, Rye nearly retching at the sound, almost sorry for the big man. Men on both sides took a step back, as natural as a shotgun's recoil, Slate Hair staggering, the thin man swinging again.

And down went Slate Hair.

One of the civilians ran at the thin man, but Gig caught him square in the chest with a thick shoulder and the man went sprawling onto the dirt, scrambled to his feet, turned, and ran. Seeing one man flee was contagious, and the other four ran up the hill for help as Slate Hair scratched at the ground for his teeth.

Gig, Rye, and the other two turned and ran the opposite direction down the trail, and were a quarter mile away before Gig paused to ask the thin man his name.

"Early Reston," he said.

"Well, Early Reston, I'm Gregory Dolan, and while I appreciate what you did back there, as long as you're traveling with us, I'd ask that you abide the IWW's code of nonviolence."

"Nonviolence?" Reston stopped and gave a winking half-smile. "When a mob intends to throw you in a river?"

"Especially then," Gig said.

Reston laughed—a rusty sound like an old gate swinging open. "Good God," he said, and tossed the club he'd been carrying. "I've fallen in with idealists."

3

"You think a tramp killed that policeman?" Rye asked as they circled back along the river trail toward town. They were moving quickly, in case the mob re-formed—single file, Gig in front, then Early, Rye, and Jules.

"Not a chance," Gig said.

Early Reston agreed: "If a bum did it, they wouldn't wait a day to raid the camp."

Jules said, "And they'd come with more than sticks."

"Then what's it mean," Rye said, "them rousting us like that?"

"Means the bosses know we plan to shake off the yoke of slavery," said Gig in his jawsmithing voice. "To wit, they aim to lay us low before Monday."

Early laughed. "To *what* now?"

Gig said Monday was the IWW's Free Speech Day. And that the police were hoping to intimidate them into not doing it. "You should stick around," he told Early.

"And give those cops another shot? I don't think so."

"Well, that might be for the best anyway," Gig said, "if you can't refrain from that kind of thing back there."

"Oh, I can refrain from having men throw me in a river."

Gig smiled. "I meant your reaction."

"I know what you meant." Early covered his eyes against the sun. "So, Gregory Dolan, are you a big man for these Wobblies?"

"Nah." Gig seemed both embarrassed and pleased at being taken for a union leader. He was on the free speech committee, he said, but was not an elected officer. "I simply share the belief that since all wealth comes from labor, labor ought to share in the wealth it produces and not merely be its fuel—"

Early Reston grinned. "And do you have opinions that John Locke didn't write first?"

"Maybe." Gig stopped and could barely contain his own smile. "Tell me, what kind of student of bum economics are you?"

So Early Reston told his whole story: he grew up in Shelbyville, Illinois, studied mining engineering at Purdue College, and went to work on the front range of the Rockies, where he met and married a Colorado City girl. Though not a union man himself, he walked out in sympathy with the Western Federation of Miners' strike in '03. When the National Guard was sent in, he was arrested with the strikers and spent three weeks in a detention camp. Released, he went home to find his pregnant wife dead on the kitchen floor, "our stillborn son half out of her."

They walked quietly along the river trail awhile.

"That is why," Early said, "Gregory Dolan of the Irrational Workers of the World, I tend to take a harder view of these things. Doesn't matter how good your speeches are, if someone comes to knock Early Reston, he's gonna get knocked back."

It seemed to Rye that his brother usually had a famous saying at the ready, and as they moved down the trail, he went with an old favorite: "Whoever fights monsters should see to it that in the process he does not become a monster."

Early Reston squinted as they walked, the same grin on his face. "Well, go on, you well-read son of a bitch, don't stop there."

"For if you gaze long enough into an abyss—"

"The abyss gazes back," Early said. "And that's me, friend. The abyss smiling back."

Rye had never seen anyone compete with Gig in the quoting of famous men. This Early Reston was like Gig meeting his match and his best friend at the same time, and they went back and forth about this fella Nitchee, or that one Marks, or some guy Russo, who Early said believed that "liberty with danger is preferable to peace with slavery."

"Tommy Russo?" Rye tossed in from behind, thinking of a young Italian they'd picked apples alongside.

"Jean-Jacques Rousseau," said Gig over his shoulder, less to educate Rye than to show off for his new friend. "His *Discourse on Inequality* is basically the Wobbly pitch after a bath and a glass of port."

This caused even Jules to laugh, and Rye felt left out, as he often did when Gig broke out the union talk. He'd been listening to this Wobbly pitch for almost a year, but he'd never been entirely sold. Carpenter, millwright, machinist—plenty of unions Rye could see them joining for steady work and a slice of the pie, but the IWW seemed more tramp church than true labor outfit to him. Gig said this was "small thinking" on Rye's part. "This is about more than you and me making enough to buy some vacant lot, Rye-boy. It's about equality. It's about the worker owning the means of production."

That seemed awfully unlikely to Rye—like a beggar hungry for bread getting the whole bakery. And the idea that you could make men equal just by saying it? Hell, it took only your first day in a Montana flop or standing over your mother's unmarked grave to know that *equal* was the one thing all men were not. A few lived like kings, and the rest hugged the dirt until it cracked open and took them home.

On the trail in front, Early Reston was making a similar point. "To my way of thinking, your one big union goes against human nature *and* human history."

"But it *is* history," said Gig, "the coming revolution of the working class."

Early turned back and winked at Jules and Rye. "I think you and I had different history books."

Then Gig smiled back at his little brother, too, as if to say, *Ain't this grand?* And it was grand, thought Rye. He imagined everyone had a picture in mind of the word *America*—flags or eagles or George Washington's wig—but from that moment on, he thought he'd imagine waking on a ball field with his brother, fighting off a mob, then marching into town in a moving debate of economics and justice.

"What do you think, Jules?" Rye asked.

They had fallen back a few steps, the old man glancing over the hillside at the mouth of a stream. Hangman Creek ran through the farm near Rockford where they'd worked together, and Jules had told Rye how it came to be named fifty years earlier, when the valley was filled with nothing but Indian villages. During the Coeur d'Alene War, a Cavalry colonel named George Wright rode along the Spokane River, destroying every village and food cache he found. He also captured eight hundred horses, the full measure of the tribes' wealth. Twelve miles upriver, Wright ordered them shot. At first, they led each animal out separately and put a bullet in its head, but realizing this could take days, Wright had the soldiers fire directly into the herd, ponies falling in heaps, eight hundred wailing horses shot dead while the Spokanes watched from the foothills. After that, missionaries guaranteed the safety of any chief who would talk peace with Wright, but each time one rode into camp he was arrested. And when a Yakama brave named Qualchan came to plea for his father's release, he and his party were immediately hanged.

In Rockford, Jules told Rye the story of these two places, the Horse Slaughter Camp on the east end of town and Hangman Creek to the southwest. He called them *Père Blanc et Mère Blanche*, and even though it was French, Rye didn't need a translation: In a city named for the people driven from it, everything called civilization was born of those two parents.

"Jules?" Rye said again. "You got thoughts on this union business?"

Jules looked up from the stream as they climbed the hill. "When I was a boy," he said, "before any of this, I worked upriver for the old French ferryman, Plante, at the only crossing for a hundred miles. This was after Wright raided our village, and my mother begged Plante to take me on so she'd have one less child to feed. I had a trapper grandfather on my father's side, so Plante agreed. He taught me French and English and was the one called me Jules. I slept in a shed behind his cabin and cleaned horseshit off the ferry decks and cleared brush from the shore. I worked for Plante from my sixth year until my fifteenth and was never paid a dime, but I was fed and given a place to sleep."

Just ahead of them, Gig and Early turned a switchback.

"One day," Jules said, "two men rode up on the far shore. I roped the barge over and loaded the men and their horses. But they were outlaws, and when we got halfway across the river, they threw me off, cut the cable, and stole the barge. I swam to shore and woke Plante, and he and I tracked the barge downriver, but one of them rode it right over the falls. And when we got back to camp, Plante beat me for losing his ferry."

In Rockford, Rye had heard Jules answer questions this way, with winding stories that tailed off before their conclusion. He wasn't sure if it was the Salish way or the French way or Jules's way, but he suspected the story's meaning was like an undercurrent beneath the surface, the opposite of how Gig and his union friends told stories, skipping the story part to go straight to collectivism or syndicalism. Jules seemed to want Rye to figure out the ism himself.

Finally, Rye could wait no longer. "What's it mean, Jules?"

Jules gave a laugh. *"Un homme dans un bateau."*

"Come on," Rye said, "you know I don't speak nothing but English."

"One man to a boat," Jules said. "We all go over alone."

They broke over a rise then, and caught up with Gig and Early, the four of them moving toward the stout brick skyline of that smoke-capped city.

4

There was no place like it then, Spokane—such hell and hair on that town. A full day's ride from anywhere, isolated between mountain ranges on the stair-step deck of waterfalls, it took Rye's breath away the first time he railed in: basalt cliffs jutting like teeth from pine-covered hills, train bridges latticing the valley, and in the center that big river, which carved a steep, tree-lined canyon that led from the silver mines and forested mountains of Idaho to rich Washington farmland.

It was a boomtown that just kept booming, doubling in size every six years, going from a few hundred to a hundred-some thousand in just thirty years, until the only place bigger in the state was that ugly harbor blight Seattle. Spokane felt like the intersection of Frontier and Civilized, the final gasp of a thing before it turned into something else—the Last Rush Town, Gig called it, for the silver rushes in the foothills, but also the rush of railroad and bank, school and merchant, brick, stone, and steel, old-growth timber turned to pillared houses, hammers popping nonstop against the wild, a mad rush to log and pave the whole world.

Downtown, the money turned west at Howard Street, to banks, clothiers, clubs, law offices, and gilded hotels, Louis Davenport's fine restaurant and the Hall of Doges, the marbled Spokane Club, bricked

roads leading to grand neighborhoods of mining and timber barons
and the men who banked and doctored and lawyered them.

The eastern half of downtown was all skid and tenderloin, six
blocks by six blocks of drink, dance, rent-a-room, liquor-and-chance,
opium, garter-bird weekend beds. Gig said that in the years before
Rye found him, he had railed from San Francisco to St. Paul and
every town in between, and for his money, of which, admittedly, he
had none, Spokane was the best city of them all.

It grew on Rye for different reasons: the quiet neighborhoods
and the way you could look up brownstone canyons and see, at the
end of even the busiest street, a pine-covered hillside. And he liked
the idea of one day building their own house among the fruit trees
behind Mrs. Ricci's boardinghouse. But however much the Dolan
brothers had grown to like Spokane, the city didn't exactly return
their affections—seeing them as just two more bums in a city thick
with them, a point Gig argued this way:

A bum wanders and drinks.
A tramp wanders and dreams.
A hobo wanders and works.

That second part was open for negotiation, but no question, Rye
and Gig wandered, out of necessity or character or both. Maybe
they'd have stayed in one place if they'd been born wheat farmers
or gentlemen grocers and not the sons of a man like Dan Dolan,
who came from Ireland, where the family name Dobhail meant unlucky in Gaelic and apparently translated perfectly to America, Dan
doing a year in debtor's jail before finding work as a shovel mucker,
at which point he sent word back to County Leitrim that Ahearn
Dobhail's youngest was a budding American silver baron in need
of a bride. Neighboring villages pooled money to send their most
disagreeable old maid, who was all of twenty-two, and for whom
two men had left Ireland rather than engage her. She arrived in Montana after two weeks on boats and trains and wagons to find this

played-out convict a decade older than advertised, her first words "I pray there's enough of you left to make a baby."

"Your mother arrived with grievances," Dan Dolan used to say, "and plans to send me out with the same." And so she did after four children, Rye the last, eight years old when his da dropped dead on the steps of a tavern, the very definition of Irish hell: dying walking into a bar. Rye's mother fell sick not long after and took to her bed— *poor Dan this and poor Dan that*—in her sickness creating a love for the ages, or maybe that *was* love: grievance to grieving to grave. With their da dead and their ma sick, the union books closed, mines and railroads sloughing off workers, the Dolan siblings had no choice but to leak away, first doomed Danny, then poor Lacy, and finally, Gig, who couldn't bear the shame of being a healthy young man not working the mines and walked off one day without a word.

Gig always said that in another life he'd have been an actor, and that's what led him to "the theater capital of the west," Spokane's gem, the redbrick Auditorium Theater, encrusted with ornate balconies and barnacled boxes over the Biggest Stage on the Planet, sixty feet wide and forty-six deep. Ten other theaters progressed downward in size and culture, west to east, Pantages to Orpheum to Comique, powdered plays and piano concertos on the west end, European horns and pince-nez monologists in the center, and farthest east the disreputable variety houses showing the likes of Ursula the Great and the Famous Fighting Fitz, who battled five men and then punched a horse to the ground. These spectacles ran up against saloons and gambling houses, faro and opium, shelters for wayward girls, betting halls and drinking halls and sporting halls and social halls, a hall for every vice and veteran of war, Spanish and Civil, and unions, too, do-gooders and service clubbers, Salvation Army and Temperance League and merciful Souls of Mercy—cause and effect, disease and cure all swirled up in the loin, block after block of wretched glorious humanity wandering the east-end streets and alleys, hungry, thirsty, lonely beggars and bums and hands and sawyers and millers and miners and scuffs, broke brothers and failed fathers and godforsaken grandfathers, all languages, religions, and races, crib rats and saloon girls, temperance ladies, nuns and cons and pickpockets and socialists and suffragists, the wicked, broken, and unholy—Americans, them, too, every one.

But as poor as that side of Spokane was, the other was more than its equal in wealth, Browne's Addition and the bookshelf boulevards of the South Hill bursting with grand estates, mansions that covered whole blocks, their houses gabled and gilded and turreted and corniced and columned and dormered and portico'd and butlered and drivered and maided, and good God go hungry, a man walking those streets would be crazy not to ponder the Wobbly pitch—hell, why not a union of *all* men and women, especially in a world like this, where a rich handful lived in the clouds while the rest starved and slaved and slept on dirt only to be rousted from sleep by an angry mob intent on drowning you.

5

They were on a plateau above the river, in Browne's Addition, high iron fences fronting estates, hired men watching from gatehouse windows. Early was still jawing with Gig. "I just don't see how you fight a class war without the war."

Three other floaters had fallen in with them as they walked toward the smoky center of downtown and the IWW's free breakfast. Two of the men were old hands who'd put up hay near Omak with Jules, and they recounted bunkhouse stories that brought out his big laugh again. The third was a young black hotel porter who introduced himself as Everett and told Rye he was paid two thirds what white porters got and wasn't allowed in their union. "My boss would fire me if I became a Wobbly," Everett said, "but he can't stop me from having breakfast."

An electric streetcar rumbled by, tracks webbing the city, lines crackling above them like sparking marionette strings. Through the window of the streetcar, Rye saw scowling faces and imagined what they must think of this parade, Gig in the lead like some tramp general.

Across the street, a man in a coat long enough to cover a rifle straightened up as they passed, Rye remembering that a police officer had been killed two nights ago and that every cop, detective, and mining tough would be on the street in the coming days.

The doors had just opened on the big IWW Hall on Front Street, and they lined up at the canteen for breakfast—oatmeal, coffee, and wheat-flour biscuits. They took their food through the double doors into the big meeting hall, and even Gig and Early went quiet as they filled their bellies.

Rye had just gone back for seconds when the street door flew open and the big police chief, John Sullivan, came in. He looked around like he was thinking of buying the building, stood bow-legged in the anteroom between newsstand and canteen, eyes scraping the pamphlets, posters, and flyers on the walls until they landed on Rye, who was holding a bowl of oatmeal. A scowl rose on the chief's face, a good two inches behind his brush mustache—facial hair of such heft and dimension that Rye half expected it to part and reveal Ursula the Great singing to a live cougar.

"Walsh," he rumbled.

Rye could do nothing but point through the open double doors to the office at the other end of the meeting hall.

Sullivan dug in his pocket for a nickel, slapped it on the newsstand, and grabbed a copy of the *Industrial Worker*. He folded the paper and, with the headline FREE SPEECH DAY peeking out from under his heavy coat, marched through the double doors into the meeting hall. Rye had heard stories about the big chief, but he'd never seen the man up close. He walked with a rolling hitch, like he was mounted on his own hips, and the way his feet pointed out and his eyes bulged, you might think him awkward, but Rye knew the man's reputation with a stick—you did well to avoid his shadow on the street.

In the meeting hall, a dozen pairs of eyes followed Sullivan as he strode down the center aisle until he got to the stage, where another man pointed left, toward the office door. The police chief pivoted and covered the distance in three steps, rapped with a knuckle, and honked again: "Walsh!" The office door opened, Sullivan went inside, the door closed, and a dozen tramps exhaled at the same time.

Rye took a seat between Early and Jules, who were finishing their coffee. The three of them watched as Gig and two other Wobblies stood in the aisle, debating the nature of the police chief. One man said Sullivan showed courage coming in without a bunch of other cops. Another said Sullivan would "smack your ass and drive you from town himself." Still, he said, he preferred Sullivan to a cop like Hub Clegg, who "knocks you down to go through your pockets."

"Sullivan's character is beside the point," Gig said. "He runs that brutal police department, ergo, failing to hold him to account for that outfit's rank corruption is like believing the snake's head ignorant of what happens to the rat it swallows."

Early and Jules turned and nodded at each other in appreciation of Gig's speaking gifts. "Ergo," Early repeated.

"Snake's head," replied Jules.

Then Early leaned over to Rye. "Your brother's going to talk himself right into jail." He stood. "As for me, I do not want to be here when that big cop comes back out and asks what tramp knocked his boy at the river today." Then he looked over at Jules. "You'll be easy to identify, too, you know."

Jules shrugged. "I think I will stick around and see what happens."

"Suit yourself," Early said. "It's been a pleasure, boys." He offered Jules his hand. "*Bonne chance*, Jules."

"*Tout le plaisir etait pour moi*," said Jules.

Gig had seen Early stand and he stepped over. "You leaving, Early?"

"For now."

"Where to?"

Early looked like he hadn't fully considered this question. "West," he said. "Seattle, maybe. Although I've been known to hole up south of here, in Lind. You know it?" Gig nodded. Lind was a little wheat farming town two hours southeast. "Then again." Early grinned. "I might not make it past Jimmy Durkin's place."

"I'll start there," Gig said.

They shook hands, and Early clapped Gig on the shoulder. "Be careful with this bullshit."

Early was still shaking Gig's hand when he looked over and smiled. "And Rye, next time your brother won't shut up about the inherent rights of man, you have my permission to crown him with a shovel." He put his hat on. "Okay, then. See you princes down the line—" Then he walked out the door and was gone.

It wasn't five minutes later that the office door flew open and Sullivan exited as boldly as he'd entered, followed by Walsh, Little, and a thin Italian man in a brown suit named Charlie Filigno, the unhappy secretary of the union.

Wobblies stepped out of Sullivan's way as the big chief marched up the aisle to where the double doors stood propped open. He turned back to face the room like a stern priest. "I told your man Walsh and I'm telling you. Don't do this thing you're planning. One of my cops was killed two nights past—"

Walsh interrupted. "You said yourself, the killer posed as a real estate man. Does that sound like anyone here?"

"No," Sullivan admitted dolefully, as if it would be easier if it did. "But it won't matter. For me boys are in a state. One of them got jumped cleaning out a hobo camp this morning."

Rye flinched and Gig shot him a hard glance.

Sullivan held up the newspaper and slapped the free speech headline. "You do this and you will pay in bone and teeth."

He turned on his heel and marched out and a second later the door to the street slammed. In the quiet that followed, Rye looked around the room, at his brother, at Jules, at Walsh and Little, at the porter Everett and the ranch hands, at a half dozen others in threadbare clothes and whiskered faces, this army of the poor and broken, in it together now, but alone, too, each man moving toward the horizon of his own end.

The Kid, 1864

AFTER BONIN liberated the Scots' pelts, me and him rode along the lower trail on the south bank till we come to a rocky ford where this Frenchman run the cable ferry that crossed the wild river. But the barge was tied the other side and we saw no sign of the old trapper Plante.

Liberate is an awful rich word for what you done, I said to Bonin.

No dust rose behind us on the Mullan Trail and I thought maybe we had not been followed.

We'd just struck camp that morning to ride north when Bonin come with that thick pelt-pack tied to the cantle of his saddle. He said the Scots made him a bargain, and if we crossed at Plante's Ferry we could sell the pelts at Fort Colville.

But the way he kept looking back I became of a mind that Bonin had stole them pelts. I asked him outright and that's when he come up with that word liberated. A God-fearing man would've rode off and let him take his own lashings, but my own weakness and Bonin's knowledge of that strange country had my nerve.

And now Plante's Ferry lay unmanned and our plan in waste. The ferryman had a cabin the other side of the river but no one appeared

about. Even when Bonin put his hands together and called *Hallo!*
across the river, the cabin stayed dark.

We could swim the ponies, I said, but Bonin's cheeks colored as he
looked down that powerful river. Snow still shaded the foothills and
that river bulged with fierce current.

Might swamp the furs, he said. I knew the truth that Bonin could
not swim more than a thrash or two. And that early in spring, the
Spokane River might sop the pelts, pull his little saddler downstream,
and dump him in the froth.

Just then a boy appeared from the brush on the other shore, a hundred feet across from us. He was dark and little, maybe twelve years
old, with a black knot of hair, from that river band of Indians that
Plante lived among.

Where's your Frenchman? Bonin called.

I can cross you, the boy called back.

Do it then, Bonin yelled.

The boy started untying his barge.

As it was the only crossing of that river, the posted price was high:
four dollars a wagon, six bits a man, and four bits per animal. We had
no wagon, just us and our horses and that bundle of pelts.

The young Indian worked the punt toward us, using a pole to push
against the shore. Thick ropes led from both ends of the boat to pul-
leys on another rope suspended above the river and tied to big trees.
Near the middle, the current pulled at the barge, trees straining and
the guide rope bent in the center like a hunter pulling a bow.

Ashore, Bonin gave a yank to his skittish pony's bit. I wish that
boy would hasten, he said. Bonin and I looked together at the trail
behind us.

Finally, the boy settled the barge on the bank and we walked our
clomping animals onto the wooden deck. The boy was older in face
than his small body and he looked at me like he knew the trouble
I was. Bonin paid for him and his horse. You are the cause of this, I
said. So he dug out six bits for me, too.

As the boy pushed us off the shore and began poling to the other side, I saw something strange on that far bank, a glittering white mound in a clearing above the river. The boy followed my eye. Horse bones, he said.

Then Bonin straightened and pointed behind us. Dust was rising on that southern road, not a quarter mile back. Riders coming our way. We weren't half crossed the river when four men rode into view on the south bank.

Gimme the pole! Bonin yelled. But the boy would not and they tussled for it. Bonin grabbed the boy by his shirt and breeches and hurled him over the side. He hit the water with barely a ripple. Then Bonin pulled his knife from its scabbard and began cutting the guide ropes.

I saw what he meant to do. And I will give Bonin credit. It was likely our only hope. Those riders could ford faster than we could pole. But the current was strong enough that the river would float us downstream at a good pace, and since the trail departed the riverbank, we ought to make a bend or two and find a spot for a proper escape in the grassy fields on the north shore.

Even in that cold current, the boy swam to shore with easy strokes. I envied him. I wanted to tell him I was sorry, but there was much I was sorry for since Bonin and I first rode out of Kansas.

Bonin had finished cutting the guide ropes and for a moment we spun in the current, then swung free off the pulley and our barge started downstream. I laughed. Well I'll be damned, I said. That's how it was with Bonin. Scared and thrilled minute to minute. Horse bones and cantle pelts and suddenly you're running a river. My own pony stirred but I gripped her bridle and bid her quiet.

Looking back, I could see both shores: On the south, the men's horses were settling in dust, on the north bank, the swimming boy was wading out of the river. He pulled his hands to his mouth and yelled for the ferryman.

Something I ought have told you, Kid, said Bonin.

I looked over at him.

The Scots trapper and I quarreled with knives.

Those words were barely free of his mouth when I was yanked by the shoulder and heard the thudding report of a rifle.

My horse was shot through her neck. She pulled the cheekpiece from my hand and leaped from the barge, breaking the railing and causing the boat to dip and rise and Bonin's little saddler to stagger and fall off the other side, the other railing going with her, both animals now in the river and swimming to shore, mine with a wound in her neck, Bonin's with our prize pelts dragging waterlogged behind. My shoulder burned where a piece of the ball that hit my pony had burrowed into my meat and socket.

I'm shot, I said to Bonin. We were both on our stomachs, clinging to the barge. We rounded another bend and I could see the man who shot me tracking us on a trail above the south bank of the river. He'd fired from the saddle, a fancy piece of aim, and now he bore down again. A report cracked and echoed in the rocks. But this one missed and the river raced us past a cluster of boulders that rose between him and us, and the expert shot could not get off another round.

The river was in full churn and we bumped along, rising and falling over rapids and unseen rocks, our raft turning this way and that. The barge pole had gone over with the horses and we had nothing to brake or steer. We held flat to the thrashing vessel. The pain raking my shoulder with each bump.

Next eddy we'll pull out, Bonin said, though the speed of that current did not bode well for it. And still the dust of those riders trailed us from the south shore.

I called to Bonin, Was the Scots alive after your quarrel?

He didn't answer. But I knew. I knew the minute he rode into camp with the pelts. Maybe I knew the minute we rode out of Kansas fleeing conscription. I wondered if those men would treat my shoulder before hanging me.

Still the river bucked, like a new colt. Ridges and stands of trees falling away.

I cannot give account of this river except that it was wide and fast, a torrent out of the mountain lake from which it drained, a blast of angry water over hard rock bed, eager to ocean. And even when we emerged in a slower stretch or our boat snagged a tree limb, we could not disembark, for the banks were bouldered or hung with brush and no snag could hold us. The trappers on the south shore had fallen back as the trail departed, and their dust grew faint. Perhaps the speed and harshness of that river might be our salvation after all.

Bonin crawled across the boards and looked at my shoulder.

Is it bad? I asked.

I don't think so, he said. But then he crawled back to his side of the barge.

That's when I saw the dust of men on horseback on the north side of the river as well.

So now we were being pursued on both shores. Sure enough, two riders emerged at a full gallop on the north river trail, on a rise above us. One was older and bearded and I guessed him to be the French ferryman. The ferry boy was leading him on a smaller mount.

I was our doom, Bonin said.

I'll not quarrel with it, I said.

The river picked up speed again, rose and fell and twice snaked us through rapids. We clung to our barge and watched behind us, both banks, as our pursuers dropped down to the river and were forced to ride up and circle back on the bluff again, as terrain and brush warranted. I waited for the saddle-aim to try us again, but he could not get a clear shot.

I was aware then of a sapping from my wound, as if I were leaking out of my own skin. I lay with my face on the cold, wet boards and drifted in and out, rising and falling on that river, and I don't know how much time passed. We slowed once more but the current pulled us away before Bonin could get us to shore. A shoreline willow had reached out a hand for us and Bonin grabbed hold but he was left with nothing but a handful of leaves stripped from bough.

I feared I was becoming too weak to swim. The river was high and fast and freezing and the few calm stretches where we might have made shore were also reachable from the two river roads and the men chasing us—trappers on the south side, the boy and Plante on the north.

So we held tight. And rose and fell, slapped by water, scraped by rocks and limbs, my arm numb like the empty sleeve of a coat.

Shame you fell in with me, Kid, said Bonin.

I suspect my own character is at fault, I said.

We talked this way as we clung to that ferry, looking across the wet boards into each other's eyes. I can tell you, at the end, you marvel at eyes. I thought of my mother's easy blues and the bark browns of the boy who took us across the river. How many hundreds in between? And how many more I would never see, Bonin's green demons to be my last.

He seemed to know my gloomy thinking.

Listen, he said, I need to tell you about this river. There is a great falls ahead, six or seven steps, the last a rocky drop of forty feet into a canyon. In summer the local Indians gather there to fish, but now, with the river so high with melt— He shook his head.

Maybe we'll ride it, I said. Maybe we will be the first men to go over and tell about it. I smiled as I thought of the western adventures we had sought.

Bonin did not answer.

The current finally slowed a bit and the trail on the north shore dipped down to us. The boy and the ferryman descended and rode at a fast trot, the boy almost as close as when we were on the barge. Like we were traveling together, two by road and two by river. I wondered if the boy had a rope to throw.

Forgive me, Bonin said, and at first I thought he was talking to the boy, saying what I was thinking about stealing the barge. But when I turned back Bonin had slid off our punt into the river and was swimming for shore. He made that awful stroke of his, flailing, flapping, his heavy long coat spread like wet wings, the current pulling him alongside the barge. I could see his face until it went under and resurfaced ten feet away, him still trying to make shore. He glanced back my way and our eyes caught again.

Sure now of his folly, Bonin tried thrashing back to the barge and scrabbled his hands on the side. I tried to pull myself over to help but I was too weak. And the next time I saw Bonin he was just hair floating alongside our barge—and then gone.

I forgive you, I said. And even though I was the one who come up with that whole Kid nonsense, I wished Bonin had called me once more by my Christian name before he went over, just to hear it again.

I did not see the trappers on the south bank after that, but the Indian on the north shore was a fine rider, and he separated from the ferryman and rode along the bluff ahead, as if to cut me off. Water sloshed the side of the barge and I could taste my blood in it.

I thought again of my mother and wondered if my sisters had all married. I wished I could see them once more. Perhaps in another world.

Foolish thought. There is no other world. Ahead came a dip, the river carving into two channels, and I wondered if this was the first step of the great falls.

I thought again of the glory of being the first man to go over alive. And I thought about the ferry boy and the horse bones and his tribe living forever on these banks and what the boy would make of me claiming to be the first over the falls, like the first white man to see some lake or first to cross some mountain pass, naming streams the boy's people had fished for centuries.

Maybe one of them had gone over the falls and lived to tell of it. Maybe they did it all the time, like swinging from a river rope. Maybe the boy had even done it. This thought gave me hope and I sat up to see where the adventure led. I felt dizzy and had the strangest thought—I need to stay awake for this.

An island split the river and I could hear the roar of white water ahead of me. The boy and his pony were on a basalt ridge thirty yards downstream, and as I approached, I raised my good arm. He still had that curious look on his face.

Watch! I called out. I cannot say why I yelled this except I imagined that if I were witnessed now, I might continue to exist, even if only as a tale the boy thrilled his children with—the scoundrel who stole a ferry and rode it over the falls.

From the back of his pony, the boy raised his hand as I passed, and he called out to me the way you would to a friend you recognized, three short yelps as my barge passed, a song whose meaning I would never know but which I took to mean: *I see you.*

There is no world but this one. And all we want is to be seen in it.

I see you, the boy said. And I was grateful.

Then a crack and a roar and my barge seized up beneath me, front end risen like God Himself had reached down from heaven to save The Kid with His great forgiving thunder of a Hand—

But no—

I had run against a boulder, which tore the current and my vessel in two, and I was riven by sin from salvation and tumbled to the smaller end of my broken punt, clinging to its side. I looked back and could scarcely believe what had happened—I had gone over! Fallen ten feet on half a wooden raft and lived to tell it! I looked at the north shore for the boy and tried to make the whooping sound he had made—but I was weak and if this first stair step had been the easiest, what came next would surely be my end.

Behind me, the boy sat atop his pony on that rock ledge—his wide eyes mirroring my own thoughts: *Did you see that!* He began to raise his hand once more (this the end of the story he would tell his children, *As he went over, I waved*) and I began to raise my own arm in response, but before either of us could finish, the next step came and I was taken by the cold froth that awaits—

6

Tramps knew Spokane by its rail stations: the big depots downtown and James Hill's freight yard in Hillyard, a neighborhood of little houses and big saloons, dry goods and feed stores, and so many stray mutts it was known as Dogtown.

Rye was walking to Dogtown to look for his brother on the day he first met Mrs. Ricci, on the hobo highway, a trail that paralleled the tracks along the river. Between downtown and Dogtown was all Catholic—the huge steeple of the new St. Aloysius Church being built on the riverside next to the Jesuits' Gonzaga College, Holy Names Academy and the Knights of Columbus, a seminary and convents for Dominican and Franciscan nuns, orphanage, asylum, and high school, a vast Vaticanland surrounded by blocks of broad-porched Irish houses and the cottages and bungalows of Little Italy, Paddy taverns, spaghetti houses, groceries, shops, and the ghetto shacks of recent immigrants.

Mrs. Ricci's boardinghouse lay on the northern edge of Little Italy, at the base of the Lidgerwood hill. It was a one-story farmhouse with an enclosed porch and an empty lot out back where her husband, before his death, had tended three rows of beloved fruit trees. Rye first saw the Ricci place when he noticed ripe plums hanging from two stuffed trees below the hillside, behind the paint-chipped house. He thought about taking a few plums but knocked on the door instead. The woman who answered was ancient, a hunch below five feet, and nearly bald beneath her head scarf. She stuck out her bottom lip and looked Rye up and down before proposing in heavily accented English that he keep a fourth of what he'd picked

("Three me, one you"). Eventually, she let him borrow a stepladder, a bucket, and a pair of gloves, Rye not twenty minutes into emptying the first tree when Mrs. Ricci reappeared with bread, noodles, and a glass of iced tea.

She had three grown sons, but two of them lived in Idaho with non-Catholic wives who sparked such deep disapproval that the boys rarely came to see their mother. The third son was an imbecile who lived in the asylum six blocks away. Mrs. Ricci walked there to see him every day after Mass.

She took immediately to Rye, and with time, to Gig, her eyes narrowing as if he might be too smooth to trust. The previous December, the Dolans had set up cots on her back porch and opened vents to draw heat from the woodstove. Her enclosed porch became a cheap place to winter so long as they abided Mrs. Ricci's particular rules: that they not show up drunk or take the Lord's name and not correct her when she got distracted and accidentally called them by her sons' names. "Wait, am I Marco or Geno?" Gig would ask before they went into the kitchen for breakfast. "You're Marco," Rye would answer. "I'm Geno."

This would be their second winter on Mrs. Ricci's porch, and they woke there the morning of the great Free Speech Fight, buried under coats and blankets, the smell of bacon stirring both brothers from their cots.

Rye had gone there alone after Gig went out looking for Early Reston at Durkin's. Rye worried that his brother wouldn't come home at all, but he'd dragged in just after midnight, smelling of cigars and booze. "I'll tell you what, Rye-boy," Gig said as he settled into his cot, "after four whiskeys, Early's case for making bombs instead of speeches begins to make a little sense." He hummed a laugh that made Rye jealous. He wasn't sure what to say about bombs versus speeches (*How about neither?*) but it didn't matter: Soon Gig was snoring.

• • •

In the morning, Gig rose and used the outhouse first, then Rye, who paused at the door to glance back at what he thought of as *his* orchard, three rows of fruit trees, apple, plum, and pear. Leaves littered the ground beneath skeletal branches. Mrs. Ricci had agreed to sell them the lot for two hundred dollars, although they had yet to pay more than a few bucks toward it.

When Rye came back from the outhouse, Gig was dressed and arranging his things as if he were going on a trip, folding his extra shirt and stacking his three books: Jack London's *White Fang,* and Volumes I and III of Count Tolstoy's *War and Peace.* Gig had traded a bottle of wine for the first Tolstoy and had found the third for sale at the Salvation Army. There were five total, Gig told Rye, part of a larger twenty-volume set of Tolstoy's *Collected,* Gig always on the lookout for the rest of *War and Peace,* the second, fourth, and fifth volumes. Now he carefully lined his three books next to his cot as if this constituted a library.

"We leaving before breakfast?" Rye asked. "I thought it started at noon."

"Committee meeting first."

"Well, give me a minute to get ready, and I'll go with you."

"You're not on the committee."

"I'll come later, then?"

Finally, Gig looked up at him. "Rye-boy. You're not coming."

"Of course I'm coming."

"No." Gig explained that he was one of twenty men slated to speak, which meant he would probably get arrested, and he didn't want Rye getting hurt if things got out of hand with the police.

"I should be there," Rye said.

"No. You stay for breakfast. Then you can rake Mrs. Ricci's leaves."

Rye hated when Gig started ordering him around—like he was some kind of authority. "I'll eat down at the hall," Rye said. "And rake leaves tomorrow."

"No." Gig smiled. "You're gonna have breakfast with Mrs. Ricci. Then rake her leaves—" He pulled his coat on. "This isn't your fight,

Rye." He walked out the door into the backyard, Rye following right behind him.

"Wait. I spend a year listening to you go on about this business, and now it's not my fight?"

Gig turned back, face set. "I'm your guardian and I say you're staying here."

"My *guardian*!" Rye could barely believe the nerve after he'd spent the last year pulling Gig out of saloons. "What are you guarding me from, Gig? Sobriety? A home?"

It stung the way Rye knew it would. Gig turned and began walking away, muttering. Rye picked up a word here and there: *responsibility* and *bullshit* and *baby*. And the next thing he knew, Rye was on Gig's back. He didn't even remember running and he didn't remember jumping and he certainly didn't know what he hoped to accomplish, hanging off his brother like a pack, arms around his neck.

Gig threw him into the dewy grass. "What's the matter with you?"

What was the matter? This panic he felt watching his brother walk off—and suddenly, he was back in Whitehall, alone with her. "You can't just leave!" Rye spat, voice breaking, panting. He pictured their mother's handkerchief, pink from the blood he could never wash out.

Gig was staring down at him. After a moment, he offered Rye a hand and pulled him to his feet, Rye wiping his nose on his shirtsleeve.

"I'll be back before you know it," Gig said. "This thing's like a show. They'll haul a few of us to jail and we'll make a big deal of it and that's that. The IWW ran this same show in Missoula, and after a week of feeding twenty singing tramps in jail, the city dropped the whole thing."

Rye pictured the big angry police chief—a good four inches taller than Gig, with that stern brogue—and couldn't imagine the man just surrendering to a bunch of singing labor men.

"Here," Gig said, and he handed Rye his work gloves. "Have breakfast. Rake leaves. I'll see you this afternoon or, at the very worst, in a week or so."

Rye held the gloves and watched Gig's broad back recede, the scratchy window in the Whitehall apartment, his big brother always walking away. "Goddamn it, Gig," he muttered.

He went inside then, and ate breakfast with Mrs. Ricci, Gig's plate empty next to his. Rye slurped eggs onto his bread.

"*Tu mangi come un cavallo, Geno,*" Mrs. Ricci said.

"Sorry, Mrs. Ricci," he said. He tried to remember the Italian word for *sorry*. "Dispatch?"

"*Dispiace,*" she said. "*Si.*"

"Yeah, that," Rye said.

Breakfast over, he pulled on his brother's work gloves and grabbed the rake from the side of the house. The wind swirled the leaves and he worked grimly, got two piles into the burn bin and lit them, but they were wet and smoldered instead of crackling. Rye watched the gray soupy smoke curl into the sky. The wind must've been howling above the valley, because the high clouds raced like migrating birds above the smoke, as if the world were flying by. "Goddamn it, Gig," he said again. And he set the rake against the house.

7

Rye hurried through Little Italy and the Irish neighborhood, kids hanging from porches and running around big leafy yards. Normally, he'd take the river trail along the tracks to downtown, but today he felt like walking the blocks of houses, imagining he belonged, and he crossed Division into rows of brick apartments, then down Howard to the sprawling train station on Havermale Island, which split the river into two channels between the upper and lower falls.

There was a trapdoor in the north deck of the Howard Street Bridge, and Rye stood watching a work crew dump a wagonload of tin cans and other garbage straight into the churning river below—a brown city soup of refuse, sewage, and train oil. People usually just threw their trash on the riverbanks, hoping the water would take it away, but by August, when the water got low, the stench was over-powering. So the city put trapdoors in the bridges where crews could dump garbage into the center of the river, easier for the current to flush downstream.

At the Great Northern depot, Rye crossed four sets of tracks, a big passenger train steaming beneath the 150-foot tower, the four clock faces informing Rye that it was twelve minutes before high noon—the time Gig said the union's action was set to start. Across the island, on Front Street, Rye didn't need a clock to tell him something was on. Dozens of people milled outside the union hall, more arriving all the time, from flops, cafés, saloons.

In front of the hall, men stood smoking in clusters of four or five, shuffling their feet, talking in low voices and foreign tongues. Most of them wore the faded clothes and work boots of floating workers, but Rye picked out Everett and another black porter, saw high-collared suffragettes and socialist women in hats, saw craggy old men with canes and eye patches—veterans of the mine wars.

He watched from across Front Street, ducking behind a produce wagon as the strike committee emerged from the hall, Walsh and Little in front, and right behind them, Gig, looking as nervous as Rye had ever seen him. Rye's chest tightened, from fear or pride, he wasn't sure. "Goddamn it, Gig," he said again.

He felt another tug of misgiving when the last person came out of the hall—Jules walking out alone, black hair loose and falling between his shoulder blades.

The men huddled around Walsh as if he were saying a prayer, then dispersed like marbles in every direction, so they couldn't all be arrested together. Walsh led five or six men down Front Street, Rye following in a pack of onlookers before he realized Gig wasn't there.

"Fuckin' Wobs!" said a man next to Rye, but most people just seemed curious. They lined both sidewalks as Walsh walked down the center of the street. He turned up Stevens and walked between streetcar tracks, Jules and a few others behind him.

On Stevens, the crowd was thick, the carnival in full swing, a man in a turban offering to "Foresee your shocking future!" next to a barker selling ginger ale and chestnuts. People leaned out of upper-floor windows as if they'd paid for balcony seats, and others pressed in on the street, businessmen from the west side, sporting girls and gamblers from the tenderloin, laborers and barmen, reporters, nurses and uniformed Salvation Army men, hats and coats as far as Rye could see. Wobblies mixed with the crowd, too, and Rye recognized one of the ranch hands Jules knew, muttering the words he must've been given to say when it was his turn, "Mah fella workers . . . mah fella workers . . ."

As Walsh marched down the middle of this wide street, Rye saw the security men hired by the mining and timber companies; they straightened up from brick walls and light poles, or stood on stoops with their arms crossed, clubs and rifle barrels peeking from beneath their long coats.

At the south end of the block stood another line of men, six uniformed cops led by big John Sullivan. All of them had some lesser version of the chief's facial hair, bush beards or marmot sideburns, and Rye wondered if they'd chosen the force by sheer whiskers alone. If the chief had looked unhappy the day before, today he looked like he might rip the arms off the first man to speak.

That turned out to be Walsh, who took a National Biscuit crate from another man and set it on the street in front of the worst job shop, the notorious Red Line Agency. A buzz went through the crowd: *Here it comes.*

Sullivan was walking even before Walsh started speaking— "Brothers and sisters, fellow wor—!" The labor man stumbled on the box, nearly losing his balance until Frank Little caught him, patted his coat, and pushed him back up, a ripple of laughter passing through the crowd. In that moment, Rye thought Gig might be right about this being like a show at the Comique: The tramps would do their tramp thing and the cops their cop thing and everything could return to what it was, Gig with a good story to tell next time at Jimmy Durkin's.

On the box, Walsh removed his hat and spread his arms like a preacher: "We are here to stand against injustice," to cheers and boos, "in peaceful exercise of our right to speak out against the brutal tyranny of this city government and its corrupt bargain with these job agencies—"

Walsh was not a small man, and the crate made him a foot taller, but he seemed like a toy when Chief Sullivan marched up, two thick cops on either side. Rye recognized one of the cops as the bull goon Hub Clegg.

Sullivan yanked Walsh off the box and grabbed him by the neck like a chicken he might shake dead. He threw him to the ground and slammed a boot through the biscuit crate, Clegg wrestling Walsh's arms behind his back.

"Disperse!" the chief yelled to the crowd. "Next man steps on a box gets it worse! And worse for each after."

No one moved, neither Wobblies nor crowd, and the chief turned and said something to Clegg.

Then a voice in the crowd called out, "Hold the line!" and that brought a cheer, and more boos, a man calling, "Kill the bums!," more cheers and chatter, the crowd speaking all at once, drowning out Sullivan—then the people in front of Rye snapped their attention to the left as if a baseball had been lined up the middle, and Rye stood on tiptoes to see over the hats: Another box had appeared in the street, half a block north, and Frank Little was climbing on. This was the union's plan, after Walsh was arrested, to go up one after the other in different spots, force the cops to scramble one end of downtown to the other, arrest dozens of them, and fill the jail with the only weapon they had, their bodies.

"Brothers and sisters," Little began, but before he could say another word, a cop was on him and threw him to the street. He disappeared in the crowd like someone slipping beneath waves.

"Disperse!" Sullivan yelled again, and the crowd took a few steps back but didn't leave, Wobblies pressing forward, onlookers straining to see, every window on Stevens Street now full of people sticking their heads out and a man yelling from a second-story window of a lawyer's office, "This is freedom? You call this freedom?"

A few minutes later, the same man appeared in the doorway of the building, face bloodied, pushed into the street by one of the security men, his glasses skittering onto the cobblestone as he cried, "What is my crime? What is my crime!"

The crowd rumbled and muttered like it hadn't chosen which team to root for, heads swinging left and right at signs of action: To the south a young woman in a plain gray smock yelled, "Wake up! Wake up!," and a cop pulled her down the street, then the crowd swung the other way, to the north end of Stevens, where Frank Little had gone limp and was being dragged by the arms, his legs bumping on the streetcar tracks. His soapbox was still in the street, and a long-bearded man climbed up and began singing with a heavy Slav accent, *"Oh, say can you hear,"* the first lines of the workingman's "Star-Spangled Banner," *Coming near and more near—*

That man went down, too, pounded by a security goon, but another man was already on the box behind him, and Rye yelled, "Jules!" as if he might warn his friend, who either didn't know the workers' anthem or didn't like it, because he started singing in French: *"C'est la lutte finale, groupons-nous et demain!"* and a cop standing just a few feet away cocked his head in confusion. But Hub Clegg had no hesitation and stepped in behind Jules with a raised nightstick, Rye reflexively closing his eyes rather than see the blow land—but when someone near him yelled, "Oh!," Rye opened his eyes and tried to fight through the crowd.

That was when another voice, Chief Sullivan's, thundered, "Boys!" and a great surge came and this was no longer a show or a baseball game but a full-on riot, cops and bull goons mowing down Stevens, swinging nightsticks to clear the street, and people running, falling, being trampled, Rye swept up in a wave moving north, his last view of Jules a bloodied face and his hands shackled behind his back.

"Hold the line!" someone shouted, and Rye could hear another man pick up the workingman's anthem: *"Come all ye who labor"*— and that voice stopped, and a heavier accent, *"The Industrial Band throughout all the land—"*

But he couldn't see the action anymore, and there seemed to be nothing left of the Wobbly lines, just a man or two running from the cops, and the crowd heaved forward and pulled back like a living thing, Wobblies scattered to the edges, a new shift of cops running into the melee, fixing suspenders and buttoning coats, a man in a fine suit running down the street with a shotgun.

For an hour, the crowd moved back and forth down Stevens to Front, where, amid the bedlam, a man on the corner began to sing: *"Come workers unite! 'Tis humanity's fight!"* A brick flew from a third-story window and the man was dropped, then a hail of bricks came and Rye ran with the crowd out of the melee, and how long it went on, Rye couldn't say, the crowd scattering and flowing like a tide, back and forth, bricks and sticks and winded cops, singers and speakers shackled and hauled off and so much happening Rye couldn't focus on any one thing.

Until his eyes fell on a small dark-haired man in a bow tie who walked calmly through the throng and climbed on what had to be the IWW's last crate, for cops were stomping them everywhere, the man producing a mouth harp and blowing a note through it, Rye transfixed as the man took a deep breath and sang—*"And the Banner of Labor will surely soon wave"*—and for just a moment time seemed to halt, and everyone—cop, workingman, Pinkerton, and suffragist—turned to look—*"O'er the land that is free"*—for the man's tenor was glorious—*"From the master and the slave"*—pure as birdsong—*"The blood and the lives of children and wives"*—as if God had broken through the melee to allow this song—*"Are ground into dollars for parasites' pleasure"*—either that or the Italian was just too short for the cops to see—*"The children now slave, 'til they sink in their grave"*—for that's when even God lost interest and the tenor's face warped sideways, inside out, eyes and nose and lips bursting forth in blood—he'd taken a club to the head and down he went—that harsh music critic Hub Clegg on him like hound to bone.

Another man quickly stepped on the box, and Rye's first thought was surprise that he hadn't seen Gig standing there, but there he was, climbing on the Italian's tiny stage, and Rye calling, "Gig!" and lurching toward him, his brother so small up there, Rye struggling to get upstream though the fleeing people as Gig picked up the tenor's chorus, *"And the banner of labor will surely soon wave—"*

A security man took Gig off the box, and as he fell, another man swung a rifle stock at him, Rye yelling, "Gig!" And Rye had almost reached his brother when he found himself in front of the empty crate, and then he was on it, his voice thin and frightened as he picked up the song, *"O'er the land that is free—"*

He blocked the first swing with his forearm and yelped the last of the song, *"From master and slave!"* as his brother yelled, "Rye!" and something hit him in the back and he tumbled to the street, looked for Gig through the scramble of legs and feet, but a kick to the gut took what was left of his breath and Rye Dolan finally gave up and curled into a ball, covered his face with his arms, and waited for what felt like had been coming his whole short sweet life.

8

The day he left Whitehall, Rye pulled himself up into a dark train car for the first time, and when his eyes adjusted, he realized there was an old man in the corner. He was thin and gray, sitting on an old case. His left hand was missing fingers and the eye above it was nothing but a caved-in socket. The man asked Rye where he was headed and Rye said, "West, looking for my brother."

"Well. Get off before Spokane," the man said. He'd been arrested in Spokane and said the cops went hard on vagrants there. He was rolled, robbed, and knocked around for a week in a windowless cell, then, without a court hearing, one morning was simply dragged to the edge of town and dumped on the tracks by a cop who said he'd end up in the river if he ever came back. "It's where I lost this." He pointed to the scarred, flattened eyelid. "Get off before Spokane," he said again. "The tracks keep going, but there's nothing west of dead."

Rye thought of the old man's warning as he was shackled and duckwalked toward the Spokane jail. There were six of them in his line and other shackled prisoners sitting in the street or already locked up. Even with his aching back and arms, and the fingers on his right hand swollen and bruised where he'd blocked a blow, Rye had gotten off easy. The Italian singer had it the worst, whistling mists of blood through his battered mouth and nose. "That was good," Rye said to the singer, remembering Mrs. Ricci at Mass one day, "*Bel canto.*"

"Thank you," the Italian rasped.

Gig was at the front of the line and kept trying to look back at Rye, but the cop in front rapped his shoulder. "Eyes ahead!" The riot was breaking up behind them, but a few people still catcalled the prisoners as they were led down Stevens.

They passed the ornate five-story city hall and saw faces staring down from its towered and arched windows. The jail was just around the corner, along the river, a stone building with barred windows on the first and second floors. Next door, three firemen stood smoking and leaning on a new truck, watching the shackled prisoners waddle past.

At the jail, they were led into a small booking area, and a harried jailer came from behind the counter to look them over. "Goddamn Wobs," he said in a brogue that made Sullivan's sound like the king's English. Then he went down the line. "Nem?" he said. And "Edge?" When he was done, he gave a jagged smile. "Well, look at what you coonts have done now, fooked your own bloody arseholes."

Rye caught Gig's eye. His cheek was bruising up a dark purple and he shook his head and frowned. Rye looked away.

Three more jailers came into the holding area, one of them a man in round eyeglasses who seemed to be in charge. Another unshackled them and patted them down for weapons. He made a pile of belongings: coats and money and paper and pocketknives and cigarettes and any other worthless thing they carried. The Irish one kicked through the swag, picked out a few coins, but shook his head in disappointment at the rest. "Fookin' rubbish, is it?"

The head jailer looked down at the list of names and ages and then over the rims of his eyeglasses. "Where's Gregory Dolan?"

Gig raised his hand unsteadily.

"This one's strike committee," the head jailer said. "C block."

"Wait," Rye said. "Can't I go with my brother?"

This brought laughter from the Irish jailer, who gave Gig a shot in the back with his stick and pushed him through an open door.

When that door closed on his brother's back, Rye found himself really afraid for the first time: *What have I done?*

The head jailer looked up. "Gentlemen. As our good rooms are taken by your fellow Wobs, you get the pen tonight."

They were led down a back wooden staircase to a basement with nothing but a single holding cell, something left over from frontier times. There was one lightbulb hanging from the ceiling and, next to it, a pipe with an open valve spewing steam down onto what looked like fifteen men already packed into an eight-foot-by-seven-foot cell.

"Please! I'm sick!" a man cried out from inside, and then others began yelling, too, for water, to go to the toilet, until the Irish jailor raked his nightstick across the bars, rapping fingers. "Shut your fookin' traps!"

Rye couldn't believe it when the jailer with glasses put a key in the cell door and unlocked it. He meant to put them . . . in *there*? Where? Another jailer jabbed at the wall of bums with his nightstick and gestured at Rye and the others to go in. "You Wobs wanted to pack the jail—here you go."

Rye was pushed inside and pressed between three men, the stench bringing tears to his eyes. There were no sounds but breathing and

moaning, and minutes seemed to take hours. At some point, three
more men were shoved into the cell, and then two more. "Twenty-
six," the jailer said proudly, but inside was a mass fever, the bulb
went out and it was windowless basement dark, that pipe hissing
steam all night, the smell of vomit and piss, time measured in pain
and stench and thirst—then someone would snap and the others
would subdue him, for the struggle hurt them all—knees and elbows and fists and rising panic. Then the basement door opened and
a bit of stairwell light flooded in, men crying out that they had to
piss or were sick, but two cops and two jailers clopped down the
stairs, drunk and laughing. "We're going for the record!" one said,
and two more Wobblies were somehow jammed into the cell, cops
and jailers throwing their full weight against the door just to get
it closed on the crush of men, Rye mashed between stinking flesh
and iron bar, and all around him, whimpering and moaning and
gulping, as if they were drowning in rotten flesh, and someone near
him passed out, but the man just hung there between the bodies,
nowhere to fall. "Hold the line!" a man called from somewhere in
their rank, and a jailer yelled back: "Fuck your mother."

Rye jerked awake at some point in the night, bars pressed against
his face, stunned to think he might have slept on his feet, but no idea
if it was a minute or an hour. At last the stairwell door opened and
light came in, a shift change and a new jailer appeared alongside
the one in glasses. He looked at the cell and covered his mouth in
disgust. "Jesus, Carl." Then he turned and spoke to the other one
quietly: "Who approved it?" Finally, the door was opened and the
prisoners poured out; they wept as they squeezed out the cell door.
Rye looked back to see six men still inside, collapsed on the floor, the
Italian singer one of them.

They were marched upstairs and into the jail courtyard. Soon
other Wobblies from other cell blocks joined them and they lined
the four sides of the square. No one looked any good—there were
black eyes, cut lips, torn clothing—but Rye's group had gotten the
worst of it, pissed and sweated and bloodstained, and the others

looked at them with pity. Rye saw Jules in a line to his right, cough-ing and breathing heavily, staring at the ground, and Gig across the square, mouthing, *You okay?* and Rye nodding a lie: *Yeah.* Gig had been put in with Walsh and Little and the union leaders, segregated to keep them from organizing and agitating. A man next to Rye said there were more than a hundred men in a jail built to hold forty. Three jailers and six private security men with rifles stood guard on the edges.

They were given scratchy jail grays, and they changed quickly in the cold, their old clothes piled in front of them, a jailer poking through them with his nightstick. Then another man came with a biscuit and cup of water for each man. They bounced in place, wait-ing for their turn, and ate and drank like animals. After the heat of the sweatbox, it was freezing in the courtyard, and even out of his damp clothes in the jail coveralls, Rye couldn't stop shaking. Men fell and were helped up by those around them.

They had been in the dirt courtyard an hour when Hub Clegg came out with another cop, his face bruised purple, and it took a moment for Rye to recognize Old Slate Hair, the bull cop who'd led the attack on their camp, left squirming in the dust by Early Reston.

Rye and Gig caught eyes.

Sergeant Clegg put a hand on Slate Hair's shoulder and spoke kindly to him. "Ready, Edgar?" Slate Hair nodded and he and Clegg walked the lines, looking from face to dirt-scarred, bloodied face.

Rye couldn't help himself and glanced up as Slate Hair went past, the deep raspberry Early Reston had put on the big cop's face filling him with a kind of pride.

"I don't see the one hit me," Slate Hair said when he'd looked at all of them. "He was thin and older."

"What about the others?" Clegg asked.

The big cop pointed at Jules. "That old Indian was there, but he didn't do nothing but laugh. There was a kid I didn't get a good look at." Then he pointed at Gig. "But this is the one did the yapping be-fore the other one jumped me."

Clegg walked over to Gig. "That right? You a yapper?" Then Clegg turned to Slate Hair. "He's not so yappy now." Then back to Gig. "What's your name, son?"

"Gregory Dolan."

"Where you from, Gregory Dolan?"

"Montana," Gig said. "Last few years, I lived here."

"Nah, you don't live here any more than a cockroach does." Clegg had thick lips and bulging eyes, a face that looked like it was pressed against a window. "Tell me, Gregory Dolan, what Montana town had the good sense to run you off?"

"Whitehall."

"Your whore mother suck off Irish mine rats there? Or was it coolies?"

Gig just stared.

"You don't look Chinese, so I'm going with Irish whore. And your da? Whatever man lifted her skirts a Saturday night?"

He didn't answer and Clegg got even closer, so that he could've taken a bite from Gig's face if he'd wanted to. "Tell me the name of the man attacked my sergeant, Gregory Dolan of Shitfuck, Montana."

"Your man attacked us," Gig said.

"That ain't what I asked," Clegg said. "Who else was at the river yesterday?"

"I don't know," Gig said, but Clegg did not like the answer and gave him a quick jab to the gut with his nightstick.

"One more time," Clegg said. "Tell me who was there?"

"I was there," Rye said, surprised to hear his own voice.

Clegg spun. "Who said that?"

"I did." The men around Rye stepped back slightly, and he spoke in a rush to get it all out: "We were just sleeping when your man attacked us with that mob. We ran away and your man chased us and tried to throw us in the river. The man who hit him, I didn't know him, and he left right after—" Rye felt clever at his truthfulness: He *hadn't* known Early Reston's name before he beat Slate Hair.

By this time, Clegg was standing in front of him, his features even worse up close. Black flecks of tobacco spotted his teeth. "What's your name, son?"

"Ryan Dolan. I'm his brother."

"So, we got both whoreson Dolan brothers." Clegg looked back and forth, from Rye to Gig and back to Rye. "I don't see it. Must've been half a poke made this little one." Then Clegg walked to the line Jules was in. "How about it, Shitting Bull—these Dolan boys telling the truth?"

Jules nodded without looking up or making eye contact. Clegg gave him a lighter poke, in the side, Jules's face unchanged.

And now Clegg circled back to Gig and stepped up into his face again. "I suspect I could beat and sweat a buck like you for a month and not get anything. So how about I work on your little sister instead. Give him another night in the box. How's that sound, Gregory Dolan?"

Gig swallowed hard, his mouth pinched.

"Unless of course your memory has returned and you'd like to tell me who was at the river with you and attacked my man here." He got even closer to Gig. "Come on, Gregory, you got a name for me?"

"John Rockefeller," Gig said.

The blow to the gut was quick, and harder than the others, and it dropped Gig straight to the ground.

"Cornelius Vanderbilt," Gig rasped from his knees.

Clegg scratched his head with his stick. Then he shook his head, and just before he kicked Gig in the face, he laughed. "Goddamn it, I almost like you Dolan boys."

9

The second night in the sweatbox, a Wobbly named Brazier organized the cell. He had them fashion a crude ceiling with their shirts to block the steam, and with so many in the infirmary, there was a little room, and he had two men sit at a time and rest. He spoke with the cadence of a preacher: "Listen, my Fellow Workers, I want to tell you about the three stars. Not the three stars of Bethlehem. The stars of Bethlehem lead only to heaven, which nobody knows about. These are the three IWW stars, of education, organization, and emancipation. They lead to pork chops, which everybody wants."

Later, Brazier had them sing, and they kept it up all night long— *"Up with the masses"*—songs from the IWW Songbook—*"Down with the classes"*—in every flat accent—*"Death to the traitor who money can buy"*—to piss off the jailers—*"Cooperation is the hope of the nation"*— and raise their own spirits—*"Strike for it now or your liberties die."* Finally, the jailers offered to take them out to use the toilet if they would just stop.

News traveled through the cell: After a hundred were arrested the first day and fifty the second, cops began taking new prisoners to the brig at Fort George Wright. The next morning, Chief Sullivan set up a special rock pile overlooking downtown, and in daylight, lines of shackled prisoners were marched over the bridge to swing sledges for no purpose, the chief wanting both sides to see the hardship, to show the mining bosses he was being tough on the union, and to discourage new men from agitating. But some people on the street called out support to the chain gang, and three suffragists tried to give them food and water and were hauled off to the women's jail for it. A dozen more Wobblies were arrested downtown, and it might have been three times that number, but Sullivan had firemen open the hoses on anyone who tried to speak while he figured out where to put the extra prisoners.

Sullivan had separated out the union leaders to keep them from organizing, but word came down that they should refuse to work the rock pile to protest their treatment. So the next day the sledges sat idle, men's arms at their sides, or they picked up the sledges and laid them down gently on the rock pile, as if patting the stones to sleep. Rye saw Jules on the rock pile that day, coughing like he might have pneumonia, but he winked when he saw Rye. The Italian tenor was there, too, his face stitched like a baseball glove.

Brazier spread news between songs—*"You've heard this all before, it's off to the chain gang to hammer rocks some more"*—every day new hobos railing in to sing and to give speeches, one man arrested for reading the Declaration of Independence in front of city hall, another for asking a street cop if the free speech protests were still happening.

Sullivan countered their moves with his own, and after the spectacle at the rock pile, he put the prisoners on bread and water rations, and the next morning they were taken to the courtyard and "bathed" with a fire hose. The union leaders responded with a hunger strike to demand humane treatment for people they said were political prisoners. Fine, said Chief Sullivan, if three hundred singing bums wanted to starve themselves, less trouble for him. "Man don't work," Sullivan said, "he don't deserve to eat."

That particular line was read to them by a jailer who stood outside their cell each day reading from the establishment newspapers, the *Chronicle* and the *Spokesman-Review*, to show how public support was against them: "'The petty acts of the men in jail, such as throwing their food upon the floor, breaking the dishes, screaming out silly songs and pouring torrents of abuse upon the law and police department are what sane and orderly minds look for from incorrigible children and men in insane asylums.'"

Rye would have shaken his head if he'd had room to do it: crammed into a double-barred cell beneath an open steam vent, beaten with sticks and sprayed with fire hoses—and *the prisoners* were the ones "pouring abuse" on *their captors?* Then, on the fifth morning, with the three hundredth protestor arrested, the jail full and the courts backlogged, Rye discovered the latest torture they had devised for him.

He was being sent to school.

There was a vacant boarded-up building on Front Street, the old Franklin School, which had been replaced by a high school on the South Hill, and the city was using it as a temporary jail to house the slop-over prisoners until this crisis ended.

It had been three years since Rye stepped foot inside a school. He'd always felt trapped there, saddled and reined, writing numbers on a slate board or reading Bible verses and hearing what an idiot he was for getting both wrong.

At dawn, Rye and the hardier of the men from the sweatbox were marched along with twenty others down Front Street, the first flakes of snow swirling in the gray sky. They trudged to a dark and imposing three-story brick building, a clock tower rising from the center, the hands stuck at midnight. On the steps, four civilians held rifles, paper stars marking them as deputized emergency jailors.

As the prisoners were led through two heavy wood doors, Rye looked down at the words etched in stone at his feet.

"*Sapienta et veritas,*" said a tall man with a heavy accent, as if reading Rye's mind. "Wisdom and truth."

"Whiskey and trout," said another, and a laugh went through the line of men.

"Wine and tomatoes," said another, and more laughter.

"Women and trouble," said another, and even the guards chuckled at this one.

"Water and turnips if you bums are lucky," said a good-natured emergency jailer, who turned out to be a barber and held his rifle by the barrel like a walking stick.

The school was dark and cold, no furniture, no heat or light, only a single blanket for each prisoner on a hard wood floor—but at least it wasn't a dungeon sweatbox. Rye got the best night's sleep he'd had since being arrested. Brazier said they shouldn't work at the school, either, so when they refused to cut their own firewood, Sullivan said fine, let them freeze, and he cut their rations in half. One cold night, they gave in and burned window sashes and doorframes to keep from freezing. They took the doors off cabinets and closets, and in one, they found a box of old books. They burned the box but not the books, and Rye leafed through them—*Pearson's Latin Prose Composition*, the *National Compendium for Penmanship,* and *Epochs in American History,* from 1896. He ran his hands over the raised letters on the covers and felt, for the first time in his life, cheated by his lack of schooling. That night he used the thick history book as a pillow and, in the morning, read about the American Revolution in slanting sunlight through a school window.

The number of IWW men left to arrest was dwindling, but there still seemed to be four or five new men every day—the prosecutor slowly holding arraignments in front of a drunk judge named Mann who told the newspapers his job was to "rid the city of this filth." The trials always went the same, charges read, objections overruled, Wobbly convicted of disorderly conduct and given thirty days. The leaders were held on disorderly charges but also conspiracy to incite a riot, six months in prison if convicted. The women suffragists and socialists were turned loose with citations, as were the progressive civilians who got caught up, and a few people too old or infirm to do jail time. Some days the drunk judge would feel compassion, and if a union man agreed to leave town, the charges would be dismissed. Most of those rode out on rails, but when one man climbed right back on a soapbox, Judge Mann stopped offering such leniency.

On Rye's fourth day in the school, the Salvation Army came through to assess the prisoners' treatment, and the guards lined Rye up with a dozen of the healthier-looking men in the school's old gymnasium. What we called the Starvation Army grandees came in uniforms like a real army, and a man with a red birthmark on his face walked past Rye, then turned back, looking him up and down. "How old are you, son?"

Rye didn't hear the full question, and he said, "Fine, sir."

But the other prisoners all stepped forward in line to look back at Rye. The jailers, too. And the Salvation Army man got red-faced and turned back to the head jailer. "How old is *this boy*?"

It was quiet a moment, and then the quick-witted barber with the rifle walking stick said, "Rye, if you jump a train in Butte going forty miles an hour toward Spokane—" and he didn't even finish the joke before the room was laughing.

"How *old* is this *boy*!" the flushed Salvation Army man asked again.

"That is, uh . . ." A jailer had the original booking list and he looked for Rye's name on it. "Dolan, Ryan J. Sixty-one."

The laughter was pealing now, and the Salvation Army man turned to Rye and asked more gently, "How old are you, son?"

Again Rye hesitated. "What is today?" he asked.

The man told him it was November tenth.

"Oh," he said. "Well, in a week, I will be seventeen."

10

Rye was put in the back of a wagon with five other shackled prisoners and taken across the river to the new fairy-tale courthouse, light stone walls, high turrets at every corner, and a huge central tower with flags on top. The prisoners were unloaded, unshackled, and climbed an ornate staircase to a dark-wood courtroom, where Rye found out the most remarkable fact of his life to that point.

He had a lawyer.

Ryan J. Dolan of Nothing, Nowhere, having neither house nor bed, nothing a person might call a possession, somehow had a lawyer. Rye wondered if that, more than waking on a ball field or eagles or George Washington's hair, was what it really meant to be an American.

His lawyer's name was Fred Moore, and the first words out of his mouth confused Rye: "This is a travesty, Mr. Dolan, an obvious violation of habeas corpus."

"Oh," Rye said, hoping he meant the case against him.

The IWW's strategy had been to ask for separate trials, to clog the courts, and to reject lawyers, since representation might give credence to what they saw as an unconstitutional anti-speech law. But then the city began charging the protestors with disorderly conduct instead of the underlying gathering-and-speaking law, and so Fred Moore volunteered to represent the union for free. He seemed only a few years older than Rye and, except for his glasses and tweed, was nothing like Rye would have expected a lawyer to look, but like a boy who had borrowed his father's suit.

But he was aces in the courtroom, habeas corpusing again—an actual writ this time—and railing against the city having held in custody "this mere child" for more than a week, "not even putting him in the incorrigible-youth facility but beating and torturing him in a sweatbox full of adult men!"

Judge Mann was sober enough to ask the prosecutor, Pugh, "What of this?" and Pugh, a balding, confident man who *did* look like a lawyer, said Rye "gave false information during his booking and ought to be charged with that as well. His arrest was a coordinated ploy meant to embarrass the city and further disrupt the judicial system. And I would ask the court, what harm is there in temporarily incarcerating a despicable and shiftless wastrel, likely in better circumstances than his wayward and immoral life on the outside."

Rye sat still through all of this, hoping his own lawyer could match Pugh in spewing mouthfuls. And then, like one more pull from the tap, the prosecutor looked right at Rye and said, "And finally, as Mr. Dolan has lived an adult life of criminal vagrancy and broken adult laws willfully, the state recommends that he be tried and treated as an adult by this court."

The prosecutor sat, and the judge said, "Mr. Moore?" and Rye turned to his lawyer, who stared at the floor a moment, Rye worried he might be stumped.

Then Mr. Moore said simply, "Sixty-one." And he took a deep breath. "Mr. Dolan was recorded in the booking sheet as being sixty-one years old, Your Honor. The state would have you believe that a conniving sixteen-year-old looked at his jailers and thought them too stupid to tell the difference between sixteen and sixty-one. While we are prepared to stipulate to the stupidity of Mr. Dolan's jailers, the idea that Mr. Dolan tried to pass himself off as an old man to embarrass the city is ludicrous on its face, Your Honor."

This brought a murmur of laughter and then Mr. Moore was on his feet and every bit Mr. Pugh's match, railing at the "bastardization of decency and law," saying that the city would "attempt to *retroactively* remedy an egregious mistake by blaming an abused child for his own abuse, a poor indigent born under fortune's darkest cloud, an orphan boy with no home, no parents, nothing of comfort in this hard world."

As his lawyer spoke, Rye felt an odd mix of emotions—pride that someone so eloquent was working on his behalf, but embarrassment, too, a painful self-awareness that he was the hobo waif Mr. Moore was describing, and shame at the way he must look and smell, he and the other scraggly shit-souls shackled behind him awaiting their own trials. He looked around the courtroom at the men in fine suits. And he thought of Gig back in jail, every bit this lawyer's match in intellect but born, as Mr. Moore said, under fortune's darkest cloud, with no chance at fine suits and fancy courtroom Latin.

Rye slumped in his chair as Fred Moore finished speaking. Mistaking Rye's shame for worry, Mr. Moore patted his arm and said, "It's going to be okay, Ryan."

Judge Mann sighed, then flipped through some papers. Finally, he looked down at the prosecutor. "What do you say you toss this fish back?"

Then Mr. Pugh smiled as if even *he* hadn't believed his own argument, and he turned and winked at Rye as the judge rapped his gavel and said, "Charges dismissed. Mr. Dolan, you are free to go, but I had better not see you back in this courtroom, because I will not be so generous next time."

The words stung Rye: *shiftless wastrel* and *poor indigent*, beaten and jailed for eight days and then *tossed back*? All so the union could make a point, the judge joking about who got the best of it—like some kind of game?

He was moved to the backbench and watched his five teammates take the field. He felt bad for Mr. Moore, who didn't have a sixteen-year-old waif and stupid jailers for these cases and tried arguing the illegality of the law against union men gathering on the street, Judge Mann saying he wasn't prepared to rule on the merits of that—"Only the lawless behavior of anarchist rascals"—and despite Mr. Moore's energetic *ipsos* and *factos*, one by one the other five struck out, were found guilty of disorderly conduct and given their thirty days back at Franklin School.

Two jailers came in to shackle the five men—while the other team gathered at the bench in their bow-tied uniforms—and Rye felt again the horror of this game.

"Hold the line," Rye said as his teammates were led out.

"Happy birthday," one of them said back.

Jules, 1909

THREE YEARS before she died, my mother sent me to live with the French ferryman and said I should not speak anymore. I could talk English or French, since she did not consider them *speaking*. What she meant was I should leave our language behind. She said it did not belong in the world anymore and would only get me hurt. It was losing your mother and your tongue at once.

She gave me another warning. Stay out of it.

Out of what? I asked.

Everything. Listen. Walk to the side. Keep yourself. Go the other way.

And then she warned me about my laugh. I had a great whelping laugh like my father's, and she said that if I laughed at the wrong people, it would get me killed, as sure as it had got my father killed, as sure as if he'd pulled a knife.

He *did* pull a knife, I said.

But that was *after* he enraged a man by laughing at him, she said. So, if you must laugh, do it with your mouth closed. Through your nose.

After I went to live with the ferryman, I tried to stay quiet. I listened, and walked to the side. My mother died and I spoke French and English and no Salish or Sahaptin, although I still sometimes muttered words to myself.

But I could no more laugh through my nose than I could see through my ears.

She was right, it did get me in trouble, my laugh, that morning on the river with the Dolan boys and Early Reston, the man who beat the cop. I laughed with them boys and a couple of old hands I'd ranched with, and I followed them all to the union hall, even though I knew better, and we laughed and we ate and listened to speeches and I sang and laughed with the union boys for two days, sang and laughed myself right into the city jail.

After the riot, I was put in a crowded cell with seven others, we were cold and hungry, but we still laughed and sang. Then, on my fourth night in jail, a cop pulled me out alone and brought me to the empty courtyard. It was a nothing sky, gray and starless. The cop made me wait. When I was a boy, Plante used to make me wait for his anger to set, and so I hated waiting, shifting foot to foot, wondering when the blow would come. I have always found the waiting worse than the beating. Death comes for everything, but only spiders and men make you wait for it.

Eventually, that cop Clegg came out. Our first morning in jail he had come in to ask the Dolan brothers and me what happened that day at the river.

Now I'm here to talk to you alone, Chief, said Clegg. You got no reason to protect them Montana boys. Or the man who hit my sergeant that day. So why don't you just give me the man's name and I'll see to it you're let go.

I stayed quiet.

This ain't your fight.

Stay out. Don't speak. Keep yourself. Eyes down, walk the sides. But no laughter? When the world is *etrange et ridicule*?

He whispered: Come on, Chief. Give me a name. Who was it?

I wished I could make a joke like the older Dolan saying John

Rockefeller, but the cop wouldn't take that from me. Still, just think-ing it made me laugh.

At least no more waiting. Clegg hit me in the stomach and then in the chest with his baton. On the third swing I felt something give, a rib. And I caved in. There was no breath anywhere in that yard.

A jailer dragged me back to the cell and dropped me like an empty shirt. I slept all night on the stone floor.

In my sleep, I imagined my mother would come, call me by name, and be angry: *What did I tell you?* Once, when I was a boy, we saw an old French-Canadian skinner fighting with crows over a dead rac-coon. *You see?* my mother said. But I never saw. And remembering her now wasn't the same as seeing her in my sleep. Maybe old men didn't get to dream about their mothers anymore.

I woke up wheezing in the dark cell. Eight of us taking turns on two hard cots. I'd done vagrant time in the stone blockhouse, but not packed like this. Nothing in our guts but stale bread and dank water. After the beating, and the wheeze in my ribs, I worried this might finally put me in a grave box. We took shifts on the cots. One of them said, Why's the old Indian get a turn, but the others ignored him and I took to that cot like a sweet wife. They were all decent men in the cell except that one. Not a bad number, one idiot in eight. I had a cousin once who told me kindness lives in the lips, and when I got a good look at the one who questioned my right to the cot, he had only a line where he took in food and put out *merde*. He was lucky I was not in good health or I'd have put him on the stone floor myself.

After my beating, I saw Rye once at the rock pile but I was too sick to speak. *I'm sorry,* he said, but how could I blame him for my own laughter. He was a good kid and I hoped they would not beat the good entirely from him. One night I heard they moved him and some others from the sweatbox to an old school building and I was glad.

There was a Finnish sawyer in my cell, a man named Halla, and one night I must've muttered in French, because after that, he made jokes in the language whenever they brought us hunks of bread and dirty water. *Merci, garçon!* he'd chirp, and then stick his lip out in a frown and wave his handkerchief like a fancy tablecloth. *Bon appétit!* This Halla would sniff the stale bread as if it was the finest cheese and say to the jailer, *Mais mon vin, garçon? Deux Côtes du Rhone?* I would laugh every time at this, and Halla would wink at me. Once I joined in and said to the guard, *Deux steaks du boeuf s'il vous plaît,* and Halla clapped my back and said good on me, though my French was *chien de champagne*. Country-dog French. I laughed at that, too. Laughed and coughed and could not stop. Blood on my hands.

Halla said, We need to get you a doctor, Jules.

But the jailer said the infirmary was full.

At night we talked about food and women like men who had experienced neither. Halla told me about the herring his mother used to fry every night for dinner. I asked, Did you get tired of herring? He said, Never. I asked, Are the herring still in the Baltic? He looked at me like I was crazy. Of course, he said.

I told him our river once ran thick with salmon and steelhead, and at the falls, the fish rose like flies over a pond, and you could swing a drop net and catch *dejeuner pour deux*. My uncle grew so fat on fish and shade-berries that he became a bear. Fur grew all over his body and his voice became a growl.

But our fish are gone now, I said. The dams keep them away. Now our river is shit and trash and wash from the mines. On the ground, they drove all the game away with hammering and sawing, they cleared the hillsides of berries to build more houses—they killed the world and called it progress.

Halla patted my arm. Rest now, Jules. But I was dreaming and fevered and feared I was going over.

I was too sick to work the rock pile, but Clegg told the jailers I was holding out on him and they took me to the pile and handed me a pick. I always liked to work, but standing in sleet, watching shackled men *not* hit rocks, was torture. Twice I fell, and the second time I could not get up. Halla and another man carried me back to our cell. *Ne t'an fais pas, Jules*, said Halla.

Je ne suis pas inquiet, I said. I wasn't worried. I wanted to tell Halla about the boy who stole my ferry, but it was so many words, and I wasn't sure what it would mean this time. People expect a story to always mean the same thing, but I have found that stories change like people do.

I wasn't asleep and I wasn't awake. I missed my shift on the floor and I sat up on one of the cots to see Halla had given up his turn for me. In the morning, my legs felt a mile away. My face burned. Even my cough had no breath behind it.

Winter fever, said a jailer.

Another listened to my chest. Ague, he said.

Sleep. Sunlight in dreams I did not want to leave. I looked for my mother to put her face against my fevered cheek, to use my name, to chide me, anything, but still she did not come.

Halla told me I was talking in my sleep in a language he couldn't understand. He tried to repeat what I'd said but I told him that it sounded like he was speaking horse. I said, Come closer. Halla bent down so his ear was near my mouth: I was ordering us two steaks.

Halla laughed and patted my chest. *Très bien, Jules*. After a time, he said, Do you have people, Jules?

I had a wife, I told him.

I should have stopped there. But I could not.

My wife's sister had a daughter. My niece.

I should not have given the name. But I was afraid and so I gave Halla the name of my niece and her husband in Spokane.

It's okay, he said again. Sleep now, Jules.

Heat. Breath catching. Slip down a ladder. Pass into dreams, bales of hay and garden rows and a thicket of blackberries and a dog with white eyes and still no mother but an old aunt who didn't recognize me. And in my dream I could not remember enough of the language to ask for her. I could not even name all that I had lost.

Men were talking over me.

Hands on my shoulders and legs.

Halla's face. You're getting out, Jules.

Deux vin, I said.

Goodbye, Jules, he said.

I see you, I said, but in what language?

Repose-toi, maintenent, Halla said. *Mon ami.*

Night. The sky was clear. Cold clean air. I gulped it like water. Was this freedom? I was being carried on a litter, ice crunching beneath the feet of the men carrying my body.

They put me in the back of a wagon and I drifted again. Cold air. Horses crying, rustled, clopping, pulling the wagon. Ruts. Blankets. Wagon. Heat.

Then we were outside her house. Dom came out, with his big arms and his kind eyes. He spoke to the jailers. Muffled words. Yes, he said, Jules Plante is my wife's uncle. Of course.

The litter rose up the steps with me on it. And I was delivered into the warmth of Gemma's house. And then her face filled the world above me.

Hello, Uncle.

Gemma, I'm—no breath.

It's okay. Stay quiet, Uncle, it's okay.

It's what my mother would have said, too, stay quiet, Jules.

Heat from the fire. O Gemma. Lovely girl. Jewels and gems.

Sleep now, Uncle. You're home.

Her husband left the room, and she bent and whispered in my ear.

And the rest of life was dreams.

PART II

I fell in love with my country—its rivers, prairies, forests, mountains, cities and people. . . . It could be a paradise on earth if it belonged to the people, not to a small owning class.

—Elizabeth Gurley Flynn

11

She was the daughter of an Irish firebrand named Thomas Flynn and a lace-curtain suffragist named Ann Gurley, raised on the speeches of Emma Goldman and Mother Jones. At ten, Elizabeth Gurley Flynn was railing against inequity at Harlem social clubs and calling for the women's vote at her grammar school. She drew hundreds when she spoke on the street and, by the time of her first arrest, at fifteen, was locally famous, dubbed by progressive newspapers the "East Side Joan of Arc, an Irish beauty with blue eyes, filmy black hair and a fiery manner of speaking." The establishment *New York Times* took a harder tack, calling her a "she-dog of anarchy." At seventeen, Gurley Flynn joined the IWW as an organizer, rallying workers and leading strikes in Pennsylvania and New Jersey, working her way west, speaking in mining camps and earning the nickname *Rebel Girl*. She married a Montana labor man named Jones and, having just run a successful protest in Missoula, was sent to Spokane to help organize its free speech battle—at nineteen, already a grizzled veteran of dozens of union actions.

Rye's lawyer, Fred Moore, was explaining all of this as they left the courthouse after his release, but Rye was having trouble concentrating. A jailer had brought his clothes to him, and though they'd been laundered, a bloodstain still covered his shirt like a bib. As they walked down the courthouse steps, people kept staring, and Rye self-consciously pulled his coat tight around his neck.

In Spokane, the seasons could turn like a switch, autumn light one day, winter dark the next. A wall of courthouse maples burst with color the day Rye went to jail. Nine days later, the trees were frosted and skeletal.

Rye shared their mood: What was he supposed to do now? How would he explain his absence to Mrs. Ricci? Would she charge him against their wintering money for the eight days he'd been gone? And what about Gig? Who knew how long he'd be in jail or what trouble he'd face in there?

Fred Moore stopped on the sidewalk and turned to him. "So," he said, "if you're amenable to it, this woman would like to speak with you this afternoon."

Rye looked up. "Ursula the Great?"

"Who?" The lawyer looked dumbfounded. "No. Elizabeth Gurley Flynn, the woman I was just telling you about, Mrs. Jack Jones by her married name." He put a hand on Rye's arm. "But I should warn you. She can be—" He cleared his throat. "What I mean is, she has a certain way of . . . well, her nature is—" Then Rye's lawyer, who seemed never at a loss for words, laughed at his own inability to find the right one. "Let's just say she is redoubtable."

Rye stared.

"Estimable?"

Rye shifted his feet on the frosty gravel.

"Formidable?"

Rye liked having a lawyer, but the man could be as hard to understand as Old Jules on a French bender. He wondered how many words he'd have to hear before he recognized one, so he gave up and said, "Oh," thinking he would figure out what *formidable* meant once he met the woman.

Rye walked with Fred Moore across the river, which steamed like a bath in the cool air. They passed Stevens Street and the job agencies, guarded by men with downturned rifles. Down Front Street, past cafés, hotels, service halls, laundries, and bars—the street nearly empty of tramps and day workers, so many now behind bars or run out of town. A cop standing across from the IWW building took note of Rye and his lawyer as they entered. Inside, the foyer was empty, cantina closed, the cops having seized back issues of the *In-*

dustrial Worker from the newsstand and arrested the editors for conspiracy to incite a riot.

In the meeting hall, they could hear raised voices from the back office, and that was when Fred Moore put a hand on Rye's arm. "I'm sorry for taking you into the fray without a bath or a change of clothing. Miss Flynn—er, Mrs. Jones requested that you arrive bearing the evidence of your mistreatment." Then Fred Moore gently reached over and opened Rye's coat to reveal the bloodstain on his shirt. "Her idea . . ."

Rye looked down. Seeing his own dried blood made him think of Gig. "Mr. Moore, I don't suppose you'd see about getting my brother out, too."

"Of course," he said. "I will look into it immediately."

"Gregory Dolan," Rye said. "And there was another man with us, an Indian named Jules."

Fred Moore pulled out a pad and wrote the names down. "I'll see what I can find out. And I'll get you some proper clothing. You look to be about my size." He reached for the door of the union office.

"I don't suppose you got a bowler hat," Rye said. "I always thought I would look smart in a bowler."

"I'll see what I can do," Mr. Moore said, and he opened the door and Rye got his first look at the redoubtable, estimable, formidable Elizabeth Gurley Flynn.

12

She was just a kid, more *girl* than *rebel*, small and sprightly and not a line or seam in her open face. She seemed to change from different angles—a bit of the schoolgirl, a bit of the nun, a bit of the Irish saloon girl—long black hair loose to the waist, held thick by a black ribbon. She wore a long-sleeved black satin blouse with a high collar revealing a narrow black necktie, above a plain black bustled skirt—black on black on pure Irish pale. Her slate blue eyes were big and dipped at the corners so she seemed to be alternately pleading and sympathizing.

Rye wondered then if *redoubtable* meant a thing so pretty and un-expected that it actually hurt to look at. She glanced up and saw Rye and his lawyer at the doorway, but she did not announce them, instead turning her attention back to the five men standing around her, their backs to Rye.

The men shuffled and shifted their weight, hats in hand. Gurley Flynn was the only one sitting, perched sidesaddle on a small sofa, as if choosing between unworthy suitors.

The only man Rye recognized in the room was the IWW secre-tary, nervous Charlie Filigno. He was standing nearest Mrs. Jones, trying to explain in heavily accented English that they were plan-ning a second free speech action for November 29, exactly four weeks after the first. Word was going out for more soapbox speakers and floaters willing to clog the jails. They planned to keep up the pressure with news stories while they battled in the courts. "Eliza-beth has offer to give speeches to raise money—"

"A thousand dollars," interrupted Gurley. "That's how much I in-tend to raise. In three weeks, the great Clarence Darrow will be back in Boise delivering a lecture on the Haywood case, and I plan be there, to hire him to come to Spokane and challenge this outrageous anti-speech law once and for all."

Filigno cleared his throat. "Elizabeth hopes—"

"I hope to use my notoriety to raise this money, as I did in Mis-soula," she said, "until the cops there overplayed their hand by ar-resting me."

The men shifted, made wary eye contact, and a chinless man cleared his throat. "Mrs. Jones, we all admired what you done in Missoula, but you had thirty men in jail there. There's three hun-dred here. And frankly, we got concerns about allowing a nineteen-year-old girl in your *current condition*—"

"Allowing?" She laughed. "Mr. Davis, with all due respect, I have given speeches from Maine to Montana, and I have never once been *allowed* to speak."

Standing next to her, Charlie Filigno put his hand out to calm her just as one of the men, whom Rye couldn't see from the doorway, grew agitated. "Mrs. Jones, you will refrain from such outbursts—"

And that was the moment when Mrs. Elizabeth Gurley Flynn Jones thought it best to see Rye. She popped off the sofa, and that was also the moment when he understood her current condition— she appeared to be some months pregnant.

"Mr. Dolan! Mr. Moore!" she said. "Please, come in."

They did, Moore first, then Rye. The union men took a step back, repelled by his appearance, just as Gurley Flynn must have hoped. As for the Rebel Girl, she greeted Rye's lawyer, then took both of Rye's hands like he was her oldest-dearest, her white skin creamy against his rough, scarred mitts.

She spun and presented him. "Gentlemen, I trust you know the young hero of our movement, Mr. Ryan Dolan, only this morning released from jail. Ryan, these men are union leaders with the AFL and WFM—carpenters, metal workers, and miners—our *allies* in this struggle." She leaned on that word, then gestured toward Rye's lawyer. "You know our brilliant young attorney, Mr. Moore." She let go of Rye's hands and had him sit on the sofa next to her. She smiled as if this were a garden party she'd organized. "These giants of labor were just explaining to me that the people of Spokane would be scandalized to find out that engaging in sexual congress with one's husband occasionally results in pregnancy."

Rye felt like a firecracker had gone off in the room. One of the men gasped. Another snapped: "Mrs. Jones! We are simply asking for some decency! That you not make a spectacle of yourself and that you let others do the public speaking."

"Others?" she said. "What others would you suggest?"

"Elizabeth—" Charlie Filigno said.

But she wouldn't even look at Charlie, her intense dark eyes sweeping the room, challenging. "My entire membership is caged, living on bread and water," she said. "To whom should I turn for this public speaking, Mr. Bennett?"

That's when the oldest of the union men, a big mottled man with reddish-gray hair, stepped forward: "Enough, Mrs. Jones!" The way the other men deferred to him, Rye figured him to be the biggest labor boss. "I'm not your father, but I will speak to you like a child if you continue to act like one. You ask our union's support and then you speak to us in such coarse language? While brashly promoting yourself as Gurley-Flynn in the newspapers?" His face kept reddening. "Maybe that's acceptable in New York City, but here, for a married woman, it is unseemly and wrong—"

Her face flushed as well. "Mr. Cawley—"

But the red-faced man would not be quieted. "I worked alongside your husband in Butte, and I know for a fact Jack was against you taking this trip! And yet here you are, *with child*, run off from a devoted husband, sullying your reputation and that of every workingman in the west!"

Gurley Flynn drew her lips tight. "My apologies if I offend you, Mr. Cawley, but I use my maiden name because Elizabeth Jones is unknown as a speaker, whereas Elizabeth Gurley Flynn is a name whose reputation I burnished—"

Cawley interrupted again. "Your reputation is what we are here to protect!"

Again she interrupted her interrupter: "—*whose reputation* I burnished from New York to Chicago to Missoula to Spokane—"

Oh, but that got even further under the skin of the union man, and he took two steps toward her, his face going scarlet to the mottled line of his hair. "Enough! You ask for our support—now listen!"

Gurley gripped Rye's arm. She was shaking.

The man held out a copy of the *Industrial Worker*. "Your first article, you call Judge Mann 'a known bottle-tipper' and 'a lackey of the parasites!' You call the Spokane police 'hired thugs' and 'half-witted Hiberians.'"

Gurley half-smiled. "Too alliterative, Mr. Cawley?"

"Too far, Mrs. Jones! You go too far! You go too far confusing the cause of labor with that of socialism and suffrage, the Negro and Indian, and you go too far now!" He crumpled the newspaper. "My union is committed to higher wages, not a goddamn revolution! In fact, I'm not sure this outfit of yours *is* a union," he continued, "and not a menagerie! Every day the *Spokesman* runs the names of foreign savages you trot onto soapboxes!"

"Listen—" she said quietly.

"No, *you listen!*" He took another step forward, until he was right above her. "From now on, you will use your married name! And if Jack doesn't join you here soon, I will put you on a train back to Montana myself! While you're in Spokane, you will stay *off* the soap-box, off the street, and indoors at all times—"

She smiled. "So, I am not free to speak about free speech?"

But Cawley was not done. "You may deliver speeches at women's clubs, but if I hear you have been on a single street corner addressing men, or using your maiden name, I will pull my union's support. You will travel at all times with an escort, and if you publish anything in that red rag of yours, it will be respectful, and it will be under the name *Mrs. Jack Jones*. Do you understand?"

Gurley glanced around at the other men but found no allies. Even Filigno was looking at his shoes.

Cawley finally took a step back and sighed, his anger having run its course. He ran his hand through his thin hair and put his hat back on. "Mrs. Jones, I don't care if you get a nickel out of every Negro hoe-boy and half-breed Celestial whore in the state, but I will *not* ask God-fearing American unionists to line up behind a pregnant wayward wife."

The air was gone from the room.

"Gentlemen, can we—" Charlie Filigno began.

Gurley sprang up and smiled broadly. "Good point, Charlie. Let's thank these gentlemen for their support and get back to work." She turned to the mottled man. "Mr. Cawley, I assure you, my husband will be in Spokane soon. In the meantime, I will travel at all times with an escort. In fact—" She turned to Rye. "Mr. Dolan will accompany me and speak about his mistreatment."

The men all looked at Rye. "He's a boy," one of them said.

"He is a boy who was beaten and jailed for seeking honest work. I guarantee everyone who hears this Irish orphan's story will imagine their own son."

That word again—*orphan*.

"And by your own description, Mr. Cawley," she went on, "I would say that as the only white male American-born, English-speaking member of our union currently *not* in jail, he's ideal."

Rye went almost as red as Cawley. Not because he didn't like Gurley calling him ideal but because he wasn't actually a dues-paying member of the IWW.

And no way could he imagine getting up and jawsmithing like his brother.

"Mr. Dolan," Gurley said, taking his hand again. "Please. Tell these men about the treatment you endured."

Rye wished Mr. Moore were still there to give all the proper *habeas ipsos,* but the lawyer had slipped out. The rest of the men were staring at him.

"Go ahead, Mr. Dolan," she said, "tell them what happened."

"Well," Rye said, "we woke on a ball field."

He hardly remembered what he said after that—he just talked, about his brother and Jules and the slate-haired cop and Gig telling him to stay at Mrs. Ricci's boardinghouse but him sneaking off to watch the free speech riot and Walsh and the Italian singer and seeing Gig get arrested and stepping on the soapbox himself and being locked up in the sweatbox and then the school and the Salvation Army discovering he was only sixteen and the judge releasing him that very day.

"And now . . ." Rye looked over at Gurley. "I'll do whatever it takes to get my brother out, too."

The union men took turns shaking his hand on their way out, and clapping his shoulder, and then they left. When it was just Filigno,

Gurley, and Rye in the office, Elizabeth turned and said, "You did well, Ryan."

Then Fred Moore came back in the room with a stack of clothes. On top was a bowler hat. "As promised," said Fred.

The pants were fine, gray, with a matching jacket, braces, and a white stiff-collared shirt. Rye immediately put the gray bowler on his head.

"Looks good," Gurley said.

Fred Moore pulled some notes from his jacket. "I also got the charging documents for your brother, Ryan," he said. "He's being held with the union leaders, charged with conspiracy. They're seeking six months."

"Six *months*?"

"Don't worry, we'll fight it," Fred Moore said. "Your brother is not an elected union official, and since he was only on the free speech committee, we can use his overcharging to challenge the anti-gathering law."

Rye was about to ask what that all meant when Fred Moore flipped to another page in his file. "The other name, your friend Jules?" he said. "A Jules Plante was released to family two days ago."

Of all the things that had happened that day, this seemed, in some ways, the most unlikely to Rye. He took the hat off. "Wait," he said. "Jules has a family?"

Gemma

I HEARD no breathing from the other room. I touched my husband's broad back. "Dom?"

He rolled over. "I'll go see." He pulled on his pants and walked across the floor. I heard his footsteps out in the hall, and then it was quiet again. The steps moved into the kitchen, and the cookstove door opened, Dom stoking embers, a log going in. A minute later, he got back in bed. "He's alive, Gemma."

It was decent of him, but my husband was nothing if not decent. Especially about Uncle Jules. The very first time he'd shown up, dirty from the road, Dom had invited him to stay. "He's family," Dom had said. I was humbled. Not every man would let an old Indian shirttail relation of his wife's come sleep at the house each year.

Jules had Spokane and Palus parents, and a Scottish trader on one side. He was born on the river before the city existed, then sent to live with an old ferryman who ran the crossing between here and Idaho. In his thirties, he married my mother's sister, Agnella. As I told Dom that first year, Jules was the only family I had. Mother and Aunt Agnella were both dead from flu and my father long since run off.

Dom liked Uncle Jules. When he showed up after harvest, he and Dom would work together wintering the house, cutting firewood, making repairs. I knew Dom gave him money, too, even though I said a winter bed was payment enough. Jules brought presents for the girls—corn dolls and wagon-wheel rugs. He'd stay two or three weeks in November and then drag a train south to hunt work in California. Fourteen years Dom and I had been married, and Jules came for eight of them, no warning, just him walking up our road with his pack and long duster.

He always looked so big walking up that road.

But the man the jailers brought in the wagon was half that size. They said Jules got caught up in the labor trouble from the newspaper. When he became sick, Jules gave them my name and they released him to the closest thing to family, his niece by marriage.

Dom didn't hesitate when that coach arrived. He cleared a place in the living room, put blankets on the davenport, and tried to make Jules comfortable.

Jules's gaze flickered in and out, then fell on me. "Uncle Jules," I said. The girls stood in the doorway. Elena was thirteen, Maria nine. Maria had been studying Indians in school and used to pepper Jules with questions and even asked him to teach her Salish. But Jules, wary of teaching the old language, had told her French words instead. He'd held up a knife. *"Couteau,"* he'd said.

But Maria was too smart for that. "Not French, I want to learn Indian."

"That language doesn't work anymore," he'd said. *"C'est disparu."*

And now he was on the davenport in our living room, drawing what sounded like his final breaths.

"Is Uncle Jules gonna be okay?" Maria asked that first night.

Elena was the quiet one. She and I heated wet rags for his chest. We kept the fire hot and tried to break his fever and that awful rattle in his chest. Dom always said Jules could lift as much as a man half his age, extra strength coiled in that body, even with his hard life. Now he was just a weak old man. Still, he survived the first night and seemed to be improving in the morning, but on the second night he took a turn. Short, uneven breaths, and he couldn't open his eyes. Dom looked over at me. We'd both buried parents. We had the girls say goodbye before they went to bed.

"Is there anything he would want us to do?" Dom asked in bed. "People we should contact? Preparations to make?"

I said I didn't know.

"Are there leggings or something?"

"Leggings?"

"Funeral leggings? Or buckskins or something? I think I've heard that."

"How would I know?"

"He's your uncle," Dom said. "Did he ever say anything about his wishes?"

I told him that Jules didn't talk like that. He told stories. He liked to make himself laugh. The only thing I ever recalled him saying was how, when he was a boy, his people sometimes put the dead on platforms in trees. This terrified him. He thought that if he walked beneath one of these trees, someone would reach down and pull him up into it. Once, he and the ferryman's son climbed a tree to see if there were bones up there, but there was nothing. They debated whether animals had made off with the remains, or if the spirit had gone on to the afterlife. When loggers took down trees, Jules would say to himself, *Goodbye, Uncle, goodbye, Grandmother.*

Dom listened intently. "You don't think he'd want us to put him in a tree."

"No, I don't think that was the point," I said. It was hard to explain someone like Uncle Jules to a man as direct as Dom.

"What was he like then?" Dom asked.

"Jules? The same. The big booming laugh. He didn't have the trouble with liquor then. Not until Agnella died."

My mother and her sister died within a month of each other, in the 1890 Russian flu outbreak. Agitta and Agnella were only a year apart, dragged west by their miner father, Giacomo, and his wife, Gemma, after whom I was named. Grandma Gemma died not long after they arrived, and Grandpa Gio died in a cave-in when his daughters were sixteen and seventeen. Neither girl was what you'd call a looker, unless you meant to look away from, and even in a mining town, neither was beset with suitors. Mother married late, a union that lasted just long enough to produce me. She would volunteer, without being asked, that my shiftless father "flew off with a soiled dove." Then there was Jules, who met Aunt Agnella while digging fence posts near the family house in Mullan. After that, Jules was in and out of our lives, catching work on ranches and orchards most of the year, during which time it would be just Mother, Aunt Agnella, and me in the little Mullan house.

All spring and summer Jules worked farm jobs from Canada to California, but he'd come winter with Agnella and Agitta and me, cut firewood, and catch up on repairs to our little house. Once the snow came, Jules would hibernate, barely leave his chair in front of the fire, drink tea, smoke his pipe, and tell stories. I never shared much of this with Dom's family, for fear they would judge me sordid, coming from the kind of women who took up with Indians and gamblers who ran off with whores.

I sat up in bed. "There *was* one story he used to tell, about an outlaw who stole their ferry boat." In the story, Jules was twelve or thirteen, working on Plante's cable ferry. One day two outlaws stole the ferry, cut the ropes and escaped downstream. Jules tracked the men from the shore on horseback as the raft rode the current down to the falls. One fell off and Jules kept expecting the other to swim for shore. Instead the man simply rode the boat over the falls.

"Maybe he couldn't swim," Dom said.

"Maybe," I said. "But Jules said the man didn't look scared, not the way someone would if they couldn't swim. He seemed almost eager, and right before he went over the falls, he sat up and called out, 'Watch!'"

"Watch?" Dom said.

"Watch. Jules yelled from the riverbank, 'Swim, you idiot!' But the young outlaw just waved and went over the falls."

Dom waited for more, but there was no more. "And . . . he died?"

"Well of course he died," I said.

Dom just stared ahead, as if trying to picture it. "Huh," he said.

"Jules said if the kid jumped off the boat and swam to shore, he'd have been arrested and hanged. But as long as he stayed *on the boat*, his fate was his own. I think that's why Jules liked the story. And why he rode the rails instead of moving onto a reservation. I think he came to believe it was better to choose your life, and that even choosing your death was better than letting someone else choose your life."

In bed, Dom sat with this a moment. Finally, he opened his mouth to speak.

Oh, how I loved my sweet, simple husband. I put my hand on his thick, hairy arm. "No, darlin'," I said gently. "I don't think Uncle Jules would want us to put him on a raft and send him over the falls."

I woke. The sun was up. After spending all night listening for Jules's breathing, I'd overslept. It was after seven and Dom must have gone to work. I put on my robe and went out to the living room. The fire was out. Jules lay still on the davenport. The grimace was gone from his mouth. I was equally heartbroken and relieved. With Mother there had been gasps, jerks, and shudders. I didn't want that for Jules. I put my hand above his mouth. I touched his head, pushed the hair away.

Before the girls woke, I walked down the road to ask the Carvers if their boy could ride downtown to notify the county coroner that my uncle had passed.

"Your uncle?" asked Mona Carver. "I didn't know you had relations around here."

"Yes," I said, "my uncle." I walked home, snow crunching under my boots, built the kitchen fire, and lit it again. Then I went into the girls' room. I sat on the edge of their bed. Elena sat up without me saying anything.

Maria was just waking. "Uncle Jules?"

I nodded.

She crawled into my lap and wept into my chest. "I want to see him."

"He's gone, Maria."

"In heaven?"

"Yes," I said.

"The same heaven we go to?"

I did not know what to say. Most of Jules's people had gone to the reservation and got Christianity from the missionaries a generation ago. But Jules hated the missionaries and said cruelty and hope should never be served together. He'd gone to the Billy Sunday tent revivals when the old ballplayer came through town—but more for Billy's good humor and free food than the preaching.

He talked sometimes about elders who practiced the old ways. *Washani*. Dreamer Cult. But he rarely shared details except a single prophecy that he told like it was just another story: that after the shimmering people destroyed the world, knocked down the mountains, drained the rivers, and ate all the animals—the true people would be resurrected and have the land to themselves.

But did Jules believe this? I had no idea.

I suspected he did not. I didn't think Jules practiced the old ways any more than he practiced Catholicism. If Jules had a religion, I would call it the Church of the Big Laugh.

"Mama," Maria said. "*Can* Indians go to heaven?"

"If anyone can," I said.

I covered Jules with a bedsheet and sat with my girls in the kitchen, next to the fire. I could not get warm. I made tea and bread with raspberry jam. Elena ate quietly. Every few minutes, Maria would sniff.

The coroner's assistant arrived at noon with a man from the funeral parlor. Both men seemed surprised to see an old Indian in our house. I asked the funeral man if there were special considerations for Indian deaths, but he did not know. He said he could carve a feather on the headstone. "Did he have a name like Two Clouds or Bear Paw?" the man asked.

I did not know his Indian name—but I was fairly sure it wasn't Two Clouds. I suspected it bore some relation to the name the French ferryman had given him, but I didn't even know that. "Jules Plante will be fine," I said.

They were about to load the body when two young men came walking up our drive. These were not funeral men, but a boy in tramp clothes and a new bowler hat, and a young man in a fine suit who introduced himself as the young tramp's lawyer. The boy in the bowler said he was a friend of Jules.

The lawyer said he had inquired with the jail about Jules's condition and had been told that he was released and brought to the house of his niece. Was I her?

Yes, I said.

Might they see him?

"No," I said. "He died this morning."

The boy's legs buckled and he reached for his lawyer's arm. "We're too late."

The lawyer explained that he was working on this union fight— perhaps I had read about it in the newspaper—I nodded—and that he was concerned that Jules's treatment in jail might have contributed to his death.

"He had pneumonia," I said.

The lawyer said his condition had come about from being confined eight men to a two-man cell, and that he would be happy to represent me in an inquest into the circumstances of Jules's death.

As the lawyer spoke, the boy kept rubbing his face and looking at different spots on the ground. Sorrow was written on his pocked, thin face.

"What's your name, son?" I asked.

"Ryan Dolan," he said. And as if he'd been reminded by his mother, he thought to remove his hat, revealing a rat's nest of brown hair underneath. "I worked with your uncle up near Rockford. Went to the tent revivals with him."

I nodded but said nothing.

Grief can be a stingy emotion. I was in no mood to share it with a rabble-rousing lawyer and a young drifter. A horrible stain, a mixture of sweat and blood, trailed the front of the young man's shirt, and he absentmindedly turned the hat in his hands. Still, he was Jules's friend, so I invited the boy inside to pay his respects.

"He looks so small," Ryan said.

My girls peeked in from the kitchen and I pointed at them to go back. I knew they'd want to say goodbye, but I did not want them to see the old man's lifeless face, and I did not want to deal with Maria's nightmares.

Outside, the lawyer started in again. "There's a woman named Gurley Flynn who would like to write about Jules's death for the labor newspaper," he said.

"No," I said. "Thank you."

"With all due respect, Mrs. Tursi," the lawyer said, "your uncle is a casualty in the battle for free speech, and his death should not go unnoticed, nor those responsible go unpunished—"

"No," I said again. "To all of it. No."

He looked confused. "You'll at least let us proceed with an inquest. You could have a claim against the county, pay for his burial and maybe more—"

"My husband and I will pay for my uncle's burial," I said. "I want no part of this. It's not my concern, and it shouldn't have been any of his."

The younger one put a hand on his lawyer's arm to quiet him. "We're sorry for what happened, ma'am." Then he pulled at his dumbstruck lawyer, and they turned and walked away.

A light snow had begun to fall.

I watched them walk to the corner of our fenced field. We lived on the outskirts of town, and it was a quarter mile to the nearest streetcar stop. I wished Dom were home with the buggy to offer them a ride. Maybe he would listen to what they had to say about this free speech fight. Dom was a machinist, a member of that union, and his sympathies might be keener than mine.

After they rounded the Carvers' corner, I went back in the house. The coroner and the funeral man had set Jules on a litter and were ready to move him.

I pulled the blanket aside so that one of Jules's hands was exposed. "Girls," I said, and I let them come hold his hand and say goodbye. "Oh, Uncle," Maria said. Elena said nothing, just squeezed his hand. Then I sent them back to the kitchen.

"May I have a minute?" I asked the coroner and the funeral man.

"Of course," they said, and stepped outside.

The room was quiet. I took Jules's cold hand. Such heaviness in my arms—sorrow for Jules, dead on a litter in my living room. My living room. My house. My daughters. Oh, how proud he was of the life I had made, of the woman I had become. It meant everything to him, having me safe and settled, as my girls' health and happiness will mean everything to me.

Still, I was saddened by the time we had lost. The years apart, the secret we had borne the way these two men would bear Jules's dead body. The invention after Mother died, when Jules urged me to leave Mullan, saying I could pass for Italian because of Mother's coloring, move somewhere and start over, not the daughter of an Indian tramp and a Tunisian Gypsy but a good Catholic girl. I took the name Gemma from a neighbor in Mullan. Jules liked it, said it meant precious. *Jewels and Gems*, the two of us.

Jules found a woman in Spokane to take me in, and she brought me to Mass and taught me enough Italian to be my finishing teacher. Her neighbor had a nephew who had lost his first wife in childbirth, this bull of a man whose family, Tursi, was Tuscan. That was how I met Domenico. I liked the look of him the minute he came calling. Secure and sturdy. He asked for my hand after just three weeks. I hadn't even spent half my boarding money. Except for missing Jules, I was never unhappy with my decision, especially when Elena was born.

Uncle Jules was my idea, and *Aunt Agnella*, whom I invented by splitting my mother in two—kindly sister Agitta and shrewish Agnella. At first Jules fought it, said it was better if he just drifted away and allowed me to live this new life. But I insisted, and eventually he was glad for it. Especially in the last few years, with the girls, and Dom agreeable to his visits, Jules became part of our family. I think we both had a sense of peace, of landing safely on some other shore.

Jules and I were never anything but uncle and niece after that— even when it was just the two of us. I even began to believe we could separate Mother from her angry half—separate the pretty young girl who ran away from a brutal father from the common-law wife who harangued Jules for not supporting us better. Sometimes it bothered me that my daughters wouldn't know Jules was their grandfather and that they were part Indian—but what was life if not one invention after another?

Out the window I saw the coroner and the funeral man walking back toward the house.

I bent down to the old man's ear, and I said goodbye in his language, the one I had promised never to use—the one he'd feared would get me a beating or land me in a reservation boarding school. My mother hated the old tongue, "like someone choking on a bone," she said, but I always thought of it as music. Jules only taught me a few phrases, but I sometimes hummed them to myself, and I sang the words now that I knew best, for I used to say them every time he walked away in the spring—*kʷ hin x̌menč, mestm̓*—their sweet click on my tongue.

13

Rye couldn't tell if Mrs. Ricci was crying or yelling or both. *"Piccolo brutto!"* She cupped his face, hugged him, then slapped him. *"Pensavo fossi morto!"*

"Sorry I didn't rake the leaves before I went to jail," Rye said.

Then Rye's lawyer proved his value yet again; Latin wasn't his only trick. *"Mi dispiace, signora. Sono il suo avvocato, Fred Moore. Ryan era in prigione—ma non era colpa sua."*

"Prigione!"

"Si, ma non ha fatto nulla di sbagliato. Anche suo fratello, Gregory. La polizia era molto brutale! Ryan era trionfante in tribunal. Molto trionfante!"

Mrs. Ricci cupped Rye's face again. "Oh, Marco! Oh, *mio povero* Geno!"

She went to the kitchen to make him some food, and Rye showed his lawyer around back, to the porch where he and Gig slept. Mr. Moore looked at the cots, bindles shoved under them, and the few belongings they'd managed to squirrel away—on Rye's side, a pair of summer pants, a set of utensils he may or may not have stolen from a café in Pullman, a baseball he'd found in the grass, and the only thing he'd brought from Montana—a small pencil drawing his father had done of two horses. Mr. Moore looked at the picture of the horses, then turned to Gig's side of the room, extra clothing, a hairbrush, a poster advertising that bill of depravity at the Comique Theater—Ursula the Great's name across the top.

The lawyer ran his hand along Ursula's name and then reached down for Gig's prized possession, Volumes I and III of *War and Peace*, published in America in 1903 by Scribner's Sons in a five-volume set, as part of the larger *Complete Works of Count Tolstoy.*

"Those are Gig's books," Rye said. "He says it's two fifths of the finest novel ever written. He's on the lookout for the rest."

The lawyer turned the volume over in his hands.

"He doesn't usually like people touching it," Rye said, "but you being a lawyer, it's probably okay."

Fred Moore carefully put the book back with such a pitying look on his face that Rye felt compelled to point out the window to the grove of trees behind the house. "Mrs. Ricci is selling us that little piece back there. Gig and I are planning to build a house—well, we *were*, I mean, before all this started."

This didn't seem to alleviate Mr. Moore's pity, and he turned away. "I'm sorry about Jules, Ryan," he said. "And your brother. I'm going to get Gregory out of jail, and you'll be working on your house by spring."

"Spring," Rye repeated.

The back door opened just enough for Mrs. Ricci to slide a bowl of noodles and some bread out; then, without a word, she closed the door. Rye jumped up and had a forkful before he'd looked up at his lawyer. "I'm sorry. Did you want some?"

"You go ahead. Eat up."

Fred Moore said he'd check on Gig's case the next day, and he left, glancing back once at Rye's sleeping arrangements. When Rye's lawyer and his dinner were both gone, he collapsed back onto his cot. It was like an entire life had been lived in this one day, the schoolhouse, court and his lawyer, the redoubtable Elizabeth Gurley Flynn, and then seeing Jules dead like that. And to end this day here, on the porch without Gig—Rye felt lost and alone. He leaned back in his nest of blankets and fell straight into sleep, dreamless and black.

He wasn't sure how long he was out, but then it was late morning and the sun was flashing through the porch window and Mrs. Ricci was shaking him awake in frantic Italian: *"Donna! In una grande machina!"* He got the first word. *Woman.*

He sat up. He must have slept sixteen hours. He felt panic that he'd missed something. Then he remembered that Gurley Flynn had wanted to talk to him about accompanying her on the trip to raise money for the lawyer. But here? Now? Rye felt disoriented. "Tell her I'll be right out, Mrs. Ricci," he said.

"*Si, Geno*," Mrs. Ricci answered, and went back inside. She left a glass of milk and a biscuit, and Rye made quick work of them. He looked at the stack of neat clothes piled at the foot of the bed, the bowler hat he'd worn the day before smack on top.

Rye went out back and used the outhouse, cleaned up as best he could, powdered and dressed in the clothes Mr. Moore had given him, which smelled fresh and fit fine, if a bit loose in the seat. He hitched the pants with the new set of braces that Mr. Moore had provided. He had everything but shoes. He laced up his old boots and put on the gray coat. He slicked down his hair with water, set the bowler on top, and caught his faint reflection in Mrs. Ricci's back window: a *fine gentleman*—

The back door was open, and Rye walked into Mrs. Ricci's kitchen, then through the house and into the parlor. And there, sitting in a chair with her hands in a muff, looking around the room, was Ursula the Great.

"Oh, hello, Miss—" He'd begun speaking without knowing what came next, and so he said, "Great."

14

Life is slow until it isn't; Rye wondered if that was what people meant by fate, life speeding up like the view from an express train. Or maybe fate was a fancy motor car driven by a silent man in white gloves, for once Rye climbed in, there was no choice—you held on and rattled over cobblestones and streetcar tracks, around horses and carriages, nothing to do but shrug and think, *So this is it*, one day on a ball field, next a sweatbox, then snuggled into the leather backseat of a pup-pupping automobile with Ursula the Great—buffeted by wind while she squeezed his arm like she was his girl, the two of them chauffeured by this serious man in a driver's cap and goggles, who gave Rye the warmest scarf and gloves and now motored them around buggies and trucks and lampposts, heads turning like royalty was passing, for this had to be the finest car in town, and they traveled through neighborhoods and years, up the South Hill to the grandest boulevard overlooking downtown and the whole river valley.

There were other autos on the street, but those lesser vehicles were chuddering old Tin Lizzies and delivery trucks, nothing like this long, fancy dragon.

"This is the Peerless seven-passenger Touring!" the driver called over his shoulder, over the wind and the thupping motor. "Out of Cleveland! Ohio! Shipped piece by piece! Built on the spot by a specialist! Only vehicle of its kind in the state!"

Rye wondered at the kind of man who could afford to hire someone to yell out his bragging for him. "I could see six passengers," he said quietly to Miss Ursula, "but you'd have to drag the seventh."

It was ice cold in the open air, and Ursula just kept pulling him closer by his hostage arm. "Thank you for coming. I've been worried about Gregory."

"Gig can handle himself," Rye said, and wondered if it was true.

"I hope you're right." She nestled even closer.

When she glanced up at the driver, Rye took in her whole face and thought how funny the word *beautiful* was, that it could mean such different things. The stark contrast of Elizabeth Gurley Flynn's black hair and eyes against that pale Irish skin or Ursula's scarlet hair and pink lips and high flushed cheeks. She looked at him looking at her, and before he could turn away, their eyes locked, and she glanced down at his lips. Rye wondered if she did this to make men think about kissing her, because it certainly made him think that, then he felt awful for even thinking about kissing his brother's girl.

"I went to see Gregory at the jail," she said. She swallowed and glanced up at the driver. "They are being treated brutally in there.

It is barbaric. But he was happy to know you'd gotten out. He asked me to talk to you and make sure you knew that he was fine."

"Thank you," Rye said, though he was filled with jealousy and wondered how Ursula had managed to get in to see Gig when they were on lockdown.

"He also told me about the house you hope to build one day," she said.

"He did?"

"Yes, he'd like to build a real home for you, Ryan." She smiled and squeezed his arm again. Rye could feel her breath on his face.

Hearing about his brother's feelings from Ursula was strange. Like Rye was overhearing a conversation that wasn't meant for him. He had to remind himself that less than two weeks ago this woman had chosen a rich mining man over Gig.

He wished he could show her that he and Gig weren't all orphan-on-the-bum sorrow. That they were actually adventuring brothers. But he was at a loss as to how to make that case in the back of a rumbling seven-person automobile. Some nameless ache hit him, and he imagined Gig and Ursula making a house together, her cooking dinner—and felt a swirling confusion: his arm pressed in her bosom. Rye wasn't sure if he wanted to be kissed by this woman or mothered.

"What is it, Ryan?" she asked, and she squeezed his arm even tighter, and he thought, *When we separate, my arm might go with her.*

The driver shifted to go uphill and Rye had to yell over the sound of the motor. "Can I ask you something?"

"Of course!" she said.

"It's about the cougar!"

"Oh," she said, "that," and loosened her grip. She must've heard this question a hundred times, because she turned away and looked out the window. "There's meat sewn in the corset," she said more quietly. "Beef liver and offal." She shrugged. "Provides some extra here, too." She patted her chest. "The cat knows that if he growls but refrains from biting, he'll get a fine meal." And now she glanced at the driver again. "Me, too, I guess. If I growl but don't bite, I get to eat."

The car slowed then, and Rye looked up. They were on a street of mansions lined with shade trees and massive gates. The driver wheeled the Peerless Touring into a turnout. The home went on forever, dormers and rooflines making it look like three houses had collided—not just the grandest home Rye had ever seen but, he knew in that moment, the grandest home he would ever see.

He couldn't take the entire house in, but the front seemed to cover half the block. It was three stories, with turrets and balconies and rows of exterior arches. It was an unusual coral color, like a castle from another land, the buildings behind it painted the same: a carriage house, a shop, and a gardener's bungalow. Rye realized he was gaping and closed his mouth.

Thank God for the paid braggart driver or Rye never would have known the house was "constructed entirely of sandstone imported from Italy" or that its style "suggested Spanish and Moorish influences with classical elements."

"I was thinking Moorish," Rye muttered.

The driver went on about how the arches referenced an estate called Alhambra, a Spanish palace belonging to Charles the Fifth.

The driver opened the back door of the Peerless Touring and they climbed out, Rye grateful to have Mr. Moore's bowler on his head as they climbed the steps, the driver leading them to a set of double doors adorned with silver knockers inlaid with gold sculpted horses. Then he pushed on both doors and the building didn't open so much as unfold, reveal itself to Rye, the first image one that would endure for him—gold.

Gold light and gold fixtures and gold furniture, burlap wallpaper painted gold across a wide two-story landing, crystal chandeliers hanging between two grand round staircases, each with shiny black railings above a marble floor, those steps curling away into untold second-story riches. It was the most beautiful thing he'd ever seen. The tables and chairs lining the entryway, the rugs, everything was gilded on its edges. Four servants were lined up waiting, the first a young man holding out his hands for coats and hats and gloves and scarves. "Can I keep my hat?" Rye asked, worried about the rat's nest beneath.

"Of course, Mr. Dolan," the coat man said.

The lord of the house was nowhere in sight, and unsure what to do now, Rye stepped up to get a look at one of the two dazzling staircases, wide enough for ten men at the bottom but narrowing as it curled up and around. He looked deep into the black shiny railing, expecting to see himself, but whatever that black stone was, it gobbled up light and reflection like a deep cave.

"Onyx," the driver said. "Each of the house's nine fireplaces is also constructed of Brazilian onyx."

"Did he run out of gold?" Rye asked.

The bragging driver made a noise that might've been a laugh, and when Rye turned back, the driver was handing the servant his own hat and gloves and coat. Beneath his wool coat, he wore a velvet dinner jacket, and Rye thought he seemed older than he had in the car—fifty, perhaps. The other servants all faced him and waited. "Heat some brandy," the driver said, "and some tea for Ursula," one of the waiting women nodding and backing away, and Rye saw that even Ursula the Great was watching the driver, and he understood, finally, just as the man offered his hand.

"Lemuel Brand," he said. "You'll forgive me for not introducing myself earlier, but I am still getting used to motoring by myself."

Rye glanced over at Ursula, remembering her promise that night "not to bed the man," but she wouldn't meet his eyes.

Then Lem Brand waved his arm around the room like a magician and said, "Welcome to Alhambra, Mr. Dolan."

15

It seemed funny, as they walked the grounds, that Rye had imagined Lem Brand would hire someone to brag for him—he would have been just as likely to hire someone to draw his breaths. He gushed with pride over every aspect of his estate: here, a two-story carriage house with room for four premier autos and an apartment for his mechanic; there, Spanish stables for two of the finest breeding horses in the western United States; up there, a sledding hill and archery course. He described everything with such care ("a footbridge made from Amazon rosewood assembled with no nails or screws"), it was as if he'd built it with his own hands.

Ursula stayed a few steps behind as they walked; clearly, she'd had this tour before. They were also trailed by several members of the house staff, led by a thick man with bushy eyebrows who introduced himself simply as Willard and who had a pistol strapped beneath his long coat. He eyed Rye suspiciously as they walked.

They looped back into the house, where Rye was shown one treasure after another: a stained-glass window twice his height, silk curtains from Java, crystal lamps from Paris, a thirty-person dining table cut from the Bavarian forests of a "lesser duke," a Patagonia cherrywood grandfather clock that cost twenty thousand dollars. When Rye stopped to stare at a forest of tall orchids in vases, Lem Brand put a hand on his shoulder. "You have a good eye, Ryan," he said, "Anyone can buy a clock, but find fresh orchids in winter? That's the true test of a man's means."

The estate was overwhelming, and Rye felt a kind of dazzled panic—like a hungry man trying not to eat too fast. Finally, they settled into what Lem Brand called the main library, which, like the landing, was two stories tall, but felt to Rye as cozy as a pair of new socks. The walls were floor-to-twenty-foot-ceiling with books, and books disappeared into the sky, leather-bound volumes climbing and climbing, a sliding ladder to reach them all. A fire burned in the onyx fireplace. It was the warmest room Rye had ever been in—he felt sleep come on the moment he sat down, and he covered a yawn.

"Happens to me every time," Lem Brand said, the enveloping warmth coming from heated water that ran through pipes in the floor as well as the radiators, and just then a servant arrived with a tray of French cookies and gold-lined snifters of a warm, sweet drink—Rye looked up and the servant said, almost apologetically, "Brandy, sir"—which they sipped in the soft chairs.

Rye sat in this warm cookie-brandy-Ursula goodness, looked up at the walls of books, and suddenly began to weep.

Seated in the chair next to his, Ursula leaned forward and touched his arm. "Ryan. Are you okay?"

He nodded. He cleared his throat and asked Brand, "I don't suppose you have *War and Peace* by Count Tolstoy?"

Brand looked around at his books as if he'd never seen them before. Then he looked at Willard, who had been standing by the door. Willard nodded.

"All five of them?"

Willard shrugged and nodded again.

It was too much. All of it, too much, and Rye cried at the too-muchness of it. This incredible room of books—how he wished Gig could spend a single day in such a room, two stories of leather and gilt volumes and a heated floor and brandy so sweet and rich it coated your insides. The thought of his bookish brother in that stone jail while he was here—it was all just too much.

The unfairness hit Rye not like sweet brandy but like a side ache—a physical pain from the warmth of that heated floor and the softness of that chair and Gig not knowing any of it—and Lace and Danny and Ma and Da, too—Rye never could have imagined it, either. But now *he knew*, and he would know the next time he was curled up in a cold boxcar, that men lived like this, that there was such a difference between Lem Brand and him that Brand should live here and Rye nowhere.

He flushed with sadness, as if every moment of his life were occurring all at once—his sister dying in childbirth, his mother squirming in that one-room flop, poor Danny sliding between wet logs, Gig in jail, and Jules dead—and how many more? *All* people, except this rich cream, living and scraping and fighting and dying, and for what, nothing, the cold millions with no chance in this world.

He remembered last winter hopping an open boxcar with Gig

and seeing a body in the corner. He'd seen played-out bums before, but this one appeared to be a young woman, her long hair iced to the floor of the boxcar, frozen or starved or kidnapped or run off or just made dead somehow. How was it this girl was trash in the corner of a rattling freight box while Rye had hot water running through the floor and warm brandy in his guts? He wept for that girl, too, for what a learned man like Gig might've called humanity, a poor girl born in hunger and dirt, destined to die in a cold boxcar without ever imagining this room existed.

Lem Brand offered him a handkerchief, stitched, like everything, in gold. Rye stared at the handkerchief, and at Brand's clean, rounded fingernails. It was the softest thing he'd ever held to his face. Rye hated that he'd cried in front of Brand and did his best to fill the thing with dirty hobo snot before handing it back.

Brand waved that he should keep it. "I'm sorry, Mr. Dolan," he said. "I imagine it's been a strange couple of weeks for you. And now you're probably wondering why you're here." He leaned forward and Rye finally got a full picture of the man: pale, balding, wide-faced, with a trim mustache. "I thought you might consider working for me."

Rye wasn't sure he'd heard right.

"This request comes at the suggestion of my friend Ursula"—she looked at the ground—"who asked me to intervene in your brother's case. As I explained to her, I have no real power in these situations. This fight is between the police and the unionists." Mr. Brand swirled his drink. "As I told Ursula, this is a matter for the courts now. But, like many, she exaggerates the power of a simple business-man. Still, I might be able to see about getting the charges against him reduced, although, as you might imagine, I am not eager to go out of my way to help a man who makes trouble for the agencies I rely upon to provide labor and security. Not without getting some-thing in return."

Ursula was studying the heated floor. Rye couldn't imagine the thing of value he could supply in return for helping Gig. "Like what?"

"I understand you met a young woman yesterday?" Lem Brand said. "A Mrs. Jack Jones?"

Rye said nothing.

"Listen, Ryan," Brand said, "I am not a political person. This business with the Wobblies and the police, I don't like it. Were it up to me, I'd put every English-speaking man in Spokane to work. I am a businessman, and this is bad for business. But I also have responsibilities, and partners. And to satisfy those responsibilities, I need information. That's all I'm asking from you. Information."

"What kind?"

He shrugged as if it were nothing. "Plans, meetings, developments. Say a union organizer like Mrs. Jones comes to town. Basic news of the street."

Rye looked down at the glass in his hands.

Brand leaned forward. "I wouldn't ask you to put anyone in danger or do anything that goes against your ethics."

Ethics? Did Rye have those? He'd slept and shat in people's yards and stolen their food, he had been drunk and sacrilegious and disparaging. Was the peak of tramp ethics seeing a dead girl on a train car and not going through her pockets?

"I only ask two things," Brand said, "that we keep this in complete confidence, which is to your benefit as well as mine. And that you answer my questions honestly. That's it. For that, I will do my best to intervene in your brother's case." He looked over at Ursula. "And as long as your information is correct, I will pay you twenty dollars a month."

Rye took a drink to keep himself from making a noise. He didn't imagine he'd had twenty dollars' worth of information in his whole life.

"For instance"—Brand pulled a twenty-dollar note from his pocket as if it were nothing—"tell me about the man who beat up the police sergeant on the river that day."

"Early?" Rye asked before he thought better of it. "What about him?"

"Where is he now?"

"I don't know." Rye chewed his lip. How did Brand know about Early? "He said he was going to Seattle."

Brand leaned forward and handed him the twenty. "See how easy that was?" The bill was crisp and flat, like it had been pressed. Brand leaned back in the chair and watched him. "Your father worked the Golden Sunlight strike in Montana."

Again, Rye wondered how he could know. He nodded.

"I owned that mine," Brand said. "I worked it myself after my father died. Started on the muck line and worked my way into the sluice and the mill. These agitators—your Gurley Flynn, she doesn't care about men like your father or me. Or you. All they want is revolution. You're a pawn in that.

"Look, I'm not saying you always get a fair deal in mines and timber camps. But you'll get worse from them. They come from Berlin, from drawing rooms in New York City. Do you think they care about you? About this job-shark business? They want to upend everything. Blow up the world. Don't take my word for it. Ask Gurley Flynn. Ask her where this all ends. Ask, if you get rid of the job agencies, get a higher wage for workers—will that ever be enough?"

Rye looked down at the floor.

"People like her, they only want to get you killed and then go on to the next battlefield, because that's what they really want. A war. I've seen it for twenty years. They call themselves WFM or IWW or socialists or syndicalists, they rile up the locals, get you arrested and killed, then go back to New York and tell their friends how they fought in the revolution out west."

He was getting *himself* riled up, Ursula shifting uncomfortably like she'd heard this all before. "Do I use workers?" he asked. "Yes. I use them to extract silver and to fell trees and to pull beer in my saloons. But I *pay* them for it. And that's all I want to do, pay good men for good work, the way I was once paid to dig silver. Do you know the difference between me and them, Ryan?"

He shook his head.

"This?" Brand waved around the room, the house, the grounds, the mines and hotels and saloons, the world that he owned. "I want *you* to have it, too. I want you to have every opportunity I had. With them, nobody gets a chance at anything."

This was when Ursula finally spoke. "Ryan?"

He looked over at her and could see she must be tired of Brand's ranting.

"Do it for Gregory," she said.

If Ursula thought she had to remind Rye of his brother during Brand's speech, she was wrong. He wondered just what sort of ethics a person needed to survive so long in cages with cougars. Rye looked down at the twenty-dollar note in one hand and a glass of brandy in the other. He took a deep breath.

Ursula the Great

A WOMAN owns nothing in this world but her memories—a shabby return on so steep an investment. The First Ursula taught me this. The other thing she taught me was how to climb in a cage and sing to a mountain lion.

I was the Second Ursula. I met the First in the spring of 1909. She'd been doing the act for ten years, nearly half her vaudeville life. By the time I met her, she was putting her stage makeup on with a putty knife, dying her hair every morning, and every night wrestling her rangy tits into corseted captivity like two escaped criminals. Then she would walk onstage and try not to get eaten by a cougar.

It was a bear, the first creature Ursula performed with, and the reason she was called Ursula, "*Ursa* being Latin for bear," according to her fatstack manager, Joe Considine, who hired me to replace her. This was in Reno, Nevada, where I answered a simple newspaper ad for "Actress, singer, calm demeanor."

I was from an East Coast performing family, my mother an opera singer, my father a playwright. Just two years earlier I'd wowed six hundred a night on the San Francisco stage as Fanny LeGrand in *Sappho*. But two years is a hundred in actress time, and I had chosen badly in romance and found myself in Reno in a limited engagement called desperation. That's when I saw the ad.

For my audition, Joe Considine led me to the stage of an empty variety saloon, and I sang, "A Woman Is a Woman but a Good Cigar Is a Smoke." I wasn't even to the second *puff* when Joe said, "And can you dance?" and I showed him tap and a high kick and he said, "And what about your tits?" and I asked if we could keep those out of it, and he said, "Then how do you feel about animals?"

I met the First Ursula the next afternoon backstage at the theater where she'd been performing for the last month, co-billed with an Orientalist seer. She wore a flowing gown of reds and oranges, her hair wrapped in a scarf, four dollars in costume jewelry on her fingers and neck. Behind her, her costar lay in a ten-by-ten cage, asleep in a narrow slant of sunlight beneath a high window.

Ursula seemed resigned to giving up the act, and gamely showed me the tricks, although, from what I could tell, the main trick was to not get mauled.

"Why are you leaving?" I asked.

"I am not *leaving*," she said. "I am being replaced. A week ago, Joe informed me that he was taking out an advertisement for a new Ursula. And look, here you are."

I chose not to apologize. "Why would he replace you?"

"As he explained it to me, our receipts are down, the show is rarely extended beyond our two-week contracts, and he has begun to suspect my age is an issue in marketing this spectacle."

"So, you're too young," I said.

"Yes, very good." She smiled. "No, according to Joe, a more mature Ursula reminds them of their mothers and wives, and they have begun to cheer for the cat."

"What is the age," I asked, "when a woman becomes more entertaining as meal than singer?"

"I am thirty-six," she said, "or so."

Or so. No way First Ursula had seen thirty-six this century. Not that I held any reverence for the accurate measure of one's age. I had told Considine I was twenty-four, a number I had scrupulously maintained since turning twenty-five a few years earlier.

First Ursula was slated for three more shows while she trained me, and after that I would assume the role, meaning I had only two performances in Reno to get the act down. After that came a two-week run in Boise, followed by Butte and Missoula, then it was on to Spokane in the fall, where we had an open engagement at a theater First Ursula said was the finest house in the best city this side of San Francisco.

It was called the Comique and it was owned, in secret, by a mining magnate named Lemuel Brand—secret, she said, because "his wife remains blissfully unaware of his fondness for actresses." She was quite taken with this Brand, whom she described as "a cup of charm in a gallon of largesse." Brand's wealth came from silver-mining the Coeur d'Alenes and the rather broad range of vices his workers spent their money on—cathouses, saloons, hotels, opium dens, and theaters in Spokane's tenderloin, positions he held behind a series of paper partners. "Lem likes to say that every dollar that goes out in payroll," Ursula said, "comes back through bed, brothel, and booze."

Ursula and Lem Brand had carried on for her entire two-month run in Spokane. He'd even made her a promise: that when her career was over, she could manage one of his flop hotels and turn it into a proper boardinghouse. She planned to open its doors to old variety-show actresses like herself, to teach them secretarial and operator skills so they wouldn't be reduced to taking on loggers at four bits a throw. Of course, she said, a hotel full of former actresses also appealed to a patron of the arts like Brand.

That's why she was staying with the show as far as Spokane, so she could dismount the stage for the next segment of her life. She had even picked out a name for her boardinghouse: the Phoenix.

That morning she'd sent a telegram to Brand saying that she would be coming to Spokane with the show, was eager to see him, and hoped to discuss taking over the management of his hotel. "I am ready," she told me. "I have been at this for too long."

"May I ask," I said, "what happened to the bear?"

"Ah, the bear." This question softened the corners of First Ursula's eyes. "Boryenka. He fell quite in love with me, I'm afraid. Backstage, he would growl whenever Joe raised his voice. Onstage, he would sit patiently, panting like a dog, his eyes following me everywhere. He was heartsick, and he would moan for me to come into his cage, to sing to him, to stroke his jowls. He was so gentle the audience began to laugh.

"Joe found it unseemly the way the bear looked at me. I suggested we play it as a comedy, the bear my suitor, perhaps add a wedding scene, but Joe feared the ministers would be scandalized by us suggesting what happened in the wedding bed, or worse, that audiences would be disappointed *not* to see that. Of course, I had fallen quite far in the theater, as you apparently have, too, dear, but I was not about to become one of *those* acts." She smiled gently. "In the end, Joe sold the bear to a traveling circus out of Denver, and we went with a mountain lion after that."

Mountain lions were more reliable for snarling and baring teeth, Ursula said. But she still missed Boryenka. "I understand he is quite a star in the circus." Her eyes drifted to the window. "The last I heard, he had learned to play the banjo while riding a bicycle. He is quite a talent."

Those first few days in Reno, First Ursula showed me the basic staging and blocking: come out, sing my first number, and dance three laps around the cage. Then open the door and go inside for the next song. She showed me how to sew raw steak strategically into the corset to enhance my profile, and how the cat would growl and wait while I ripped off the corset, and that a quick throw was the real trick, for if I hesitated and held the meaty corset in my hand—

Then, with my back to the audience, singing in full voice, I was to grab the robe hanging from the stand at the back of the cage. Depending on which city we were in and its variety-theater laws, I could either show my tits or not. She had not shown hers in a year, "but this is more for gravity's sake than for decency's."

One other thing to remember: The robe stand could be used to fend off the cat should things go badly. This was the way she described being attacked by a cougar in front of a screaming throng— "should things go badly"—the loveliest bit of theater decorum I'd ever heard.

We had a fine time in Reno, First Ursula and me. I'd watch her perform and then we'd stay up late in her hotel room, sharing stories while we drank a strange plum wine that she had acquired a taste for in Spokane's Chinatown.

In the mornings, she would go to the front desk of the hotel to see if Lem Brand had answered her telegram about the Phoenix. When, after three days, no answer came, she sent a second telegram, and then a third, but these also went unanswered, and as the week wore on, I felt an aching sympathy for her.

On the fourth night, we stood backstage together. There was no announcement that the actress playing Ursula was changing; the barker simply said, "Ursula the Great!" and I went out instead.

There was a whistle, some light applause. We'd spent most of our rehearsal time on the bits with the cougar, for obvious reasons, and while the show itself was simple, I found myself overtaken with a surprising and savage bout of stage terror.

The heat of the lights, the growl of the cat, the smell of workingmen in the front rows: It all combined to make me nauseous. I hit my notes and the cougar was professional enough, but I left the stage thinking I might not be cut out for this. There were only three things these yokels wanted to see: Two of them were my breasts and the third was a cougar attack; the singing and dancing to which I had devoted my life were very much beside the point.

I came off after that first performance feeling bereft, what she called having "fallen so far in the theater" weighing on my soul, and that is when I saw First Ursula, standing backstage, her hand over her mouth.

"Dear God," she said. "Your voice."

Since the rehearsals had focused on staging and safety, I hadn't really invested in the songs and had almost forgotten the effect my voice could have at full release, its unlikely power and register, which at one time had secured parts and performances for me at the best theaters in San Francisco.

"Thank you," I said, and she said, "No. Thank *you*," and began to cry. She enveloped me in a shuddering embrace.

We separated and she looked out at the dingy Reno theater. "These dusty heathens have no idea. You could be singing in Paris for monarchs."

"Well, I *am* at the Palace," I said, and waved a hand at the bar of the Palace Theater and Gambling Club of Reno, Nevada. This, too, was rewarded with an embrace. The show was now mine. I was now Ursula.

On our last day together in Reno, First Ursula and I had breakfast at the hotel, and she checked once more for a telegram from Lem Brand; there wasn't one.

"Why don't you have the operator ring him?" I asked.

She said the telephone was a "brutish form of communication," and that Lem Brand not answering her telegrams was, of course, answer enough, and the one she had secretly been expecting all along. "I suspected the Phoenix was a fantasy the moment he mentioned it," she said. "A man will say anything on the windward side of a bed. But I *chose* to believe it. And I don't mind indulging in the fantasy that a wealthy lover might reward a woman with whom he has shared such intimacy. Perhaps I could have been a wife somewhere with a loyal husband and nine perfect children—but I would have to indulge *that* fantasy. Compared with that business, this was a harmless bit of theater."

We stayed up all night drinking plum wine.

"What will you do now?" I asked. "Do you have family?"

She said she was from a Philadelphia stage family—her father an acrobat, mother a singer. She was the youngest of six performing siblings—tumblers and musicians. But she was a late bloomer in looks and in talent. As each of her siblings ventured off into show business, Ursula stayed behind to care for their parents. When she was in her teens, her father fell from a tightrope in Cincinnati and suffered a debilitating head injury that required nearly nonstop care. That was when she met Joe Considine, who had come east looking for showgirls willing to perform in the saloons out west. She auditioned and left with him the very same day without telling anyone.

"And you haven't talked to your family since?" I asked.

"No," she said. "It's been—" Perhaps remembering that she had shorted her own age by at least a decade, she finished, "several years."

I said it was cruel, Joe Considine whisking Ursula away from her family as a young woman and then summarily firing her once she got old. She said Joe was too simple to be cruel, and that he had offered her severance, fifty dollars and a train ticket east. She said she was going to take him up on it.

"I'm going to tell Joe I won't perform until he gives you a hundred-dollar severance," I said.

"You're a dear," she said, patting my arm. "You make a fine Ursula."

"But not *great* yet," I said.

"You are far more talented than I ever was," she said, and her eyes welled with tears again. I began to object, but she put a finger to my mouth. "Please. It would be unseemly for you to argue. Your voice *hurts*, it is so lovely."

We were quiet a moment.

"I will send you a postcard from wherever I land," she said.

We finished the last bottle of plum wine and talked until dawn. We became loose with our stories, and at some point she began listing old lovers' attributes. Instead of their names, she referred to them by avocation: The bullfighter was a groveler, the sea captain equipped like a horse.

And what of the mining magnate, Mr. Brand? I asked.

I should not have brought him up, for the very mention of his name brought sadness to her eyes and she simply shook her head.

I told her about my own weakness in that area: my penchant for a certain kind of younger man I referred to as "meat," an actor here, a stagehand there, culminating in the dashing young playwright I fell for, who turned out to be more swindler than scribe, and who went to the bathroom at a restaurant in Sparks and never returned, sticking me with the check, a week's hotel bill, and a wrecked heart. And because he had stolen from my old theater and I'd stood by him when I had thought him wrongly accused, I could never go back to San Francisco.

"I'm sorry," she said, and she put her hand on the side of my face.

It was almost dawn when First Ursula asked if she might kiss me. Before I could answer, she leaned in and did it. Then she lay down in front of me and faced away. I held her from behind. She was frailer than I'd imagined. In a beam of streetlight through the hotel window, I could see age spots on her shoulder, little fissures around her eye, the gray seams in her clownish red hair. When she began shaking, I whispered, "It's okay."

I woke alone midmorning, Joe Considine rapping on my door. "Ursula?"

He did not seem alarmed or surprised that I was in her room. "Train leaves for Boise in two hours," he said. "They're loading the cat now."

I asked about First Ursula.

"Gone," he said. She had come down early to breakfast, dressed and packed, and accepted his offer of fifty dollars and a ticket out of town. Then she caught the Union Pacific headed east toward Denver. "She left two hours ago."

We did two weeks in Boise, then two in Butte, and after that, Missoula. In each city we headlined with two or three local opening acts—musicians, comedians, the occasional freak and animal trick. We started slowly but were extended in Montana, the notices hinting at just enough scandal that we filled the seats without riling the ministers. Meanwhile, the cat and I were developing a real rapport—sometimes when I sang, she seemed to growl on key.

In each city, I checked for a postcard from First Ursula, but none arrived.

Finally, we moved to Spokane, our passenger car emerging from mountain forest into a river valley laced with bridges and railroad tracks, a lovely train station on an island in the center of a rocky channel. First Ursula was right: Spokane had a thrumming vibrancy those other cities lacked, and the Comique seemed a fine theater, URSULA THE GREAT across the whole of the marquee, in letters thrice the size of the next act, a blind accordion player named Rico Roma.

Lem Brand was waiting to greet us onstage at the Comique, hat held over his chest. He gave a bow like he was meeting royalty. I cannot say what I expected after so many weeks imagining him, only that he was less of it. He was perhaps fifty, although he was the kind of man who would have looked fifty at thirty, bald and lumpish, soft in the manner of one used to hiring other men to do his work.

"My goodness, Ursula," Brand said, "you are more beautiful than even Mr. Considine's rather vivid description."

Behind me, Joe laughed and said, "Isn't she something, Mr. Brand?"

"Welcome to the Comique," Brand said, and he gestured to what looked like three-hundred-some-odd seats. "I hope you will consider dining with me this evening," he said. "It's a tradition that, as the theater's benefactor, I show new performers a bit of good old-fashioned Spokane hospitality."

"So the blind accordion player will be joining us, too?" I asked.

Joe cleared his throat behind me.

"No," Brand said, taken aback.

"That's too bad. And what about your wife?"

That limp-rump Joe Considine hissed at me: "Margaret!"

I turned and gave Joe the sharp eye. "Ursula, you mean," I said, reminding him of his own rule that I stay in character even when not onstage. "Please, Joe, Mr. Brand and I are having a conversation. Perhaps go check on the cat."

Joe slunk away. When I turned back, Lem Brand's face was flushed and wore a stern expression I imagined he gave the miners and valets and maids and countless others in his employ. And me, too, his eyes said, I shouldn't forget I was on the payroll as well. "My wife is away," he said. "In Boston, visiting our son at boarding school."

"Perhaps she could join us next time," I said.

"Perhaps," he said, the word nearly choking him.

His anger roiling, I saw the moment to turn things. "In that case, a private dinner sounds divine. Just the two of us. Perhaps you're thinking we might even become friends and dine regularly. Is that what you had in mind, Mr. Brand?"

He was clearly confused by my change in tone. "Yes," he said. "I . . . Yes."

"Good," I said, and smiled softly. "Then, as your friend, I hope you don't mind if I ask for the smallest favor before we meet again."

"Favor?"

"Yes," I said. I reached out and took his arm. "After which I will be all yours."

He swallowed.

Then I brought up the telegrams First Ursula had sent from Reno and how there must have been some mix-up at the Western Union office, because surely if her cables had been properly delivered, he would have answered them.

"Yes, a mix-up," he said.

"I thought so," I said. "You must be so eager to find her."

"Find her——"

"To fulfill your agreement! It must be disheartening to know a *friend* is out there with the misconception that you have cast her aside. You must be so eager to remedy it by making good on your promise."

"Yes," he said, his eyes on my pale hand on his hairy wrist.

"Then it is decided! Once you've tracked down Ursula, you and I will have the most splendid dinner, Mr. Brand."

"Lem," he said.

"Lem," I said, "indeed." I nodded. "I greatly look forward to it." And with that, I bowed, turned, and began walking to my dressing room.

"Wait," he said, "do you know where she is?"

I looked back over my shoulder. "I don't. I believe her family is from Philadelphia. But I should think a man of your stature would have a private detective you could engage on this question, perhaps even one on staff?"

"Yes," he said. "How about a name, at least. A name would help."

Christ. He didn't even know her name.

"Her name is Ursula the Great," I said.

We killed in Spokane. The cat roared. The house roared. I belted. The lights, the opening acts—from the first performance we were a hit. And when one of the city's five newspapers called me "a spectacle of indecency," Joe raised ticket prices thirty percent.

Of course, there is always a catch, and the one in Spokane was called Gregory. I found him wandering the theater one day, delivering boards to a carpenter, and I played at mistaking him for an actor and we bantered and I asked if he might bring a bit of that lumber to my dressing room.

He turned out to be a union man, a budding socialist, an adventurer, or, by clearer light, a day laborer and train vagrant. If memories are an unwise investment, this was burning money.

But what can I say? He was beautiful. And I have always been weak for physical beauty in men. My sister always said I was born with a man's lecherous eye and made stupid by my base attractions. She said it would lead to my ruin. "Well," I told her, "then let's get on with it."

He was a man of broad marbled shoulders, deep-set blue eyes, thick black hair, roping arms, and a full chest that tapered to a waist nearly as slender as mine. His skin was cooked a golden crisp beneath the shirt I coaxed from him and tossed on my dressing room chair. At times I have found the beguiling ones to be less energetic at play, perhaps too used to getting their way. But this Gregory was my equal in hands and hunger, and my goodness, the carnal afternoons we shared, the first I'd had since the grifting playwright left me.

He was a conversationalist after, which I also liked. Our legs tangled in my hotel bedding, he presented himself an avid reader, a socialist and intellectual, although I suspected he was somewhat vagrant in that department, too, limited by the six or seven books he'd happened upon while tramping.

But it was his talking about his brother that really got to me. He was raising the boy since their parents had died, and when he described the house he wanted to build them someday, it was all I could do not to have another go at him. I could imagine First Ursula shaking her head at my sentimentality. To be made stupid by a man's beauty was foolish enough.

One night I told Gregory to bring his little brother by the show. I was a nervous schoolgirl all that day, but afterward, I returned to my dressing room to find a different man waiting there for me—that overripe squash Lem Brand, thin hair slicked across pale forehead, a rich bouquet of fresh flowers in his hand.

He smiled. "I must say, you surprised me the other day."

"Must you?"

"I'm not used to such wit in a woman, nor such impertinence."

"Thank you," I said, as if this were a compliment.

He looked around my dressing room, then back at me. "You said that when I found her, you would have dinner with me."

I felt a tug. "You found Ursula?"

He nodded.

"Will you give me a moment to change?"

"Of course," he said. "Meet me in front of the theater."

After he was gone, I hurried down the hall to the stage door to get rid of poor Gregory and his brother. A man like Brand could cause terrible trouble for them, so I intended to chase him off mercilessly, like a stray, for his own good. But in his eyes I lost my nerve, and the shadow of his little brother at the end of the alley—it affected me greatly, and I apologized and gave what promises I could. Empty as they were, I *wanted* them to be true. I ached watching Gregory slink down that alley, hands deep in his trouser pockets.

I returned to my dressing room and changed, a cold iron taste in my mouth.

There are things a woman must do, my sister used to say.

A woman owns nothing in this world, Ursula used to say.

Roar, the mountain lion used to say.

Brand was waiting outside, beneath my name on the theater marquee, near a large touring automobile. He held the door, I climbed in, and he drove us all of three blocks. The auto was the point, obviously, for it was an unseasonably warm night and we could have walked as easily. "That's quite a machine," I said.

"Thank you," he said, as if he'd invented it.

It was a fine restaurant with stucco walls and white tablecloths. The dinner service was ending and chairs were being put up for the evening. I followed Brand through the main dining hall to a small private room with formal settings for two. All around were marbled pillars and red curtains.

Waiting for us in the room was a side of security beef who introduced himself as Willard. He was holding a folder.

"Willard's a retired Pinkerton," said Brand, "and the head of my security. I told him you were the kind of woman who would want documentation, so he prepared this dossier."

Willard wouldn't meet my eyes and, with a nod, backed out of the room.

"I was hoping we could eat first," Brand said. "I have just come from a meeting about some pending labor trouble that upset my stomach, and if you don't mind, I should at least like to *pretend* that you are eager to dine with me."

"Oh, but I am," I said, and sat next to him, the two of us on one side of a long table, like a king and queen receiving official visitors.

For the next hour, waiters swarmed us. We were served a French red wine, a fine local beefsteak, scallops from Seattle, and gnocchi that might have been pinched from the ass of an Italian angel. Brand told me about the theater scene in Spokane, about the battles he was having with a union organizing the men he would prefer remain unorganized, about the ministers who wanted to tame the city he would prefer stay untamed, and about a spineless mayor who seemed to think a modern city could be constructed only of parks and churches.

He was surprisingly good company, and I told him so, though not the surprising bit. I said how nice it was to be in a city that employed actual chefs and not the blind syphilitic camp cooks who had tried to poison me in Montana.

Our plates were being taken away when Lem Brand asked the headwaiter to hold our desserts a moment. "You've been kind," he said to me, "and you have waited long enough." Then he reached over and opened the file on First Ursula.

Her real name was Edith Hardisson, he said. She was forty-six years old. She was not the youngest child of an East Coast stage family but the oldest of six, daughter of a clerk and his wife from Independence, Missouri. Her parents were members in frightful good standing of a devout chapter of Reorganized Latter Day Saints, and they betrothed her at fifteen to a widower and pig farmer from their church, but Edith ran away before the wedding.

Mr. Willard could find no trace of her for the next six years, until a twenty-two-year-old Edie Hart was arrested at a labor camp brothel in Minnesota. There were also arrest records in Virginia City, and Cripple Creek, Colorado, which was where she met Joe Considine, who first put her onstage as a saloon singer and, later, turned her into Ursula the Great.

"She told me she was from Philadelphia," I said, "that her father was an acrobat who cracked his skull falling off a tightrope."

He smiled. "She told me that her father was a cowboy in Buffalo Bill Cody's traveling Wild West show and that he impregnated her French mother, and when she turned sixteen, she came to America to find him."

I could see on his lumpish face that he was as disappointed in this banal report as I was, and I reminded myself that even if he had been shabby in not returning her telegrams, Ursula had once thought enough of the man to share his bed.

I paged through the report myself: After she left Reno, First Ursula took the train to Denver, where she apparently went to the offices of one "Putnam and Gold Traveling Circus." The circus was performing that week in Iowa, so she inquired of the circus booking agent about purchasing an animal she'd once worked with, a performing bear named Boryenka. The booking agent explained that Boryenka had been dead for a year, put down by his trainer when he began to go blind. The booking agent didn't recall Ursula being overly upset by the news of Boryenka's demise, but they spent some time reminiscing about the bear and agreed that he was a rare talent, the booking agent saying the animal had grown so adept at the banjo in his last years that his facility rivaled that of a human player.

Edith spent another week in Denver, Willard wrote, eating and drinking until her money ran out.

I kept flipping pages, Brand narrating as I read.

"Finally, when she had nowhere else to go, she went back to Independence," he said. "It was not a pleasant homecoming, and she stayed only two days. Her father is deceased, and her mother and sisters rejected her. Now she is in Des Moines, Iowa, at an SRO hotel, working as a waitress and"—here Brand cleared his throat—"augmenting her income in ways I asked Willard not to include in this report."

The report fell to my lap. *How far you have fallen. Your ruin.* For a moment I could barely breathe. I looked down at the floor.

"You had to know I wasn't going to bring her back here," he said.

I looked back up at Brand.

"So I began thinking," he said, "there must be some other reason you brought up my agreement with Ursula. And I realized that if I were in your position, I would do the same." Brand reached into a valise next to his chair and produced another document. He handed it to me. There was a wax seal on it. It read *Spokane County* and *Official Deed and Bill of Sale*. The building was listed as the Bailey Hotel, Spokane, Washington.

"This is the hotel we talked about her running," he said. "Fifty-two single-occupancy rooms that rent for five dollars a month. But that's just on paper. We get three dollars a day from the thirty or so women who ply their trade in cribs on the alley side. That's where the real money comes from. From that, I pay the police to look the other way.

"The legal owner is a man named Burke. I pay the taxes, and the upkeep, and I give Burke ten dollars a month to serve as a front for my interests."

I looked over the document. It was two pages long. At the bottom of the second page were two lines transferring ownership from Burke, who had signed below his name, to my legal name, Margaret Anne Burns. The contract was dated that day. Brand held out a fountain pen.

"Of course, you'll get a better deal than Mr. Burke had," he said.

Then he pointed to a paragraph in the contract. "This deed transfers twenty percent of real ownership of the building to you, as well as that percentage of monthly income from the property. You'll be responsible for twenty percent of upkeep, improvements, and taxes. This stake requires no cash investment on your part but will be in exchange for agreeing to assume management of the property and being its public face. You have the right to sell your stake at any time, but I retain first right of refusal to match any offer."

It was quiet in the private dining room. My investment in the hotel was clear. His eyes sought out my chest and I felt my rib cage tighten, like I was still wearing the meat-filled corset.

I looked up into his eyes. Whatever First Ursula had seen there, she was right: A woman owns nothing of this world.

"Thirty percent," I said.

He smiled, crossed out 20 on the contract and wrote 25, then initialed it. "And you will pay Burke five dollars a month for two years," he said.

"I will pay Burke two and you will pay him three," I said.

He held out the pen. I took it. He pointed. "Here," he said, "and here. And here."

When we were done, I set the pen down. It weighed forty pounds.

Then dessert came. Bread pudding.

16

At midnight, Rye met Gurley at the Great Northern station for the overnight to Seattle. She wore her usual black dress with bulky black coat, hair tied back with a black ribbon. She carried a red and gold carpetbag. So he wouldn't have to travel with his bindle, Rye had borrowed a boxer's bag from Fred Moore.

They settled in second class and Rye sat by the window. He'd never been *in* a train, only *on* one. It was how he'd traveled to Seattle the first time, lying in deep grass with Gig, ducking railroad bulls, then running down a Northern Pacific freighter just as it picked up speed outside the yard. They had spent a miserable seven hours hanging ladders and riding blinds, but even so, there were worse ways to go. Class existed among tramps, too; Rye had seen Negro hoe-boys from Texas clinging to the trusses a foot above the tracks.

But now, how could he go back to riding on trains after he'd been inside one, nestled in this soft seat, lulled by the thumping rattle of the ties?

When he jerked awake, he realized he'd missed most of the trip. The sun was up and Gurley wasn't next to him. The snow had held off and they'd made good time through the mountains, easing down Cascade switchbacks into a lush valley. Log piles and shipyards rolled past the window—farms and stacks and waterfront hamlets, and then the train slowed and they crossed a bridge onto the isthmus that held that great shithole of prosperity, Seattle.

Last time here had been a disaster for them. Gig had been sold a dock job by an employment shark, but it turned out to be unloading a contraband barge with no manifest, and on day two, when dockworkers with union badges showed up, Gig understood he was

scabbing a union job. He beat it off the pier and found Rye scroung-
ing for food in alleys. They were stranded four days down the Seattle skid, wet and cold, under a low gray ceiling. If the sun rose that
week, Rye missed it.

Seattle was like an infection that started at the water and spread
up the verdant hills. The smell of stewed harbor turned his guts: salt
flats, log pulp, and fish guts stirred by a tide that gently rocked the
city's sewage back and forth. Gig said it was why he preferred a river
town, because it took your shit *away.* "A man shouldn't have to worry
about his morning business coming back for him in the afternoon."

Rye hadn't cared for the people, either—a humorless breed of fish-
ermen and dockworkers, and tight shop owners. In four days, they
found no work and little in the way of generosity, and finally grabbed
a rattler back out of town.

It felt entirely different now, arriving inside a warm passenger compartment, staring out his window at the city around him.

"See that?" asked a man with a British accent from the seat behind him.

Through the window, Rye watched a crew of workers using water
cannons to blast at a steep hillside, sluicing away the dirt in muddy
streams that left a few houses perched on a jagged man-made cliff.

"They are flattening Denny Hill," said the man, his face pressed
against the window. "Farewell, Rome of the West, the City of Seven
Hills is now six."

Rye wasn't sure what to think of any of this.

The train rattled along Elliott Bay, then through a tunnel behind
the piers, and at last into King Station south of downtown, its huge
clock tower rising into the low gray clouds.

Gurley came back from the dining car with a man and a sandwich. The sandwich was wrapped in waxed paper, the man enduring
a Gurley lecture, ". . . not trying to convince you of anything except
that which you claim to believe," and without a beat, she handed
Rye "turkey and cheese," then back to the man, "while you fret over
a few extra pennies going to the poor," then to Rye, "they were out

of mustard," then back to the man, "the rich live on untold millions in interest and inheritance, all of it unearned, by your own definition a free handout and proof of your inherent hypocrisy, now I hope you will pardon my candor and my brusqueness, but good day, sir," and she dropped into the seat next to Rye. "Did you want coffee?"

Rye spent the day like this, in this revolving door of Gurley's considerable energies, first at the train station, where she introduced him to a tall union man, "James Garrett, IWW Puget Sound organizer, this is Ryan Dolan, sixteen-year-old orphan the Spokane police very nearly beat to death—" Garrett escorted Gurley to a female boardinghouse and Rye to a flop around the corner where he dropped his bag in his room and went down to the lobby to find Gurley and a red-faced man with a notebook and pen already in deep conversation.

"I'm telling you, it's not like Missoula. If that was a skirmish in the free speech war, this is Antietam," Gurley said, and without pause, she touched the red-faced man on the arm. "Olen Parr, this is Ryan Dolan, sixteen-year-old orphan beaten and arrested in Spokane for nothing more than standing on the street, and then crowded into a sweatbox with thirty other men."

"Son of a bitch." The man looked down to write in his notebook. "Is that so?"

"Well," Rye said, "twenty-eight, but . . . yeah."

"Son of a bitch," the man said again.

"Olen, walk with us." Gurley rose and, her hand falling easily on Rye's arm, spoke over her shoulder at Olen as they walked through the cluttered lobby. "Ryan here was on bread and water for two weeks, and he is only sixteen years old and an orphan to boot."

"Is that so?" Olen muttered. "Son of a bitch." Rye wished she'd go easy on the young-orphan talk, which made him sound like a baby left on her doorstep.

As they stepped through the door, she said to him, "Olen is the editor of the *Socialist* newspaper."

On the sidewalk, Olen looked stricken. "But I'm not anymore, Gurley."

"What?" She stopped, turned.

"You didn't hear? I split with the Socialist Party in July, and went with the Socialist Workers Party, but then I left them, too."

"What? Why?"

"Well, we got into it with the Central Branch at the state convention over their platform, those uptown sons of bitches handcuffed us and pushed the Pike Street radicals aside, so I walked out and joined the SWP for two weeks, but those petite bourgeois sons of bitches were like a knitting club, so we finally had our own goddamned convention."

"You quit the socialists to have your own socialist convention?"

"Then National failed to recognize us, so we quit altogether."

"You quit the Socialists? Olen, you edit a newspaper called *The Socialist*."

"Like I said, I don't anymore. I'm in the Wage Workers Party now. We started a newspaper called *The Workingman Paper*, but we only printed two issues. Now it's called *The Agitator*."

Gurley stared at the ground for a moment. She looked over at Rye, who had no idea what to make of any of this. He tried shrugging with his eyebrows.

She abruptly started walking again, hand on Rye's arm, Olen at full pace behind them. "Well, you should still write about Ryan here, a poor orphan fighting for justice and for freedom of speech—"

"And to get my brother out of jail," Rye interjected for the first time.

"Yes!" she said. "And for his equally courageous brother. That's what we need you to write, Olen, that we came to raise money to launch a second free speech day in Spokane and to hire a lawyer of national caliber to eventually get those five hundred brave men, including Ryan's only living relative, out of that horrible jail!"

"Five hundred. Son of a bitch." Olen was back to scribbling in his notebook. "Is that so?"

Gurley tapped Olen Parr's pad with her finger. "Five hundred workers whose only crime was to speak freely in the street and to seek a job without paying a crook for it! The cops filled the jail and filled the brig at Fort Wright, and they locked poor Ryan here in an old school with no heat and no electricity."

"And he's an orphan, you say?"

"Son of a bitch," Rye muttered to himself.

"The police don't even wait for them to speak now," Gurley continued. "Man climbs off a train or asks for directions, they shackle him on the spot. It's tyranny!" She turned them around a corner, the sidewalk rising up a hill so steep that the side door was on the second floor in front of the building. "You need to see for yourself, Olen. Come! Write about it! It's a great story. An outrage."

"Well, we have a committee meeting next week to vote in our bylaws, but I might be able to come after that."

"That will be too late."

"It's the bylaws, Gurley."

"Well, for God's sake, at least write *something* about our trip, Olen. You can do that, can't you?"

"Well, sure," he said, his face flushing.

She tapped his pad again. "In ten days, we're planning a second free speech action. A week after that, Clarence Darrow is speaking in Boise, and Ryan and I aim to travel there, raising money along the way to hire Darrow to fight this travesty! D-A-R-R-O-W!" She pushed Rye through the revolving door and said back over her shoulder, "Publish, Olen!" She squeezed Rye's arm and said quietly, "What a waste of blood."

Rye glanced back to see Olen Parr through the spinning door and hear the man's last muffled question: "Gurley, are you *pregnant?*"

17

Seattle's IWW Hall was half the size of Spokane's—cramped above a Pioneer Square dry goods store, stage half hidden by beams. The room was dark and smoky, a bog of beards and hats, legs crossing and uncrossing. Rye sat with Gurley in the front row as a local speaker went first—a *snerfling, erming* lumber bum who couldn't put three words together—Rye unable to concentrate without imagining the whole town with the same flu bug.

Back in Spokane, Gurley had assured the union men she would leave the agitating to others, but throughout the day Rye saw this was impossible. In meeting after meeting, she swept into the room and took it over, whether it was filled with socialists, suffragists, or society women. She got thirty dollars here, fifty there, and a commitment of four women to come to Spokane and help feed the union men. All leading to the main event that night in the IWW Hall, flyers in Pioneer Square announcing: "The Rebel Girl E. Gurley Flynn (Jones) Speaking Tonight 7 p.m. on Spokane Free Speech War." Onstage, the local organizer was finishing: "*Erm*, I said my peace, and now the person you come to hear, Mrs. Jack Jones, previously known as, *snerf*, that fiery girl rebel out of New York and Chicago, Elizabeth Gurley Flynn."

She came out to musty applause, purposefully striding toward the crowd like she might dive in, her toes stopping at the stage edge. She leaned forward. "Listen," took a few breaths, "brothers and sisters, have we ever seen such trying times?"

She went through a list of outrages, fifteen-hour workdays and women dying at their sewing machines, men crushed in cave-ins while their families got nothing, copper kings and shipping magnates living like royalty while poor workers couldn't even afford a flop bed, families in tents and hovels, workers given no rights and tossed aside when they were too broken or sick or old to work.

"Listen," she spoke softly, so the crowd had to lean in, "I know you believe in a better world—" Then she raised her voice and sat them back in their chairs. "But belief without the will to fight is *nothing*! And I'm here to tell you the fight is *here*! Now! In Spokane!" She gestured at Rye and he stood. "This is sixteen-year-old Ryan Dolan, beaten and jailed for trying to *speak*, for imagining his hard work might one day get him a foothold in this life. He came here with me today to plead for your help and help for his own brother, a political prisoner in a Spokane jail—"

They'd rehearsed this part, Rye facing the crowd and telling his story as he always did, starting, "We woke in a ball field—" and continuing to the mob's attack, Gig's beating and arrest, his own arrest, the sweatbox, rock pile, bread and water, and then getting out, finding out his friend Jules was dead and that his brother was facing six months in jail, maybe more, for doing nothing more than standing on a crate and singing. And that was why he was here, raising money to hire "the great Clarence Darrow" to help get Gig and the others out of jail.

"Thank you, Ryan." She gave him a nod that he'd done well, and he returned to his seat. She'd added Jones to her name on flyers and posters, but it was all *Gurley* onstage now, striding about in her big black coat to hide her pregnancy, and which made her appear to float, ethereal, fine dark features on a thin pale face. "This is the fight, brothers and sisters! And it's not just in Spokane!" She worked the space like a boxer, corner to corner, perched forward as though looking through a high window. "It is anywhere these robber barons own the land *and* the industry *and* the agency that sends you to work there! Anywhere men and women are forced to live on the street. Anywhere a handful of copper and timber kings steal the wealth created by the labor of tens of millions and then beat and arrest the very men they've robbed for simply asking why!"

Rye had seen his brother jawsmith, and he'd seen Walsh talk an angry crowd out of busting up a job agency, he'd seen storytellers like Jules, and traveling quacks and palmists, and he'd seen the dazzling center fielder Billy Sunday keep a thousand hobos rapt with his jokey preaching ("Goin' to church don't make you a Christian any more than goin' to a garage makes you an automobile").

But he'd never seen the likes of Gurley up there.

The crowd was nodding, perched to erupt, but Gurley wouldn't pause, and she rode their murmuring *yeses* to a rising chorus. "Brothers and sisters, look around this room, at our bodies, our blood, the *fuel* for *their machine*! We can use the same fuel to start *a movement*! These bodies! This blood! To demand fair pay! Basic medical care! Rights for women, Negroes, Indians! To demand nothing less than the American right to speak out against corruption! Against greed and unfairness! Join us on the front lines, donate money, help young Ryan Dolan and his brother, for when we've won in Spokane, we'll bring the fight here, to Seattle, to San Francisco and Fresno, to Portland and Minneapolis, we will fill a room like this in every building on every block in every city in every state in this country! And our righteousness will spill into the streets, into the lumber camps and mining halls! Join us in Spokane on November twenty-ninth to fight their corruption with our peace, and room by room, street by street, city by city, on rails and docks, in factories and farms, anywhere a workingman or -woman is cheated from a dollar and clings to a freight ladder for life and livelihood, we will stand as one and say, 'No more! We demand a better world!'"

Rye was sitting when all around him people rose up, stomping, cheering. A bucket passed, slopping change and small bills. Gurley, speech over, was swamped by men and women wanting to talk or to touch her, but as Rye stood nearby watching, she ignored them all and walked to the edge of the stage and called over a ragged-looking young woman who had been sitting off by herself.

The woman looked to be twenty at most, no stranger to trouble, an opium girl or rustle boxer, Rye guessed. He had noticed her just before the speech, matted hair and a fresh black eye. Now, while the crowd milled, Gurley bent down, took the young woman's hands, and said something to her. She pulled away and said in a louder voice, "You can do it." Then she walked along the stage, thanking people as the raggedy woman made eye contact with Rye and hurried from the union hall.

Most people waiting at the stage just wanted to thank Gurley or to hand her an envelope with a donation it. These went so swiftly into the big coat that Rye thought she'd have made a good sleight-of-hand grifter if she hadn't been such a terrific union agitator.

A few people wanted to talk to Rye, too—a woman in a bonnet asking about his brother, an older man thanking him, a floater saying he'd be in Spokane at the end of the month for the next free speech action. One woman said she had a sister in Spokane, "Agnes Poole? Married to a furniture man? Carl Poole? I don't like Carl much, no one does. Do you know him?"

Rye was relieved when a tall man in a Stetson grabbed his arm to make a plea for sabotage instead of peaceful protest. "Son, you know all this talk ain't worth a well-placed spike in a tree."

"That's what I've tried to tell him," said a familiar voice.

Rye turned to see Early Reston, still as a rock in a stream in that crowd, hands in his trousers pockets, hat tilted forward.

"Early!" Rye left the saboteur and walked over.

"Look at you," Early said. "I leave for two weeks and you go become a famous radical."

They had a tussling handshake and Early put a hand on Rye's shoulder and became serious. "I'm sorry about your brother. And Jules." He shook his head. "I should have made him come with me."

Early said that after leaving Spokane, he'd made his way to Seattle and was scraping up day jobs when he saw on a poster in Pioneer Square that Elizabeth Gurley Flynn was in town to talk about the trouble in Spokane. "I figured Gig might be caught up in this, but I didn't imagine I'd find you here." He chewed his bottom lip. "I hope what I did to that cop didn't make things worse for you fellas."

Rye shrugged. "They were going hard at us anyway."

"Well, I'm still sorry for it, Rye."

Their reunion was cut short by raised voices.

Rye turned to see an older, gray-haired man yelling at Gurley from just below the stage. The man was possibly hard of hearing, or just angry, because in his opinion, her speech had "devolved into a screed about women's suffrage!"

"A screed—" she said.

"Yes, a screed!" the man said. He reminded Rye of the older labor bosses in the union office, yelling at Gurley like she was a child. "A screed that hardens the listener's heart against the merits of what could be an otherwise honorable message, the cause of justice for the poor!"

Rye could see that from the edge of the stage, Gurley was smiling at the old man. He marveled at her calm but thought he saw something else in her eyes, too—a hint of mischief. "With all due respect, sir," she said, "I do not believe justice will ever be truly possible, economic or otherwise, for *any* human being, until we have once and for all emancipated the vagina."

The man sputtered. He took a step back and was still sputtering, red-faced above his priest's collar, when he rushed past Rye and out the door.

18

They had raised nearly $250, a fourth of their goal, the Seattle IWW leader, Garrett, pointing out that they might've done even better "if you hadn't decided to end the evening by yelling profanities at a priest."

"*He* was yelling," she said, "I was quite calm."

In addition to the money, a dozen men had promised to come to Spokane for the second free speech protest, including, to Rye's great surprise, Early Reston.

Rye had just introduced Gurley Flynn, "Early here was the man at the river I was telling you about who got some good licks in the day we got rousted," when Early surprised Rye by taking off his hat and bowing.

"You are some speaker," he said to her. "By the time you finished, you'd half convinced me to come back to Spokane and join up."

"Just half?" she said.

"Maybe more than that," he said.

Rye looked sideways at Early.

"I'd do it for Gig," he said. "And you and Jules. You all took a beating for me."

"Why don't you come with us now," Gurley said. "To Montana. I'm supposed to travel with two men anyway, for security, and Ryan speaks well of you." She said she had union funds to buy him a train ticket.

"Yeah?" He looked at Rye and then back to Gurley. "Well. Okay. But I'm not singing. And if some cop comes at me with a nightstick, I can't promise I won't—"

"No," she said. "No violence. That's the one rule." She put out her hand. Early stared at it a moment, as if not used to shaking with a woman.

"All right," he said, and gripped her hand. "But I'm still not singing."

When everyone had left the hall, Gurley took Rye's arm, and he walked her down the busy street toward her boardinghouse.

"You did a fine job today, Ryan," she said.

"You're the best speaker I ever heard," he said.

She took the compliment without comment. Rye remembered what Lem Brand had said, that Gurley didn't care about workers like him. "But I wanted to ask. Do you think you could change one thing in your speech?"

She stopped walking and turned to face him.

"You keep calling me a sixteen-year-old orphan," he said.

"Oh, I'm sorry." She touched her chest. "Is it terribly demeaning? At times the story overwhelms me and I get carried away."

"No, I understand that. It's just . . ." He hesitated. "Well, today I'm seventeen."

The hand that had been on her heart now covered her mouth. And when she removed it, she was smiling. "Come on," she said, and she pulled him up Second Avenue, through the mist, dodging the streetcar-auto-and-horse-hustle. At Yesler Way, she steered him into a building with a fancy scripted sign: G. O. GUY DRUG STORE.

Gurley spread both hands on the soda counter and beamed. "My gentleman friend and I are celebrating, and we would like two ice cream sodas."

Gentleman friend! Rye watched the man at the counter produce two big glasses, thin at the bottom, wide at the top. He pulled vanilla sodas from the tap and dropped two plops of ice cream in each, the soda fizzing around them.

They carried their ice cream sodas to a wrought iron table, Rye reluctant to take a bite. He'd had ice cream and he'd had soda and liked them so much separately that he worried they'd be ruined together. But the soda made the ice cream melt slowly and the ice cream made the soda colder. It was creamy and delicious, and he felt another pang of guilt about having such a treat while his brother sat in jail.

Gurley was stirring hers slowly. "My mother used to take us for ice cream sodas when she earned a little extra from sewing. We didn't tell Father." She hummed at the memory and finally took a bite. "Ryan? Do you ever think back with regret on the choices you've made?"

He wasn't sure how to answer that. *Had* he made choices? He hadn't really thought of it that way. Since his mother died, he'd bounced from job to flop to train—sleep here, sleep there—was that a choice? There were things he felt bad about, stealing chickens from an icebox, letting a tramp press against him on a cold night, but really, the first *choice* he remembered making was to step on the soapbox after Gig got knocked from it.

Then Rye thought about Lem Brand's warm library, the twenty dollars in his hand. There was a choice. And a regret. He had tried to tell Brand nothing important that day—only things that were already in the newspaper—but he knew what he'd done was wrong. He looked up at Gurley now, worried that the guilt was written on his face. But she was lost in her own thoughts.

"When I was fifteen, my mother took me to see Vincent Saint John speak about the labor troubles in the west. He was dashing. I couldn't stop staring at his mangled hand—he'd been shot in a dispute in Minnesota." She laughed, then leaned forward, confiding. "It's a grave disappointment: the discovery that you have a *type*."

Not long after that, she said, a note arrived at her house from a Broadway producer named David Belasco. "He'd read about my arrest in the newspaper, and he invited Mother and me to see a play he was staging, *The Girl of the Golden West*, about a frontier saloon woman who falls for a notorious outlaw. It was a terrible play, although I must confess some stirring when the outlaw came on. Blanche Bates played the girl, and I recall my mother saying, 'Well, at least her bosom can act.'"

Rye glanced around the soda fountain, but the only person listening was an older man with a bulbous red nose, wearing a tweed suit, who sat over Gurley's shoulder. He had lowered his newspaper at the word *bosom* but now lifted it back up.

"After the play, we were led upstairs to Belasco's office, and he asked if I might be interested in a career as an actress. He was producing a play about a young labor activist, and he thought having the real 'East Side Joan of Arc' could generate great publicity. 'No, thank you,' I told him, 'and anyway, I'm from the Bronx.'" Gurley shook her head at the memory. "Mother was furious with me. Here was my chance for an independent life, on the stage! But I told her I would choose my own path and that she should not pass off her unlived ambitions to me.

"The next year, I went to my first IWW convention. That trip changed me, the factories, the mining camps, the great stands of forest and mountains. I just wanted to keep traveling, going west, one more train stop. I did not want to go home, Ryan. It was like . . . falling in love."

She smiled at the memory. "And that's where I met Jack. He was a miner and a union organizer on the Mesabi Range. His eyes, oh, I can't tell you. So when Vincent Saint John suggested I take a speaking tour of the west, starting in Minnesota, I jumped at the chance.

"But my parents were furious, and Mr. Saint John came to plead my case and to reassure them. He said I would stay in decent boardinghouses with matrons and that he would have two men assigned to my security. As he explained all of this, though, my mother just stood in our living room with her arms crossed. 'And who,' she said, 'will you assign to protect these men from her?'"

Rye blushed again and looked down.

"I was so humiliated! I dragged her to the kitchen and we yelled at each other, but she wouldn't budge. I had just turned your age, seventeen, which she thought was too young to travel to rough labor camps and western towns alone. Besides, she reminded me, I had promised that I would finish high school. I couldn't believe what I was hearing. *High school?* Should I ask Jack Jones and Vincent Saint John to wait a few months for the revolution while I took my exams in comportment and had my final piano recital? Or perhaps my mother preferred I stay home and marry a Newark bookkeeper who would spend the rest of his life fumbling at my skirts while I learned to boil cabbage?

"Mother threw her arms in the air. At the very least, I could admit there were choices in life other than bookkeeper's wife and miner's whore!"

Rye glanced around the soda fountain. The old man in tweed was peering over his newspaper again, but Gurley didn't seem to care, in mid-performance, replaying this fight with her mother.

"I yelled back at her, 'At least a whore has the good sense to get her money up front!'" Gurley shook her head. "Oh, it was a horrible thing to say. My father had never been much of a provider, except of stories. Mother slapped me. And I slapped her back. And she slapped me again. And I knew better than to go another round with Ann Gurley. We faced off like prizefighters in the kitchen while the great Vincent Saint John sat patiently in our parlor, awaiting my answer and listening to my father dither on about some speech he'd given about home rule back in 1890.

"That's when my mother's face changed. It was as if, in that moment, she suddenly became an older version of herself, and the rage drained from her eyes.

"'I am going, Mother,' I said.

"'I know you are,' she said. And she looked around this kitchen, this place she worked twelve hours a day, cooked three meals and sewed and darned for extra money, where she would live and die, and where I would have died, or some kitchen like it, had she not raised me to break out. She sighed and took my hand and said, 'Give 'em hell, Gurley.'"

Rye's ice cream soda was long gone, the glass licked so clean it barely needed washing.

"Look at me going on," Gurley said. She slid her glass forward. "Please, finish mine. My stomach is unsettled."

"No," Rye said, "you should eat it."

"For your birthday," she said, "please."

A woman passed by smiling, and Rye became aware that they must look like sweethearts, him in his secondhand lawyer's clothes and bowler, Gurley in her big black coat—a young couple sharing an ice cream, not a pregnant nineteen-year-old revolutionary and a seventeen-year-old orphan who was days removed from a jail sweatbox. He imagined them as real sweethearts, and the thought caused him to blush.

He looked around the room, but no one else seemed to be looking at them. Even the tweed man with the bulbous nose had gotten up and left. Rye finished Gurley's ice cream and they left the drugstore. Outside, a woman was leaning on a light post. She straightened when they came out.

It was the woman with the black eye Gurley had spoken to after her speech. "I followed you from the hall," she said. "I hope that's okay."

"Of course," Gurley said. "Ryan, this is Carol Anne."

Carol Anne wouldn't even look at him.

Gurley turned to him. "I'm sorry, Ryan, would you excuse us a moment?"

She walked the woman halfway down the block. On the sidewalk, people made a wide berth around the thin woman, but Gurley held her hand, nodded, and listened. Then Gurley reached into the pocket of the black coat, pulled something out, and pressed it into the woman's hands. The woman shook her head no, but Gurley nodded as if she were insisting. She patted the woman's hand and seemed surprised when she suddenly gave Gurley a hug.

The woman continued down the street. When she rounded the block, Gurley returned to Rye and took his arm again and they began walking back toward the hotel and boardinghouse.

"Did you see her eye?" she asked.

"Yes," Rye said.

"Her sister's husband did that and much worse, I'm afraid. She would be in danger if she didn't leave, so I advised her to catch a train and get out of town immediately. She has family in California, cousins, so she's going there.

"Oh, and another thing," she added. "I had believed we raised two hundred fifty dollars tonight, but due to a bookkeeping error, it was closer to two hundred."

They had reached the door of her boardinghouse. Rye could see through the window the house matron sitting next to a fire with a cup of tea. "A bookkeeping error," he said.

"Yes," she said.

Rye looked at her closely. How had he imagined they might be sweethearts? She lived such a different life, not just married and expecting a child but commanding a union fight against a whole city, this *slip of a girl* who fired up rooms full of workers and decided on a whim to pay a poor beaten girl to get out of town. It seemed silly that he had imagined what it might be like to kiss her. What he wondered now was what it might be like to *be* her.

"I hope it was the priest's money," Rye said.

She stared at him a moment and a wide smile slowly spread on her face. "I don't believe he donated," she said.

"Too bad," Rye said.

She enveloped him in a hug. "Thank you, Ryan," she said into his ear. "I needed this. Happy birthday."

Rye watched her walk up the steps, the matronly figure in the window rising to greet her.

He walked down the street to his own dank hotel, got his key from the ghost at the desk, and went up the narrow stairs to his room, still feeling the pressure of her hand on his arm. So strange, the turns of life. Gig in jail, him here in Seattle with someone like Gurley.

Rye turned the key and slid inside the door. A man was sitting on his bed.

"Who are you?" Rye asked.

He was an older man, sixty at least, in a gray tweed coat and trousers, with a great flourish of a tie. But it was his red, veined nose that drew Rye's eye, and he recognized him as the man from the drugstore.

"How was your ice cream, Mr. Dolan? To your satisfaction, I hope?" He spoke with the western remnants of a British accent, like something fancy covered in dust. Rye remembered the voice from the train seat behind him when they'd arrived in Seattle, pointing out the window at men blasting away Denny Hill.

"Who are you?" Rye repeated.

"I've been sent to collect the debt you owe Mr. Brand."

Rye was confused. "He wants his twenty dollars back?"

The man laughed. "No. He does not want his twenty dollars back."

None of it made sense to Rye. "Who are you?" he asked a third time.

"Oh yes, forgive me, where are my manners?" The man stood and removed his hat and held out his hand. "My name is—"

Del Dalveaux

SPOKANE GAVE me the morbs. Right blood blister of a town. Six-month millionaires and skunk-hobos, and none in between, Spokane a gilded carriage passing by peasants bathing in the very river they shat in.

Last place I wanted to go, but the job was the job, so I packed three shirts and lingered a minute over which barking iron to take (in the end I went small, loud, and kicky, the .32 Savage automatic). I caught first-class Denver to Billings, my first day sober in a month spent crossing Montana, then two hours over the Idaho panhandle toward the Washington border, and that's when the old morbid voice rattled up: *Careful, Del—*

At Hope, I slipped the porter a buck for a whiskey, then another when the train slowed the last five miles, forest, foothills, farms, and finally, Spokane.

I couldn't believe how the syphilitic town had metastasized. Smoke seeped from twenty thousand chimneys, pillars to an endless gray ceiling. The city was twice the size of the last time I'd hated being there. A box of misery spilled over the whole river valley.

I was half rats by the time we settled in the station. The voice again: *Go home, Del. You don't need this.* But my doctor wasn't likely to take reputation as payment. *You can do this*, I said back. Ten years a Pinkerton, ten more with Allied, and twenty a freelance, I had survived worse.

And money was good. The kind of money I hadn't seen since the mining wars, this Brand offering me prime pay (*Dear Detective Dalveaux, My associates and I would like to inquire* . . .) and a bit of my old station in the letter, but also I suspected the job lived on the outskirts of what I was willing to do—and I'd done plenty: undercover with the Molly Maguires in my youth and the unionists in middle age. I had broke, beat, and buried men.

Spokane had a fancy new train station since I'd been through, built on an island just this side of the falls, three stories of brick and optimism. On the platform, I made the mistake of looking up, and a ripe ass told me I was gazing upon the biggest clock west of Chicago, 155 feet tall with four nine-foot faces. The ripe ass also said Spokane had the biggest beer hall and the biggest theater stage in the world, and I fancied shooting him in the teeth if he didn't shut up. I can suffer any fool, but a booster turns my guts.

"You know what else you should see while you're here?" he said.

"Is it only you," I said, "or is every man in this town an insufferable cunt?"

Before he could answer, a thick lug in a driver's cap stepped forward from a line of porters. Stared at my nose. A lot of things a man can hide, but not that grog-blossom map of life. "Mr. Dalveaux? Please follow me, sir."

I stepped after the driver, but I noticed his socks were silk. His arm swung cuff links. Good Christ, this tiresome business. A fancy monger pretending to be his own driver, cap and all, reaching for the bags like a servant.

How to play it? Get rumbumptious or let him have his fun? I went down the middle, didn't want him to play me, but didn't want him canked yet, either: "Thank you, Mr. Brand," I said, and he looked surprised over his shoulder. I liked the defeat on his face—his racket was queered *and* he was stuck carrying my bags. How's that for a red nose, muffinguts? He muttered some rot about safety and anonymity, but I could tell he'd just wanted to reveal himself like a posh magician—*Look, it is I, Lemuel Brand!*

We were followed by his security lug, who climbed in a tail car. Brand and I settled in a big touring auto—him driving us into that hopeful downtown, past a curling streetcar packed with people, hutching wagons and sputtering Tin Lizzies, much more traffic than last time, on suspiciously wide streets up a hill to a big gaudy house overlooking his rank kingdom.

He laid out a whole speech in the car: "city on the verge of— dangers of socialism—East Coast agitators—immigrant filth— concerned mine owners and business leaders—real Americans—jail full of vermin—mayor's hands tied—in support of police—moral responsibility—commercial interests—future in the balance—last stand of decency—"

"And is that why you brought me here, Mr. Brand? My decency?"

He looked over. Did not so much as smile.

We parked and got out of the touring. The security brute climbed out of the follow car and gave me the old agency-man once-over. I opened my coat to show my gun so the lug wouldn't feel the need to pull it from me.

"Dalveaux," said I.

"Willard," said he.

Three other men worked the edges. This Brand was spooked. Or just had money to burn. He offered to show me the grounds, but I declined, much to his disappointment. I was already feeling one of my harder thirsts.

His lecture had reached the part about him representing "a consortium of industrialists, mining and timber men looking to fight back against the anarchists and unionists."

"Consortium," I repeated. Nothing better than a *consortium*. Ten rich hens to pluck instead of one.

He explained that the Spokane police chief had been properly tough with the Wobblies in the first round, and if they stayed tough until spring, the tramps would give up and go back to work, and trouble would take care of itself. But there were "pockets of weakness in the city's resolve," and a new union organizer had arrived, a girl. "The consortium hopes to augment the actions of the police while keeping this young woman organizer from getting a foothold."

"So it's augmenting you want," I said. "Why me? Plenty of augmenters here. Indeed, there were three national detective agencies with shops in Spokane—Thiel's thugs and Pinkerton's too-smart-for-their-own-goods and Allied's bargain boys. Any of them could *augment*, plus at least four regional head-knock shops. Why go all the way to Denver and old Del—this part I did not say—ten years far side of prime?

"First, this can't be local," Brand said. "And it can't be one of my men. No tracing it back. It needs to be off the books. And made to look . . ." He searched for the word. "Natural. You came highly recommended for that."

Then he said a name. Rich Spokane monger. Nasty job I had done for him last time I was here. During the low period. The kind of thing the Pinkertons and better agencies wouldn't touch. A woman-in-the-way kind of thing.

Christ this town.

We went up the steps, and as if to wave off my conscience, Brand swept his arm at the entryway. "Welcome to Alhambra, Mr. Dalveaux!"

"Like the Spanish castle."

He looked stunned, and if he hadn't hired me already, he'd have done so on the spot. "Well. I must say—you live up to your reputation."

These mining guys. Knew so little and wanted to believe so much. How hard was it to find the name of his bloody house?

I followed him through a fancy landing, beneath dual staircases, to a two-story library. Books that hadn't been cracked since they were shelved. Give money to a monkey and he'll fill his cage with bananas. Give the same money to a dim American and he'll build a show library every time.

Brand had a bottle brought in. Brandy. I stared at it while he mentioned again the Spokane mining prince I'd done the job for a few years back—son of a prominent family in a rub with a hotel girl—a dove run by some cop in town—told the boy's father that the girl was pregnant—father deciding it was cheaper to pay old Del once than this rat cop over and over—*Can you make it seem . . . accidental*—

On and on, anon, anon, begat, begun, begone. The brandy stared back.

"And so, in talking with my colleagues, you seemed a good candidate for the kind of thing we need."

"Which is?"

"Which is . . . the kind of thing we need."

His tone surlied me—or the bottle did, just sitting there, doing none of us any good. And the sour taste of that other job: hiring the girl, getting her drunk in her crib behind the tavern, pouring booze and lye down her throat until she drowned. Easing out of the room. Took a peek-feel as she died and she wasn't even pregnant—likely just a play this dirty cop made against the wealthy kid. But the girl was gone now, while the rat cop, shit kid, and old Del, we all woke up next morning and breathed air. In a better world, I'd have done them, too, the cop, the kid, the dad, but that wasn't the job. The job was the job and the girl had to go. And Del—a little more of him in the process.

Finally, Brand handed me a glass of brandy.

"They're planning another major action, November twenty-ninth," he said. "They're going around giving speeches, raising money, recruiting bodies to fill the jail. They want to hire Darrow."

"Sure they do," I said. After he got Big Bill Haywood acquitted of a murder conspiracy in Boise in '07, every jailed radical prayed at night to Clarence Darrow.

"We would like their efforts . . . hindered."

Hindered? The only thing I hated more than a booster was a euphemism. *Augment? Hinder? I ought to augment his chin with my right fist and hinder his dick with my left.* I drained my glass.

"I was thinking," Brand said, "what if, at some point of their travels, their party was relieved of whatever funds they'd raised?"

"You want them robbed," I said. Euphemisms.

"Is it considered robbery if the money is intended for an illegal purpose?"

"Yes," I said. "How much money?"

"The money isn't important."

"The money's always important."

"The money is important only in that it conflicts with our larger purposes. You can keep the money. What I'm wondering is if the presence of the money provides an opportunity to . . . make one thing look like another?"

I finished my brandy through gritted teeth, thinking: *You don't hire a man forty goddamn years in this thing and tell him how to make one thing look like another thing.* Just like you don't go into a restaurant and hand the chef a recipe for a bouillabaisse. You order bouillabaisse and you let the goddamn chef do his goddamn job. You don't hire Del for a dirt bath and say *make it look like a manicure.*

"You have names?"

"I have dossiers."

Good Christ. Dossiers. Save me from these mining men—little girls playing dress-up in their mother's wardrobe.

He handed me a file. *Dalveaux* typed on the outside. Six pages. Four names: two tramps, brothers, *Gregory* and *Ryan Dolan*, twenty-three and almost seventeen. Montanans. Arrested in the labor trouble. The younger released. The older, Gregory, still in jail. He'd done some speaking for the IWW and was known to "consort" with *Margaret Anne Burns*, aka Ursula the Great, thirty-two although she claimed twenty-four, actress in a wild cougar act. It was the joke of a place like Spokane, how many whores listed themselves as "actress." Still, if it was real, I wouldn't mind seeing this cougar thing. It occurred to me that Brand might have a personal angle for this job, too—a stake in the cadge.

There was a third bum, but the information was thin, nothing but a name, *Early Reston*. He'd taken a few punches at a Spokane cop. With this one I was to use caution because he was dangerous. I nearly laughed at the idea of a dangerous bum. So he'd decked a cop? There were raccoons I'd take in a fight with a Spokane cop.

That left the labor woman. The only one I knew. At least I knew *of* her. Every detective in the west knew Elizabeth Gurley Flynn. Saucebox spent the last two years riling up camps from Seattle to Minneapolis. Labor cunny roused more rabble than jaws twice her age. I'd had my boy Paul in St. Paul tail her back when she was working the Minnesota mining region, and he all but fell in love with her. After that I'd heard some miner married her and knapped her up. Good for all involved. Best way to turn a nineteen-year-old problem like that was put her in a kitchen with a babe on her tit. But now she was back on the road?

"What do you think?"

I looked up. Brand was smiling. "The bums won't be a problem."

"The older brother is still in jail."

"It will be easier when he gets out. Fewer people involved."

"I see. And what about this Early Reston? He beat up a cop pretty bad. When it comes to it, I would advise taking him down first."

When it comes to the bouillabaisse, I'd stew the lobster with tomatoes first. "Like I said, the bums won't be a problem." I held up the page and pointed to Gurley Flynn's name, not wanting to say it aloud. "This one's a problem."

He nodded. "The job you did for my friend—"

"I don't mean because she's a woman. I mean the attention. It would be four times the price." I held up four fingers. "Plus expenses."

His eyes widened. "I see." It was more than he'd planned, and I worried I'd started too high. "Well." He took a swallow of his drink. "Maybe it won't come to that. For now I just want them located, followed, and—"

"Hindered," I said.

"Hindered," he said, "although, should the opportunity *present* itself—"

I cleared my throat. Should the opportunity—I *was* the opportunity, opportunity and chance and fate, that's why you called Del. Dirt bath. Eternity box. That's the opportunity I provided.

"There is one other thing you should know," Brand said. "Last week I made an entreaty to the younger brother."

"You did *what*—"

"An entreaty? An offer—"

"I know what an entreaty is."

Brand shifted in his chair. "Last week I brought Ryan Dolan here and I floated the idea of hiring him, having him on retainer. For information."

"Information?"

"Specifically, I wanted to know if Early Reston had rejoined their party."

I stared.

"I . . . I had Ursula bring Ryan to me. You see, I was seeking information—"

I held up the file. "You had one of *these* people . . . *brought here?*"

He cleared his throat at the depth of his mistake. "Ursula wanted me to get the older brother released, and . . . it seemed like an opportunity to—"

"What if he told someone? What if Ursula told someone?"

I could see this hadn't occurred to him. Christ, this euphemistic stupid scaramouch. I closed the dossiers. They weren't half bad.

That's what made them so bad. I looked up at Willard, standing with his hands crossed in the corner. "A minute with your boss?"

He looked at Brand, who nodded. The lug left the room.

I closed the file and ran my finger over the label. *Dalveaux*.

Brand saw me looking at his handiwork. "I imagine you'll be hiring other men for this operation? Perhaps I could be your—"

"Shut your bone box."

His breath went short.

I walked to the fireplace and pitched the dossiers into the fire. "No more paper. No more *dossiers*. No more fake drivers and no more trying to hire the men you want me to plant. Right?"

He nodded weakly.

"I will hinder. Follow the girl and plan the robbery. Meantime, you go back to your *consortium*, and if it's dirt baths you want: It's a thousand per bum and three for the girl. Nonnegotiable. From now on, you and I speak only by telephone. Twice a week. I ring you on Monday and Friday. I tell the girl on the line my name is Grant.

"If it's just the robbery, you don't take the call. If it's a dirt bath you want, you come on the line and propose lunch. If it's the labor cunny, you say, 'Can we have lunch Monday, Mr. Grant?' If it's the dangerous tramp Reston, you say, 'Lunch Tuesday?' The entreaty brother, 'Lunch Wednesday?' If it's the whole party, you ask for dinner—"

"Dinner," he said breathlessly, his trousers no doubt tightening.

"Say you want just the girl and the dangerous tramp, you say—"

"'Mr. Grant, can we have lunch Monday or Tuesday?'"

"Right. And the younger brother and Reston?"

"'Mr. Grant, can we have lunch Tuesday or Wednesday?'"

"And if you want all of them done, you say?"

"'Mr. Grant, can we schedule a dinner?'"

"Good." It was over the top, pointless secret agent business, but he ate it up. That's what he was hiring—a story. Any mining goon could plant three tramps and a knapped-up labor girl. This rust-guts wanted a play. So, Del played, and hoped this lunch-on-Tuesday gully-fluff would keep him occupied and out of my way.

"Any questions?"

"What if I actually want to have lunch?"

I cleared my throat. "We will not be having lunch. Anything else I should know?"

He hesitated a moment, and the old voice said, *Oh, get out, Del*, but I hadn't made this kind of money in a decade, and then he said, "No, that's it."

I didn't think he'd ever ordered this before. He was overwhelmed, a scared schoolgirl with Del's hand up his skirt.

I reached over and took the bottle of brandy. "Now have your man drive me downtown. I need to get some sleep. And have a girl sent up. Something young."

"Yes," he said.

"Right, then." I offered my hand down to him. "Charmed."

The man looked up, took my hand, and I shook it. And I squeezed the blood right out of that fat claw.

PART III

When I first came into this burg, I had a cold hunch, and I kept having it. Something was due to happen to me in this place.

—Wallace Stegner, *Joe Hill*

19

On the way from Seattle to Montana, they stopped in Spokane for a day. While Gurley checked in at the union hall, Rye and Early went to see Gig in jail, but the IWW leaders were on a hunger strike and weren't allowed visitors.

"You could write him," Gurley said on the train the next day, and she got a card and envelope from the purser. They were on the Northern Pacific, on their way to the Coeur d'Alene Mining District for a day of speeches.

Rye stared at the blank card. He had never written anyone a letter.

"Tell him to break out of jail and come find us and we'll raise hell together," Early suggested.

In the end, Rye decided simply to tell Gig what had happened since he got out—although he knew he couldn't write all of it, about Ursula bringing him to Lem Brand's house and the twenty dollars he'd taken for information, or the strange detective, Del Dalveaux, appearing in his Seattle hotel room. Instead, he wrote:

Dear Gig,

I'm sorry you are still in jail. I am traveling with Elizabeth Gurley Flynn raising money for your defense and for the others. She wants to hire a crack lawyer by the name of Darrow who I pretended to know of but I don't. He must be even better than Fred Moore who is the lawyer who got me out. I never met a girl like Gurley Flynn. She is an excellent speaker tho you should of heard what she said to a priest. We had ice cream sodas one night. (Very good.) We have already been to Seattle and I talked in front of two hundred people

*and now we are taking the train to Wallace and then to Missoula.
(Inside the train.) Early is with us too. He came to hear us in Seattle
and we tried to see you in Spokane but they wouldn't let us. Early
made a joke that you should just break out of jail. I know you feel
bad that I got knocked around and arrested that day and put in the
sweatbox and mixed up in all this. But it's the proudest I've ever
been climbing on that crate next to you.*

Yr brother Ryan

He sealed the letter in an envelope and wrote Gig's name, care of
the Spokane City Jail.

From the seat in front of him, Gurley turned back. "Listen, before
we arrive, I need to tell you something about Al Bolin. To prepare
you."

She said that Al was an old union pick, blown up in an anarchist's
bombing in the '99 labor wars. That in spite of his injuries, Al was a
top organizer, and they should count themselves lucky he'd agreed
to be their guide for two days of fund-raising in Wallace and the
mountain mining towns of Idaho and Montana.

"Al can be a sight, and it takes a moment to get used to him," Gurley said. "So try not to stare, though neither should you look away."

Early sat up in the seat behind Rye. "How am I supposed to look
and also *not* look?" Rye liked having Early along. It reminded him of
traveling with his brother.

"I mean that you should behave normally," said Gurley.

"Well, that's what I'm saying," Early said, "looking and *not* looking are fairly normal behavior for eyes."

"You'll see," she said.

Al Bolin was waiting on the platform when they pulled into Wallace,
and Rye saw right away that normal eye behavior was going to be
impossible. The man lurching toward them was six feet tall on his

right leg and six-four on his left; a four-inch peg had been nailed to his right cowboy boot to make up the difference. His arm and shoulder on the right side were diminished too, half gone, like his portraitist had lost interest.

But it was his face that Rye couldn't keep from staring at: the cave-in that constituted the right side of Al Bolin's burned, mottled mug, the eye patch and torn nostril, the gnarled mouth, and the hole where his right ear should be. A metal clip was punched through his cheek like a bull's ring and held his jaw together on that side. When he offered Rye a hunk of stained bone with two scarred knuckles for a handshake, Rye hesitated.

Bolin said, "Best shake it, kid. The good one I use for fighting."

Introductions over, they followed Al through the depot and out to a dirt street in front of the station. For a man half blown up, Bolin walked like he was in a footrace. He generated surprising speed on the block of wood, and Rye hurried to keep up with him as he strode into downtown Wallace, a picturesque valley town nestled between impossibly steep mountains. There weren't three thousand people, and there were twenty horses for every automobile on the street, but Wallace was what passed for civilization here—schools, hotels, and restaurants, center of a spiral of two dozen smaller mining and logging towns that disappeared up in the mountains.

This area had been the site of a fierce labor war a decade earlier, culminating with a gang of angry, underpaid miners hijacking a train at gunpoint, loading up two hundred men and eighty boxes of stolen dynamite. The "Dynamite Express" picked up more men in every little town and rail platform until a thousand of them hung off the cars, men whooping and waving rifles as the train steamed to the Bunker Hill mine, where they shot the first security man they saw, then lit the boom sticks and blew the mill and a handful of scabs and managers off the world. Their work done, they took the train back to Wallace, got drunk, scattered, and went to bed. The mine owners appealed to the Idaho governor, who sent the army to put down the rebellion, and a thousand union men were thrown into detention camps with no trials, guarded by buffalo soldiers meant to inflame them. The governor paid for this in the end, getting blown up in his house near Boise five years later.

Wallace also had the most famous tenderloin this side of San Francisco, a block of brothels and cribs just north of Cedar and Sixth, along the South Fork of the Coeur d'Alene River. Temperance and clergy were cleaning up other red-light districts, but in Wallace, the brothels were seen as a necessity by the town fathers to keep the miners mining and the loggers logging. The city legislated and regulated the houses, and it wasn't uncommon to open the newspaper and see the mayor presenting flowers to the madam who'd donated money for a new streetlight.

"That's Block Twenty-three, where our whores is kept," Al Bolin said as they walked past a cluster of brick-and-stone buildings along the river.

Gurley had already given a speech in Coeur d'Alene and one in Smelterville. This last speech was to be here in Wallace, at dusk on the street from the back of a buggy up against that wall of mountains. The national IWW office had advertised the event as Gurley and Big Bill Haywood, the hero of the old mining wars, acquitted of assassinating the Idaho governor in 1907, but Big Bill never made it out of Chicago, so it was just Gurley and Rye.

A small crowd of lumberjacks and miners, socialists and suffragists had gathered, maybe sixty people. Rye's job was the same as always, matter-of-factly tell his story when she called on him, after she'd riled up the crowd with her socialist talk, when she got to the part about "the criminal mistreatment of workingmen by the thugs in the Spokane Police Department. And here with me is a victim of that abuse, a young orphan recently turned seventeen . . ."

"We woke in a ball field," Rye said each time, and then he stood and removed Mr. Moore's bowler and told his story as plainly as he could. He was careful not to exaggerate, to stick to real details, and not to make sweeping political statements. He always ended with the death of his friend Jules and the Salvation Army man asking his age. This last bit got gasps and angry *tuts* from folks, although Rye couldn't see why it was so much more barbarous to beat on a sixteen-year-old. Or why it was worse than them killing poor Jules.

As he spoke, Rye noticed Early leaning against a wagon at the edge of the square. He wore a smirk that stung Rye.

When it was done, most of the crowd scattered, and Rye, Early, and Al Bolin met Gurley behind the wagon where she'd spoken. She was plainly discouraged. They'd collected only about fifty dollars, barely two hundred total from three speeches in Idaho, less than they'd gotten at one event in Seattle. And only a handful of volunteers had said they *might* come to Spokane.

"We're speaking to the wrong people," she said. "Socialists and retired men, women's clubbers. I'm not getting through to the actual workers. This is not some dry Sunday lecture. It's a fight with dirt under its nails."

"That's why I want to take you where the workers are," said Al Bolin. He said he'd added one stop to their tour. Instead of going around the mountains, they were taking the Great Northern through the mountain pass for a noontime talk in the border town of Taft.

"Taft?" Early looked up sharply. "Wait, we're going to Taft?"

"Sure," Al Bolin said. "You don't have to be in Missoula until five, and Taft is where the workers are. Probably two hundred of them just sitting up there. Timber work's shut down for winter, and the rail jobs are winding down. You want workingmen, they're in Taft."

"What's Taft?" Rye asked.

"I like this," Gurley said. "Let's do it, Al."

"Jesus," Early said, and he turned and walked away.

"Wait, what's Taft?" Rye asked again.

But an old miner with a sideways foot had just limped around the wagon to talk to Gurley. He began telling her about the day in 1899 when troops marched down Sixth Street. Gurley nodded politely. He went on, "They built a bullpen down on the river, rounded up every man in town, and locked us up there. No trials. Nothing. You remember them days, Al?"

"If I didn't recall it, my body would," Bolin said, "just like yours, Jeff."

Rye backed away from this conversation to go find Early Reston. That look on his face earlier while Rye spoke: It was eating at him.

The sun had gone down and there seemed to be twice as many people on the street now. The mountains were pine-blanketed walls on every side of him. Rye followed some men through the brick downtown to Sixth Street, where a block of saloons was broken by a single café.

He stuck his head in each saloon, and he finally found Early in the fourth, leaning on the rail with a half glass of beer. He turned and saw Rye. "Why, look, it's Eugene goddamn Debs!"

Rye could feel his face redden again. "Were you laughing at me out there, Early?"

"No!" Early straightened.

"It's not easy, getting up there talking."

"Of course not. Rye, I was not laughing at you." Early looked around for the bartender. He clicked his teeth like he was calling for a horse and pointed at the bar in front of them. The thick bartender gave Rye a harsh sideways look, but Early chided him: "Don't be like that. Did you not hear the man's speech? He's got no mother, and his brother's in jail in Spokane." Early winked at Rye, spun a coin on the bar, and a glass of beer quickly landed on the rail. "A peace offering," he said. "Drink up."

Rye took the pint glass and tipped it, the tart foam reminding him of the sweeter foam around the ice cream soda he'd had with Gurley.

Early took a long drink of his own. "I guess, if anything, maybe I was thinking it was strange seeing you up there because you seem to agree with me about this *one big union* business. I thought it was more your brother's folly than yours."

Rye took another drink.

Early leaned over. "This utopian one-for-all bullshit . . . if it wasn't for your brother and that cyclone of a girl, I don't think you'd be doing any of this. I guess that's what I was thinking."

Rye felt a tightness in his chest, loyalty to Gurley and to Gig, but something else, too, which had been growing since the riot.

"Come on. Tell the truth." Early closed one eye. "You don't actually believe the story Gurley is selling out there, do you? I mean, that it's *possible*?"

"I don't know, Early," said Rye. "Does it have to be possible to believe in it?"

Early stared at him a moment, then gave a short staccato laugh. "Jesus, Rye. That might be the best defense I've ever heard from one of you utopian shitheads." He gave a small, appreciative nod and pointed at Rye with his glass of beer. "And are you willing to go to jail again for something impossible?"

"Yes, I am," Rye said, wondering if that was true.

"Okay, then. If you're going back to jail anyway, wouldn't you rather do something to *deserve* it, something big?"

Rye looked around the saloon. It was full of men like them. He imagined a street of saloons in a state of saloons in a world of saloons, a million men spending their last dollar on a glass of frosty forget. It was all too much, this way of thinking. Rye took another drink, the tartness not bothering him anymore.

"I got a question for *you*, Early," he said. "What the hell is Taft?"

20

It wasn't even a town but an overgrown work camp that had sprouted three years earlier when the Chicago, Milwaukee, St. Paul and Pacific Railroad decided to connect the last transcontinental line. They mapped a route eighteen miles shorter than any competitor, but that meant going over, and mostly through, the steep Bitterroot Mountains of Montana and Idaho. Thousands of men came to the woods to lay track, spike ties, clear trees, and build dizzying trestles two hundred feet over virgin forest and canyons. They dynamited and hand-dug thirteen tunnels, the longest of which ran 1.7 miles through a granite peak. On either side of that endless tunnel, the St. Paul Pass, grew a pair of squalid work camps, like the front door and back door to hell, Grand Forks, Idaho, and Taft, Montana.

At their peak, each bustling camp housed more than a thousand men and nearly as many barmen, gamblers, and prostitutes, spread out in fifty or so rough-hewn wooden buildings—saloons, brothels, hotels and casinos, a barracks, chow hall, sawmill, and a sprawl of crib tents where the sorriest played-out jangle girls sat open-legged on dirty cots waiting for men too drunk to climb the brothel steps. Neither place had what you'd call streets—just crude wood buildings thrown up alongside the train tracks, where every night dirty, bearded men seeped from the woods to spend a day's wages. Behind this one square block were the men's shacks, lean-tos, and tents, trailing up the wooded hillsides with no more planning than sprouted mushrooms. Taft himself had visited as secretary of war in '07, before becoming president. He called the camps a "sewer of sin" and "a sore on an otherwise beautiful national forest." In response, the Montana side gleefully voted to take his name.

If Spokane was half-lawed, at least there was half. Taft and Grand Forks were built illegally on National Forest land, so neither had police nor government, and vice grew wild and untended there. An hour after frustrated forest rangers closed a saloon, three others opened. Taft did have what locals called a hospital—a dank cabin where a sawbones separated men from their smashed feet and gangrenous arms and where it was rare to leave better off than you arrived.

With no police, order was kept by the bosses of Baltic work gangs—Serb, Croat, Montenegrin, and Slav—who drove off the Chinese, Negro, and Indian workers and took over the camps. These bosses made deals with the job agents and foremen to control hiring, and they took a dime from every man's paycheck. The gangs also policed each other, settling disputes quietly, with fists and knives and hammers. No one would ever know how many killings took place in the mountains in those three years, but the previous spring, forest rangers had counted eighteen corpses in the melting snowbanks outside Taft.

"I'd like to register my official objection," Early said that morning as they boarded the Northern Pacific train from Wallace.

But Gurley had already been convinced by Bolin that with log and rail work down for the winter, Taft was the best place to recruit floaters to join the Spokane protests.

Early leaned over to Rye. "Nothing to recruit there but the drips."

The train slowed as it slid through Grand Forks, and they looked out at a cluster of half-burned log buildings along muddy paths. A prostitute had recently set fire to the camp to cover up the murder of a sadistic barman. "And that's the nicer of the two camps," Early said as they left Grand Forks and entered the endless black tunnel, bound for Taft. It was dead quiet in their car through the mile and two thirds of darkness.

Finally, they came out of the tunnel on the Montana side. Taft was a scar, half the buildings empty, roofs caved in by snow. No one greeted them on the platform, and in the center of that mud-and-ice square were only two human beings, and those two barely, a couple of slack-mouthed booze sacks perched on empty kegs waiting for the saloons to open.

"It looks like this during the day," Early said to Rye. "But the player pianos start jangling and the men come out of tents and shacks, straight for the saloons and cribs. We won't want to be here after dark."

It already felt dark to Rye as Bolin led them along a narrow trail between peaks toward a dark barracks hall. They walked single file down a rutted path, clumps of trees felled on either side for strips of roughhewn cabins. Smoke tipped from the tin chimney of the log barracks in front of them.

At the door, the smell hit Rye. "Here we go," Early said.

The faces inside were whiskered, sooty, dull. They wore dirty long johns and work clothes—loggers, rail spikes, and tunnel rats out of work until spring. They sat on sleeping pallets or leaned forward on the few rickety chairs they hadn't burned for heat. An old boiler had been turned into a woodstove in the center of the room, and it burned so hot its iron sides glowed red. Yet no matter how close he stood, Rye couldn't shake off the Bitterroot cold.

"Well then," said Al Bolin, and he clomped to the center of the room next to the stove. With as little fanfare as possible, he made the introduction: "Boys, here's Elizabeth Gurley Flynn, the labor girl out of New York I said about."

No applause, just quiet stares from the thirty or so men in the room, a third the number Al had promised. Rye's eyes and nose had adjusted, and he watched as, again, despite the setting, Gurley brought the fire. "The ruling class will keep you in slavery until you demand freedom!" she said. "Come stand beside me in this fight!" But unlike the other crowds, these hard, hungover men just stared. She introduced Rye and he told his usual story of getting knocked around and surviving the sweatbox. The shadowed faces didn't seem to register any of it, and Rye wondered how many of them even spoke English. They watched with bored, hungry stares—like hawks trying to decide if that mouse was worth the dive.

Gurley gave another pitch for them to come to Spokane for the November 29 free speech action, and when they'd finished, Al Bolin hobbled into the center of the room, tilted his ranch hat back, and said, "Well, boys, give a hand to these folks come to tell you about this business." They did, a couple of short claps. Then Al Bolin said, "You're welcome to come ask them questions and wish them luck as they travel on to Missoula to continue raising money for this thing."

At the door, Early Reston straightened. Rye felt his unease and watched his friend's eyes sweep the room and finally fall back on Bolin, who was backing away toward the rear of the building. They both watched as Al slid out a side door.

"Where's he going?" Early said, and he went out the front door to catch up to Bolin. Rye was frozen. He couldn't follow Early and leave

Elizabeth alone. He could see why Early was alarmed. Why had Al made a big deal of them raising money? And why, when he'd introduced Gurley, had he mentioned the "New York girl I said about"? *When* had he told them about her?

Rye made eye contact with Gurley, who also seemed to sense something was wrong. Then he looked at the travel bag at her feet. She had hundreds of dollars in there from their fund-raising, plus whatever she'd brought for expenses on the trip, more than enough to stir those hawks.

"We'd love to take questions, but we should get going on to Missoula," Gurley said, and she edged toward Rye and the door.

"I got a question," a voice called.

"We really should be—"

"How much money's in the bag?"

A thick man stepped in front of the door just as Gurley reached Rye's side. She cleared her throat. "Whatever funds we've raised are intended for the legal representation of those labor leaders in the Spokane jail."

"How come you didn't ask *us* for money?" said a tall man with gray-blond hair. "You think we ain't got any to give?"

"We'd be honored to have your contributions"—Gurley looked at the two men by the door and then back at Rye—"to challenge the unconstitutional law against speaking on the street—"

Another man with a thick accent cut her off. "How much money—"

Gurley persisted: "As I said in my speech, we hope to hire—"

"How much?" the man came again.

"—the great Clarence Darrow—"

"How much fuckin' money!"

Rye's eyes darted around until they landed on the shirt of a small dark-haired man standing next to him—his white undershirt was stained yellow, with a bib of crusted brown blood below his chin, like he'd eaten something alive.

Then the tall man with graying blond hair stepped forward until he was right in front of Gurley. Something about him seemed authoritative, and he spoke with an accent Rye couldn't place. "Mind if I look in your bag, miss?"

Rye took a half step between the man and Gurley. This caused the man to turn slowly and look sidelong at Rye. A toothy smile crossed the tall man's face. With the heat from the woodstove, the awful breath of the tall gray man, and the ripe of the men around them, Rye felt bile rise. His only defense might be to vomit on the man.

"Well, look at here," the blond-gray man said. Rye could feel Gurley's hand in the center of his back, supporting him or cautioning. "The orphan boy wants a go."

Thirty minutes of speeches and socialist talk and *rise-up-brother* and the room hadn't made so much as a peep. But now the men laughed.

"This money belongs to the Industrial Workers of the World," Gurley said, "and I would ask—"

The man was faster than Rye would have thought—and in what felt like a single move, he swept Rye aside, into the burning old boiler stove, and grabbed at the bag. But Gurley wouldn't let go and they tussled over it.

Rye pushed off the burning stove. He saw Gurley gripping the bag's handle, started toward her, but felt his arm yanked and twisted behind his back, and then something sharp pressed against his cheek. The man with the bloody shirt was holding a big deer skinner against his face, the knife scratching Rye's cheekbone.

"Not in here," the gray-blond man said.

Gurley still wouldn't let go of the bag's handle. "Listen—" And that was when the man hit her, open-handed but full, not a child's slap but a shoulder-rotating heel-of-his-hand swing that knocked her off her feet and slid her into the legs of some of those other men. And now the man held the bag alone.

Gurley looked up from the wood floor like a cornered badger, like she might leap up and rip that man's head from his neck. "You would steal from people who come to help you?"

"I don't recall asking for your help," he said. "Any of you men ask for this bitch's help?" He opened the bag and flipped through the clothing and held up some underthings for the others to see. "What have we got here?"

Then the gray-blond man pulled the money from the bag, held up the cash for the others to see, and threw the bag to the floor in front of Gurley. The money disappeared into his lumber coat. "Best get on, you two," he said with a vicious half-smile, "before it gets any colder out there."

Rye knew then what he meant by *"Not in here."* The minute they stepped out that door, the knives would come. They'd been robbed, and now these hounds would make sure there were no witnesses. They would rifle his pockets and try on his boots as the last of his squirming life spilled out in a snowbank. As for Gurley, Rye didn't want to think about it.

He looked helplessly at the door, wishing he'd never agreed to this, wishing he and Gig were sleeping in Mrs. Ricci's house, wishing Early Reston could come back in with a gun and save them, wishing he could overpower the man, take his knife, protect her.

From the floor, Gurley carefully pulled herself up and gathered her clothes. In the midst of those wolves, she carefully folded her things and put them back in the travel bag. She appeared to be in no rush. She patted at her red-black hair and at the rising mark around her eye. If she was feeling Rye's panic, she didn't let on. Her hands were steady. She wasn't crying, nor did she look particularly frightened.

She took a deep breath, reached back, and pulled the ribbon tighter around her hair. She took in the faces around her. And then she spoke, her voice changed. Lower, steadier. She wasn't jawsmithing or high-handing—she was just talking.

"You think I'm a fool." She slowly buttoned the travel bag. "Some Sunday temperance lady with no idea where she's landed." She looked directly at the man with the knife against Rye's face. "I know where I am. And listen: I've been to worse. Iron camps in Minnesota, Pennsylvania coal towns, Butte copper mine so deep I could smell the earth's mantle." She looked around again. "And I know *you*. I know you don't give one shit for the *brotherhood of men* some stupid union cadge comes up here selling. Fine."

Rye couldn't say what it was—her language, her posture—but he felt a shift and the men stayed quiet. "But whether you want me to or not, I am here to fight for you stupid sons of bitches. For your jobs and your booze and your right to be as stupid and poor a son of a bitch as any rich, stupid son of a bitch. I'm here to fight for your backs and for your arms, and for the freedoms you're too goddamn stupid to use. To come and go as free men, as goddamn *Americans* no matter where you were born, to make your way in this world without some robber baron owning you.

"But I will be *damned* if I'll let *you* end it all *here*"—she choked up and cleared it away—"in this *place*," and Rye felt the hum of her anger in his throat, in the whole room.

Gurley's lips hardened and she took on a mocking tone. "'*I didn't ask for your help, Gurley.*' Fuck you!" She said it right into the gray man's face. "I fight for any man who labors, and I will fight *against* anyone who gets in my way, and that *includes* you! All of you! You want the money? Fine! It's yours."

She stared at the gray-blond man as if daring him to say something. Then her eyes swept the room, landing on every eye that would meet hers. "Now maybe you think you still have business with us. Maybe you think you can do what you want, that no one cares what happens to some Montana tramp and a pregnant Irish girl—"

All eyes went to her heavy dress and coat.

"But I will tell you this: If I'm not in Spokane leading this second free speech action five days from now, it *will not happen*! And then, make no mistake, *you* will have chosen sides. You'll have chosen the side that lives off your blood and tosses you aside like trash.

"But if you want to give those bosses a poke in the *fuckin'* eye?" She grinned. "Let us go. Let us go finish our thing and fight for you, and next week I promise to make those rich bastards feel every bit as terrified as you've made *me* feel. Now, if there's nothing else, we've got a goddamn train to catch—"

And with that, Gurley turned and started for the door, the man guarding it so surprised that he stepped aside, and Rye, hurrying after her, pulled away from the man with the knife, bent to grab his bowler off the ground, and ran to catch up.

21

The frosty ground crackled as they walked quietly up the trail, Gurley first, then Rye, taking small steps, not daring to look back at the barracks or up the dark-shadowed hills on either side. They got a good thirty feet before Rye remembered to breathe.

"Bolin set us up," Gurley whispered. "And where's your friend Reston?" Hot anger emanated from her.

The hundred feet seemed to take an hour to walk, every tree a threat, the shadows terrifying, until they came over a hump in the dirt and there was Early, walking toward them from the cluster of buildings with a big woman who seemed all bosom and revolver.

"See," said the woman with the gun. "I told you them boys wasn't all bad."

"No, you said not *all* the boys were bad." Early Reston still had his hands in his pockets, as if nothing had happened.

"Well, that's true, too," the woman said.

"Where'd you go?" Gurley demanded.

"I ran after Bolin," Early said, as if it were obvious. "Then I went to get help." He tilted his head at the woman without removing his hands from his pockets.

"Where's Al?" Gurley asked.

"He took off into the woods," Early said. "I think he was in on it."

The woman was named Effie and she was the madam at the brothel above the Swanson Bros Saloon. She brought them up the back stairs into what she called the parlor, a small bare front room with no furnishings save an old couch with torn upholstery. Early went out to make sure the signal was down for the next train to stop, and Effie sat Gurley down and tended to her eye. She had Rye gather some snow in a handkerchief and told Gurley to press it to her face on the train ride to Missoula. Then she took out a makeup brush and began applying her craft. "You're a pretty girl," she said.

Rye had never seen paint on Gurley's face, and he ventured she didn't need it, so drastic were those dark lashes and brows against her Irish pale.

"Don't worry, honey, I've treated my share of these," the woman said. "Shouldn't raise a bruise. You were fortunate it was with an open hand. A fist is harder to hide."

Gurley's own hand came to her mouth then, and two tears made tracks in the coat of paint on her face, as if she'd just realized what had happened.

"Don't go and do that," Effie said. "That ain't helpful."

"I'm supposed to see my husband in Missoula tonight," Gurley said.

Effie looked down the length of Gurley's body. "Honey, are you pregnant?"

Gurley nodded.

"What are you doing out here?"

Gurley still couldn't answer.

"What are you, about five, six months?"

Another nod.

"Well, don't worry about that, neither. I seen girls fall down two flights of stairs couldn't shake a child loose, once it gets hold up there."

"I lost one before," Gurley said, Rye surprised to hear this.

Effie kept tending the eye. "Well, like I tell all my girls, don't go crying for a thing misses out on *this* business." She turned to Rye next and put a bandage on his bleeding cheek. "Why, this one's just a baby himself."

They sat in Effie's parlor for almost an hour, before a train squealed to a stop on the platform. "All *a-goddamn-board*," Early said. With Effie covering them from the window, they rushed down the stairs, across the muddy square, up onto the platform, and into the passenger car. They sat there, breathless, watching the trail to the barracks, waiting for men to come pull them off the train. Minutes later, the Milwaukee's engine lurched and the train pulled out. They watched out the windows. Gaslights and shadows loomed in the saloons. Smoke billowed from the wood barracks where the wolves had robbed them. It was dead quiet on the car and no one said a word, long after the cluster of rough-hewn buildings had fallen away.

22

Gurley stared out the window as the train rattled over a bridge across the Clark Fork River.

Rye sat next to her. "Are you okay, Elizabeth?"

She turned as if surprised it was him. "We fell in love on a train," she said. "Minnesota. Hibbing, Biwabik, the iron camps north of Duluth. My first trip west of Chicago. I loved seeing the world through a train window.

"It was Jack who insisted we get married. For my own safety, a single girl traveling through these parts. He was thirty. I was just seventeen. I thought I was so grown up." She laughed. "I used to see the coal steam shovels off in the distance and imagine they were dragons, that Jack was my prince, and we were exploring this mysterious land together." She glanced up at him, embarrassed. "My romanticism is my great weakness, Ryan. But you probably guessed that by now."

"If you have a weakness, I haven't seen it," Rye said.

She hummed a small laugh and looked at him fully, her wet dark eyes dipped at the corners. "Thank you." Then she turned back to the window. "When my mother found out I'd gotten married, she said, 'Well, now you've done it. Wasted both our lives.' Even Vincent Saint John thought it was a bad idea. 'Look at you, Gurley,' he said, 'you fell in love with the west and went and married the first man you met there.'"

Rye wished he knew what to say about any of this.

She touched his arm. "I'm sorry, Ryan," she said. "I'm being morose. Will you give me a moment with my thoughts?"

"Of course," he said, and he moved a few rows, to where Early Reston was drinking from a flask he'd borrowed.

"The purser is from the town next to mine in Wisconsin," Early said.

"I thought you were from Indiana."

Early glanced over his shoulder. "Well, he doesn't know that." He nodded ahead at Gurley. "How's she doing?"

"Morose," said Rye, adding it to his list of words to look up.

"Taft would make anyone morose. But I warned her. Going to Taft and not expecting trouble? It's like jumping in a lake and hoping to stay dry."

"They almost killed us, Early."

"Yeah, but they didn't."

"Because she talked them out of it."

"She *can* talk."

Rye felt defensive of her. "What's that supposed to mean?"

"It means she can talk. That's all."

"Why do you think Bolin set us up like that?"

Early didn't hesitate. "Money."

"He'd get us killed for a little bit of money?"

Early shrugged. "Everyone does everything for a little bit of money."

"You don't believe that," Rye said.

"Sure I do. Money and sex. That's why we do everything. The desire for sex can be quenched at least for a few hours by having sex. But give someone money? They just want more."

Rye shook his head. "Not everyone is like that. I'm not like that."

"Come on!" Early laughed. "You and your brother got yourselves arrested over what? A dollar!"

"It was not over a dollar!"

"Sure, it was. Same dollar that got Jules killed."

Rye's hands balled into fists. "No! It was about free speech!"

Early seemed amused by Rye's defensiveness. "Yeah, and what were you free-speeching on? The dollar you didn't want to pay a job shark."

"It was the principle!"

"Yeah. And the principle was a dollar."

Rye wished he had Gig here to debate Early. "It's not the same! Arguing for basic pay versus a guy taking money to sell out the people he's helping." As soon as he said it, Rye flushed with guilt, thinking about Del Dalveaux questioning him in Seattle, and Lem Brand's twenty-dollar note, still rolled up in his sock.

"Is it? I mean, that girl up there, she is a whirlwind onstage, don't get me wrong, but in the end, what's she really jawing about? Getting you bums a few more dollars. That's all."

Rye shook his head again. "You didn't hear her in Taft, Early. She was amazing. No, it's about a lot more than that."

"Sure it is." He held his hand up in surrender. "Hey, don't listen to old Early. I got nothing against that girl and her little union. It's as good as any other thing." He offered the flask to Rye, closed one eye and considered him. "But ask yourself this, little brother. Why is this conversation making you so upset? Two possibilities, I see, and they are not exclusive to one another. One, because you're getting sweet on her. And two, because you've had these thoughts yourself—I see it on your face." Early leaned in closer. "This thing she's out here doing? It's nothing but a show. I suspect you know there's a more direct way to accomplish things."

It was quiet, just the sound of the rails beneath them. Rye took the flask and had a pull to keep himself from saying anything.

"Look," Early said, "in case the first possibility is true, let's not talk about her at all. Let's say," he stuck out his bottom lip, "there's a castle. And a king in the castle. And he's an ass, because, well, kings are asses. Takes too much in tribute. The other knights and noblemen hate him. They say, This fella is getting rich off our fields and the tribute we get from the peasants. They scheme and plot and one day they slit his throat. Replace him with a new king. But pretty soon the noblemen say, Well, goddamn, the new king is as shitty as the last greedy son of a bitch. So they whack his head off, too, and they put in a new greedy king. Kings killing kings. You know what that's called?"

Rye shook his head.

"Shakespeare," Early said. "Now let's say you're on the other side of the moat, and you got these peasants watching one rich king bump off another rich king, thinking, *Wait, this ain't changing anything.*" He gestured at Gurley. "They gather behind some charming rebel who leads the peasants in revolt, and they behead *all* the shitty knights and princes and noblemen."

Rye just shrugged.

"Here is my point—the peasants own the castle now, and *they* become the greedy sons of bitches. It's all the same. What I'm saying is maybe the king ain't the problem. Maybe what it is"—Early took another pull from the flask—"is time to blow up the whole goddamn castle."

23

A felt cowboy hat rose from a bench in the Missoula depot and the man beneath it ambled toward them, Rye assuming this was Gurley's husband until he saw that she was looking around the man for someone else.

"He ain't here, Elizabeth," the man said. He shook hands with Rye and Early. "Arn Burkitt, IWW local vice president." Arn handed Gurley a letter. "It's from Jack."

As Gurley opened the letter, Burkitt told her that her two speeches in Missoula had been canceled.

"Why?" she asked without looking up from the letter.

"I'm under a lot of pressure here, Elizabeth."

"What pressure, Arn?"

"I'd rather not say."

Finally, she looked up. "Pressure not to let"—she read from the letter—"'a pregnant, wayward wife' take the stage?"

"It just don't play well here, Elizabeth, Jack wanting you back in Butte and you out here speaking on street corners. Makes us look barbaric. And it makes you look . . ." He didn't finish this thought. "It ain't just Jack. The other unions object to having you speak, Elizabeth. The AFL, WFM—"

"I know who they are," Gurley said. "So, you're saying we just let those men rot in the Spokane jail, surrender to the forces—"

He cut her off. "Don't jaw me, Elizabeth. I know what you can do. And it worked here. Cops blinked. But they ain't blinking in Spokane. No one wants that here. Five hundred in jail, Walsh and Little on a hunger strike. Hard enough to get men to sign up for red cards, you want 'em to sign up for bread and water and beatings and rock piles and a year in prison, too?"

She looked away. "Are you saying I should give up, Arn?"

"I'm saying that after your second arm gets bit off, it might be time to stop poking the bear."

"Yeah." Gurley sighed. "Time to start *kicking* the son of a bitch."

"I'm sorry," he said. "Nothing I can do."

"Arn, they sent me to Spokane to organize and raise money to hire a national lawyer to challenge this law. We are a week away from the second free speech action, and you're sending me back with no men, no money, nothing."

"What do you mean, no money?"

She looked down. "We ran into some trouble in Taft."

"What in God's name were you doing in Taft?"

Gurley's eyes trailed around the busy depot—travelers greeting family, porters handing luggage to travelers. "Doesn't matter," she said.

"I'm sorry, Elizabeth," Arn said. "I'm at a loss here. This is all I can do." He reached in his back pocket and handed her three train tickets. Two second-class tickets to Spokane. And one to Butte. "Time for you to go home."

Del Dalveaux, 1909

THE HOTEL clerk handed me a message from Bolin. Flaccid old lobcock wanted me to call a number. I had the girl on my end connect us.

Right off, Al said, "It didn't go, Del. Taft didn't go."

The girl on my end was chewing nails.

"They took the money is all. And let 'em go on to Missoula."

I said nothing.

"It's a lazy bunch up there is the thing."

I said nothing.

"And there were surprises."

Said nothing.

"Wasn't like you said."

Nothing.

"So what I figured now is——"

I snapped my fingers and gave a nod to the girl, who yanked the call.

I was ripe enough with that whorepipe Bolin to grab the next rattler to Wallace and beat him to death before he could hobble off.

But first I needed to deliver the news to Brand. And the thought of telling that fat church bell anything but "It's done" and "Goodbye" sank my guts. Goddamn Spokane.

I caught a hansom to his house. Algoddamnhambra. The stones on that man. His doorman said he was having a drink at his club, so I had the cab take me there, to a pillared building above the river where I found the man smug in a gauzy library, having Scotch and cigars with what he called the consortium—half a dozen fat whiskered high-collared white men sunk like nails into plush chairs in front of a fireplace so big three of them could've held hands and walked into it. Butter on bacon, that room was: white marble floors and velvet chairs, Negro waiters behind the rich men, and two bored security men along the wall. Thirty millionaires in Spokane and six of them sat right here, like potted plants in this gilded room, ripe prig-pipes playing chess with the whole town.

Low chatter rose from the chairs—a set of whiskers complaining about the mayor hiring the Olmsted brothers to map a new park system. "I said to Pratt, you'll spend a million dollars to have some New Yorker tell you to put grassy fields where our grassy fields are."

The other men laughed, and one said, "What's your complaint, Charles, if they pass the bond, they'll buy up your scabland, hire your crews to build the parks, and you'll end up with half the money."

"He's complaining because he wants *all* of it."

I wondered how many I could get in that fireplace before the security men stopped me.

Brand's back was to me, so I edged into the room, past more wall portraits of bristled white faces. He looked up and saw me, smiled, and began to speak, "Oh, Mr.——" before he remembered my admonition and brought his finger to his lips. I tilted my head to the hallway, stepped out, and waited for him.

When one of the waiters walked by with a tray of cognacs, I snagged one, drained it, put it back.

Finally, Brand came out in the hall. He was bleary-eyed drunk. Worse, one of the other men in the library had come with him and stood nearby, a few steps back. He was thin and pale, with a few long hairs pulled over his pate like wild grasses on a beach.

Brand chattered: "I'm sorry, Mr. . . . *Grant*. I know you said not to mention your real name, but Mr. Tate here is my dearest friend and closest ally, and I promised I would introduce him."

I opened my mouth to say it wasn't a good idea, him introducing us, but drunk Lem Brand had already turned to his mate and waved him over: "Bernard, come, meet the famous detective"—and now he whispered—"Del Dalveaux."

Christ.

"Such a pleasure!" This Bernard was drunker and more gal-boy booster than even Brand. "And how are you finding our fine city?" he asked. "I have heard it described more than once as the London of the West."

"Have you?"

"Because of the rivers, I mean. The Spokane and the Thames."

"Yes," I said, "those are both rivers."

"I hope someone has taken you to the Auditorium," he said. "It has the largest stage in the world."

"Perhaps you could tell me about it another time," I said. "I really must speak with Mr. Brand."

"Of course," he said. "Anarchists and dynamiting bums—we appreciate the work you're doing—Lem here has kept us all abreast and has told us of your great reputation. But it must have been quite a surprise when you found out that Lem's driver was Lem himself!"

"Mmm," I said, a bullfrog's croak.

Lem Brand jumped in then. "But we've got them on the run, don't we, Del? Chief Sullivan squeezing from the top and you and I from our end."

"Mmm." I felt the sweat on my brow—wiped it with the back of a spotty hand. I had aged ten years in a week in Spokane, and I was old when I arrived. "Speaking of which, Mr. Brand, I really must speak to you in private."

This was too much excitement for his friend Tate. "Of course! In-filtrations and espionage, much to discuss!" He fluffed the tails of his coat as if he were a partridge and backed away.

"You have a report from our operation in Montana?" Brand asked. Still playing secret agent. "Was our dinner for three a success?"

"It didn't go," I said.

"What do you mean?"

"I mean it didn't go."

"Wait. None of them?"

"It didn't go."

"You said Reston, at least. You promised!"

"It didn't go. The Serb took their money, but it wasn't right for the other."

"You said this was the place—"

"It was *a* place."

He was quiet. More than disappointment on his face, desperation—

"I'll take care of it," I said.

"You said this Serb gang—"

"My man there—"

"You said the farther from Spokane—"

"Right, it would have been—"

"Are they coming back here? Are you planning to do it here?"

"I don't know yet."

His face reddened. "When will you know?"

"I'm gathering information."

His irritation became something else. Fear, maybe. "Are they here now?"

"As I said, I'm gathering information."

"Yes, I heard that!" Brand's face constricted, mouth tight, and he spoke quietly. "I hope I didn't make a mistake." His eyes going straight to my grog-blossom nose again. "Hiring reputation over youth."

My shoulder twitched with the desire to punch his fat mug. "You may of course hire anyone you like. But as long as I am here, I will take care of it. Now, if there is nothing else—"

He grabbed my arm. "Mr. Dalveaux—"

I looked down at his hand. He let go of my arm.

I barely made it out of there with my breath. I seethed on the street. Muttered. Walked until I found a rat tavern and fell in—had a beer, a whiskey, and two more before I could breathe. The last one I sipped, and that's what started my thinking: *So Brand wants youth over reputation? The jobs you do for these sons of bitches. I infiltrated the Molly Maguires and the WFM, and this prig questions me about a union girl and a handful of tramps.*

I could do these three in my sleep.

The point, of course—in the old days *Del would have done the job himself.* Trusting it to Bolin had been soft. Lazy.

I was replaying my mistakes while the bartender dragged a drunk out of the place by his underarms. He edged the man through the door and dropped him on the sidewalk in front of the tavern. Came back slapping his hands together to get the bum off. "Been quiet, with so many in jail," he said from behind the bar.

I settled up. Outside the tavern, I saw the man dumped on the sidewalk, sleeping it off, legs draped over the curb, head bent like he'd cocked his ear to a joke. I looked back in the tavern. The bartender was wiping down where I'd sat. Below me, the bum slothered like a hog. There was an old hitching post in front of the building. I bent over and lifted the sleeping man's head, leaned it against that post like a pillow. The bum was maybe forty, skin and bone but for his gut, thin hair, rotted teeth. I lifted my leg and stomped down on his neck. Two more to his ripe melon, one each for Brand and his friend, but on the third stomp, I felt something in my ankle give and I limped away, cursing that slick tramp head and my own temper.

• • •

Bolin was easy. Same Sixth Street saloon in Wallace where I'd paid him and where we'd planned the whole thing with the tall gray Serb from Taft.

He wasn't surprised to see me. He would've checked the train tables the minute we stopped talking. Twelve years I'd worked with that ogre and still he gave me a jump—shriveled arm and leg and boiled face and that metal ring holding the gristle of his jaws together.

He sat at a table with a fresh beer, facing the door. A dozen other men were there. Bolin would think he was safe. Nothing better than a man feeling safe. Two men at the bar shifted as I walked in. So Al had at least two men, Dwang and Snool, pointless work, their eyes following me as I stepped to the bar. I pressed between them at the railing.

I said to the barman, "Do you have Scotch, or just that piss whiskey?"

While he poured, I leaned forward on the rail and spoke to the apes on either side. "I might not kill Bolin, but if I do, it's my business. Either of you makes a move and you'll go next, right?" I opened my coat on the .32 Savage.

I was alert, three quarters sober, a twitch from tears. I took a sip, stepped from the railing, turned, and smiled friendly, first at Dwang, then at Snool.

"Boys," I said. I walked across the floor and sat next to Bolin at his table. He'd put an empty chair on his good side—where he wanted me to sit. I grabbed the chair and carried it to the other side of the table. His shite side.

"Looking good, Al. New scars?"

"I figured you'd come."

"Fucking genius."

He pointed at my whiskey. "How many of those you had, Del?"

"Every single one of them, Al."

"Look, there was nothing I could do. In Taft."

"So you said."

"Didn't go is all. Sometimes things just don't go."

"So you said."

"The Serb got his money and I guess he lost interest in the other."

"Right."

"It was a drunk crew. Nothing to be done."

"You could've done it yourself."

"It never occurred to me that the Serb wouldn't. Son of a bitch killed his own nephew over two bucks."

"So why didn't he?"

"The girl got to 'em, Del."

"What do you mean, she got to them?"

"After they took her money—what she said got to 'em."

"What did she say?"

"I don't know, exactly."

"You weren't there?"

"Well, no, Del. I cleared out. I set it up and I left. I figured thirty men could handle two bums and a girl. And I didn't think you'd want me connected to that business. What good would I be to you later if I lost my cover?"

"What good are you to me *now*?" If my ankle didn't ache from the bum-stomp earlier, I might have meloned Bolin's rotten face, too. What a mistake, giving him this job. *Old and tired, Del, you are.* "Where's my money, Al?"

"I have it. I decided—"

"You decided?"

"I decided I'm keeping half for my trouble."

I laughed. "Those boys in Taft have *your* money, Al. Go get it from them. My money was for the job you didn't do."

"Well, I'm keeping two hundred."

I laughed again.

"Okay, one hundred. I have to get out of town, Del."

"I'll get you out of town for nothing. Out of every town."

"I'm keeping a hundred, Del."

I looked up. The apes were staring. Barman, too. And one at the door. So that was at least four. Christ, Bolin was spooked. But in a place like this, *more* wasn't necessarily better. Give me one good man over four rattled mettle fetchers any day. Especially for close work. The bark of the Savage would be to my advantage, the question was order: which first. *Dwang. Taller ape. Do that one and everyone stops to watch that man curl around his guts and then Snool, and that's when I turn and do Al, slow, no rush or panic, then see if any other man makes a move, although in my experience, those three will be plenty—*

Al interrupted my thinking. "There were surprises, too. You didn't tell me the girl was pregnant. And you could've told me Brand had another man inside."

I turned and looked straight into Al's mangled face. I did feel compassion for him, carrying that mug around. And it was true, I hadn't told him Gurley Flynn was pregnant. Had I thought Al wouldn't follow through if he knew that? Or was it some kind of guilt over the other Spokane job I'd done? I also hadn't told him about the younger Dolan. I was slipping. "I should've told you about the kid."

"What kid?"

"Ryan Dolan. He tell you that Brand has him on retainer?"

"What are you talking about?" Bolin asked.

"What are *you* talking about?"

"I'm talking about the Pinkerton."

"The what?"

"The Pinkerton. Reston. The guy playing a bum. What if we'd done him in? The shit they'd rain down on us? Even in Taft you can't just go kill a Pinkerton. You should have told me, Del."

I was quiet.

"You didn't know," he said.

"You're sure?" I asked.

"Yeah, I'm sure. He slipped out and followed me. Knocked me down in the snow. Asked a bunch of questions about who paid me.

Said he'd been on the job almost a month, that Lem Brand hired him to go deep."

Jesus. How many men did Brand have on this job? I thought back to the dossiers. Was it possible he didn't know Reston was the man he'd hired? Back when I went deep, I used fake names. Or was it darker than that? Had Brand wanted me to take out a man he'd hired? Was possible with him. Christ, planting a Pinkerton could've ended me. You can plant a dozen mutton-shunter cops, but you start killing Pinkertons, they will hound you to your last day.

And even if Brand hadn't known Reston was his man inside, he would've known he *had a man inside*. And he didn't tell me that. I had asked him, "Is there anything else?" and he had stalled. Told me about the kid but not another detective inside.

"You look like a man with troubles, Del."

I shrugged. "Put my money on the table, Al."

He sniffed. Then, thinking he had the upper hand, he put a small stack of cash on the table. I swept it into my pocket without counting it. "Now the other half."

"Like I said, I'm keeping—"

I grabbed the metal piece that held his jaws together and yanked it like a kid on a carousel. I pulled his face down to the table and, with my other hand, pulled the .32 Savage from my waist and leveled it below the table at the two men by the bar railing. They came up straight, but their hands were up and out, as if calming an angry animal. I held Al's face down by the ring in his cheek. "Where's my money, Al?"

He fiddled in his coat and set the rest of my money on the table.

A dozen years I'd known Al Bolin, since I worked him inside the WFM, back during the silver wars. I liked him. He had courage. Easy to turn a coward, but a coward's work left much to be desired. A man like Bolin, you only had a small shot of turning him, but if you did, he was gold. He was inside for me when an anarchist blew up a

safe house—Al the only survivor. In the hospital, his wounds bub-
bled and seeped, but when he came to, I was there to whisper in the
hole where his ear used to be: *You're gonna come out of this, and when
you do, come and find me*. He did and I took care of him. Gave him
money and opium, and when he could move again, I got him work.
Paid him to watch meetings and stoke a riot in Havre so my employer
there could convince the police to crack down on the union.

Still, I should've known better than leave a job like this to him.

I held my finger in the ring through his cheek like the trigger guard
of a pistol, his head on the table between us, money in front of his
nose. He looked up at me with his good eye. I spoke quietly. "Now. To
show that I am not a vindictive man, take twenty back."

He did.

"That's for a train ticket out of here and a hotel somewhere. Now
take another twenty for your troubles."

He did.

"And another ten to buy your apes a beer and a meal."

He did.

I took fifty dollars from the stack, pressed them into his hand. "And
that's from me, Al. For old times."

The rest went in my pocket. I had given him the hundred he'd asked
for, but *I'd* done it. I did not let him make Del Dalveaux look ripe for
prigging up the back avenue. His face still on the table, Al squeezed
the hundred in his hand like it was my throat and stared up at me with
that one good eye. I leaned in and whispered in the hole where his ear
used to be. "You're gonna come out of this, and when you do—go
fuck off, you half-roasted shitsteak—"

I gave the metal ring the slightest tug, then I let it go and his head
snapped back like it was a tree branch. I stood slowly, the gun still
leveled at Al's two men.

Al rubbed the bad cheek and smiled with the other one. "One of
these days, Del, someone's going to bury you, and not a single living
soul will be sorry."

Wasn't often I couldn't come up with a proper retort to these western cunts, but Al batty-fanged me on that one. Of course, the old half-miner didn't know about the doctor in Denver and the bump on my skull, but still—it was a cruel thing for one friend to say to another, and I stewed as I backed out of the bar into the street.

And now? Find Flynn and the young Dolan tramp and plant them where they stood. Collect five grand from Brand and ask about this Pinkerton he apparently hired and wanted dead. Or better, take the Pinkerton with me to see Brand.

I got a room with a girl in Wallace, but the situation had me lobcocked and she went to sleep unruffled. I was visited all night by visions: Bolin and the hobo's neck and the pregnant girl in Spokane I drowned, on and on. At three, I sent the girl away and dressed to catch the first train back to Spokane. A cold dark walk to the station, no sign of Bolin or his apes.

God of morbs, pulling back into Spokane that morning I felt low, and I nearly wept as we eased into the station. Was I never to be free of this place? In the seat in front of me, a man said, "First time to Spokane?"

I just stared at him.

"Make sure you see the Auditorium," he said. "Biggest theater stage in the whole—"

I leaned over the seat and punched him in the throat.

Hell with Spokane, hell with Lem Brand and his consortium of prigging gentlemen, with the doom doctor's diagnosis in Denver, all of it. I had money from two weeks' surveillance and the money I took back from Al Bolin. Maybe I could quit. Let Brand keep his bonus for the dirt baths. I had a daughter in Lexington, I'd go live with her and fish and read books to her boy. He'd be, what, five now? Eight?

Porters were helping the man I'd punched. I hurried off the train and went to my hotel. I had the clerk make a phone call to the Allied office in Missoula, to ask a favor of an eye who worked the Anaconda with me ten years ago.

"What are you doing out here?" he asked, heavy on the word *doing*.

I told him, and thirty minutes later he called back. He said Gurley Flynn's Missoula speech had been canceled and his man at the train station had Dolan and Reston railing back to Spokane today, on the Great Northern 1356, scheduled to arrive at one p.m. I checked my pocket watch: eleven-forty.

And Gurley Flynn?

"Sent back to Butte to be with her husband," the man said.

I felt a great lightening then, glad to be free of that woman. I have never liked killing the lesser sex and prefer not to. Half the world being women, you can't avoid it, but still it unsettles me. Even a shrill dollymop like her, better for everyone if she's making pasties in Butte and avoids my shadow the rest of her life.

I limped to a restaurant across from the Great Northern station and got a corner table by the window, where I could wait for the train from Missoula. I could at least drop the Dolan kid, fix that mistake, collect a thousand. If Brand wanted, I could even come back and do the brother when he got out of jail.

Fog had rolled in and the Great Northern 1356 was running late. The waiter delivered my eggs and I ate them as I watched out the window, carriages and autos beginning to pull up to the station. It had me imagining Lexington, my daughter greeting me.

The waiter came by to take my plate away, and I asked for a whiskey, but he said, "We have the luncheon out, sir," and I said, "I know it's lunch, I want a bloody whiskey for my lunch," and him, "I'm not allowed, sir," and my flush rose again, and that's when I looked out the window to see people spilling out of the train station, porters loading bags onto hansom cabs, folks hugging on the street in front. I tossed my napkin on my plate.

But I was stumped. Gurley Flynn and Dolan were coming out of the train station together, her in a black cape with a carpetbag, him in that same ill-fitting suit with his bowler hat. So she'd come back after all. Well, that would be more money. But where was Reston?

I reached into my pocket for a dollar coin, dropped it on the table, and was about to stand when a shadow fell and I looked up to see Early Reston.

"Del Dalveaux," he said, like we'd met before.

It is the strangest aspect of aging—how faces blur, a language you no longer speak. Up close this man seemed familiar, but perhaps the way a common face is reminiscent of others—thin, weary, plain—an age that might be twenty-five or forty-five, so ordinary in appearance that only another agency man would appreciate the difficulty of achieving such anonymity, like walking in snow without making a footprint.

"You have me at a disadvantage," I said, my hand finding my .32.

"Oh, I doubt that," he said. "Has any man ever had the great Del Dalveaux at a disadvantage?" He took the chair next to mine. "Brand hired you?" he asked.

"Indeed," I said, my hand square on the Savage grip. "And you?"

"Yep. A month ago," he said. "Wanted me to work both sides, rile things up, get the union throwing bombs and the cops busting heads. He wanted to avoid what happened in Missoula, the cops and mayor going soft."

"Well, no one's gone soft," I said.

"You hire me to rile—I rile." He looked away. "Maybe too much."

"You think that's why my employer didn't tell me about you?"

"He didn't?"

"No. I thought you were just one of the bums."

"Really? He didn't tell you?"

I shrugged. "Would have been good information to have."

"For me, too."

"I'm sure. A snake, isn't he?"

"Did he do the driver bit with you?"

I laughed. "And the dossiers?"

"Jesus," he said.

"So, what office are you out of?"

"Office?"

This confused me. "I thought you were a Pink. Are you freelance?"

He chuckled like there was a funny story in that, and shifted in his chair and looked around for a waiter. "I'm going to have a drink. You want one?"

Out the window I could no longer see Gurley or Ryan Dolan. I craned my neck. I'd find them later. "It's lunch. They won't open the whiskey," I said.

"Of course they will." Reston spun toward the passing waiter, "Excuse me," but the man skated by without stopping, and when Reston turned back, it was with a lunge, the blade sliding between ribs and nearly lifting me off my chair. I felt more pressure than pain, a thrust-lift-swipe in my chest and lung, the man's full weight—not jerking but easy and practiced, like a butcher cutting rib roasts, and what felt like eight inches of steel in my side and God I was dead on my chair—

My hand had come off the handle of the .32. I scrabbled for it, but it was gone.

Reston was leaning on the knife—*Ah, there's the pain*—I yelled, coughed, and sputtered, but he was standing, bent over me as if concerned about my condition. He spoke with—was that an attempt at an English accent? "Oh, Del, what's the bother?" Left hand on the handle of the knife, right reaching around his backside to tuck my gun into the back of his pants—can a man admire his killer's method? Except for the shite accent—

"Oh my, you're coughing blood, Del!" He called out to the bar: "Stay back!" He put that right arm around me, helped me to my feet. "My brother is consumptive," he said. "I need to get him some air."

The waiter gave us a wide berth, as Reston must've known he would, and he had me upright, pulling me out the door, the waiter held it for us, Reston's right arm over my shoulder holding me up, his left reaching across his own body into my suit coat, onto the hidden handle of his knife, which jutted from my side and which he used like the tiller of a boat to steer me.

I got out a weak "Help" to the waiter, but Reston said, "I'm trying, Del, I'm trying to help," and he gave the knife a slight twist, the pain buckled my knees, and I cried out again.

"My brother is quite ill," he said as he lurched me down the block, over the curb, and into the street. "Consumption, stay back," he repeated, knowing TB could explain the blood, and that people would steer away from a man coughing it up. He was so convincing that I almost wished he *were* my brother taking care of me—*Oh, Del, dead Del, god Del*—and I cried out again.

"Quiet now," he whispered. "Won't be long."

I faked a stagger, mustered some last fight, and gave him a sharp elbow, and followed that with a fist, and was almost able to spin away from him, but that knife was heavy in my side and he gave another turn to the handle and *oh-goddamn-weeping-sorrow-goddamn* pain—I could do nothing but collapse against my brother and surrender to it.

"None of that," he said.

"Fucking Brand—" I muttered, for that was my true killer—luring me to this hell-city and hiring me to kill my brother and God I wanted my brother to go and kill Brand next—*God weeping sorrow*.

"Quiet, now," he said. "Tell me, are you a religious man, Del?"

"No," I managed.

"That's good," he said, "because I don't believe we have time for rituals."

Oh God weeping pain

"I'm sorry. I know it hurts," he said. "Try not to talk or breathe too deeply. We're almost there. Stay quiet and I'll help you along."

Oh weeping God

"You shouldn't have drunk so much, Del!" he called out to someone who must've seen us staggering, and him half-carrying me, for he was having trouble supporting my weight now.

I wished I could stop my weeping. Was this how it had felt for the people I'd planted? Jesus, the horror. At least I was quick. And the shame of it. I could have gone to see my grandson and daughter in Lexington. Oh, that little girl running into my arms. Shame *weep shame* goddamn Spokane morbs, sorry for it all, sorriest for me, *shame weep God panic weep shame weep*.

We walked east and then turned north. He had me step over railroad tracks. We were moving toward the river.

He laid me down in some wild grass and the pain nearly undid me. I opened my eyes. We were in a little grassy strip between railroad sidings, just above the south channel of the river. He was crouched, a little winded from carrying me so far.

"Exhale," he said, and when I did, he pulled the knife from my side, and I felt blinding pain and then a loosening and a relief, that blade and handle out of me. But the burbling of blood in my breath was enough to know I would drown one way or another. He took my hand and pressed it against the wound. "Hold your hand here. And take shallow breaths. It's okay now. I will put you out quickly once you answer some questions."

I opened my eyes. He was standing above me, wiping clean the blade, which was smaller than I'd have thought, long and narrow, barely wider than an ice pick. The sky was low and gray behind him.

"What are you going to do?"

"Me? Finish the job I was hired for and go collect my money."

"I didn't know"—*wince weep shame*—"he said you were a dangerous bum—said you punched a cop."

"Oh, I did more than that," he said.

It hit me then. "The cop who was shot?"

He said again, "You hire me to rile, I rile."

It became clear then: Brand hires Reston, but he kills a cop, so Brand hires me to fix that problem. I pictured his *consortium*. "If anyone found out he hired you—" I didn't finish the sentence.

"Hey! Look at there." A smile crept over Reston's face. "The great Del Dalveaux has solved his last crime."

Weeping sorrow.

"I'm sorry, Del," he said, and started to come at me again.

"The kid," I said. "Brand got to him, too."

This stopped him. "What?"

"The kid. Dolan. I met with him in Seattle. He's the one who told me you were going to Wallace. Brand bought him for twenty bucks."

The look on his face. "Ryan?"

"Yeah." I hoped he'd kill the kid. Hoped he'd finish the whole lot, the bums, Gurley Flynn, Brand. I imagined him going door-to-door, killing the whole city, marching those millionaires into that big fireplace, all that pig-fat wealth crackling and melting, him killing every booster and setting fire to that bloated theater stage. I imagined the whole city gone, and it was a great feeling, picturing Reston wiping the morb town from the planet. He was like no Pinkerton *I'd* ever known, those priggish bookkeepers—and I felt a terrible respect for whatever he was—

"You're not—" Even to my own ears, my burbling words made no sense. "I need to—" I stared at the sky. Old prayers.

"Okay, quiet, now," he said. He bent over me and blocked the sky, looked in my eyes—such warm eyes, you'd never know—and then I felt one of his hands open my coat. He reached for my wallet, but I got the strength to push his hand away. Terrible form while a man still breathed. Would he go for my fillings next?

"Sorry, Del," he said. "You're right."

Oh blessed weeping shame—"Wait," I said, "wait—" *Oh cold morbs*—and he bent again and covered my eyes, and I tried again, "W—" but he drew the blade across my throat and the warmth spread and my arms went out in wide embrace and that's when—

24

Rye stared out the window as they crossed the Idaho border. Winter air had blasted down from Canada and dropped the temperature forty degrees in two days. A thick band of fog belted the valley. That morning, a freight train had slammed a junk wagon at a foggy crossing, its cowcatcher tearing an old dray in two, and so the Great Northern 1356 slowed to a crawl. The passenger train eased into Spokane like a man feeling his way into a dark room—ghost buildings, pale faces in the mist.

They'd left Missoula before dawn, Gurley spending the whole trip writing articles for the *Industrial Worker* and penning letters to supporters. She'd decided at the last minute to come to Spokane instead of going to Butte and had convinced the train agent to exchange her ticket. "I'll go home when this is done," she told Rye.

"What about your husband?"

"He knows who he married."

The closer they got to Spokane, the more energized she became. She read lines from her articles aloud. She looked up from her writing to tell Rye new ideas. Five days wasn't much time, but she could go to nearby granges to rally farmhands; wire organizers in nearby towns for immediate help; recruit better in Chinatown and among the Negro hotel and street workers, and at the new Balkan hotel. In the meantime, she'd give a daily speech in the hall, maybe even on the street.

"I'll give the first today," she said.

She sounded a little frantic, Rye thought, and he worried something was wrong with her. "Today?"

"We'll be back by noon. I'll speak at seven."

"I just mean, you don't want to take a day to rest?"

"I don't have a day, Ryan. We have to keep the pressure up."

"But you said yourself, we have no money and no bodies."

"The other side doesn't know that," she said. "We could have another five hundred floaters coming to town."

But they didn't, and Rye thought about his conversation with Early, who sat two rows back, slumped in his seat, hat pulled over his eyes. He'd spent most of the trip like this, after a few hours in a Missoula saloon. He was still drunk at five-thirty in the morning when they boarded the train, and announced it would be "my last official duty. All due respect, I tenderly tender my resignation."

Now, as they pulled into the Spokane station, Early coughed, leaped up like he'd remembered an appointment, grabbed his pack from the luggage rail, and patted Rye on the shoulder. "I'm off, kid," he said. "Take care." He tipped his hat to Gurley. "Good luck, believers," he said, then darted down the aisle. The train hadn't even come to a full stop when Early dropped to the platform outside. Through the window, Rye watched his friend slide away again.

"He does that," Rye said.

"We don't need him," Gurley said, Rye thinking, *Maybe it's time to blow up the castle.* He helped Gurley up and got both of their bags down from the luggage rack. She rose belly first, pushing on her lower back. With the other hand, she took Rye's arm, and he carried their bags through the crowded station, like husband and pregnant wife, past newsboys hawking the dailies and men selling ales and sandwiches. By the time they were outside, Early was long gone. *Like being friends with a storm cloud,* thought Rye.

Cars and carriages lined the station curb like cattle at a salt block. Rye walked Gurley through the smoking, shitting traffic and across the bridge, two icy blocks to the union hall, which was empty, desolate.

"Where is everyone?" Gurley asked.

They'd only been gone a few days. The door was open, but there was no one in the canteen or the newsstand. The big hall was empty, too. Finally, they found Charlie Filigno in the cold meeting room, playing cards with the cook and the newsstand clerk.

Filigno gave Gurley the grim update: union coffers depleted, membership flat, cops patrolling the streets and rail yards, picking up anyone with a foreign accent and running them out of town before they could protest. No one had been arrested in four days. The union was basically out of men, word having gone out among the floating class that railing to Spokane meant a beating. The last editor of the *Worker* had been arrested three days earlier and, like the editors before him, charged with conspiracy for luring protestors to Spokane.

Charlie shrugged. "We can't run this without a paper."

"I'll edit the paper," said Gurley. "We'll publish this afternoon."

Filigno looked at the other two men. "Publish what?"

Gurley tossed the articles she'd written on the table, the pages scattering the cards from their poker game. Rye had read them on the train—announcing the second free speech action and promising waves of support from Seattle, Idaho, and Montana. There was no mention of the robbery in Taft or the canceled speech in Missoula, just a story about full donation buckets and men promising to come fight. Filigno read aloud: "'We welcome the ranks of organized labor in our battle against the corrupt Hibernian Police Chief Sullivan and his brutal bunkmate, the Drunken Judge Mann, these monstrous minions of the mining millionaires.' Elizabeth—"

She smiled. "I know, the alliteration."

She told the cook to fire up the canteen so that floaters could see they were open, and she told the newsstand clerk to take her stories to be typeset. She scribbled headlines on top: SECOND SPEECH ACTION IN SPOKANE! and GURLEY FLYNN TO SPEAK TONIGHT! The one-page paper would feature these two huge headlines, the second story announcing, "Elizabeth Gurley Flynn, organizer for the Industrial Workers of the World, is giving the first of a series of speeches leading up to Friday's Free Speech Action tonight at 7 p.m. Will detail city's brutality and the Union's response. Free, at the IWW Hall, 240 Front Street, Spokane. Apple, cherry, mincemeat pie & coffee."

"Tonight?" Filigno looked up at Rye as if to ask, *Is she okay?*

"It's one o'clock," she said. "If we get this typeset and run the press, there's no reason we can't get newsboys on the street by five."

"And the pies?" asked the canteen cook.

"You have six hours to figure that out," she said. She took the cards from the cook's hand and tossed them on the table. A pair of eights. Rye couldn't believe her energy, after all they'd been through, and more than that, how the hardship in Montana seemed to have fired her up even more. She sent Rye to gather newsboys to distribute the *Worker* and to get copies of the daily newspapers to see what news they'd missed while they were gone.

It was a cold and foggy afternoon, the sun skirting the hills and a snow so light and dry that Rye couldn't tell if it was falling or blowing up from the street. He fixed his coat around his shoulders and buried his hands in his pockets, but still the cold took his breath. He walked to the train station first, where a regular clutch of newsboys was selling dailies.

They formed in crews around an older boy, and Rye recognized the leader of this crew, a kid named Lidle, who ran six younger newsboys and who liked to hang out in front of the union hall. Although he was a foot shorter than Rye, Lidle was only a year younger.

"Hey, Ryan. I like your bowler." Lidle self-consciously patted his own nest of unruly brown hair.

Rye explained to Lidle what was happening. In a few hours, they'd need five newsboys to go out and sell a hundred papers each—a special edition of the *Worker*. They could keep the money they made, and they'd each get an additional nickel for putting posters on walls and light poles.

"I'll take care of it, Rye," Lidle said. He still had copies of the afternoon *Chronicle* and the morning *Spokesman-Review,* so Rye got one of each.

Rye hurried back to the hall, glad to be out of the cold. Through the front door, he saw the old cook in the canteen, busily stirring pie filling. He went through the doors into the main hall. At the end of the hall, the office door was open, and Gurley and Filigno were bent over the table, planning. Rye plopped down in the pews to look through the newspapers for IWW stories.

But the union's fight was old news now, the front pages on to a brakemen's strike and the announcement of a big heavyweight bout in New York between the old champ, Jim Jeffries, and the new one, Jack Johnson. A *Chronicle* cartoon portrayed Johnson as a baboon training with fried chicken, and a local story had the six hundred colored troops at Fort George Wright planning to bet heavy on Johnson.

Rye flipped to the *Spokesman*'s Labor News page and found a short bit headlined FOREIGN BUMS LEAVE; DISAVOW IWW. After being served bread and water for Thanksgiving, three men had told the judge they were no longer with the union. "We was tricked into this," one of them was quoted as saying. The story gleefully pointed out that more than sixty men had now been released after agreeing to disavow the union and immediately leave town. After a high of five hundred in lockdown, the numbers were falling.

The *Spokesman-Review* also had a small story about the successful prosecutions of four union leaders on conspiracy charges. These were one-day summary trials in front of six-man juries, in spite of the objection of what the paper called "the young Socialist mouthpiece Fred Moore." Walsh and Little had both been found guilty and sentenced to six months' hard labor in the state prison, as had the first two editors of the *Worker*, James Wilson and E. B. Foote. The last line of the story listed the upcoming conspiracy trials of four more union leaders this week, "those involved in organizing the Nov. 2 riot." The last name on the list was Gregory T. Dolan.

In the empty hall, Rye's head fell to his chest. *Six months?*

He felt like such a fool. Lem Brand had said he'd get Gig out early. And Rye had believed it.

He thought he might get sick.

He looked around the dark union hall.

In the office, Gurley had straightened up from the table and was staring at him. "Ryan?"

Christ. What were they doing here? What were they pretending they could do? He thought of Early: *You don't believe this shit, do you, that it's possible?*

And Lem Brand: *You're a pawn.*

And Gurley? Did she ever have a plan other than having them throw themselves at the cops and rotting in jail? They had no money, no men, no pressure, no Clarence Darrow, no hope.

Gig was going to jail for six months. Or worse, he'd die in there, like Jules had. And if Gig did get out, what would he be like? He'd been gone a month already, on hunger strike for part of that time. Rye looked around the empty union hall. He felt like his chest might collapse.

He stood and left the newspapers open on the pew.

Gurley came to the office doorway. "Ryan, is everything okay?"

He lurched toward the door. "I just need some air." By the time he reached the street, Rye felt like his sternum was cracking. *Six months.* He gasped at the cold air, needles in his lungs. What would he do? Tramp around and try to find work himself? Where would he go? Rye doubled over but couldn't catch his breath. He glanced to his left and saw a policeman on the corner, watching the hall.

It took a moment to recognize the big cop, Clegg. "Hello, Dolan. Back from Montana already?"

Rye couldn't speak, his breathing shallow and pained. He turned away from Clegg and hurried down Front Street. He passed a couple staggering on the street, passed a saloon, a café, a Chinese cleaner.

He passed the newsboy, Lidle, followed by three other boys, like quail crossing Front Street. "Hey, Ryan, we're ready."

He waved at them from across the street but kept moving, turned south on Stevens, wavering against the flow on the sidewalk, people headed for east-side saloons. He passed job sharks, hired guards on stoops, and an alley where two women stood smoking outside their storefront cribs. He had no idea where he was going. He just kept thinking the word *home*, although he didn't think it existed without Gig.

He looked back once to see if Clegg had followed him.

But no one was there. Had he imagined the big cop?

He slowed, his breath returning to normal.

He looked up. He was on Sprague Avenue, in the fancier part of downtown, where a better class of steam escaped people's mouths.

25

Tramps didn't venture into this part of downtown without getting hassled, so Rye pulled his coat tight and lowered the bowler on his head, trying to blend in, just a man on his way home from work. Even with Mr. Moore's coat and hat, though, his dungarees and boots gave him away. At Howard Street, he paused for an electric trolley car, its overhead wires crackling, and he was spellbound by the pale-lit, ghostly faces inside the car, people headed to families and meals and fires. Automobiles and horse wagons filled the streetcar's wake, and Rye stood at that intersection for a long time, staring at the tracks. The whole country was laced together with tracks. He could get on a train and end up in New York City if he wanted, and this felt like another reverie, or a premonition.

The world was becoming a single place.

He moved deeper into the west side, fancy hotels, restaurants, and theaters. He found himself on the sidewalk in front of Louis Davenport's frilly white stucco restaurant, pillars at the door, arched windows—inside, the bright lights gleaming off crisp white tablecloths and sparkling on gowns and shoes. He couldn't stop staring—the light inside was like a vision of heaven.

Three men in fine suits and leather gloves were walking into a cigar shop next door. At the curb, a young man in tails was helping a drunk woman in a gown into a brand-new automobile. Another man was leading a woman in a fur into the restaurant, and casually slipped the tuxedoed doorman a dollar.

A day's wage for opening a door.

Rye stood on the sidewalk and turned a slow circle, taking it all in. It was dusk, early supper hour, and men were leaving offices for a beer together, or taking their wives to a meal before the theater.

Right now he and Gig would be lining up at a Starvation Army soup kitchen or warming their hands over a rail-yard cook fire or, best case, huddled in their coats on Mrs. Ricci's sleeping porch, hoping she'd invite them in for dinner.

"Come on, *get!*"

Rye looked back over his shoulder. The Davenport's doorman was shooing him. He wore a heavy coat over his tuxedo and was waving a gloved hand as though Rye were a stray dog. "Come on, kid, move it." He was probably only nineteen or twenty himself, hair slicked on either side of a widow's peak.

But what caught Rye's eyes were the young man's hands, encased in a pair of the warmest-looking gloves he'd ever seen. They were heavy black leather and reflected the diamond sparkle of the restaurant. Rye looked around at people on the street, some of them turning to watch. Everyone's hands were gloriously gloved in fur and pelt and lined leather. One woman wore what looked like a pair of otters to her elbows.

The doorman clapped his gloved hands and made a muffled sound. "Hey! You deaf? You can't be on the sidewalk. No begging here."

Rye looked down at his own icy red, calloused hands—pure rebuke, dead giveaway. "I'm not begging," he said, "I'm just walking."

"Then keep walking!" The man started toward Rye. "You can't be here."

"Where'd you get your gloves?"

"What?" The doorman gave Rye a shove, and he lurched into the street.

Rye sat down on the sidewalk and began unlacing his boot.

"Don't do that, kid! Don't make me call a cop."

Rye reached in his sock and came out with Brand's twenty-dollar bill. He'd carried it there for over two weeks, the safest bank in the world, a hobo's sock. "I want to buy some gloves," he said.

The doorman grabbed him by the collar, lifted him, and walked him to the end of the block. "I don't care if you want to buy a Ford, you can't do it on my curb." He gave Rye another shove, pushing him down the block. "Now get, before I crack your head open. You'll put people off their dinner."

Rye staggered down the block, one boot untied, gripping that rank bill in his hand. It had been like an infection in there. He'd thought about donating it to Gurley's bucket but hadn't—thank goodness, or a thief in Taft would have it. It occurred to him that he'd kept it for another reason. He'd convinced himself that as long as he didn't spend the bill, maybe he could deny what he'd done, betrayed his friends.

But he had betrayed them. He had told Lem Brand their plans, and in his Seattle hotel he'd answered Del Dalveaux's questions: *Where are you going next? Is Early Reston with you?* He had betrayed them and then tried to convince himself that he hadn't, or that it was harmless information, or that it was the only way to help Gig.

But it was a rock in his conscience, this twenty-dollar bill. And Gig was spending six months in jail anyway.

Rye stared at the wrinkled bill. A stray thought: *If I spend this, I will no longer have it.* This was the crazy thing about wealth: You only *had* it if you didn't *use* it, but if you didn't *use* it, there was no value in *having* it. It was like a riddle. No wonder some men died with more money than they could spend in a second life while other men starved. And him: *a fool with twenty dollars and ice-cold hands.*

He kept walking west, paying particular attention to the gloved hands of the men and women on the street, gesturing in conversation, climbing on streetcars, opening doors. Finally, he followed a man in a smart suit and warm gloves up a set of stone steps and straight into the dark wood door of a store called Bradley & Graham's, Fine Clothing and Rich Furnishings.

It was a corner shop, warm and gently lit. Rye stood in the doorway, unable to move. An older man in a fine suit with a kerchief in his breast pocket looked up, smiled grimly, and began approaching, but before the man could speak, Rye held up the twenty-dollar note. He sputtered, "Gloves?"

The man looked down at Rye. His plain, thin suit coat, or rather, Fred Moore's plain, thin suit coat, was dusty and worn from ten days on the road. It wouldn't have come from a shop like this even when it was new, of course. And his once fine gray bowler had worn edges and a big grease stain on it. Still, that note in his hand was legal tender, and the salesman seemed perplexed by it. He was maybe sixty, with eyeglasses and a gray beard. He glanced down at the bill.

"It's real," Rye said.

"What's your name, son?"

Rye answered, "Ryan Dolan, sir," and wished he hadn't added the *sir*.

"And what kind of gloves are you looking for?"

Rye considered again his red, stinging, work-scabbed hands, the mitts of a sixty-year-old man sewn to the arms of a boy. His clothes usually came from the Catholic charity bin or the Starvation Army, and he'd only ever bought one new item of clothing, a pair of warm socks from the bin at Murgittroyd's. He could probably get a pair of gloves there for four bits. Or, if he was feeling fancy, go to the Emporium's Saturday sale. One time he had walked into the Crescent, hoping to pinch a biscuit at the lunch counter, but a security guard had hustled him out. He wondered how much gloves were at the Crescent. *Two bucks?*

"Well," he said finally, "the warm kind?"

"I could sell you a pair of ten-dollar ermine-lined gloves." The man lowered his voice. "Or I could be a decent fellow and send you to Murgy's, where you could find a pair almost as nice for under a dollar."

Rye looked around again. He must be in the finest clothier in town. Rich men sat in velvet chairs while other men retrieved items for them. Here, they didn't pick over bins for the things they wanted, but got served like guests in a restaurant. A handful of wooden dummies were dressed like they were attending a wedding. There were no prices on anything, no bins announcing six for a dollar, Rye guessing that if a man had to ask how much something cost here, he could not afford it.

He had a feeling similar to the one he'd experienced in Lem Brand's house—despair that this world existed, and that, normally, he could no more afford one-dollar gloves than he could ten-dollar gloves. That nine dollars, like nine levels of class, existed between the very limit of what he could imagine and what men like Lem Brand bought without a second thought.

"Is that your most expensive pair, then, the ten-dollar jobs?" Rye asked.

"The ermine? No," the salesman admitted. "The ermine comes from the stoat, a kind of weasel. But you could spend as much as you want, really. If you want mink, for instance, I could order you sable fur gloves for twenty or thirty dollars a pair."

Rye shook his head. How naive to think that only nine dollars separated Brand and him. "And do you ever sell them twenty-dollar gloves?"

"Of course." The salesman leaned in. "There's a pair of forty-dollar gloves I could order from Milan. I have sold two pairs this year."

Rye looked around the store again. A man and his wife were staring at him, the wife seated, the man behind with his hand on her shoulder, as if he might protect her from whatever Rye was surely carrying.

When Rye looked back, the salesman was chewing his cheek. "You're one of those Wobblies," he said.

Rye didn't answer. But at that moment, he felt done with it all—done with the beatings, done with Taft, done with Lem Brand and Ursula, done pretending they could stand on soapboxes and draw justice out of the air. Early was right. Rye didn't believe in anything but a job, a bed, some soup. A simple farmhouse behind Mrs. Ricci's boardinghouse. Gig out of jail, living with him.

And in that moment, all he wanted was to go back to the doorman in front of Louis Davenport's place and clap at him in the warmest gloves in the world.

"I was there the day of the riot," the salesman said. "I saw you, shackled in the street. I remember because you seemed younger than the others. Reminded me of my grandson. I'm sorry what they did to you. The police here—" He shook his head but didn't finish the thought.

Over his shoulder, two other salesmen looked their way.

"Are the ten-dollar gloves warm?" Rye asked.

"They are very warm," the salesman said, "but really, I think—"

"I'll take two pairs. One for me and one for my brother."

The salesman smiled but did not budge.

"And can you wrap his pair?" Rye said. "I'd like it to be a gift."

The man hesitated. "Son, you should know, these gloves are not going to be nine dollars warmer than the gloves at the Emporium."

"Yeah," Rye said, "maybe they will be to me."

26

It was after five, and outside it was tunnel dark. Just two hours before Gurley's speech, and Rye rushed to get back to the union hall.

As he walked, he looked down at his hands, almost stunned to see the rich brown gloves, a band of white fur at the wrist like a bird's plumage.

How would he explain this? A month's wages for two pairs of gloves? Gig's pair was in a slender box with a bowed ribbon. He'd be in jail for six months, and then, what, Rye gives him a pair of white-fur-lined gloves? In July? *I've lost my mind,* he thought. He wondered if Bradley & Graham's would take the gloves back.

He turned down Stevens Street and saw one of Lidle's newsboys, a skinny black kid already hawking the *Worker.* "Second Wobbly action!" the boy was yelling. "Free pies tonight at the IWW Hall!"

Rye felt an auto on his left. It was driving slowly next to him. He glanced back and saw the big headlight eyes of a Model T grille. Then the car pulled around him and onto the curb, curls of smoke from the exhaust, the red ash of a cigarette glowing in the window. The driver's-side door creaked open and a man rose above the car's roof. It was Brand's thick security goon, Willard. He tossed the cigarette butt. "Get in."

Rye stood still. "I can't. I have to be at the hall."

Willard sighed and, as if thinking, *This job,* reached into his coat pocket and set something on the roof of the Model T. Rye couldn't see it but guessed by the heavy clank it was a pistol. "Get in," Willard said. "It's goddamned freezing out here."

It was barely warmer inside than out. Willard sat back in the driver's seat, his breath coming in heavy bursts of steam. They rumbled along in silence until he finally looked over. "Nice gloves."

Rye looked down. "They're weasel."

"And the box?"

"A second pair."

"In case you lose those?"

"Something like that."

There was almost no traffic. Willard offered Rye a cigarette from a box he pulled from his coat, but Rye shook it off. Willard stuck one in his own mouth, popped a match across his thumbnail, and lit it. He sighed again, a sound that Rye took to mean: *Sorry for this business.*

"I have to be at the hall in an hour," Rye said.

Willard said nothing. They motored up the South Hill, the snow getting heavier and the wind through the open side window stinging Rye's face. This was nothing like the first trip to Alhambra. No hats or scarves, no soft Ursula to hold his arm, just Rye and Willard in an icy automobile.

The gate to Brand's driveway was closed, guarded by two men

in long coats and earflapped hats. One of them was holding a rifle against his chest, the other had his gun strapped over his shoulder. They were standing around a burning ashcan in front of the gatehouse. The one with the strapped rifle walked over.

"How's he doing?" Willard asked.

"Birdshot," the man said, and wiggled his fingers.

"He alone?" Willard asked.

"She left an hour ago."

Rye wondered which *she*. Ursula? Brand's wife?

They were waved through. One man watched from the window of the carriage house gate. Another man guarded the front door of the house. "What's going on?" Rye asked.

Willard parked the T, killed the motor, and opened his door.

There was no tour this time, no doors thrown open, no Amazonian redwood or African onyx. Willard led Rye into the house, the front-door security man nodding them through. Down a long hallway, past a dark dining room, they went through a pantry and into a plain room behind the kitchen.

At the servants' table sat Lem Brand, a glass of something dark and a half-eaten meat pie in front of him. He was on a stool, facing a leaded-glass window, coat off, suspenders over an undershirt, reading what looked like a stack of letters.

"Mr. Brand," Willard said, but he didn't answer. "Mr. *Brand*," he said, louder.

Brand finally turned. His face was pale, shiny with sweat.

"I'll be in the study," Willard said.

Brand pointed with the papers to a stool on his left. Rye remained standing. "How are you, Ryan?" Brand asked. "None too worse for wear, I hope?"

And if Rye hadn't known before, he knew then: Lem Brand was behind what had happened in Taft, what had *almost* happened.

"I'm not a man who apologizes very often," Brand said. "But things occasionally get beyond my control." He took and let go a deep breath, as if that had been the apology. "Where's Early Reston?"

"I don't know," Rye said. He cleared his throat. "And I wouldn't tell you if I did."

Brand flinched. He held out the pages he'd been reading. Rye hesitated, then took what looked to be some kind of report. The first page featured a photograph of a young man with the words: "Ennis R. Cooper. Pinkerton Agency. San Francisco, California. May 1, 1894." There were other names listed below that one: William Baines. Ennis Crane. Thomas Baines. William Crane. Ennis David Baines. Ennis Thomas. Thomas Reston. Ennis Reston. And the last one. Early Reston.

Rye's thoughts came together like badly shuffled cards. "Wait." He looked up from the pages. "This is Early?"

Brand took a drink of the whiskey.

Rye looked back at the photo. Could it really be him? Suddenly, he was having trouble remembering Early's features. He could recall his hat, his clothes, a certain look in his eyes. But was this *his face*? It seemed close, sure, but it made Rye realize how strangely similar all faces were—nose, mouth, eyebrows—really, what made a person himself?

"I hired him two months ago. I was told he could go deeper than most agency men. Rile things up, get the union throwing bombs and the public turned against them, keep the police from going easy like they did in Missoula. We agreed to a price, half up front, half to be paid later." Brand swirled his drink. "He told me, 'When it's anarchy you need, best to hire an anarchist.'"

Rye flipped through the pages—interviews, newspaper clippings, an arrest report.

"He went too far, though, and I came to regret it. So I sent my man Willard to figure out what, exactly, I'd hired: a detective posing as an anarchist or an anarchist posing as a detective. The stories you hear: that he's an agent who got in so deep he forgot which side he was on. Or that he was never on a side. The Pinkertons won't even acknowledge that he worked for them. And the rumors? That he planted bombs. Caused a cave-in that killed six miners. Blew up a town marshal. Killed a labor man's pregnant wife."

Rye looked up from the report.

"And some say it was *his wife* who was killed. Or that there was no wife, it's just a story he tells. That he's killed scabs and millionaires and loggers and bounty hunters and children. The stories are like his names—every possibility and combination. Or he's just a thief who doesn't care about anything. That's Willard's thinking—that he's in it for the sport. Or the money."

Rye recalled his conversation with Early on the train—*Everyone does everything for a little bit of money*—

"This was delivered to my house this evening." Brand handed Rye what appeared to be an identification card from a decade earlier. It read: "Dalveaux, Delbert, Allied Detective Agency." It was the old detective Rye had met in Seattle.

"Del was last seen downtown this afternoon. Being helped out of a café by his brother." Brand laughed bitterly. "Of course, he doesn't have a brother."

Rye handed the pages back. He tried to be firm, "Doesn't have anything to do with me," but his voice cracked.

"Sure it does," Brand said.

"I don't work for you!" Rye sputtered. "It was a mistake." He felt frantic. He pressed the box of gloves into Brand's hands.

"What's this?" Brand opened the box.

"It's half of your twenty dollars. I'll get the rest, but I'm done."

"I don't think a pair of gloves gets you out of this, Ryan." Brand tossed the box on the table. "What if your union friends knew that I had you on retainer, that you were the one who told Del about Montana?"

Rye felt sick.

"Or if your brother knew? Imagine if Ursula were to mention our meeting. How would Gregory feel about it?"

"You said you'd get him out of jail."

"I said I'd try. And I will." Brand reached in his coat, took out an envelope, and set it on the table. "But I need you to get this message to Early Reston. Or Ennis Cooper, or whatever his name is."

Rye stared at the thick envelope.

"It's five hundred dollars," Brand said, "the second half of what I agreed to pay him. It might not be enough, after what happened, but tell that I'm willing to reopen our contract, settle our differences. Tell him to give me a number."

A number. Rye thought about the armed men outside. Early's fake names, the stories, it must be unbearable for a man like Brand, so used to being in control. "You're afraid of him," Rye said. "You're scared to death."

"*Of* death," Brand said, "yes, like any man."

Rye looked from the envelope to the stack of pages to Del Dalveaux's ID card. He remembered the questions Brand had asked, and then Del's questions—how many of them had been about Early. "It was *him* you were after—Early? In Taft?"

Brand muttered something into his drink.

"So it wasn't even about Elizabeth or the union?"

"It was both," Brand admitted. "She is a problem. My partners certainly thought so. And I wouldn't have minded solving that, too." He shrugged as if they were talking about mice in his barn. "But I got greedy, two birds . . ."

"And me?"

Brand shrugged again, which Rye took to mean, *You? You were nothing.*

Rye's arms went slack against his sides. He looked down the long hallway. Then he turned back to Brand. "No," he said. "I'm not going to do it. I'm done with all of this." He started to walk away.

"That's not really a choice you can make," Brand said to his back. Then: "What if I get your brother out two days from now?"

Rye turned again.

Brand was holding the envelope out. "Take this message to Early Reston, I'll get Gregory released, and you and I are done forever. No one will ever know what you did."

Rye stood in the hall, breathing heavily. "I don't even know if I'll see Early again."

"I'm willing to bet you will."

Rye stood staring at an envelope with five hundred dollars in it. He just needed time, to think. "I have to get back to the union hall."

Brand turned and looked at the grandfather clock behind him. "I'm afraid it's too late for that. The raid will have already started by now."

Gurley

Lﬞ ISTEN: I come for the fight. I come from rebels, from blood nationalists, Molly Maguires, fiery socialists. I come from a New York suffragist and a New England quarryman, Irish parents who saved me the humiliation and hypocrisy of *Our Blessed Church* so that I might see the world clearly and burn with other fires. I have sought a paradise in *this life*, from the window of a train traversing a starkly beautiful land where a man's skin is still criminalized and a woman's body enslaved, where workers are thrown away like coal slag.

Injustice burns in me like a fever. Take away the Catholicism, and a little Gaelic heart like mine still beats martyr's blood.

From the first days of grammar school, I was haunted by an adage the nuns had us copy on our slate boards: *There but for the grace of God go I.* The sixteenth-century reformer John Bradford was said to have uttered those words upon seeing a criminal led to his execution. Bradford was clearly on to something, because he *did* go eventually, burned at the stake for a crime that is my own, stirring up a mob, although I'd propose his real offense was another of mine: first-degree aggravated empathy.

I was thinking of Bradford as I sat in the Spokane I W W office that cold winter night, an hour before I was to speak. Two loud crashing sounds came from outside, yelling in the main hall, the sound of doors being bashed in.

Charlie Filigno and I stood and looked at each other.

"Raid," he said simply.

I thought for a moment of those five hundred already in jail in Spokane, and the millions fighting every day around the world for fairness and justice, risking limb and life, and I repeated Bradford's words like a prayer (*There but for the grace . . .*) as the yelling drew closer and an ax cleaved our office door with a great cracking sound, the wood exploding in chips and splinters.

The broken door was flung from the hinges, and I could see in the great hall that cops were smashing windows and having at our printing press, and another man was taking a splitting maul to the small piano. I put an arm out to keep Charlie from moving, from getting beaten.

And then that awful Sergeant Clegg stepped through the broken doorway into our office. He smiled. "You're under arrest for conspiracy, you fat labor cunt."

"I assume you're addressing me," I said, and smiled calmly, in my mind editing the devout Bradford with a brevity and clarity he would have had to admire as those first flames licked his feet: *There—go I.*

They aimed to finish us. I don't know how else to say it. Ten stick-wielding police thugs sent to arrest a pregnant girl and glum Charlie Filigno, a handful of newsboys and an old cook making pies. They meant to shutter us forever. Less than an hour after we sent newsboys out to announce my speech and the second labor action, the police were ready with a full raid. I suppose they'd been waiting for it, having weathered our first attack, jailing five hundred, scuttling our attempts to raise funds and recruit. Now came the death blow.

After Clegg, that brute police chief, Sullivan, came inside. "Afternoon, sister." He held up a newspaper with a story of a speech I had given to the Women's Club of Spokane. "You're under arrest for furthering a conspiracy inside the city limits."

"Speaking is an act of conspiracy?"

"Calling for violence against the city is."

"I have called only for peaceful protest. You're the ones beating men and breaking down doors, *Acting* Chief Sullivan."

He had two cops drag us outside in the swirling dry snow. We stood on the sidewalk, Charlie, me, and our old cook, Alan. Across the street, they were arresting newsboys, three twelve-year-olds led by an older boy named Lidle, the cops treating them like a gang of criminals.

A crowd was gathering on the street. "Are you seeing this?" I yelled as the cops broke windows and threw pie pans in the street. "These are your police! Arresting children!" Two cops dragged our printing press out into the street, where they resumed beating it to scrap. They carried out chairs and pots and pans, coffee cups and plates, and smashed them on the sidewalk. They confiscated posters, newspapers, and threw everything into a smoking burn barrel.

Fred Moore had arrived and was pacing in the snow, *cease-and-desisting*, but the cops weren't paying him any attention until Clegg pointed with his stick and said that if he didn't shut up, he'd be charged, too, with resisting arrest.

"Am I under arrest?" Fred asked.

"Not yet," Clegg said.

"Then how can I be resisting?"

The riddle was too much for Clegg, who turned back to the newsboys.

Finally, to keep me from jawing on the street, Sullivan had a cop load me in the back of a wagon, onto a hard bloodstained bench. I put my head in my hands. There were rings for shackling hands, and the wagon smelled of horse and sweat and piss. I thought of my mother back in New York and what she would think, her pride and disgust and fear always mixed up. And I thought of Jack, in Butte, sitting at our table, waiting for me to bring him his dinner, and for just a moment, I wished—

It was freezing in that wagon, and through the frosted back window, I could see them leading newsboys away while cops battered the last of our doors and chairs. A small cop with a red beard climbed in and sat next to me. A moment later, Chief Sullivan stuck his head in and smiled.

"Well, look at this," Sullivan said to the other police officer. "We've managed to do the impossible: We've shut up Elizabeth Gurley Flynn."

The bearded patrolman laughed. I've always been surprised at how it stings, the laughter of small men. The smaller the man, the more the laughter hurts, as if saying, *I may be nothing, but you are less.*

The wagon rumbled over streetcar tracks, and they took me to the women's jail, where I was unloaded and booked on a charge of "conspiracy to incite men to violate the law." I asked to see my lawyer, but the clerk stared as if I'd asked for a cannon. "You'll see him tomorrow," he said, "when you're arraigned."

A pigeon-toed jailer led me down a long, dark hallway. He turned once and looked me up and down, as if considering a purchase, and I felt a wave of disgust. Unlike most cities, Spokane did not employ a jail matron, Chief Sullivan saying jail was no place for a decent woman to work. This sloth led me to a heavy iron door, a single electric bulb illuminating it. "Back up!" he called through the door. Then he keyed it open. A few socialist ladies had spent the night in the women's cell in Spokane for our cause, and I'd heard them describe it as a cold, dark dungeon, filled with prostitutes arrested on late-night raids for not having the twenty-five-dollar fine ready.

True to form, two tavern girls were lying on cots when I came in. One of the women was facing the wall, skirts bunched, her back to me. The other was younger and sat up when I came in. "You're that Elizabeth Gurley," she said with a heavy Austro-Hungarian accent. "No, I seen you speak one day."

I had been in jail cells before, but this one made New York's hold-

THE COLD MILLIONS   221

ing pen seem like the Waldorf Astoria. Heavy rock walls and an iron door—a freezing draft and a faint light through two barred windows, a stone floor beneath us, and on my cot, a single blanket, thin and scratchy as old leaves, and a pillow that was little more than rice in a sock.

"Here, you take mine," said the woman with the accent. And she held out her blanket to me.

"I couldn't," I said, "thank you."

She raised her skirts and showed me what looked like men's pants beneath them. "My barman give me these before the police come yesterday."

"He knew the police were coming?"

She whispered: "My barman is behind to pay the police—" She shrugged. "He get the money, buy us back tomorrow, hope tomorrow—"

The other one rolled half over to shush her. "Katya, shut up. You'll get us in more trouble." She shot me a look.

A few minutes later, Pigeon-Toed was back and the heavy door opened. "Elizabeth Jones," he said. He led me out, back down the dark hall, to a room with no windows.

The prosecutor Pugh was sitting at a table, Sullivan against the wall. They sat me at the table across from Pugh. The needling prosecutor read from a thick notepad as he slowly questioned me for the next hour. Who was funding our chapter? Who sent me? Would I confess to conspiring to violate the anti-speaking law, to inciting violence, to causing a riot, to disturbing the peace? Did I know that I faced two years in prison? How many more men were coming to protest? How many had I rallied in Seattle? In Wallace? In Taft? Was it true that Vincent Saint John was planning to come to Spokane? And what about the murderer Big Bill Haywood? Was my husband, Jack, bringing mining toughs from Montana? Who was leading this conspiracy?

My face heated up as he spoke, anger blessedly replacing my fear. "I am conspiring to exercise my right to speak freely, if that's what you mean." I began interrupting his questions. "Bill Haywood was framed by Pinkertons and acquitted of murder. You should read the newspapers, they are quite informative." I laughed as he pressed me: which *men* were coming, which *men* were leading the fight, which *men* were pulling my strings. Even the sentence he threatened me with, two years in jail, was for conspiring to incite *men* to violate the law.

"And what if I promise to incite only women?" I said.

Mr. Pugh was unamused. "You do not seem to appreciate the severity of this situation, Mrs. Jones."

"Nor you, Mr. Pugh."

Sullivan came off the wall. "See—now this manner of yours is what I don't understand, sister. The shrillness. Disrespect. It doesn't have to be this way. You could be ladylike. You're not bad-looking, not one of those dried-up milk cows like Emma Goldman or Mother Jones."

"They are champions of—"

He acted as if I hadn't spoken. "I don't see why you'd throw your life off like this. Do you want to have your husband's baby in jail? Raise it among fallen women when, with a little cooperation, Mr. Pugh might be convinced to contact your husband and have him come get you? Forget this whole mess?"

"My husband is proud that I am fighting for—"

"No, no, no. Don't start with me. I'm not talking about that." He bent so that he was at eye level. "I don't see your husband as a man at all, *Mrs. Jones*. I don't approve of your rabble-rousing, and I would forbid my wife from making a whore's spectacle of herself—but if she did? If it was my wife out here? I would sure as hell not let her fight alone."

This cut me, as he must've known it would, and I felt even greater shame at the sharpness of it. He'd found the spot that stung, the romantic girl who once rode toward dragons with her prince. He had *not* come from Butte. Three weeks I had been here and nothing. Not so much as a letter.

For a moment I couldn't breathe. And then I could.

"My husband has nothing to do with this," I said. "Just as whatever poor girl you have enslaved back at your stove has nothing to do with your rank corruption. As for 'whore's spectacle,' ask your wife what bargains she made to live in *your* house, *Acting* Chief Sullivan."

A storm went over his face, and then a surprising vulnerability.

But I was not done. "And when your pretty wife answers, watch her eyes closely, because whatever she says, there will be another truth she won't speak, for fear of breaking her *acting* husband's fragile heart."

Sullivan straightened. "Take this trash to her cell."

My anger had dissipated, and with it, hope. I lay back on the cot in my jail cell. I could not sleep. The only light came from the small barred windows. The breathing of the older woman in the cell was labored, and as soon as the door closed, I began to hear the scurrying down the hall of large, industrious rats.

There were faint voices, too, men's laughter, the opening and closing of cell doors. I thought of Chief Sullivan and of Jack. Why *hadn't* Jack come?

The saloon girls snored beneath their thin blankets.

And then, at some point in the night, the heavy door pushed open and a man with a gas lantern came in. It was a new jailer, one who hadn't been on the earlier shift, a man with gray teeth and a patchy beard that covered his cheeks.

"Who's up?" He held his lantern over me. "This one?"

"Not for that," said Katya, the younger girl, with the accent. "Leave her alone." She rose with a sigh.

This repeated three more times, like an uneasy dream. The heavy jail door would open, and the gray-toothed jailer would come in and take one of the women away. "Sweetheart's here," he said to the unfriendly one. She rose without making a sound and, twenty minutes later, plopped back down on her cot.

"Sweetheart's here," the man would say again, and now Katya rose with a deep sigh, left, and returned half an hour later.

At some point, I must have slept, for at dawn I woke to find a different jailer sitting on my bed, a younger man, his hand on my cheek. "Cold, are you?"

I sat up straight. I had two blankets on.

"Leave her be!" said Katya, who must have put her blanket on me after I went to sleep. She rose and walked over. "I am coming."

It was almost an hour before the jailer brought Katya back. She carried two pieces of stale bread and two cups of coffee. I sat up and she gave me one of the measly breakfasts. The jailer brought another hunk of bread and a cup of coffee for the quiet woman in our cell, but she faced the wall, her back to him. "Hey," he said, and when she didn't budge, he set the coffee and bread on the ground in front of her.

I sipped the cool, oily coffee and gnawed at the hard bread.

"When will your baby come?" Katya asked.

I looked down at my belly, surprised each day by how evident my condition was becoming. "April, hopefully," I said. "I lost a baby last year, so . . . I don't know."

"Lost a baby." She looked me up and down. "Lost a baby," she repeated in a singsong way, as if trying to place the phrase. "Lost." Up close, she was thin, with black hair and lovely pale skin. Her eyes were dark and mirthful. "You have choose a name for baby?"

"Not yet," I said.

"After your husband if a boy? Or your father?"

"I hadn't thought of it."

"My father's name. It is Oleksander. You know this name?"

"Alexander," I said. "Yes."

"*O*-leksander," she corrected. "Is very good name. Very strong for boy."

"You should take this back," I said, and I handed her the blanket.

"No, please," she said. "You." And I could tell it meant something to her, that I use the blanket.

"Thank you," I said. "Can I ask you—last night, is it always like that?"

She shrugged. "Is here, is there, is same, yes? Different boss but same." She held up the bread. "Food is worse."

The other woman had stirred, and she cleared her throat as she rose. "I swear to God, if you say another word about it, Katya—"

"Be quiet, cow," Katya muttered.

The other woman sat up now. "You're gonna get us killed." She took a drink of the coffee and stood. She shook her head. "Christ's sake, you two." She walked to the corner of the cell, raised her skirts, and squatted over a bucket in the corner.

Katya patted my arm and stood to return to her own bunk. "Oleksander," she said quietly. "Very strong name."

By the time of my arraignment that morning, Fred Moore had done champion lawyer work. The newsboys—after four hours of threats and questioning by the police—had been released to parents and orphanages. No charges had been filed against the old cook. "Not unless the state plans to charge him for dry pie crust," Fred said. Only Charlie Filigno and I were being held, on conspiracy charges.

Fred said he'd gone around town all night trying to raise the money to bail me out. He'd approached the other labor leaders—AFL, WFM, even the porters' union, but everyone had told him no. One man had said that he would, but his wife found me indecent. Instead, the entire six hundred dollars—against an outrageous bond of six thousand—came from a single woman of means, the wife of a wealthy doctor in town. I recalled meeting her at a women's club luncheon where I'd gotten such tepid applause that I'd blamed the members' white gloves.

"Keep the money for the fees you haven't charged," I said. "Leave me in here."

"Elizabeth, you know I can't do that," Fred said. "Not in your condition."

The small courtroom was packed with onlookers and reporters craning their necks to see me. "What do you say, Gurley?" one reporter yelled.

"I say the time has come for the working classes of Spokane to stand up to this thievery and brutality!" The reporters bent and wrote like I was the president. Then the jailers brought in Charlie, who was bearing it quite well, in fact, even looking somewhat relieved to be on this side of things instead of doing the impossible job of running that dying union all by himself.

The charges were read, and Mr. Pugh offered as preliminary evidence the seized copies of the *Industrial Worker*, quotes I had given reporters and lines from earlier speeches I'd made, and my plans for the second free speech action. All listed as parts of the conspiracy to break the law against speaking on the street.

"An illegal law," I said, and Fred put his hand on my arm to quiet me.

Then Fred entered the pleas for Charlie and me—not guilty—and began arguing against the legality of the raid, "the unprecedented violation of not only the rights of these defendants but the rights of an entire community, Your Honor—"

"Enough, Mr. Moore," the judge said, and rapped his gavel, "you'll have plenty of time to bore this court later."

When Fred explained that I planned to pay the bail, the prosecutor, Pugh, asked the judge to stipulate that my release be conditioned on my not speaking publicly or in any way further antagonizing police or city officials.

"If your plan is to shut me up, you'd better keep me in jail," I said.

There was laughter, and again the gavel rapped. "Mrs. Jones, you will refrain from making speeches, and you will address this court with respect."

"I will respect this court when it respects my rights."

The judge pointed the gavel. "Mr. Moore."

Fred's hand landed on my arm again, and I went quiet for him. Then the judge remanded Charlie over to custody and said, "Against my better judgment, and with strict regulations on her behavior, Mrs. Jones is released until her trial date."

"You should have left me in there," I said to Fred.

"I can't do that," he said again.

There was a copy of the *Chronicle* on our defense table and I read the headline: OFFICERS SEIZE IWW LEADERS IN DARING RAID: ARRESTED INCLUDES WOMAN.

"*Daring* raid," I said to Fred. "*Includes* woman? Who do they think was running the show?"

But if our goal had been to get back in the newspapers, it worked. The *Chronicle, Press, Spokesman-Review*—IWW stories were all over the front pages: FEMALE AGITATOR ARRESTED WITH OTHER WOBBLIES, and OFFICIALS RAID UNION HALL, and even a story about the newsboys being arrested: YOUTHFUL PRISONERS KEPT CROWDED IN A DELINQUENT ROOM ALL NIGHT.

"They've gone too far," I said to Fred Moore. After a month of the cops painting us as foreign agitators, it didn't look good for them to go after a bunch of poor Spokane newsboys and a pregnant red-cheeked Irish-American girl. "It's too much."

Outside the courthouse, a handful of reporters had gathered. I allowed Fred to help me from the building, thrust forward my pregnant belly, and made sure to shiver in the cold as Fred led me through a cluster of men with notebooks. He had warned me that I was not to comment to these reporters outside the courthouse, not to say anything that might aggravate the police and prosecutors.

"You do understand that I *came* to aggravate police and prosecutors," I reminded him.

"She has no comment to make," Fred said, helping me into a waiting coach.

I covered my mouth. I went weak-kneed. I did everything but pass out from the vapors. "Mr. Moore is correct, I will not speak about my case, out of respect for the judge's orders," I said, "but I cannot be silent about the plight of this city, and those poor newsboys, held and sweated all night in a crowded delinquent cell! Are the people of Spokane going to stand by while the police arrest children now?" I touched my belly as if to remind them another child lay here.

Fred eased me into the coach and climbed in with me. And like some prison Cinderella, I was spirited away. I asked Fred to take me to the union hall, but there was nothing left of it, boarded up and empty. In fact, said Fred, the city council had passed an ordinance banning the IWW from operating within city limits.

"Can they do that?"

He laughed bitterly. "We're beyond the point of asking what they *can* do. It's a question now of what they *won't* do."

Something else was bothering me. "Have you heard from Ryan?"

"No," he said. "He wasn't arrested. Why?"

"It's nothing," I said. But I kept picturing him leaving the union hall, in a hurry, just an hour before the raid. I did not like what I was thinking. I sat back in the coach and looked out the window at the reporters, at men in suits moving in and out of that fairy-tale courthouse. At the bustle of this burgeoning city. Cars and horses and streetcars, apartment buildings going up, a scurry of construction and destruction. Layers and layers. This place was a termites' nest.

"What do you think of the name Oleksander?" I asked Fred.

He looked up. "Alexander? I think it's nice." He gave the driver the address of the boardinghouse where I was staying. "I'm taking you home to rest now," he said.

"I don't care where you take me," I said, "as long as it has a typewriter."

27

The night of the raid, Willard motored Rye back to Mrs. Ricci's house. They drove past the union hall so Rye could see for himself, Willard craning his neck, too: doors and windows broken, glass and wooden splinters all over the sidewalk, an ashcan smoldering on the corner. Two men were boarding up doors. No sign of Gurley or anyone else.

"Can we stop?" Rye asked, but Willard kept driving. He crossed the river, drove through Little Italy, and parked on the street down the block from Mrs. Ricci's house. He sighed—and something about the sound, almost an animal grunt, felt sympathetic to Rye.

Willard reached in his coat and handed Rye the envelope with Early Reston's five hundred dollars in it. "You got a safe place for this?" he asked.

"No," Rye said.

"Right," Willard said. Then he handed him the box with Gig's gloves in it.

Inside the sleeping porch, Rye looked around for a hiding place before finally sliding the envelope and the gloves under his cot. He barely slept. He heard noises, sensed shadows across the yard. He dreamed that Early was behind him on a train.

In the morning, he heard voices from the kitchen and sat up in bed just as Mrs. Ricci's older son, Marco, was stepping onto the enclosed sleeping porch.

Marco was short and square, wearing a big wool coat, with curly hair below his hat, around his ears. "Cold out here," he said. Any heat came from two vents cut in the kitchen wall. "Anyways, Ma says you could use a job."

Marco said he had a friend named Joseph Orlando who ran a machine shop on Garland Street, on the North End. The day before, his stock boy had whacked off a couple of fingers with a table saw, and they needed someone to fill in. "Joe said the kid's a real goob," Marco said, "but if the goob comes back to work tomorrow with eight fingers, you're probably out a job."

"That's fair," Rye said.

Rye got cleaned up and dressed, and Marco chuddered him up the Division Street hill in an old Model N.

Marco kept glancing over. "Hey, where'd you get the gloves?" he finally asked, probably thinking they looked stolen.

Rye looked down at the gloves and the band of white fur hinting at the luxury inside. He was like a tramp in a tiara. "Murgittroyd's," he said finally.

"Fancy gloves for Murgy's," said Marco.

"They're weasel," Rye said.

Marco parked the auto on Garland Street, in front of a business called North Hill Fittings and Machine Shop.

"One other thing," Marco said. "Ma said she agreed to sell our orchard to you and your brother. You know that won't happen, right?"

Rye said nothing.

"How much you pay her so far?"

"Not much," Rye said, "six dollars, maybe."

"I'll have her apply it to your boarding costs." He shrugged. "Anyways, that's all I can do. But there's no way we're selling that land to . . . well, to you."

Rye thanked Marco, got out, and went into North Hill Fittings and Machine. Joseph Orlando was a short, wiry man who toured Rye around the store with great pride. He seemed to be under the impression that Rye was Mrs. Ricci's nephew, and Rye didn't correct him. The first building was a storeroom where Rye would get the bolts and bushings and other parts that customers needed while Joseph took their orders and their money at the front desk. Joseph explained which parts the shop manufactured, which they ordered, and how many were needed to die-and-cast. He showed Rye where to find invoices, order sheets, and inventory forms. Rye could barely keep track of the pads, flanges, washers, and pins, let alone the paperwork, Joseph spending five minutes alone on bolts—rim bolts, hub bolts, spindle bolts—and he was about to confess that he might not be smart enough for this job when Joe said, "But a broom and a mop are the only tools you'll need to master today."

Then Joe led him to a second building, behind the first one, a machine shop where two men ran cutters and grinders, threaders, presses, lathes, taps and dies, and the table saw that had taken the goob's fingers. "Stay away from that goddamn saw," Joe said.

Joe's brother, Paul, worked in back with a big machinist named Dominic; Rye's job was to go between storefront, storeroom, and machine shop. He liked being around the machines, the smell of oil and metal. Dominic was especially nice, stopping his drill press and raising his goggles to explain to Rye what he was doing. That day Rye cleaned up metal tailings and rubber shavings, oiled the saws and presses, and mostly fetched nuts, bushings, and bolts to take up front. He swept the floor so clean the men could've eaten dinner on it.

"Kid's a fast learner," said Dominic at the end of the day, and Joe agreed and said he wouldn't mind if the eight-fingered goob found other employment. He gave Rye a dollar for the day and another half for what he called "a bonus for coming in on short notice." He said, "Check back Monday; if the goob don't show, the job's yours."

"Thank you," Rye said. He put the money in his pocket and pulled on his coat, his bowler, and his ermine gloves.

Big Dominic was getting dressed to leave, too, and he looked at Rye and opened his mouth to say something, but Rye cut him off. "Weasel," he said.

Back at Mrs. Ricci's house, she fed him dinner like he was part of the family, *"Mangiare!"* she said when she caught Rye thinking about Gig, staring out the window with his fork in the air. After dinner, Rye built them a fire and sat drinking tea and reading the afternoon *Chronicle*, like a regular fellow home from work.

There was a front-page story about the raid and Gurley's arraignment: "With the arrest of the petite and startlingly pretty agitator
Mrs. Jones, and the permanent closure of their hall, the city has
struck a final blow against the IWW's dangerous insurrection."
Rye read the phrase "petite and startlingly pretty agitator" again,
as if Gurley were a debutante. The *Industrial Worker* had been shuttered for good, the story went on, and more than a thousand copies
burned. The paper was banned within the city limits. Any printer
who took it on would do so under threat of prosecution. Eight union
officers and five newspaper editors had already been found guilty of
conspiracy and sentenced to six months in county lockup, with the
preliminary trial for Gurley Flynn and Charlie Filigno set to start in
two weeks. In the meantime, she was under house arrest, forbidden
by the judge from publishing or speaking publicly about the case.
"We've whipped the IWW," Police Chief Sullivan was quoted as saying. "We took the fight to them and it's over."

It certainly felt over, Rye thought as he stared into the fire. There
was no mention of Gig in the news story, and he wondered if Lem
Brand had lied about getting his brother out of jail.

He slept uneasily again, repeating over and over in his mind what
he'd say to Early if he came back (*Look, I don't want any trouble for Gig
and me . . .*).

In the morning, another skiff of snow had fallen, like sugar onto
a biscuit. After breakfast, Rye swept Mrs. Ricci's steps and walked
downtown along the old hobo highway. It was rare to walk the trail
and see no one, but with so many men in jail or wintered up, Rye felt
alone in the world. He emerged in the fuel and freight yards east of
downtown, then walked the tenderloin into the center of downtown
and eventually to the building where Fred Moore had a small office
on the second floor, and where Rye took off his bowler and asked to
see his old lawyer.

Fred came out of his office in shirtsleeves. He clapped Rye on the
shoulder. "What great timing, Rye," he said. "I just got some news."

"How's Gurley?" Rye asked.

"Climbing the walls," said Mr. Moore. "We've got her preparing for trial, but she'd rather be out there fighting."

He led Rye back to his office and explained that, two weeks earlier, he'd petitioned the court to dismiss the conspiracy charge against Gregory, since, unlike some other union leaders, he wasn't an elected officer. Moore had argued that since Gig had already been found guilty of disturbing the peace, he should be released after thirty days, like the other nonleaders arrested in the original free speech riot, and not charged again with conspiracy.

"It was a sound argument," Fred said, "but the last thing I ever expected was this judge responding to a sound argument."

While the lawyer spoke, Rye was looking down at Mr. Moore's desk, at what appeared to be a coffee stain on the swirls of dark wood grain.

Fred cleared his throat. "Do you understand what I'm saying, Ryan? The judge ruled in our favor. Thirty days is today. Your brother's getting out this afternoon."

Rye looked up to see Fred Moore's disappointment at his reaction. "Oh. That's great news. Thank you, Mr. Moore."

Fred smiled and shrugged, rearranged some papers on his desk, covering the coffee stain. "I haven't had a lot of victories to celebrate in this fracas, but I'm two for two with you Dolans."

"No, it's great," Rye said. "I was just surprised is all." Even if he *could* tell Mr. Moore about his deal with Lem Brand, Rye realized he wouldn't want to take away his lawyer's sense of accomplishment.

"The city is altering its strategy," Mr. Moore said. He explained that the first prisoners, like Gig, had done their month in jail for disturbing the peace and were being released, hundreds more expected to go in the coming weeks. These men had been beaten and put on bread and water, or had gone on voluntary hunger strikes, and most were in no shape to protest again. Others were eager to move south for work or bed down for winter. With the union rethinking its strategy and the *Industrial Worker* shuttered for good, the protests had dwindled to the occasional hobo who made his way past the railroad guards. So now the city could concentrate on prosecuting the leaders and sending them to state prison.

"After your brother's release, the only two left are Filigno and Elizabeth. If Pugh convicts them, it'll be a clean sweep."

Mr. Moore got his hat and coat, and he and Rye left the office and walked the four blocks to the jail. It was a cold, sunny day, few people out on the streets. There was a café a block from the jail, and Mr. Moore gave Rye two bits and suggested he wait there. "I don't know how long it will take to get him released."

Rye was relieved not to have to go to the jail. He sat in the window of the café with a cup of coffee, watching people in scarves and heavy coats hurry down the sidewalk, trailing dusty clouds of light new snow.

Everything Rye had done the last month had been with this in mind—the day his brother got out of jail. Meeting with Ursula and Lem Brand, going to Seattle with Gurley to raise money to hire Clarence Darrow, talking to Del Dalveaux, Wallace and Taft, Early Reston and Brand's man Willard—all for this moment.

But now that it was here, knowing that all it had taken was a flick of Lem Brand's wrist, Rye felt demoralized. It didn't matter what he did, what Gurley did, what Fred Moore did, what any of them did. Somewhere there was a roomful of wealthy old men where everything was decided. Beliefs and convictions, lives and livelihoods, right and wrong—these had no place in that room, the scurrying of ants at the feet of a few rich men.

It made him think that Early Reston was right, in his way—even if Early wasn't really Early—that maybe it was the castle that needed to be blown up, and that was when Rye looked up and saw, through the light haze, his lawyer walking down the street with a tall, gaunt man in a snow-dusted coat, a patchy beard climbing his sallow cheeks to his bruised eyes.

Rye rose and met them at the door, and he and Gig fell into each other. The smell was overpowering, and Gig was bones beneath his baggy coat. He tried to speak, but all that came out was a squeak, then "Rye-boy," and then he was crying and Rye was crying, and for a long time, they just did that.

28

The eight-fingered goob decided he wasn't cut out for machinery work, and on Monday, Rye became the full-time stock boy of North Hill Fittings and Machine Shop. Each morning Rye got up, checked the envelope under his cot, and said goodbye to Gig, who had spent the weekend days curled up on his cot and the nights sitting in front of Mrs. Ricci's fire. "I'll be back around six," Rye said as he put on his coat, hat, and gloves. Gig said nothing.

Rye loved being a workaday guy: Grab a grip on the streetcar, arrive before eight, and wait for Joe to open the shop. "You don't have to beat me to work, kid," Joe said, Rye smiling: "I don't mind." He'd hang his coat, put on his shop apron, turn on the lights, warm the machines, and watch everything come to life, a rhythm to all of it, the flow of customers, the banter with Dominic, the precise order of cleanup at the end of the day. He liked to anticipate which parts customers needed, showing up with a toilet flange before the plumber from Millwood had a chance to ask for it. This garnered a nickname from Joe—*Seer*. A mechanic's wagon would pull up and Joe say, "Seer?" Rye gazing into the future: "Hub roller bearings."

Joe's brother, Paul, rarely spoke except to ask for things he needed. But Dominic, the big machinist, was even friendlier than he'd been on Rye's first day. He asked where Rye was from and about his parents and siblings. "Well, you've had a tough go," he said when Rye told his story. By Wednesday, he was inviting Rye to share his prodigious three-sandwich lunches, which he spread over the cutting table as carefully as a surgeon. And by Thursday, when Dominic's wife found out the new stock boy was eating a half-sandwich from her husband's lunch every day, she began putting a fourth sandwich in the basket. "Soon she'll just send the whole loaf of bread," Dominic said.

But Rye worried about leaving Gig alone all day. His brother was hollowed out by thirteen days on hunger strike, on top of the beatings and privations of jail. Rye couldn't believe how frail he seemed; even Gig's hair was thinner. He had a bath at Mrs. Ricci's, and a meal, but after that, he slept all day, rising only to pick at his food and sit by the fire Rye built each night, a blanket around his shoulders, his new fur-lined gloves on his hands. "Thanks" was all he'd said when Rye gave him the fancy box with the gloves in it. He didn't even ask where they came from.

At night, Gig's breathing was raspy and uneven. He made noises in his sleep like he was being startled. The only time he spoke was late at night, when the brothers lay in the dark. Once he talked about the hunger strike: "We started after they put the rank and file on bread and water. The jailers thought this was pretty rich, so instead of our normal rations, they sent out for steaks and potatoes, fresh vegetables. They'd leave our fancy meals outside our cells all night. Then, after lights out, the rats came. We'd lay there listening to those rats eating our dinner."

Another night, he talked about Jules. "I met a Swede who was in his cell, said Jules went out good and strong, laughing, making jokes. Two other men I knew died in there, one with diabetes, the other I don't know what he had. When the cops saw someone dying, they'd release the man so they wouldn't have to explain a corpse in jail. The man with diabetes didn't even have a family. They just released him to some woman who agreed to take him in for a dollar a day. He only made it two days, but I heard they gave her five bucks."

The next night, he said simply, "I shouldn't have gotten us into this, Rye."

Rye didn't hesitate. "It was the best thing I ever did, Gig."

"Nah, it was pointless," Gig said. "Little kids shitting our own pants trying to teach our parents a lesson."

"Don't say that," Rye said.

"It's the truth," Gig said.

Rye had been waiting for the right time to tell Gig about Early, about Lem Brand and Ursula, about Del Dalveaux, about what *he* had done—but Gig seemed so broken by what had happened that Rye was worried about how he'd react if he knew the truth. He imagined his brother calling him a spy, or running out to confront Ursula, or going to try to kill Lem Brand or something crazy—so he decided to keep quiet until Gig had regained his strength.

They barely talked about the union. Each night, Rye brought newspapers home from the shop to read by the fire after dinner. Gig might flip through the sports and theater sections, but he had no interest in stories about the IWW. Rye devoured them, especially stories about Gurley.

She was everywhere, granting interviews in the labor-friendly *Press* and the establishment *Chronicle* and *Spokesman-Review*. To get around the judge's ruling that she not speak about her case, she talked about the city's arrest of the newsboys, "poor twelve-year-olds hauled off by the Spokane police goons to be sweated like bank robbers!" When all charges against the boys were dropped, she proclaimed victory: "The city's war against children is over. Maybe now they will declare a cease-fire against its workers, too." She railed against the decision to ban the *Industrial Worker*, saying that, as the sixth editor of the newspaper (with the first five now convicted of conspiracy), "I have no intention of abiding by this clearly illegal order! They've already detained and sweated and confined me, so I'm not sure what I have to lose, except my constitutionally guaranteed right to free speech."

"You'd like her, Gig," Rye said. "She's got a lot of fight."

But Gig said nothing. He sat, each night, as close to the fire as he could get, staring at the crackling flames.

One day, a week after Gig got out, Rye was downtown, making a delivery for the shop, when he walked past the big new Carnegie Library. It was a stately two-story pillared building—more like a church than any church Rye had ever seen. He stepped inside the big doors and watched well-dressed people move among the tall stacks. He felt intimidated. He was about to turn and leave when a young librarian, all neck and no chin, approached and asked if he could help in some way.

Rye explained that his brother was in the process of reading Count Tolstoy's *War and Peace* but had only read volumes one and three so far.

The librarian looked confused. "Books one and three? Of the four?"

"I thought there were five."

"Ah. I see," the librarian said, nodding. "I'm guessing he's reading the '03 Scribner. Tolstoy's collected, of which *War and Peace* makes up five of twenty volumes." The librarian made a face as if tasting something rancid. "It's a reprint of Gottsberger, from 1886, translated from the French by Clara Bell. Don't get me wrong, Clara Bell is a real talent, her Dante impeccable, but an English translation of a French translation of a Russian novel? Isn't that more like reading a rumor than a book?"

It seemed as if Rye was supposed to laugh, so he did. This pleased the librarian, who took him by the arm. "Come on. I want to show you something." He led Rye to a tall bookshelf near a window overlooking the river. With a practiced movement, he eased three volumes out inches from the other books, so that they seemed to float out from the shelf. They had dark blue boards, the color of a lake in winter, with a lighter blue and gold design down the spine, and a gold inlaid crown on top with the raised words WAR AND PEACE, TOLSTOY I, II, AND III, and below that what appeared to be a blue and gold heart-shaped scepter.

They were the loveliest books Rye had ever seen.

"Aren't they something?" the librarian asked. "The 1904 McClure, Phillips and Company edition. The four books and epilogue are in three volumes, translated *directly* from the Russian by Constance Garnett." He leaned in as if sharing a secret. "She nearly went blind doing the translation."

The librarian handed over the first volume and Rye opened it, careful with the onionskin title page. He looked around. "Is it . . . I mean, can I just . . ."

The librarian seemed uncertain what he was asking.

"I don't know how this works," Rye said.

"A library?" The man smiled.

That day, Rye checked out Volume I of Constance Garnett's newer translation of *War and Peace* and proudly presented it to Gig as they sat by the fire. Rye tried to explain all the librarian had told him: "Reading a book translated from Russian to French to English is like— It's like—" But he couldn't remember the librarian's droll comment. "Anyway, it's not as good," he said. "But the man at the library said this is the best one. And I can check out the next volume when I return this one."

Gig said nothing. He looked pained. He held the book to his chest. "Rye, I don't—" He shook his head. "You can't keep doing this. Gloves. And books. I'm not—I can't." He just shook his head and didn't speak again. He went to bed that night without cracking the book.

Gig was still asleep the next day when Rye left for work.

As Rye walked toward the streetcar, he saw a familiar car parked at the end of the block. He leaned in the window and startled Willard, finger up his nose to the knuckle.

"Jesus!" Willard said. "Make some noise, kid."

"Sorry," Rye said. "Shouldn't you be—" He didn't finish the sentence but thought, *Better at this?*

Willard reached in his coat and offered him a cigarette, but Rye shook it off.

"Anything yet?" Willard asked.

"From Early," Rye said. "No."

"And the money?"

"Still there."

Willard looked at him suspiciously. "And has your brother heard from Reston?"

"No," Rye said. "Gig hasn't left his bed."

Willard looked concerned. "Is he bad off?"

"He'll be fine," Rye said. "He just needs some rest."

But that night, when Rye got home from work, Gig was gone. Rye checked to see that the money was still there—it was—then ate dinner alone with Mrs. Ricci. Afterward, Rye sat by the fire reading the papers for stories about Gurley and the union. There was a story in the *Chronicle* about police raiding a printer in Hillyard, confiscating and burning three thousand copies of the *Industrial Worker*. The newspaper had tried to publish "a crude and libelous story alleging wholly fabricated charges against city officials, an account so vile as to shred the very cloth of decency that shrouds this city," the *Chronicle* story said. Even the labor-friendly *Press* wouldn't characterize what was in this scandalous story that had gotten the *Industrial Worker* confiscated, except to say that it had been written by Gurley Flynn, and the judge in her case was considering revoking her bail because of it.

Rye went to bed and was asleep when Gig finally staggered in sometime after midnight, smelling like booze and vomit and woodsmoke. He moaned and farted his way under the blanket on his cot, and a few minutes later, he began vomiting again. Rye ran over and tilted Gig's head over the side of the cot. He got a basin and went to the outhouse, came back, and cleaned the floor, Gig muttering the whole time: "Leave me alone." Rye tried washing his face, but Gig pushed his hands away. "Goddamn it, Rye, leave it. I didn't want this. Any of it."

He was sleeping it off, still snoring, when Rye left for work on Saturday.

The shop was only open until noon on Saturday, and Rye was distracted all morning. When his shift ended, he hurriedly hung his shop apron and sprinted to the streetcar. And when he got home that afternoon, Gig was already gone again. Mrs. Ricci had no idea where he'd gone, just that "He wake up. He walk away." Sitting on Rye's cot were the ermine gloves and the beautiful blue edition of *War and Peace*, Volume I.

29

Rye walked downtown, along the hobo highway, looking for Gig. He stuck his head into a couple of east-end saloons, tried Dutch Jake's and Jimmy Durkin's place, but couldn't find his brother anywhere.

Finally, at dusk, he gave up and walked to the lower South Hill, where Gurley was staying in a fine Victorian house with a progressive lawyer and his wife. A police wagon was parked across the street, but as he got closer, Rye saw the cop bundled up inside, sound asleep. He walked to the house and rang the bell.

A stout man with a gray beard and a pipe answered the door, and Rye removed his hat. "I was hoping Mrs. Jones would see me."

"You a newspaperman? You look awfully young."

"No, I'm a friend of hers. Ryan Dolan."

The man let Rye into the foyer and excused himself. A minute later, he came back. "She'll see you in the drawing room."

Rye followed the man inside and sat nervously on a leather chair in the drawing room. He put the gloves in his bowler. He looked all around the room. Then he saw something strange: a high shelf, built above the windows, with knickknacks on it, fancy plates and clocks. He was staring at it, wondering why someone would build a shelf so high, when she came in.

"Hello, Ryan," Gurley said. Her hair was pulled back, and she was wearing nightclothes with a heavy robe over them. "I was having a bath."

Rye blushed. "I'm sorry," he said. "I shouldn't just come by."

"I'm glad you did," she said. "What were you looking at?"

"That shelf." He pointed. "I've never seen one so high."

She looked up. "The plate rail?"

"I guess," he said. "I was just wondering why someone would build a shelf so high you can't reach it."

She smiled. "And I've been wondering when you might come see me."

"I'm sorry. It was the first chance I got." Rye told her about the job he'd gotten and about Gig getting out of jail. "He's not himself," he said. "It's like they beat the Gig right out of him."

"That's too bad," Gurley said. She looked at the window. "It's odd the police just let you come in. They've been running off union members ever since that flap with the *Worker*."

"Yeah, I read about that in the *Chronicle*," Rye said.

She shook her head. "A newspaper celebrating the censure of a newspaper!"

"I read about your trial, too. Does Mr. Moore think you have a chance?"

"Not much of one," she said. "He keeps reminding me the city has sixteen straight conspiracy convictions against every IWW leader and editor, and of course, I am both. Six-month sentences for every leader or member of the strike committee." She looked up. "Except your brother."

Rye wondered if that was suspicion he was hearing in her voice—why did the cops let Rye in, why wasn't Gig charged with conspiracy? He looked at the ground. "Well," he said, "I wouldn't bet against you."

She said nothing.

Rye was unsure how to ask his next question or if he even should. "Has your husband come?"

"No," she said. "Maybe for the trial." Then she cleared her throat. "He knows who he married," she said again, but it was flat this time. She looked up at the plate rail that had transfixed him earlier. "Sometimes I think I've gotten everything wrong, Ryan. With Jack. The union. Spokane. You see something as corrupt as the job sharks in this town, something as clearly wrong as police cracking heads over free speech—and you say, 'Well, if we can't win that one, what can we ever win?'

"But nothing here is as it seems." She held up one end of a blanket. "You think the union is over here." She held up the other end of the blanket. "And the mining companies and cops over here." She pulled the blanket taut. "But they're all the same. Pull one string and the whole thing unravels. The sharks, mines, flops, brothels, taverns, cops—it's all one fabric. How do you fight that? Go right at it? Or come at an angle? Fight hard or fight smart?" Her voice cracked. "I don't know. I honestly don't know, Ryan."

It was similar to what Gig had said. That it ran too deep. Rye thought of what he knew, about Lem Brand, and he wondered if his brother was thinking similar things, sitting in some saloon, pointing to his empty glass. "Maybe after a while you don't fight it," he said.

Gurley was staring at the gloves in his lap. She took a deep breath. "Fred Moore is afraid we've had someone on the inside, giving them information."

Rye swallowed.

"Sixteen union leaders sent to state prison, more than three hundred other convictions for disturbing the peace. But you and your brother are out."

His mouth went dry. "Elizabeth—" he began.

"Ryan, I have to ask, the night of the raid, where did you go?"

He had come here to tell her everything, about Brand and Del and Early, about his own mistakes—but now, sitting across from her, he didn't know where to begin. He held up the gloves. His voice broke. "I went to buy these."

She looked directly at him, her mouth tight, eyes implacable. Rye felt as if she were seeing right through him, that whatever he'd come to admit, she already knew. For a moment he couldn't speak, but he also couldn't look away. He felt gutted and, inexplicably, wished she would never stop staring at him.

"Elizabeth," he began, "I didn't know—"

She looked down at her lap. "It's okay, Ryan."

"I thought I was just—"

"Ryan, please don't—"

"I thought I was helping Gig—"

She held her hands up. "Don't say any more." She looked back at the plate rail. And then she looked at him. "Would you do something for me?"

"I would do anything for you," he said.

30

The cop watching the house was leaning on a porch pillar when Rye came out. "What were you doing in there, kid?" He was tall and thin, with a scar running over his forehead and right eye.

"I'm her friend," Rye said. "I just came to see her."

The cop said, "Take off your coat," and Rye did, handing it to the cop, who went through the pockets and sleeves.

"She's under house arrest," the cop said. "She's not allowed visitors except her lawyer. Turn out your pants pockets."

Rye did, and a confetti of lint and crumbs came out. "You were asleep when I came up earlier," he said.

The cop shot him a look. "I wasn't asleep. I wanted you to think I was."

"Why would you want me to think you were asleep?" Rye asked.

The cop couldn't seem to think of a reason. "Lift your shirt."

Gurley had told him the cop would probably search him this way. They were desperately trying to keep her from publishing her story about what she had seen during her night in the Spokane jail. "It's outrageous," she said. "They arrest these girls for not paying off the police, and if they can't pay the fines, they force them to work it off in jail. They're essentially running a brothel in there, which is why the chief won't hire jail matrons. It's the worst-kept secret in the city and yet no one will touch it." She had tried to give the story to local reporters, but none would print it or even characterize Gurley's allegations. "There are some things you just can't say in a newspaper," a *Press* editor had told her. When she tried to publish a piece in the *Industrial Worker* detailing what she'd seen, police had confiscated and burned thousands of copies and charged the printer with conspiracy, lewd conduct, and libel. Even Fred Moore was leery of handling the story for fear of being held in contempt or involved in a libel suit.

The cop poked Rye with his nightstick and had him lower his pants. He patted him down and, when he was satisfied Rye wasn't smuggling any papers out, told him to fix his clothes and move on. "Okay. Go on, get out of here."

Rye took the streetcar back to Mrs. Ricci's house. Gig still wasn't there. Out on the sleeping porch, Rye reached under his cot and pulled out the envelope Lem Brand had given him for Early. It was a plain off-white envelope, no writing on it. He'd never even looked inside. But the envelope was unsealed. Rye took a deep breath and opened it. There was a typed note addressed to "Ennis Cooper," apologizing for "events that got out of hand" and offering to "abide by our original agreement." The note suggested Cooper "communicate through the boy what we might do to further keep our arrangement confidential and beneficial to us both."

Clipped to the note were ten fifty-dollar bills. Rye thumbed them. A fifty was even fancier than the twenty-dollar note he'd carried in his sock for two weeks. Rye wondered if Marco would reconsider selling his mother's orchard for this much money. He took the top bill and put the others back. He turned it over in his hands. It was issued by the Seaboard National Bank of San Francisco, stamped in blue, with a photo of Secretary of State John Sherman in the upper-left corner.

Rye found a pen and paper among his brother's things. He tore the paper in two and on one half wrote, "Gig, I'll be back Sunday. Rye." On the other half, he wrote, "IOU. $50. Ryan J. Dolan." He put that note in the envelope with the other bills. Then he tucked it back between his cot and blankets. He shoved the fifty-dollar bill in his pocket, grabbed his hat and coat and his gloves off the bed, and started out.

He walked through the orchard, even though it wasn't on his way, the icy ground crunching beneath his boots. He stood in the cold trees a moment, imagining a house among them. Finally, he started walking, catching the old hobo highway to downtown. He thought about looking for Gig in his usual saloons, but even if he found him, he'd be long past drunk now and probably just tell Rye to leave him alone. So he went straight to the train station, arriving in plenty of time to catch the overnight. The Great Northern station was nearly deserted, just three other passengers waiting.

At the window, Rye bought a nine-dollar ticket for the Cascadian. It was cheaper than the Empire Builder because it made more stops.

He was too nervous to sleep on the train, so he sat up in his seat as the train lurched off. They built up speed, and out the window he sensed more than saw the dark wooded terrain fall away amid the faint shadows of crags and ledges of central Washington. Each station they pulled into seemed ghostlier than the last, gaslight shadows of water and coal stops, rail signal switches and lonely figures on platforms, the electric lamps of rail agents in the windows. Rye had the sense of moving not just across the land but in and out of time, and at one point he fell asleep and dreamed he was old and looking back on his life.

It was morning when he jolted awake just outside of Seattle.

He stepped off the train into a wet, drizzly Puget Sound day. His second time in Seattle this month. He had bacon, eggs, and coffee in the King Street Station diner and, when he was done, asked the waiter if he knew how to find the offices of the *Agitator* newspaper.

A man at the next table knew it. "What do you want with that batty crew?" He gave Rye the names of two reputable newspapers. "I'd try the *Post-Intelligencer*," he said. "They got a cartoonist draws a dog that wears a suit and drives a motorcar."

"I have business with the *Agitator*," Rye said.

The man told Rye he believed the *Agitator* was run out of a saloon on Cherry Street, so Rye walked there. The bartender, who was just opening for the day, pointed him to a back staircase off the alley. Rye went up the rickety outdoor staircase and came to a wood door with a smoked glass window. Painted on it in red block letters was the word AGITATOR. It was a Sunday, and it dawned on Rye that no one might be at the office, but when he knocked, a woman's voice called out, "Yeah?"

"I'm looking for Olen Parr," Rye yelled through the closed door.

"He's in jail!" the woman yelled back. "In Everett!"

"What for?"

"I don't know, a week probably!" she called back. "That's up to the judge!"

"What I mean is, what did he do?"

"That's up to the judge, too!"

"Please let me in!" Rye called through the door. "I have something for him!"

"I told you, he isn't here!"

Rye looked around in frustration. "I was here a few weeks ago!" he yelled through the door. "With Elizabeth Gurley Flynn! I'm with the Wobblies in Spokane! I'm the orphan Mr. Parr interviewed!"

Finally, the woman opened the door. She was short, with wiry gray hair and glasses at the end of her nose. She squinted over the frames. "You're the orphan? From the story, I was picturing someone nine or ten years old." She was holding sheets of loose paper as if she'd been reading something.

"No, it's me," Rye said. "I just turned seventeen."

Then he removed his bowler, flipped the brim liner, and dug around in the satiny lining of the crown. "I apologize," he said, "it might be a little sweaty." Rye pulled out three typed pages, folded and mashed, from the crown of his hat.

"You an orphan magician, then?" the woman asked.

Rye did his best to flatten and smooth the pages. "This is from Gurley Flynn. She's under house arrest in Spokane, so I had to smuggle it out. They confiscated and burned the *Industrial Worker* to keep her from printing this. She wants me to ask Mr. Parr if he will consider running this story in the *Agitator*."

The woman opened her mouth—

"I know. He's in jail. In Everett. Please. Just read it."

She began reading. Slowly, her face changed. "Jesus," she said. "Can you prove this?" She looked up at him. "No, of course you can't." She read a little more and then flipped to the second page. "Jesus," she said, then "Jesus" again. And finally, "Shit."

She invited Rye in. The apartment was dark and cramped, two typewriters on small tables, and news pages clipped on a hanging clothesline. This front room was apparently the offices of the *Agitator*. Behind were a bedroom, a bathroom, and a small galley kitchen. Rye could smell onions frying.

He looked up at the clothespinned news page. Beneath the *Agitator* flag was a banner headline calling for GENERAL STRIKE! The woman excused herself and left, returning ten minutes later with two older men. Neither one said anything as they leaned over a table to read Gurley's story. When they were done, they looked up at the woman and nodded.

"Give us a minute," she said to Rye, and they retreated to the bedroom to talk. When they emerged, the woman said they would remake the front page of the *Agitator* with Gurley's allegations, and would print a special edition of the *Industrial Worker* the following week and distribute it all over the West Coast.

"You're not going to wait for Mr. Parr?" Rye asked.

The woman looked at Rye over the rims of her glasses. "I love Olen, but the man can barely knot his shoes."

Soon another woman and two men came up to the apartment, and by early afternoon, the office was a flurry of activity.

Rye stood and put on his coat. He could still catch the three p.m. back over the mountains.

"Where are you going?" the woman asked.

"Catch a train back to Spokane," Rye said. "I have to work tomorrow." Then, almost an afterthought: "And I need to go find my brother."

Gig

I T'S ALWAYS the same, first drink of the day: *uisce beatha*. Our da called it that. *Water of life*. Deep pull of air, eyes pop, and it's a goddamn clear world on the other side of the glass.

Hello there.

But here's the rub, Rye-boy. Second drink's better.

Of course, it's going to turn at some point, but when? The first is good, the second better, and sometimes the third makes me a goddamn genius or lands me in a woman's bed. To wit, it's a blind roll past two. Four, six, nine—eventually, I might wake soiled on a railroad siding or, in this case, with my wasp of a little brother on the sleeping porch floor, wiping up the *water of life* I've just gagged—me saying, "Don't goddamn do that. For once, leave me alone."

But the words don't actually come out, and when you leave that morning for your job—my baby boy brother has a *job* and is caring for *me* like *I'm* the *child*—that's when I knew I just couldn't do it anymore.

I'm sorry, Rye, I was cold and tired and done with it all.

An rud nach leigheasann im ná uisce beatha níl aon leigheas air. That was Da's old adage: *What cannot be cured by whiskey and butter cannot be cured*. I used to believe it meant that butter and whiskey were the cures for everything, but I have come to realize that saying is about

something else, about that which *cannot* be cured by whiskey or butter or anything in this world, namely, life. That steaming fly-covered
shit pile of heartache, life.

Real hunger shuts everything down. By day five in jail I couldn't remember why I liked to eat. By day ten I couldn't remember anything. Dull-witted and numb. Took a week after getting out of jail for
Thirst and Hunger to return. But they did, old friends waiting on the
curb outside the boardinghouse.

Hello, boys, where have you been?

You had a good job, Rye, and I didn't want to crumb it for you, but
Christ I had a tightness in my neck. I couldn't sit at that old Italian
woman's table three times a day, pretending to be her son and eating
slippery noodles. When you brought home that fancy volume of *War
and Peace* from the library, honestly, that was the final blow. This
was my life now? Sit by the fire and eat dinner while my little brother
borrows books for me to read in bed?

So while you were at the machine shop, I went out for a round: a
pint and a shot of *uisce*. A bartender sympathetic to our labor cause
served me up—toasted me and set me up again. And again. I told
the bartender the great realization I'd had after a month of beating
and starvation in jail—that none of it mattered. That we were flies
buzzing around the heads of millionaires, fooling ourselves that we
had power because they couldn't possibly swat us *all*.

The man could think of nothing to say about that except to fill my
glass.

After ten days of rest, and the return of Thirst and Hunger, the
old road soul began to stir. I felt the pull again, to go, fly, ride a rattler lumber rack, wind in my face on the way to some new rail stem.
Thought maybe I'd go find Early Reston down Lind way, where he
said he holed up sometimes.

I was done with Spokane. Done with jail and done with Walsh and done with his martyr Wobblies, done with your fiery girl, Flynn. Done with Ursula and her cougar and her millionaire, Brand. Done with it all, Rye, and you, too, if I'm being honest, at least for a while. Done with your faithful heart, your good job, your warm fireplace, your goddamn library card.

During the days, my thoughts would not give me rest: Why was I here? Why did I get out of jail while the rest of the committee got six months? Was Early right, was a rambling soul like mine better served by anarchy than labor union? And then, when the thoughts got heavy, I knew how to lighten them, *uisce*, and I left Mrs. Ricci's boardinghouse to drink about it all for a while, until either clarity came or the thoughts leaked away.

Like our dear departed da, I hit it hard that night, went to every sympathetic saloon in the city and asked for doubles on me troubles, Irish pubs and labor joints, and I gave the flies-on-millionaires speech, finished half-drunk glasses, bummed smokes and walked the streets, retched and pissed, and was shocked to find myself in the alley of the Comique, yelling at the doorman that inside was the most disloyal woman in the world, and he said, "Move on, drunk," and I said, "Are you the one to move me?" and he said, "Sure I am," and suddenly, there she was, the show ended, cat put away, robe pulled tight, and all my anger bled away in her eyes. I thanked her for coming to see me in jail that time, but my tongue was thick and my words jibbery, and I told her I had vowed to stay away until I felt my old self, for I didn't want her to see this wretched me, but I didn't know where else to go, drunk like this, I'd get my kid brother kicked out of our boardinghouse if I went back there and—

"Be quiet," Ursula said, and she took me by the hand to her dressing room and set me in a chair in front of her lighted mirror. I could barely look at myself there: dirty, hollow cheeks, and rat beard up to my bruised eyes. She fed me coffee and bread and meat left over from the cast room. "Look at you," she said. "What have they done to my beautiful Gregory. I just hope they left a bit of the soul in there."

This nearly made me weep, for I suspected the soul had taken the worst of it.

"What will you do now?" she asked.

"Get back on the road," I said. "Rattle out."

"Where?"

I shrugged, thinking of Early Reston. "I'm beginning to think I'm cut out more for the darker side of this thing."

"Do they employ a lot of drunks, that side?"

I laughed. "Suppose I'll find out."

"And Rye?"

"He's better without me," said I, and believed it. I told her you would do anything to survive, and good on you, the way you came up, our parents dying out from under you, the rest of us leaving you alone to scratch for food.

"Once, Rye and I were bedded in a jungle this side of Ellensburg," I told her. "The apple crews were full, so he went to bump lumps, because a begging kid does better alone, least that's what I told myself. I stayed in camp and got drunk with a couple of fellas until Rye came back with a fat lip and said he'd found an open back door and got us two chickens out of an icebox. The woman of the house had hit him pretty good with a broom, but he got away. We celebrated that little thief like he was goddamn Ty Cobb. That's the best I've got for Rye if I stay, Ursula, stealing chickens."

She smiled. "And all of this melancholy means you don't have to try anymore. Throw off your life and die in an alley somewhere. Is that the plan?"

"I don't have the particulars worked out," I said, "which alley, for instance."

I was sobering, and hated that most of all. Drunk, I could bear this lecture, but sober, it was starting to sting. "Hey, darlin', what do you say you shut up and buy an old consort a pint? For good times?"

She turned and wrote on a slip of paper: "The Phoenix Hotel" and

"Edith." And then she signed it: "Ursula." She said she'd bought this hotel and that Edith was the manager and I could stay for a few days.

I stared at the page. "You bought a hotel?"

"I am going to come see you in three days. You've got two days to get sober. If you can't do that, don't ever come see me again."

The Phoenix was the old Bailey Hotel with a new sign and, inside, a new coat of paint. I stood outside for a minute before going in. This manager, Edith, was an older woman, attractive enough, and she looked me up and down and said, simply, "Huh." She had the desk clerk give me a second-floor room in the men's wing. It was a single-occupancy bed and bureau, water closet down the hall. Better than I deserved. And all of it covered by Ursula. Best of all, there was a saloon in the basement, a private club Edith had started for men and women to get around the law that they could not consort inside a drinking establishment.

Now, if a woman gives me three days to sober up, it generally means I will spend the first two potted, and I did, eating and drinking in that basement saloon—and never once did a bill come, "Thank you, Mr. Dolan," and "It's on your account, Mr. Dolan," and I thought I might live at the Phoenix forever.

I figured you would come looking for me, Rye-boy. But there was a good shop job and a boardinghouse for you if I stayed away. And if you flew off with me? What then? Another hobo camp, another saloon, another icebox to pilfer, another cop to roust us from sleep, and in the end, another Dolan gone Drunk.

What cannot be cured cannot be cured. Not by *uisce*, or by self-pity, or love or family or anything else. I had a good two days of that which could not be cured and woke in full light at the Phoenix. I did not remember getting myself to bed. They had given me a room with a window. One of those cold sharp winter suns was cracking the shades. There was a light rap at the door.

"Yes," I said.

The door opened. It was the hotel manager, Edith, with a fresh set of clothes for me. "Good morning," she said.

"If you say so."

She set the clothes on the bureau, left, and returned a minute later with a basin of steaming hot water. Then she left and returned with another basin. Then three towels, a bar of soap, a straight razor, and a mug of shaving cream.

"Are you preparing for surgery?" I asked. "Is that the price of this room, a kidney? Because I'll gladly pay."

"You *are* funny." Edith turned and considered me. "I must say, I didn't see it when you first came in here. I just thought, *Oh, God, she's got a weakness for bums*."

This stung more than I let on.

Next, Edith brought in a chair and set it next to the bed. I lay there watching all of this without moving, without a word.

Then she left again.

And when the door opened this time, it was Ursula who came in.

I sat up. "I thought I had three days."

"Today is the third."

"Your math is suspect."

"You came to see me Saturday night. Today is Monday."

"I guess I was thinking of a day as more of a twenty-four-hour period . . . a discrete unit of—"

"Should I leave?"

"No, it's just, I'm afraid I'm not—"

"Quiet," she said. And she laid me back down on the pillow. Then she took one of the towels and pressed it down into the hot water. She wrung it out and then put the towel on my face. It nearly burned at first, then the heat seeped into my teeth. Eye sockets. My thoughts, bones, regrets, all hot and open, and I teared up beneath the hot cloth. Nothing in the world has ever felt as good. When she lifted the cloth away, she had the brush from the shaving mug, and she began putting the cream on my face. She spread it carefully on my cheeks and neck, using the tips of her fingers to clear it from my nose and lips. Then she had me hold the bowl of hot water on my chest and she gently shaved me, the whiskers falling into the bowl. She dipped the razor into the hot water and glided it across my cheeks, the pelt of whiskers falling away. She was a whiz with that straightedge, sure and fast as any barber.

I watched her eyes as she shaved me, careful and intent, looking for what she might be thinking, but she seemed as distant as if she were onstage. She shaved nearly up to my eyes and all the way down my neck. When my beard was gone, she used the wet towel again, wiped away the last of the cream.

Then she touched my cheek. She smiled. "There he is." Next she told me to stand and undress.

"Ursula, I don't even know if—"

"Just be quiet," she said.

So I got out of bed and stripped to nothing. I threw my rank long johns in a pile next to my dirty clothes. I stood before her, shaking and ashamed, flaccid, ribs sticking out. I closed my eyes and I kept them that way.

She was even more careful in the washing of my body, dipping the towels and dabbing under my arms, across my neck, my chest, over the purple and yellow of jail beatings. Ursula used the soap and the water from both basins. I kept my eyes closed and I let myself be washed and rinsed and dried by her. And when she began washing my legs and torso, I felt myself roused.

"There he is," she said again, and I felt her mouth close around me and I must have made a noise like this was too much, because she put a hand on my stomach to support me and it wasn't a minute before I was gasping and shuddering, and I let go, doubled over like I'd been kicked. When I straightened up, she went right back to cleaning me like nothing had happened.

When she was done, she went out and got one more bowl of warm water. She rinsed me again and patted me dry. She got powder and oil and cream and rubbed these into my arms and chest and hair and face. I watched her walk across the room to the bureau to get the clothes that Edith had brought earlier—her narrow waist and back, her long neck—and when Ursula returned to the bed, I was roused again.

"There he is." She whispered it this time, and she let me remove her clothes and we went at each other, soft and hard, slow and frenzied. We played like fancy honeymooners in that flophouse bed.

When we were done, she lay with her head on my chest. We talked quietly, her words buzzing my skin. She said if I managed to put some weight back on and went easy on the drink, she might see me again.

"I'll try," I said. "But maybe . . ."

There was no need to finish that sentence.

I looked around the room. "Is this really your hotel?"

"A woman owns nothing in this world except her memories," she said.

"What's that mean?" We lay there another moment, breathing each other in. If I could've stayed anywhere in the world, it was there. But I couldn't.

I looked down at the top of her head. "Tell me everything," I said.

For almost an hour, she talked. Told me where she grew up. How she became an actress. How she fell in love with a grifter. How she met Edith and how she became Ursula the Great. And how, once she'd arrived in Spokane, Lem Brand offered her part of this hotel. Through it all, I just listened.

When she was done, I asked, "Is that everything?"

"No." She laughed and fell back onto my chest. "It's never everything, Gig. But it's probably enough."

P A R T   I V

The wild still lingered in him and the wolf in him merely
slept.

—Jack London, *White Fang*

31

In the days after Gig left, Rye began to see that he was living in a particular moment in history.

Maybe this was obvious to other people, but it had never occurred to him. It was a strange, unwieldy thought, like opening a book and seeing yourself in its pages. Seemingly unrelated events— meeting Early Reston at the river that day, the free speech riot, Ursula the Great taking him to meet Lem Brand, traveling with Gurley Flynn, smuggling her story out to Seattle, maybe even Gig's disappearance—these moments seemed linked, like events leading up to a war. And he supposed that was what they were in, a war— this skirmish between the IWW and the city was part of a larger battle fought in a thousand places, between company and labor, between rich and poor, between forces and sides he wasn't sure he had understood before.

Part of this new perspective came from the fact that Rye was trying to read *War and Peace* in the evenings at Mrs. Ricci's house and on his lunch breaks at the machine shop. He'd started the book when he realized that Gig was not coming back, in the hope that it would tell him something about his brother—if not where he'd gone, at least maybe why.

Over the next few weeks, he read slowly, five or six pages a day, jotting down words he didn't know on a small notepad, then looking them up on Saturday afternoons in the big Carnegie Library dictionary. At the shop, the Orlando brothers took little interest in the book he was reading during breaks, but Dominic tried to follow along at least with the basic plot, and he would look over Rye's shoulder and ask, "What's happening in your book now?" and Rye would say, "Andrey's about to leave," and Dominic would say, "Where's Napoleon?" and Rye would say, "Still on his way," and Dominic would answer, "Well, keep me posted," and go back to his work.

One day Dominic's wife came in with a rhubarb pie for lunch while Rye was reading in the shop. He looked at the tall, dark-haired woman and she stared back at him, recognition arriving for both of them at the same moment.

"You were Jules's friend!" Gemma Tursi said.

"I'm sorry," Rye said, feeling again the sorrow of her uncle's death and the guilt of him and Fred Moore trying to convince her to further the IWW cause.

"No," she said, "I should have invited you in for a meal. Jules would've liked that." And now she smiled. "But look. I get to remedy that. Won't you come for dinner this Sunday?"

"Thank you," Rye said. He was happy for the invitation. Sundays were the hardest days because he didn't work. Rye would do chores for Mrs. Ricci and then spend most of the day reading *War and Peace* by the fire, staring out the window and wondering what his brother was doing—maybe sitting around some jungle cook fire, drinking from a communal bottle. He wondered if Gig wished he'd taken *War and Peace* with him, or if he'd found another book in the big floater library.

Rye wasn't always sure he understood Tolstoy, but he was surprised at how much he enjoyed reading him, from the first moments of Anna Pavlovna's *soiree* to meeting the beautiful Natasha and the dashing Prince Andrey and the thoughtful Pierre. He liked picturing the fancy clothing and fabulous mansions and grand palaces, larger even than Lem Brand's big house (*When Natasha ran out of the drawing room she only ran as far as the conservatory*). He tried to imagine a house so big you got tired running from one room to the next. The language seemed musical, and he found himself humming sentences like songs (*The coach with six horses stood at the steps. The coach with six horses stood at the steps . . .*).

And the deeper he got into the story, the more he began to imagine his own life as part of an epic story. It was the thing he felt the count got right, the comings and goings of all of these characters, in and out of each other's lives, as if Tolstoy were able to re-create the breadth of life as well as its depth.

Sometimes, late at night, the count's words swirled around with Rye's own thoughts, and descriptions of characters became descriptions of Rye and his brother, as if some tramp Tolstoy had created them (*Prince Andrey possessed in the highest degree just that combination of qualities in which Pierre was deficient . . .*), and it was in one of these swirling late-night thoughts (*At moments of starting off and beginning a different life, persons given to deliberating on their actions are usually apt to be in a serious frame of mind*) that Rye came to the conclusion that, instead of merely waiting for Gig to come back, he had to *do something*.

That Sunday, he had dinner with Dominic and Gemma and their two shy daughters. After talking about Jules, and remembering the stories he always told, Mrs. Tursi had asked about Rye's family.

Rye explained that they were all gone except his brother, whom he'd tramped around with the last two years but who had recently lit out on his own.

"And no idea where he might have gone?" Mrs. Tursi asked.

"No," Rye said.

But then he realized he did have one idea.

And the next day, after work, he took the streetcar downtown and walked to the Comique Theater.

Rye stood beneath the dark marquee: HELD OVER—THIRD FABULOUS MONTH—URSULA THE GREAT.

The show ran Tuesday through Saturday nights, meaning Monday was her day off. The theater doors were closed and locked, but Rye walked around to the side door, which was propped open with a garbage can. The big security guard was nowhere to be found, but when Rye looked inside, a janitor was in the dark hallway, emptying smaller trash cans into the big one.

"I'm looking for Ursula the Great," Rye said.

"No show on Monday," the janitor said without looking up.

"I was wondering if you know where she's staying?"

"I know it ain't this broom closet."

"It's just . . . I think my brother might be with her."

The janitor looked back. He was sixty or so, bald with drooping brown eyes. "Oh yeah, I saw him. Few weeks back. Looked like a big drunk you." He straightened up. "Tall raggedy bum, pissed as a fish in gin. Our doorman was about to kill him when Ursula came and took him back to her dressing room, I think to sober him up."

"Do you know where they might have gone after that?"

"Maybe she fed him to the cougar?"

"Please," Rye said. "I need to find him."

The janitor looked him up and down. He chewed on his cheek and sighed. "She stays over the Savoy."

It was only a couple of blocks away, a nice hotel above the Inland Bar. Rye asked at the front desk for Ursula the Great. The clerk didn't even pretend to look in his book. "Nobody under that name."

"I don't know her real name," Rye said.

"You're looking for Ursula?"

Rye turned. The woman in front of him was older than Ursula, maybe fifty, dressed in a black coat over a red dress and a yellow and red scarf tied around her head, a shock of gray hair visible in the front.

"I'm Edith," the woman said. "I was just bringing Ursula some soup."

"Could you tell her Ryan Dolan is here?"

She smiled. "Of course."

A few minutes later, the woman returned with Ursula the Great, in a long mustard-colored coat and a fine feathered-and-bowed hat, dressed in the dead of winter as if she had just come back from a picnic. She reached out and took his hand. "Ryan. How are you?"

"I'm fine. I've been looking for Gig."

"I haven't seen him in . . ." Ursula looked at Edith.

"Three weeks?" Edith suggested.

"Yes, thank you, Ursula." And with that, Ursula turned back to Rye. "He came to see me one night. He was quite . . ."

Edith helped again. "Skimished."

"Yes. I put him up at my hotel for a couple of nights."

Rye was confused, not least by Ursula calling this other woman Ursula. "Your hotel?"

"The old Bailey Hotel. Edith here manages it for me."

Rye remembered the Bailey as one of the worst flops in town, a five-dollar-a-month SRO and a row of whore cribs on the second floor.

"Gig stayed there a couple of nights, maybe three?" She looked back at Edith, who nodded. "But I haven't seen him since then, Ryan."

"Do you know where he went?"

"He just said he wanted to get back out on the road."

"Without me."

Ursula looked at Edith again and then back to Rye. "He doesn't want to ruin the life you've made for yourself. He's proud of you."

Rye scoffed.

"Ryan," she said, "your brother has always felt a great deal of responsibility for you. It was difficult having to take care of you after your parents died."

"Take care of *me*?" Rye's face flushed. "He ran off! I pulled him out of bars and cleaned him up. I take care of *him*!"

"I'm sorry, Ryan," Ursula said calmly. "And you're right. You *do* take care of him. Imagine for a moment how much worse that is for him."

Rye's chin fell to his chest. She was right. He didn't want to go back out on the skid. And he knew Gig couldn't stay away from it. Rye wondered if loving another person was a trap—that eventually you had to either lose them or lose yourself.

He cleared his throat and looked up. There was nothing else to say. "Thanks."

He turned to leave, and was a few steps down the hall when Ursula called after him.

He turned back. She looked pained. This wasn't the Ursula who had squeezed his arm and taken him to see Lem Brand. He couldn't place the look on her face.

"It's easy to be disappointed in people," she said, "but we do our best. And maybe what a person *is* and what they *do*—is not always the same."

"Yeah," he said. "But maybe it is."

32

The newspapers were filled with the upcoming trial of Elizabeth Gurley Flynn and her explosive allegations against the city. Each day after work, Rye brought home copies of the *Press*, the *Chronicle*, and the *Spokesman-Review*, sat by Mrs. Ricci's fire, and followed the latest developments. At the shop, Dominic would see Rye grab the newspaper and ask, "How's your girl doing today, Ryan?" On Sundays, Rye would tell Dominic and Gemma stories about what Gurley had done on the road, talking them out of trouble in Taft and telling an angry priest that, "um, female parts" should be emancipated.

Her case had become the biggest story in the west after her exposé was published by the *Agitator* and in a special edition of the *Industrial Worker*, distributed in western Washington and over the border in Idaho. The story, in turn, was picked up by progressive newspapers, and then by mainstream papers all over the country, which hinted at her "bestial and barbaric accusations."

Still, within weeks of her arrest, the whole country knew that a pregnant nineteen-year-old labor agitator was accusing Spokane police and jailers of misusing women, extorting madams, pimps, and saloon owners, and then, if they didn't pay the cops, jailing prostitutes and making them "work off" their fines.

Chief Sullivan insisted that her charges were "scurrilous lies" and that there "has never been a single complaint" filed against the women's jail. And when the *Press* unearthed two earlier complaints similar to Gurley's, Sullivan said those were scurrilous lies, too. When the *Chronicle* followed up with a story that, for two years, Sullivan had resisted appointing a jail matron, and that he'd rejected women's groups who had offered volunteers to do the job, the mayor said he had no alternative but to promise a thorough investigation.

Gurley's corruption story also began to shift the city's sympathies. Religious groups and temperance reformers picketed the courthouse, demanding action. They showed up, too, at the home where Gurley Flynn was under house arrest, and with the police unsure what to do, she came out and gave an impromptu rally from her front porch. By early February, as her trial was opening, both the Spokane Garden Society and the Spokane Women's Club had offered to testify on her behalf, saying that they'd found nothing untoward in her message.

When the trial started, reporters, portraitists, and photographers came from as far away as New York and Washington, D.C., to do drawings and hand-colored photos of her striking, youthful face and her hood of black hair—this pretty young martyr fighting alone against an entire corrupt Old West town. They drew her from the shoulders up, tastefully, as she had entered her eighth month of pregnancy.

As the story spread throughout the country, Spokane's boosters complained in letters to the editor that the city's reputation was suffering, that Spokane was in danger of becoming known as a backwoods outpost where the police traded in vice and harassed young women who objected. Prominent businessmen suggested replacing Acting Chief Sullivan and launching a full review of police practices.

What was bad for the city was good for the IWW, and it attracted new volunteers and donations, although, because the union had been banned in Spokane, new members were routed to the closest IWW office, thirty-five miles over the border in Coeur d'Alene. Emboldened, Gurley announced that the next Free Speech Day in

Spokane would be March 15, no matter the outcome of her trial or her pregnancy. "If I'm in jail, I will exercise my right to speak there, and I will listen at the bars for the cries of freedom coming from the streets outside."

Hobos even began venturing back to town, the *Press* running a story about two floaters from the Taft, Montana, labor camp who had walked all the way to Spokane to donate sixty dollars they'd raised for Gurley Flynn's defense.

All of this made the conspiracy trial of Elizabeth G. F. Jones and Charles L. Filigno the biggest spectacle in the west. By the time she took the stand to testify on her own behalf, in late February, Gurley was startlingly pregnant, her lawyer helping support her as she rose in the courtroom. She made the most of her two days on the stand, delivering lectures to simple yes-no questions like "Where were you born?"

"All of my life, from my early childhood in New York and near Boston, where my father worked, to my more recent travels in the glorious west, I have seen my people, my family and my class, suffer under the inequalities of a system that produces paupers at one extreme and multimillionaires at the other, and nothing in the middle but space. That's why I am in this work."

The judge interrupted her speeches and argued with her and on the second day demanded, "What makes you think you can say whatever you want about anyone?"

She gave her shortest answer yet: "The Bill of Rights, sir."

Someone applauded, and the judge rapped his gavel and asked where had she gotten the law degree that allowed her to do *his* job, interpreting the legal application of constitutional amendments, and Gurley responded not to him but to the jury and the courtroom: "They are written in plain English, anyone can understand them. They were written not for lawyers but for the people."

The prosecutor, Pugh, worked hard to remind the jury that the IWW was made up *not* of young, charming Elizabeth Gurley Flynns but of suspicious foreigners like Charlie Filigno. Soon Pugh was stretching out Filigno's name to four syllables in every question he asked: "On January eleventh, Mrs. Jones, did you and Mr. *Fil-ig-i-no* send this telegraph to the Butte office of the WFM?" and "Does this article accurately reflect the radical views of Mr. *Fil-ig-i-no* and yourself?"

"Well, you should ask Charlie his views," she said, "but if calling for fairness and justice is radical, then I am about the radicalest woman in the world."

Pugh tried everything to shake the witness, one day asking if her husband was in the courtroom, and when she began to answer, "No—" he interrupted with "And what do you suppose Mr. Jones thinks of his wife traveling to labor camps and mining towns in the company of such unsavory men?"

"Well, I don't know," she said, "but if he *doesn't* like it, I doubt he'd like it any better if I traveled with *savory* men such as yourself." Over the laughter, Pugh asked if her husband would find it so humorous, "you summoning every foreign scoundrel and savage to Spokane to harass our poor citizenry."

Gurley didn't answer right away. "I guess I'm wondering how you arrived at this theory that I can summon men from all over the world yet can't seem to convince my own husband to catch a train and come here?"

Pugh was more effective cross-examining grim Charlie Filigno, mostly by asking forty different ways where Filigno was from. "Sicily," he'd answer each time. "And your country of origin, then, Mr. Fil-ig-i-no?" "Sicily." "So you arrived here in 1906 from—" "Sicily." Pugh asked long, involved questions meant to confuse the union secretary and expose his weak command of English. "Are there not, in fact, criminal elements of the Industrial Workers of the World in this very city who have resorted to violence, beating up police officers, threatening public figures, committing untold numbers of crimes to further the cause of your radical agenda—in fact, wouldn't you say, Mr. Filigno, that as secretary of the Spokane IWW, that despite your union's repeated claims of nonviolence, you personally have done nothing to deter these individuals and, in fact, have expressed only the utmost respect and sympathy for your vile com-patriots and countrymen?"

Fred Moore rose in objection: "Your Honor, if the prosecutor is done testifying, perhaps he could ask a question." While Moore's objections were never sustained, Pugh agreed to rephrase that par-ticular question: "Remind this court again where you are from, Mr. Fil-ig-i-no."

Rye followed the trial in the city's dailies, his view of who was winning depending on which paper he'd just read, as if each were covering only one boxer in a match, the establishment *Chronicle* and *Spokesman-Review* cheering the hits that Pugh got in, the labor *Press* making it seem that Fred Moore and Gurley Flynn were mopping the floor with him. Still, Rye became increasingly nervous as the trial wore on, as countless union flyers, newspapers, and telegrams were entered as evidence that Gurley Flynn and Filigno were try-ing to cause a riot in the city. In an editorial, the *Spokesman-Review* vaguely referred to her pregnancy by noting that jurors are "clearly scandalized by this brash woman wearing the bustle wrong" and that the city, "having achieved eighteen straight convictions against union leadership, appears headed for nos. nineteen and twenty."

Finally, on a Friday in late February, both sides rested, and the judge announced that on Monday, the case would go to the jury.

As Joe closed up the machine shop that Saturday, Rye nervously asked if he might have Monday off to go down to the courthouse to be there for the verdict. By then, the whole shop knew Rye had been involved in the Wobbly riot back in November, and while Dom and Paul were union machinists and expressed support, Joe was uneasy about having hired a kid from an outfit as rough as the IWW.

"The goob only had eight fingers, but at least I never had to worry that he'd dynamite the place," Joe said.

"I would never do something like that," Rye said. "And anyway, Wobblies don't dynamite things. That's more the anarchists you're thinking of, Joe."

"You aren't one of them, are you?"

"No, Joe!" Rye said. "I don't know what I am." He thought of his brother and of Early Reston, out there somewhere. "Except the shop boy at North Hill Fittings and Machine."

Paul and Dominic watched from behind the counter. Finally, Joe said, "Well, you can't wear *that* to court."

Rye looked down at his worn work shirt and dungarees. That afternoon he took the streetcar downtown to look for a new shirt. He was in an unprecedented position in regard to money. With Gig gone, and Marco insisting that their six-dollar down payment on the orchard be applied to room and board, Rye was paid up at the boardinghouse until May. Mrs. Ricci had even let him move inside to the warmer first-floor bedroom. Since he was earning nearly ten dollars a week at the machine shop, and Mrs. Ricci provided his breakfasts and dinners, and Gemma Tursi sent his lunches to work with Dominic, Rye had money for the first time in his life. He'd even opened a bank account.

He stood on the corner of Post and Riverside, hands in his pockets, staring into the window at Murgittroyd's. The all-everything drugstore had a single row of stiff, boxy suit coats in between the pocket watches and fishing boots. A white $4 sign was pinned to the first jacket. A streetcar rattled past, and Rye left the window to walk down to the Crescent. He looked in that window at a rack of $13 sackcoat suits, gray, with a fine crosshatching of blue thread. A card on the floor of the window display read: THE HOME OF DIGNIFIED CREDIT. Had any phrase ever sounded better than *dignified credit*? Still, more than a week's salary for something he might wear once? He glanced up the street and kept moving, eventually finding himself back on Sprague, at the window of Bradley and Graham's, the corner shop where he'd bought his fancy gloves. He stared through the glass at swaths of fabric and pieces of vests and pants, a coat with tails that didn't have a price on it. These suits weren't even built yet. What would they cost? Fifty dollars? A hundred? The levels between people.

"Well, hello there. Ryan, was it?"

Rye turned and saw the old salesman who had helped him. He was putting his hat on as he came out of the shop.

"Sorry," Rye said, "I was just looking." He started to move along.

"It's all right," the salesman said. "How are those gloves holding up?"

Rye looked down at his bare hands. He'd left the gloves at home. "Fine."

"What are you looking for now?"

"Nothing," Rye said, then added quickly, "I wanted a new shirt, but then I started looking at suits."

"A suit! Well, yes!" He looked Rye up and down. "Every young man should own a suit." He gestured to his store. "But honestly, you shouldn't go here for that. Enough I sold you those gloves. We can get you a nice suit for much less."

The man's name was Chester, and he talked the whole time as they walked down Sprague. "Normally, I'd suggest having a bespoke coat made, something distinctive yet classic, and build the components around it. But you're a young man, thin and active, your body's still growing. I think we can find something on the rack for much less. I'm thinking high neck, shorter lapels, to display your height. I'd go narrower than a morning coat. Single-breasted vest. A tailor will try to talk you into better wool, but it's a working suit, for God's sake, we don't need to strangle a merino lamb for you to look swell on the streetcar!"

They went to a midlevel men's clothier called Burks and Feyn where Chester knew the salesman. "Kid's had a rough go, Dale," he said. "Give him your discount."

"Give him *your* discount!" Dale said.

"Come on! I'll owe you. I know you have something good back there."

Finally, the salesman sighed, measured Rye's arms and chest, and emerged with five coats. The salesman and Chester talked about them, Rye trying to follow. Even the words sounded rich to Rye—

the *Regent*, the *Winston*? Worsted? Tweed? Herringbone or hounds-tooth? Berrycorn or birdseye? Rye found it dizzying, embarrassed by how much he liked all of it. He nodded. He blushed. He listened.

"Okay." Chester was in Rye's ear. "Last question: pockets." He showed Rye the first jacket. "Patch pocket. Simple. So called because it's sewn on the coat just like a patch. Opens at the top. Eyeglasses, house key. Versatile, smart." He switched coats. "This is a flap pocket, same thing but with a flap on top of the patch. And this—" He gestured to the third coat. "*This* is style. The jetted pocket, sewn *inside* the coat so that all you see from the outside is this slit opening. Add a third pocket below it, here, a theater ticket pocket, a key pocket, and this says, 'I am a gentleman, a morning-to-night, go-anywhere, do-anything gentleman.'"

Rye could see it. The clean line. The slant to the pocket. He whispered to Chester, "How much do you think—"

"Eighteen," said the salesman, glancing at Chester, "but sixteen this week and . . ." He lowered his voice: "I could do twelve as long as—"

Chester cleared his throat.

"Fine. I could do ten," the salesman conceded. "You're a bastard, Chester."

Chester smiled, swept around, and lowered the coat onto Rye. It settled on his shoulders like the first snow on a hillside.

"Of course, you can't wear those boots," the salesman said.

"No, you'll need shoes," said Chester. "And that old hat will likely have to go."

Rye turned back to the mirror. He felt a rush, and then some shame, at just how badly he wanted to be the gentleman in the glass.

33

Rye sat on the streetcar, a long cloth bag draped over his lap, in it, his new suit and tie, white shirt, and calfskin dress shoes. The bag was, itself, nicer than most of his clothes. He ended up keeping the bowler, out of fondness, the salesman agreeing to spiff it up for him, running a de-linter over it, shining it with oil, and buffing out the grease stain. Rye bought the clothes on credit, five dollars down, the rest due over six months, though he wasn't entirely sure how much *the rest* entailed.

He got off the streetcar and walked the four blocks toward Mrs. Ricci's house, the clothing bag slung over his shoulder like a sailor returning from duty. It was a cool, snowless afternoon, the street full of welcoming smoke from neighbors' fireplaces.

He was approaching Mrs. Ricci's when Rye saw a figure through the window of the sleeping porch—Gig! Sitting on his bed in the dark. Rye ran around the side to the back door, and the silhouetted figure turned.

But when he opened the back door, it was Early Reston sitting on his brother's cot. "Hey, Little Brother."

Rye stared dumbly. Early looked different. He'd grown a close beard, streaked with gray, and was wearing a suit of his own, rough tweed, Rye thinking of the photo of the Pinkerton agent, Ennis Cooper, and all of those names he used.

"What've you got there?" Early stood and took the clothing bag from Rye.

"A suit," Rye said.

"A suit! Well." Early unbuttoned the bag and felt the fabric. "Fancy! Look at Rye Dolan. You switching sides, Rye? Like a snake shedding his skin?"

"I needed something to wear to court Monday. For Gurley's verdict."

"Ah, right. Mrs. Jones's verdict. You do recall that she's married, right, Rye? And with child? And about to go to prison. Fancy a challenge, don't you?"

Rye blushed and took back the clothing bag.

"Sorry," Early said. "Was that mean?"

"I'm supposed to give you something," Rye said. "From Lem Brand."

"How is our old friend?" Early asked.

"I don't know," Rye said. "I told him weeks ago I'd give you this message, and after that, I didn't want anything to do with him."

"Did you grow unhappy with your position?"

Rye flushed. "I didn't have a position. It was a mistake. I didn't know—"

"You didn't *know*, Rye?"

Rye said nothing.

"Come on—what didn't you know?"

Rye just shook his head.

"You knew," Early said. "We always know. Whatever happens, we know."

Rye hated that *we*, as if they were the same kind of man. "Your letter is inside. Can I—"

He wasn't sure he needed permission, but Early nodded and Rye went through the kitchen to his bedroom. There was a bread knife out on the counter, and for a moment, Rye thought about grabbing it. In the bedroom, he hung his new clothes in the closet. He'd used Lem Brand's envelope as a bookmark, and it was sticking out from a page early in the second volume of Constance Garnett's translation of *War and Peace*, which Rye had recently checked out, after returning the first. He walked back with the book and handed the envelope to Early, who sat back down on Gig's cot.

"Aw, I didn't get you anything," Early said. He opened the envelope, and thumbed through the bills. "You believe this son of a bitch, acting like nothing happened, like he didn't try to have me killed? I almost admire him."

"I borrowed some, but I paid it back," Rye said.

"Of course you did," Early said. He unfolded Lem Brand's note and read it, occasionally shaking his head. "He'd like to stick to our original agreement. I'll bet he would. The original agreement where I don't come find him, cut out his fucking liver, and feed it to his kids." He held up the note. "Tell me, Rye, did he seem scared?"

"Yeah," Rye said. "He did."

"Good," Early said. "Armed men?"

Rye tried to remember. "Two at the gate. One above his carriage house. Another at the door. And his man, Willard."

Early read the note again.

Rye watched Early's face. "Who are you?" he asked quietly.

Early looked up. His eyes were cold. "Who are *you*?"

"No, I mean which side—" But Rye didn't finish the thought, for he knew Early could turn that one on him, too.

Early took a deep breath. "I'm on *my* side, Rye. Always have been. Like any man, if he's being honest."

Early stood, folded the money, and shoved it into his pocket. Then he folded the note and put it in his small suit-coat pocket, the ticket pocket, Rye remembered, although that detail felt wrong now.

Early looked around the sleeping porch. "Cold out here. I can't believe this is where you boys lived."

"I sleep inside now," Rye said.

"Do you?" Early looked around the room and landed on Rye again. "And tell me, now that you're a man of means, with his own suit and a good job and an indoor bedroom, what side are *you* on, Rye?"

Rye said nothing.

"Come on. What stuff are you made of?"

Something about the question reminded him of a line he'd read in *War and Peace* the day before—Pierre contemplating his life. Rye opened to the page and handed the book over, pointing to a paragraph.

Early cleared his throat and read, "'Sometimes he consoled himself by the reflection that it did not count, that he was only temporarily leading this life. But later on, he was horrified by another reflection, that numbers of other men, with the same idea of being temporary, had entered that life with all their teeth and a thick head of hair, only to leave it when they were toothless and bald.'"

Early looked up and smiled with what Rye thought might be amusement or condescension. "You surprise me, Rye," he said. "Every time. You really are the smart one, you know that?" He flipped through the book, considered its spine. Then he held it to his chest. "And are you ready to stop being temporary?"

Rye shrugged.

"Because I need you to do something."

Rye opened his mouth to say no.

"It's for your brother and me," Early said.

"You've seen Gig?"

"I have," Early said.

"How is he?"

"He's fine," Early said. "He's gotten his strength back."

"Is he here? Can I see him?"

"After you do this favor for me."

"What is it?"

"I need you to deliver a message back to Brand."

"What's the message?" Rye asked.

"Tell him I said yes. I will abide by our original agreement. But I want five thousand dollars, not five hundred. After that, he'll never hear from me again."

Rye felt sick, pulled back into this.

"Tell him to give you the money Monday morning. I'll meet you in front of the courthouse at noon. You give me the money and I'll give you all the evidence of my deal with Brand, the paperwork, his idiotic dossiers. But tell him that if anyone follows you, the deal is off. And he can spend the rest of his life waiting for a visit from me."

"And then I can see Gig?"

"We'll all go for a beer afterward." Early smiled. "First round's on me."

Rye could do nothing but nod.

"Look at that." Early handed *War and Peace* back. "The old gang rides again."

Gig

I STEPPED off the train when it slowed outside Lind, in the gold rolling hills of the Palouse. It was midwinter and the wheat fields were stubble-cut, dusted by frost. The sun was out, though, lighting up old barns and wagons, an abandoned plow. I was alert and alive, and I walked into that town the king of all possibility.

Do you remember, Rye-boy, that part of tramping? The track-side stroll into some new burg, nothing weighing you down but a pair of gloves, a shirt, extra socks, maybe a book bindled in your bedroll. On the lookout for smoke from a camp cook fire. Anything could happen with a town in front of you, maybe a Lind maiden takes you to bed, or you find some old pal from down the line, or, at the very least, strike it up with a barman who has read a thing or two in his life. The world feels open for business. I'm not sure what else you could even ask for.

In Lind, there was a two-story redbrick bar and grill called Slim's, and I went there with the ten dollars I'd gotten from Ursula. I saw they had Schade from Spokane, my favorite lager, and I said, "I'd favor one of them Shoddies," and spun a dollar coin on the bar top. Beer-not-whiskey the closest I had to a plan.

I inquired of the barman, aptly named Slim, about work and a room.

"The room will be easier to find than the work," he said. "Wheat's all up. You are . . . let's see." He consulted his pocket watch. "Six months late."

"Or," I said, "I am six months early."

Slim had a bed upstairs as long as I needed it—he looked at me—"or as long as you can pay twenty cents a night."

"I can pay fifteen," I countered, and he said, "Why not," no doubt figuring I'd spend the rest of my money on beer anyway. "I'll take it for tonight," I said.

"What brings you to Lind," he asked, "other than the rods of a freighter?"

"Oh, I'm no rod man," I said. "I don't have the nerve for it, holding an undertruss for two hours with those rocks kicking up. I prefer flying on top, a flatcar if I can get it, though today I came nestled like a baby bird in a soft grainer."

"A discerning hobo."

"Only kind," I said, and gave him the real reason I was in Lind. "Say, you wouldn't happen to know a man named Early Reston?"

"No," he said. "Don't think so."

I started to describe him—and then realized it would be like describing a stalk of wheat, thin and pale and, well, that's it. "I'm an old friend of his from up Spokane. He said to look him up if I was ever here."

"Well, you are here," he said. "I'll give you that."

I finished my beer, then walked the town, which took only a few minutes, three blocks this way and three that. I returned to Slim's, had a plate of liver, and took to that upstairs bed. With food and board, even easy on the beer, I'd spend Ursula's ten dollars in less than two weeks. She'd offered more, but pride had kept me from taking it. I slept restless that night, agitating about the way she had washed and shaved and bedded me. I dreamed of buying new clothes and going back and taking her in my arms again.

The next day, I tried a couple of farms around Lind, but nobody had heard of Early. The next town over was Ritzville, seventeen miles north. I walked half toward it, then caught on a hay wagon the rest. Ritzville was a Volga German town, and I ate a fine plate of sausage and potatoes in a café. I inquired about Early, but the cook there had never heard the name.

At the next table, a man leaned over and asked if I was looking for work.

"Almost always," I said.

He ran a scrap mill on a creek just outside town and had orders for raw boards and firewood. But his hired man had left for the week to bury his father down in Oregon. "It's only five days, but I can give you six dollars," he said.

"And a room?" I asked.

He said there was a wood boiler in the sawmill, and I could sleep there and he would bring me a meal in the morning and one at night. But, he said, if I went near his house or if I went into town to booze it up, I was finished.

Not in top negotiating position, I accepted his offer.

The man's name was Schulte, and he struck me as dour and incurious. His sawmill was little more than a shop with a rusty boiler that powered an old steam drop saw, like something he'd brought with him from the old country.

I tried to engage him in conversation, but he worked quiet. At night in that cold shop, I found myself thinking of you, Rye-boy, and wishing I'd taken that volume of Tolstoy you checked out. It was a thoughtful thing, bringing me that book, and I should've thanked you instead of going off drunk like I did.

On the second day, I asked if Schulte had anything to read in the house. He said they were strict Anabaptists. "Only the Good Book."

"I have never found that to be a particularly good book," I said, and if I've ever gotten a colder response from a joke, I don't recall it.

Three days I sawed and edged and treated boards, split logs and loaded up the wagon, but Schulte insisted on doing the deliveries himself. Each time he set off for town, his admonition about staying away from the house got harsher. If I went near the house, he would have the sheriff run me off the property. If I went near the house, he would get his shotgun and shovel and bury me upstream. If I went near the house— "Yeah, I get it, Schulte," I said.

The fifth or sixth time someone tells you *not* to do something, it becomes the only thing you've ever wanted to do, and when he left in the wagon, I lit a smoke and walked halfway up the drive. I glanced at the simple wood-framed house and wondered what manner of woman he was protecting in there. But something about the gray house felt oppressive, too, and I kept my distance. Finally, on the fourth day, Schulte came back from town and said his hired man had returned early, but as I had done a fine job and minded his admonitions, he would pay me all six dollars. He had one more delivery to make and would take me back to Ritzville on the way.

We loaded the wagon with cut tamarack and butt ends, and I grabbed my bindle and climbed on the seat next to him. We approached the house, and I glanced over without turning my head. Like a lot of lumbermen's houses, his was doomed to go unfinished and unpainted, windows and doors not even properly framed. As we passed, a young woman came onto the back porch, thin and lank-haired and, I assumed, his wife. She was carrying a massive boy child, arms under his butt, his head over her shoulder. The kid was eight or nine, far too old to be carried like a baby. He was in a diaper so big it might have been a tablecloth, and his long legs hung like loose skin. He made a flat sound like a lamb.

"Cornmeal and lard," the woman said simply, and Mr. Schulte said, "Yes, Sarah," and clicked at his team, the horses lurched, and she said, "Goodbye, sir," and I nodded, and then she carried that huge baby back into the house. I felt for Schulte then, and even found myself regretting my joke about his Bible, for I suspected he made good use of that faith.

In town, Schulte stopped his wagon in front of a hotel on Main

Street, took off a glove, and offered me a worn hand. "God bless," he said. "I am going to pray for you, Gregory."

"Thank you," I said, and normally, I would have made some joke, *Ask him for an extra pint*, but I did not. I just watched him ride that loaded wagon through town. A squalling sleet was moving in, so I went inside that Ritzville hotel to bunk up for the night.

I had a meal and two beers and then one more, and the barkeep said they had whiskey downstairs, and who should show up but my old pal Thirst, *Get in here, you son of a bitch*, and he talked me into four of those dirty glasses, and I woke the next day sick and already down half my pay from the Anabaptist lumberman with the giant baby. If I didn't leave Ritzville, I would be busted fast. At the café, another farmhand agreed to run me partway down the Lind road, and I walked the rest, over wet rolling hills, into needles of driving icy rain.

I dropped happily from the upper road down into the draw where that little farm town lay like eggs in a nest. Walked through that brick downtown and stepped happy into Slim's toasty bar and grill. I called out, "Heaven!"

"You again," Slim said. "What happened to you?"

"Worst thing possible," I said, "work." I pulled off my soaked coat, hat, and gloves and laid them next to the boiler, spun another dollar on the bar top, and said, "The usual, Slim."

"Can a man have a usual if it's only his second time in my bar?" He pulled me a glass of Schade.

"Well, as we're about to get engaged, that beer and me, I would say yes."

I sneaked in a cup of bean soup amid two more drafts, and the bar grew more crowded, two hands coming in, and then a couple of old farmers with their sons, younger men debating the upcoming boxing match between Jeffries and the champ Johnson. I was in the mood for a book or at least a smart conversation, but I just nodded in agreement when the more evolved of the boys said the champ was likely to kill Jeffries and that the old alfalfa farmer should've stayed on his farm.

"Not a chance," the other boy said. "Jeffries lost a hundred pounds to come out of retirement and fight for the white race."

"He's come out of retirement to fight for a hundred thousand dollars," said a familiar voice behind me, "that's what he's come back for."

I turned and there was Early Reston in the doorway. He had grown a beard and was wearing a new-looking rain slicker. Otherwise, it was him, that welcome plain stalk of wheat. "Hello, Gig," he said. "I hear you've been looking for me."

We had a drink and a good clap of the shoulders. I told him about the riot, about jail, about Clegg beating us, about the hunger strike by the union leaders.

"That must've taught them quite a lesson," he said, "you fellas starving yourselves that way. Did you think of knocking yourselves in the heads, too?"

"They had that part covered pretty good."

He said he'd gone to Idaho and Montana with my brother and with Gurley Flynn, and I said yes, so I'd heard.

"I gave your union a shot," he said, "but it wasn't for me. Too much traveling preacher in that business, and I'm not sure I believe in Gurley Flynn's religion any more than I believe in the others."

I said, "I've become something of a union agnostic myself."

He considered the whiskey in front of him and then turned to me. "And how are you with an automobile, Gig?"

I told him I'd operated a truck once or twice in log camps and farm jobs. "I'm no mechanic, but I know my way around a wheel."

We paid up, Slim nodding goodbye at Early without ever having said a word to him. My clothes were dry and I settled into my coat, buttoned it to my neck. Outside, the rain had stopped.

Early went straight to a Tin Lizzy parked on the street, the cover and front glass on it.

"This your Ford, Early?"

"For the time being," he said. He climbed inside, set the hand brake, and adjusted the float while I primed and cranked the handle under the grille. The first pull nearly broke my forearm, but then the engine caught.

When I came around, Early was in the passenger seat. "Let's see what kind of driver you make. That's the only opening I got right now."

It took me a moment to reacquaint myself with the instruments. "Switch over the magneto," he said, and I said, "Uh-huh," and tested out the three pedals on the floor, brake on the right, reverse in the middle, and clutch on the left. A hand brake was between my legs, the up-down hand throttle next to the steering wheel.

"Clutch all the way down for first. Up for high, and neutral in the middle."

"How long you had this car?" I asked.

"Just got it," he said.

I lurched it a block but had it smooth by the time we left Lind. I veered us off an old wagon road, northeast toward Spokane. It was icy cold, even with the top and front glass on, and we had to yell over the wind. I worked the accelerator with my hand, got us up to top speed, and it felt good to be gliding at pace, flying under our own power.

On such a black night, the two lamps in front of the car cast an unsettling cockeyed glow, lighting up a tree here, a basalt column there, like we were tunneling into the earth. The two-track road crossed a shallow creek bed, ice crackling under the tires, but the car handled the rough terrain. We shadowed the railroad tracks awhile, driving at an angle below the humped ties. We passed the lights of Ritzville and I thought of old Schulte and his wife and his son just up that creek north of town. I wondered if I could ever manage a life like that—or if it was another jail.

We skirted Sprague Lake and caught a lumber path that spilled us out on the state road. On good gravel, we could hear each other speak.

"You're a natural driver, Gig."

"Thank you." I had to say, I did like piloting that Ford and thought I ought to learn the mechanical side of it. Maybe that would be the job for me—a way to be on the road but not jumping trains or sleeping in fields.

We rattled an hour on that state road, until the lights of Spokane began to show over the horizon. We stopped to refill the tank from a five-gallon can he kept on the floorboard of the backseat.

"You're living in Spokane?" I asked as I poured the gas. "Why the hell did I go all the way to Lind looking for you?"

He said, "Why the hell did you go looking for me?" There was a real question in it, perhaps even some suspicion.

"Well," I said, "I almost died in that jail, or thought I would. Singing and refusing to eat or work. We were doing nothing in there but irritating the cops and their rich bosses. Like flies at a picnic. And lying there, starving, I thought back to the last time I felt anything like a man. And it was that day on the river, when you knocked that cop back and I hit the other man with my shoulder. That was the last time. So I came looking for you."

We climbed back in the Ford and kept on. I could feel him looking over at me. We rounded a corner and came onto the Sunset Hill, overlooking the valley that contained Spokane, all those electric lights and the brick and steel and wood and smoke and, through the center of it all, the deep river gorge.

"You want that feeling again," Early said.

"Christ, Early." I looked over. "You bet I do."

The rest of the drive, he explained what he was doing. He'd put together a small crew, three men. They were making two bombs, to be planted the same day. Meeting up with me and hearing my story had given him a new idea for the targets, he said. He'd been thinking the police chief, Sullivan, "but we'd probably have better luck getting to your friend Sergeant Clegg."

"And the other?"

"Lem Brand."

I thought of what Ursula had told me—and maybe what she hadn't told me—about getting a stake in Brand's hotel. I got a tightness in my chest but said, "Well, I can't think of two men who deserve it more."

We skirted the north end and drove along the ridge below Beacon Hill east of town. There was an outcrop of boulders, an old Indian site where a natural spring burbled up. Early had a place just beyond that. An old spa had burned down there in the '90s, in an area too rocky for grading or farming. That was where he'd been hiding out, in the spa's old outbuildings, not five miles from Mrs. Ricci's place.

He had me pull off the road onto a faint drive, trees on both sides, the car rattling over rocks and dry brush. We drove through a windrow of aspens toward what appeared to be a simple block bunkhouse next to a small shop, smoke curling from a tin chimney, the door propped partly open with a brick. Early had me park the Model T next to the shop, and I killed the motor. We were close to town but separated by a wisp of river and those clusters of boulders.

We climbed out and I could hear the gurgling water beyond the trees. Two men came out of the shop. One had been at the riot in November—a thin Negro who introduced himself as Everett, then shook my hand and said, "I remember you and your brother from the free speech day."

"You get a month for disturbing?" I asked.

Everett nodded. "In the brig at Fort George Wright. Got fired from the hotel where I was working."

The other man, white and thin-lipped with small pinpoint eyes, stuck out his hand and said simply, "Miller." I got a cold chill off of that one.

"Miller I knew from Montana and Colorado," Early said. "He's

a top powder man. Knows his way around a fulminating cap, too."
Before I could say anything, Early patted me on the back. "And this
is Gig, our driver. And a good man to have in a row. Assuming you
can get him to shut up."

I followed the three of them inside the shop. There was a woodstove heating the place and a lantern lighting this front room. But no
bombs. The whole room was covered in pelts—deer and moose and
bear and raccoon and skunk and beaver and some smaller animals
I couldn't name. There must have been a hundred dead animals in
various states, their fur and hide mounted, stacked, tacked to boards,
hung on walls. The tables were covered with knives and pliers and
fleshers and other tools for skinning and tanning and stretching. I
stared into the black eyes of a lynx, stretched flat and mounted on a
board.

Early pushed the wall at the end of the hide room, and a section
opened into a narrow room with no windows. We squeezed in. Everett brought a lantern, and now I could see why they needed a top
powder man. There were loose sticks of dynamite, some cotton balls
and medicine stoppers, and what I recognized as mercury and silver
blasting caps, all spread out on a wooden workbench. Next to it were
two old carpetbag satchels, the kind a salesman might carry.

Early explained that the bombs would be small and portable, each
contained in a satchel, to be delivered to two locations at the same
time—the police station and the Spokane Club. The cases would be
packed with four sticks each, about two pounds, enough to kill but not
so heavy as to raise suspicion, like, say, a twenty-pound case would.
"It needs to feel like someone's work satchel," Early said. Because of
that, they were carving out any extra weight from the cases—metal
frames, hinges, even thinning the leather.

In the tops of the satchels would be loose papers, and beneath,
sticks of dynamite strapped to the bottom of the case with blasting
caps pressed into them, the caps covered with cotton soaked in a cya-
nide of potassium and sugar. A small medicine bottle of sulfuric acid

would be secured above the blasting caps, sealed with a cork. When the valise was opened, a wire attached to the latch would pull the cork out, leaking acid and soaking the cotton, causing the caps to detonate and the dynamite to explode.

"Two pounds won't take down a building," Early said, "but I would not want to be in the room where it's opened."

Early said the packages would be delivered by Everett, who had saved his porter's outfit just for this. They would be left at the police station and the Spokane Club when the recipient wasn't there but was expected soon. We would be well on our way out of town when the valises were opened and then——

"Boom," said Miller.

Early watched me to make sure I was up for it. Was I? He said there was one thing they needed from me. Miller wanted sharp metal to pack around the dynamite, to make the small bombs more lethal.

"We could use nails, of course," Miller said. "But something even lighter would be better. Metal shavings."

"I told them you know someone who works in a machine shop," Early said.

I looked down at my shoes. "I'll take care of it," I said.

I had once tried to get a day job at a tin shop east of downtown, where they did pressing and metal shearing, and that night I took a bucket and walked the hobo highway until I got to their warehouse along the river. They had a slag and scrap pile behind the shop, and I picked through it for the thinnest, lightest pieces. I nicked up my hands pretty good on those sharp metal bits. The thought of those pieces flying around into mens' bodies made me feel sick. But I knew what Early was asking—*someone who works in a machine shop*—and there was no way I was going to let him involve you, Rye.

Miller picked through the bucket and said the pieces were perfect, and he packed them in the sides of the valises, underneath the compartment with the fake paper. He was careful not to get them near the wire or the stopper holding in the acid. "Accidentally cut that stopper and—"

"Boom," said Everett.

Finished, the two valises looked harmless: thin leather upright carpetbags with two straps and a locking latch on top. There was a small key for each.

The plan was simple. Everett would deliver the first satchel to the police department, for Sergeant Hub Clegg. He would deliver the case at eleven, three hours before Clegg's night shift started, and would tell the cop at the desk that it was from one of the saloons where Clegg made his usual pickups.

"And how do we get the other one to Brand?" I asked.

"I had an idea about that," Early said. "I was thinking maybe your friend the lion tamer—"

"No," I said, "no way. I'm not going to involve her. I'll take it myself if I have to, and open it in front of him."

"Okay. That's fine." Early patted me on the arm.

"And it's a cougar," I said.

"We'll come up with something else," Early said.

It was quiet. We sat around drinking and playing cards, and Early came and went a few times in the Ford in the ensuing days. I wasn't sure what we were waiting for or what he was doing on those trips. Miller said he was likely out stealing, that Early was a master thief. Finally, on the last Sunday night, he returned with a bottle of whiskey. "Tomorrow," he said. The verdict was being read in the big IWW case. It would be the perfect day.

He shook our hands and patted us on the shoulders. He gave each man thirty dollars to make his escape.

"Where's this from?" Everett asked, fanning the money.

"You wouldn't believe me if I told you," Early said.

We poured a glass of whiskey and toasted each other, talking about what we'd do next. Early said not to get too specific in sharing our plans, for if one of us was picked up, he didn't want that man to be able to implicate the others.

Everett said he was headed south. "Too cold up here. I'm gonna get me a girl and winter her up." Miller, too, said he would head for warmer parts.

"And what about you?" Everett asked me.

"He's coming with me," Early said. "We're gonna outlaw a little." He winked at me and I thought it sounded fine, the two of us flying around the west in that Ford, the world quivering at our approach.

But that night I couldn't sleep. As a kid, I had thought for a while that I might become an actor, travel the country doing monologues and playing characters. Was that what I was doing now—acting? Playing outlaw? Anarchist? Or was I becoming the real thing, maybe losing my mind like the madman who shot McKinley?

There were satchels with bombs in them. People would be killed. Innocent people, maybe. Clegg and Lem Brand, I bore them as much ill will as one human could bear another, but there was no guarantee someone else wouldn't get hurt, too. Early kept saying this was a message we were delivering, that things were broken, that this was the only way to fix it, that we weren't delivering bombs but ideas.

You're fooling yourself, I thought as I lay there, trying to sleep in the front room of that little blockhouse. *You aren't some actor, some learned man. Some kind of traveling philosopher.*

This is what you are.

My last thoughts before sleep were about you, Rye-boy. I became rather melancholy, worried that I would never see my brother again. And the hardest part was knowing it was the best thing for you.

We rose quietly Monday morning in that little house, everyone alone with his thoughts except Miller, who whistled cheerfully. We all dressed plainly except Everett, who put on his porter outfit.

At nine, Early and I drove Miller to the train station and Everett to a café across the street, where he would eat his breakfast with the first satchel. Everett had just jumped out of the car when Early thought of something and chased him down with some last-minute instructions. He came back to the car. "I forgot to give him the key."

After breakfast, Everett would deliver Clegg's case to the police department, the key sealed in an envelope with Clegg's name on it. The case would hopefully sit under the night sergeant's desk until he started his shift in the afternoon. After Everett had delivered that first case, he would meet Early and me at the county courthouse at eleven-thirty, and we would give him the second case, which he would deliver to Lem Brand at the Spokane Club, where one of the waiters had told Everett that Brand ate lunch every weekday at two p.m.

Everett would then go back to the train station, where Miller would be waiting with a change of clothes and a ticket for him. Everett would change and he and Miller would leave on trains in opposite directions. Early and I would head west in the Ford. If all went well, we'd be long gone by midafternoon, when the cases were opened.

Back at the house, Early grabbed the second satchel and placed it gently in the backseat. I smoked as far from the Ford as I could get, while Early cleared the shop and the bunkhouse of any signs that we had been there. He burned our garbage in the woodstove, and I watched the gray smoke roll out into the sky. It was one of those startlingly clear days for February, cold endless blue.

I filled the Ford's tank with enough gas to get us back to Lind, and filled two more gas cans in case we needed to drive farther. I put our packs in the backseat, between the gas cans and the satchel.

"It'd be a good day to not crash this machine," Early said. I cranked the Lizzy and climbed in. A northeasterly had blown into the valley, and gusts rocked us as I drove toward downtown. "Watch the bumps," Early said, and he checked his pocket watch. Eleven. The first satchel would have just been delivered.

We drove past the train station. If there was any problem, Miller was supposed to be standing outside. But he wasn't there. I drove up

Howard Street, past taverns and theaters, and although it was a quiet morning, it made me think of Ursula and wild old Spokane.

I thought of you, too, Rye-boy, and I wished I'd gone to see you once more, to apologize for the way I was after I got out of jail. These last days, I wanted to say goodbye. You'd be working up at the machine shop all day. Even if the cops figured out I was involved, there'd be no way to tie you to it. And then, when things calmed down, six months, a year from now, maybe I could come back. Maybe Early and I would have outlawed our way to such wealth that I could buy that little orchard behind Mrs. Ricci's house for us. Or hell, maybe I'd buy her whole block.

At Riverside, we turned west, pausing for a horse and carriage. Early tipped his hat to two women waiting on the corner. They smiled and I wished I had a minute to get out of the car and charm them up in my old manner.

"Take Monroe," Early said.

The Monroe Street Bridge was a high steel span on the west side of downtown, crossing the deepest part of the two-hundred-foot gorge, just past the waterfalls. The deck was strung with power lines, and down the center ran two sets of streetcar tracks. It was a swaying, shaking old bridge that the city was planning to replace in the spring with a new concrete span. We rattled across it and landed on the north side of the river, the massive Spokane County Courthouse rising on our left. It looked like a French castle, cream brick, with a dozen spires rising from its red gabled roofs and, in the center, a 120-foot tower with American and state flags on top. It always looked so out of place across from downtown, alone on that north bank like the citadel of some neighboring kingdom.

Early had me cross the railroad tracks and drive past the courthouse once, then around back, while he checked things out. We came up from the south and idled on Madison, a tree-lined road across from the front of the courthouse. I pulled in under a bare maple. I looked around for Everett but didn't see him.

There was a commotion outside: maybe three dozen people milling about, newspaper reporters and photographers, protestors with placards. Must have been why Early chose this place—it was a circus—the end of the trial of Gurley Flynn and Charlie Filigno.

"Give me your hat," Early said, and I swapped my flat cap for his fedora. "Keep the car running. I'll be right back."

"You think something happened to Everett?" I asked.

"No," Early said. "Change of plans."

"What are you talking about," I said. "Who is—"

And then I saw you.

You were thirty yards off, standing away from that clutch of people beneath a maple tree. You were wearing a fancy suit, gray-blue, with shiny new shoes, a vest, and a necktie looped into a perfect knot. Who taught you to knot that necktie without me there to do it? You shifted your weight and I could see it then, my God, you just wanted to belong.

You looked like a man dressed for a fancy club—

"No," I said to Early, who was reaching around the backseat for the second satchel. "Not Rye."

"Gig, he'll be fine," Early said. "It's the only way."

"Jesus, Early, no."

"He *wants* to do this, Gig."

"No."

"He's the one who can get close to Brand. It's gotta be him, Gig."

"How can he get close to Brand?"

He looked over at me. "Jesus, think for just a second, Gig. How is it you got out of jail? When the rest of that crew was getting six months, how did you get out in only a month?"

"I wasn't an elected official—"

"Come on! Rye did that! He's been Brand's guy on the inside from the beginning. Him and Ursula."

I closed my eyes. *It's never the whole truth. But it's enough.*

"And now he wants to make up for it," Early said. "He's carrying five thousand dollars from Brand. We take that and he takes this satchel to Brand. He'll be long gone by the time Brand opens it."

I looked up at you, Rye-boy, in your fancy suit. And you saw me.

"Five thousand," Early said. "Think of what we can do with that." And then he reached into the backseat for the satchel again.

34

On Sunday, the day before Gurley's verdict, and the day before he was to meet Early at the courthouse, Rye took a streetcar up the South Hill, walked six blocks, and stood shivering at Lem Brand's gate, on the street below Alhambra. A young man stepped out of the gatehouse. He asked Rye to wait, and a minute later, Willard came down the driveway in his Ford. He gestured and Rye got in.

"Mr. Brand's out of town," Willard said.

Rye delivered Early's message: "He wants five thousand, and for that, he says he'll give Mr. Brand the evidence of their deal and disappear forever."

Willard wrote in a small notebook as he said, "What evidence?"

"He didn't say."

"Five thousand?"

"Yes. Delivered to me Monday morning. And then I give it to him."

Willard wrote all of this down. Then he sent Rye back to the gatehouse and drove back to the main house. Rye stood with the guard, who kept blowing on his hands, even though he wore gloves. "Do you like your job?" Rye asked.

"Are you kidding?" the man asked.

Willard came back down the drive ten minutes later. Rye got in the car again.

"Okay," Willard said. "I bring you the money Monday, and you give me whatever papers and evidence Reston has regarding his deal with Mr. Brand?"

"He wants the money first," Rye said. "Then he gives me the evidence. And I bring that to Mr. Brand at the Spokane Club in the afternoon."

Willard wrote all of this down. "Where are you meeting Reston?" he asked without looking up.

"I'm not supposed to say," Rye said. "I'm supposed to tell you that if you follow me, the deal is off."

Willard wrote this down. "And what assurance does Mr. Brand have?"

"I don't know what that means."

"How do we know this is the end of it," Willard said, "that Reston won't keep coming after him?"

"I don't know," Rye said.

Willard wrote this down. He looked over his notes. "Okay," he said, "give me a minute." Rye got out and Willard drove to the house again while Rye stood with the guard in the small guardhouse, just a few feet from each other.

"You got a job?" the guard asked Rye.

"I work in a machine shop," Rye said.

"You like it?"

"Yeah."

The guard said, "Huh," as if he'd taken some wrong turn in life.

"Can I ask you something?" Rye asked. "Is Mr. Brand really out of town?"

The guard glanced at the house, then back at Rye. He shrugged with one shoulder.

A minute later, Willard drove back down to the guardhouse. "Get in."

Rye did and Willard drove him back down the South Hill, through downtown, over the river, toward Mrs. Ricci's house. "I'll bring you the money at eight o'clock tomorrow morning," he said. "Mr. Brand wants you to tell Reston that the only reason he's agreed to this was that unfortunate business with Del Dalveaux. This closes the books between them forever. If, for some reason, Reston resurfaces, or tells anyone that Mr. Brand hired him, Mr. Brand will spend the rest of his fortune hunting him down and killing him and his compatriots."

He cleared his throat. "And Mr. Brand wants you to know that we'll start with you."

"I'm not—" Rye started to say.

But Willard held up his hand, as if embarrassed to have delivered such a threat. "Don't worry about it, it's just what people say."

Rye looked out the window at the deep sky, thinking of Prince Andrey lying wounded in the battle of Austerlitz, believing he was dying, realizing too late his own insignificance, the emptiness of valor and honor, the finality of death.

They drove in silence for a few blocks. Willard parked in front of Mrs. Ricci's house. He offered his hand and Rye shook it.

"After this, tell Mr. Brand it's over. I really am done."

"Sure thing, kid," Willard said.

35

Rye had beef and cabbage with Mrs. Ricci and a new short-term boarder she had taken in, a thin Canadian salesman with a long, open face. "What line are you in, Mr. Dolan?" the Canadian asked.

"Machinery," Rye said.

"There's the future," the man said. "Machines will do it all one day." He held up a bite of beef. "A machine will raise the cow and a machine will kill it and another will cook this steak and another will serve it to you. A machine will chew it up and take out the gristle and dribble it down your throat like a baby bird. Another machine will digest it for you. I'll be gone, and you, too, my young friend. We will be on an assembly line, and then we will be part of the assembly line, and eventually, there will just be a machine."

Rye wasn't sure what to say.

"Sta' zitto," Mrs. Ricci said.

"Exactly," said the Canadian man.

After dinner, Rye sat by the fire and read a chapter of War and Peace.

"What are you reading?" the Canadian asked, but when Rye held up the book, the man gave no reaction and went back to his newspaper. Rye had trouble concentrating on the book, and he went to bed early. He fell asleep right away but woke well before dawn and lay in bed waiting for morning.

With the sun just beginning to spill across the horizon, Rye rose and went to the outhouse. He cleaned and powdered himself, wet down his hair. He began to get dressed in his new suit. It was winter. Was he supposed to wear his long johns with a suit? He worried they would be too bunchy under his pants, so he put on summer undershorts instead. Then he put on the smooth suit pants, running his hand down the crease in the center. He put on the stiff white collared shirt, braces, the vest, the thin new socks, and the shiny calfskin shoes. He laced and knotted the shoes tight around his feet. He put on his coat. And his bowler. And finally, he grabbed the necktie. Chester the clothier had given him a quick lesson on knotting it, but that had been in front of a mirror, and he couldn't remember the steps. And there was no mirror in Mrs. Ricci's house. He felt a moment of panic. He could never loop this tie without a mirror. And anyway, what even was the point of having such clothes if he couldn't see himself in them?

Mrs. Ricci was making breakfast for the Canadian salesman when Rye came out of his bedroom. "Sharp suit," the Canadian said. "Single-breasted vest, elegant cut, fine, fine, where'd you get it, the Crescent?"

"Burks and Feyn," Rye said. "Downtown?"

"That's a thirty-dollar suit if I've ever seen one, nice, nice, very nice."

Rye's face was burning. He could ask the Canadian for help with the tie, but the man bothered him. Maybe Mrs. Ricci had helped her sons knot neckties. But she just stared at him, spatula in hand, bacon grease popping behind her.

"I can't eat this morning, Mrs. Ricci," Rye said, "no *mangia*," and he went into the front room, peeked through the curtains, and saw, at the curb, Willard's Model T idling in front of the house.

Rye unlocked the front door and walked out, went down the walk. He knocked on the passenger door and startled Willard again.

"You can't keep doing that," Willard said. He ran his hand along the right side of his face. "Glaucoma. No peripheral vision."

"How was I supposed to know that?" Rye asked.

Willard looked Rye up and down. "Christ. What happened to you?"

"Gurley's verdict is today. I want to look nice."

"Well," Willard said, "you do."

Rye held out the necktie. "Do you have any idea—"

"Sure. Get in." Willard had Rye sit in the passenger seat and face away, toward the house. "Double Windsor?"

"Whatever it's supposed to be," Rye said, embarrassed that he'd bought clothes that he couldn't even operate.

Willard lifted Rye's collar and draped the tie over his neck. He lowered the collar and narrated as he looped it. "Okay. This is simple." He put his hands over Rye's, and they did it together. "Over the top, around, over, through the loop, around again, and once more through the hole. Then pull tight. Adjust. There you go."

He patted Rye's shoulder and sat back in his seat. Rye settled in and Willard handed him a fat envelope. "You want to count it?"

"Not really."

"Good. Put it in your inside pocket."

Rye did.

"I'm going to be at the courthouse, watching."

"No, Willard, he said nobody—" Rye began.

"I know what he said. You won't know I'm there, and neither will he."

Rye felt less than confident.

"I'm not doing this for Brand," Willard said. "He doesn't even know. He's scared stupid of this Early Reston, or Ennis Cooper, or whoever he is. Thinks he's a ghost. But I know he's not. I worked with sons of bitches like this. He's no anarchist, no ghost. He's not even a detective. He's just a thief and a murderer."

"A murderer?" Rye felt a chill.

"He's killed at least two men, easy as swatting flies."

"Who?"

"Doesn't matter," Willard said. "But I want you to know, I'll be watching in case something happens."

"But what if it's in your peripheral vision?" Rye asked.

Willard sat for a moment before a corner of his mouth went up and he made a noise—"Hmm"—that Rye realized was the closest he had to a laugh. The big man patted Rye on the lapel of his jacket. "You look good, kid. A real gentleman."

36

Willard dropped Rye off two blocks from the county courthouse. It was a cool, clear day, wind agitating a row of young maples lining Broadway in front of the courthouse, which sat on a knoll across the railroad tracks, above the river gorge.

Outside, people were milling about, Wobbly organizers from Idaho and Seattle, tramps from all over, cops, men in work clothes, goateed socialists, newspapermen in fedoras, women from church and temperance societies, lawyers in worn workaday suits with winter rubbers pulled over their shoes. Rye looked down at his own shoes, so shiny they seemed to be lit from within. Rye was the only one here who had come dressed for a *soiree*.

He felt so foolish. What had he expected? Some kind of pageantry? He blamed Anna Pavlovna, Prince Andrey, the Rostovs. Now here he was, dressed in fancy new evening wear, with five thousand dollars in his breast pocket—what had Early said, *Who are you?* It was a fair question. He wondered what Gig would think of him now.

He looked for Willard in the crowd, or his Model T on the street, but didn't see either. He followed some lawyers up the wide courthouse steps. His whole idea had been to come see Gurley on the day of her verdict, but this was all so much more elaborate than he'd imagined, like some kind of production he was attending, like Ursula the Great at the Comique. But if that was the case, who was the cougar?

Up the stairs and inside the courthouse, a uniformed cop was stopping everyone. He asked if Rye had credentials, and Rye said, "For what?" and the cop sent him down the hallway to stand with other hangers-on. Apparently, every seat in the courtroom had long ago been assigned. Rye had imagined this would be like his own courtroom appearance, with just a few onlookers, Mr. Moore, and the prosecutor, Fred Pugh. But the whole building was packed, corridors full of newspaper reporters and lawyers, unionists and curious people from all over the country. Rye found himself pushed to the end of a hallway with a group of lawyers around a spittoon, none of them with decent aim. A splatter of tobacco juice crossed the bow of one of Rye's new shoes, and he dropped to wipe it away with his bare hand.

These lawyers were a scraggly bunch, reminding him of a pack of tramps around a cook fire. They were debating how badly the union was going to lose—six-month to one-year sentences the consensus, although a lawyer with a massive boiler of a gut said Pugh planned to argue that these were the masterminds of all the trouble and to seek exceptional sentences of five years. "The judge would have them drawn and quartered if the prosecutor could find a precedent," he said.

One of the lawyers said that Gurley Flynn had succeeded in distracting from the state's case, but the heavy lawyer leaned in and confided that it didn't matter because Pugh's own neighbor was the jury foreman "and he's got no sympathy for unions, bums, foreigners, or wives who run out on husbands." Another lawyer said Gurley had so angered the judge that the jury's instructions had basically been about how far they could go in sentencing. The third lawyer pointed out that Pugh had won every case against the IWW this year and wasn't likely to lose the biggest yet.

All of this angered Rye, and he had the urge to tell the spitting lawyers that Pugh hadn't won them *all*, that Fred Moore had gotten at least one Wobbly out of jail, but he kept his tongue.

People moved in and out of the hall, but the cops wouldn't let anyone go upstairs. They stood for over an hour, and then a commotion arose, people yelling from the floor above, newspapermen like birds startled off a wire. *"A shocker!"* someone yelled, although Rye couldn't tell which way, someone yelling, *"Guilty!"* and someone else yelling, *"Acquitted!"* He tried to get closer but was pushed even farther back as the hall was filled by more reporters and onlookers, a sea of fedoras, and a cheer went up and then there was some angry yelling, and Rye might not have known what was happening except a newspaperman turned and yelled right into his face, "Filigno's guilty, Gurley Flynn's let go!"

Rye was pushed against the wall and he saw the prosecutor, Pugh, come down the staircase, red-faced and furious, chasing after a man in a gray suit. "You let the worst of them go free!" On the steps, a man who was apparently a juror turned to the prosecutor. "Aw, she ain't a criminal, Fred. You want us to send some pretty Irish girl to jail for being bighearted and idealistic?"

There was more yelling, people pushing, and someone stomped on Rye's new shoes, scuffing them. He stood at the end of the first-floor hallway for another half hour, with the lawyers chattering about this great upset—a defeat for the city, shame for the mayor and Police Chief Sullivan, who now could not ignore Gurley Flynn's allegations about the jail.

Then, from down the hall, Rye saw Fred Moore descend the stairs, his arm around Gurley, who looked angry, nothing like a person who had just been acquitted. Rye was surprised at both how pregnant she was—her belly well out in front—and how small she seemed in the crowd around her. She was yelling back up the stairs to a scrum of reporters following her. "We should have both been convicted or both cleared!" She vowed to appeal, and at Rye's end of the hall, the spittoon lawyers began debating whether a defendant could actually appeal her own acquittal.

"I don't think that's even possible," one of them said.

"We are not done fighting for justice here!" Gurley yelled. "Nor am I done exposing the venal corruption of the police and prosecutors, and the millionaire mining concerns that own them!" At that, Mr. Moore pulled Gurley by the arm, and the whole spectacle moved down the steps and spilled out the doors.

Rye tried to follow, but people coming down the staircase kept pushing him farther away from Gurley and his old lawyer. He'd hoped to see her, to talk to her, to say, to say—

To say what?

In the commotion, his own thoughts froze him: *What were you hoping to say?* Rye stood stone-still in the swirling crowd. He had created a whole fantasy in his mind—her seeing him dressed like this, thanking him for delivering her story to the *Agitator,* for saving the movement. She would no longer see him as a mole and a traitor, a desperate, unsophisticated orphan bum, but as a *man* who had done the right thing.

And how far did this fantasy go? That she would no longer be married and pregnant? That Lem Brand wouldn't still be rich, that Charlie Filigno wouldn't be going to prison, that the speaking ban wasn't still in effect and the IWW still banned? That his brother wasn't off somewhere being a drunk? That Early Reston wasn't out there waiting for him? He'd read in the newspaper that since the free speech riots, the number of job agencies had actually grown, from thirty to forty. What good were they doing out here, any of them? Even her?

He thought of Count Tolstoy's book and how, after the horrific, bloody battle of Borodino, the war just seemed to peter out, ending not in bravery but in retreat—exhaustion and the change of seasons having as much to do with the final Russian victory as any decisive action. Was that just the way of things? Rye found himself wishing he could talk to Gig about it.

But then he remembered: Gig hadn't read that far into *War and Peace.* Only he had done that.

He felt disoriented as he stepped out into the brisk February air, the sky above him chalky blue, the wind shaking the bare tree limbs. From the top of the stairs, he could see Gurley down at the curb, surrounded by reporters and well-wishers, people calling, *"Gurley!"* And a few others calling, *"Whore!"*—a blur of faces and voices and the trees shaking and then she was eased into a long automobile by good Fred Moore, the lawyer calming the crowd: "That's enough! No more questions!"

But right before she slid into the car, Gurley happened to glance up, and she must've seen Rye on the courthouse steps, because she smiled just a little and raised her hand to wave—

Or did she?

He could never be sure, because then Fred Moore climbed in the car and it pulled away, stopped for a man crossing the street, and sped off.

Standing there, alone on the courthouse steps, Rye thought that history was like a parade. When you were inside it, nothing else mattered. You could hardly believe the noise—the marching and juggling and playing of horns. But most people were not in the parade. They experienced it from the sidewalk, from the street, watched it pass, and when it was on to the next place, they had nothing to do but go back to their quiet lives.

On the wide marble steps, someone bumped Rye and he moved down the staircase to the sidewalk. On the lawn in front of the courthouse, the crowd lingered, argued, made cases to people who couldn't hear a word the other side said. Rye looked east to the big clock tower above the train depot. It was eleven-twenty, ten minutes before he was to meet Early Reston and give him the money in his coat.

Newsboys were already selling *extra* one-sheets from the *Chronicle*, and Rye bought one for a nickel, amazed at the speed of news nowadays. The verdict had been less than an hour ago, and here he was, holding a story about it in his hands. He walked away from the courthouse with the paper, leaned against a tree, and read the

coverage of his friend's trial. There were three big headlines: IWW
GETS DOUBLE DEFEAT! and IRISH REBEL GIRL CUT LOOSE! and ITALIAN
AGITATOR TO PRISON!

"The IWW has this day been twice defeated," the writer opined.
"By the conviction of the violent labor leader Mr. Filigno, the power
of the law and the action of civil authorities is upheld. By the acquittal of pitiable Mrs. Jones, the organization loses its most delightful
chance to coax money and sympathy from people in remote parts of
the nation."

But it was the last line of the story that Rye knew would infu-
riate Gurley, and which made him go red with anger, too. "May it
be hoped that Mr. Jones now will come from Montana and take his
wife back to enjoy the beautiful home life which it should be every
American woman's privilege to enjoy."

Rye looked around. The crowd was still here on the lawn in front
of the courthouse steps. He thought about that line—*the beautiful
home life which it should be every American woman's privilege to enjoy.*
He thought of his mother, of Mrs. Ricci, of Ursula the Great. Then
he turned to the back page of the special edition. It was filled with
advertisements. So many companies had wanted to be part of this.
Soap and pocket watches and corsets and combs and potatoes and
writing desks and fine linens and *Remnants! Remnants! Remnants!* and
one particular ad that caught his attention and seemed somehow as
important as the news story on the other side: "SKILLED DENTISTS,
CROWNS, PLATES, AND BRIDGEWORK, $5 EACH, EXTRACTION, 50 CENTS."

So, it was ten times harder and more expensive to fix things than
it was to extract them, to just take them out—this seemed like some
philosophical truth that even Count Tolstoy would have to admit.

Rye folded up the newspaper, put it under his arm, and looked up.

A Model T was idling on the street across from him. Early Reston
was in the passenger seat. And his brother was on the driver's side.
Rye's first thought: *When did he learn to drive a car?*

"Gig?" He took a step toward the Model T.

But the car lurched out of its parking spot into the street. It turned a tight circle, then slowed for a moment, the passenger door flew open, but no one got out, and the car sped up, veering away from Rye and the courthouse. It looked like Gig and Early were fighting inside the cab.

The car swerved wildly as it sped away from Rye. It barely missed hitting a light pole, then a buggy, and then the car veered straight down Madison Street, the open passenger door flapping like a broken wing, back toward the web of railroad tracks, and just beyond them, the river gorge.

Gig, 1910

HE REACHED back for the satchel and I popped the hand brake, yelled, "No!" and jacked the throttle. The car jumped and Early fell back in his seat. He looked over at me with a half-smile. "And what do you think you're doing?"

"Not Rye!"

He smiled wider and reached for his door handle, but I cranked the steering wheel to the right and he fell against me. I spun the car in a circle away from the courthouse. I was unsure where I was going—just going.

I'd always been going. Since I left Whitehall, maybe since birth. Always running. But in that instant I saw my brother in his new baggy suit—*my God, the kid just wants to* be *somewhere*—I was felled by regret and wonder—*where was I going all those years? why couldn't I just be still?*

"Come on now, Gig," said Early.

And I said again, "No. Not Rye."

He made a quick thrust with his left hand, and I felt a tightness in my chest and let go of the throttle—my God, he'd put a blade in me, in my rib cage, the snake was murdering me—he was a goddamn murderer—and I wondered if I'd always known what kind of man this was.

We were barely moving now, listing like a boat in chop. He grabbed the satchel and reached for his door again, but I knew something else: that even with his knife in my side, and after a month in jail, I was still stronger than he was, and as he opened his door, I reached over with my right arm and pulled him into a headlock. I held his neck as tight as I've ever held anything, cranked my arm like I owned his skull, his hat tumbling to the floor of the car as I held his face just below the knife handle, and then he swung at me—but with his head down, he had no angle and couldn't get anything behind it. I squeezed his treacherous neck as if juice might come out.

With my knee, I kicked the throttle lever up and the car began moving faster, Early squirming and fighting with me, and I sensed in him a shift as he realized how hard I would go to keep him away from my brother.

We ripped down Madison, struggling and squirming in the cab, the car veering and shaking, him grunting and choking and slapping at my legs, my face, anything—still no force behind his blows. I let go of the wheel with my left hand to give him a quick pop to the nose and then grabbed the wheel again.

He pawed at the knife, maybe to stab me once more, but I had his neck so tight he could do nothing but kick wildly, one leg out the flapping door, the other forward into the windshield, which cracked and buckled, and now he was crazed, like a dying animal, like anything dying, I guess, and still I squeezed that goddamn neck, choking him, and me, too, choking on the pain in my chest, so sharp now that I cried out, and he cried out, a hacking, bleating sound as we bounced over the first set of tracks—

We rattled over the second set and I hit the roof of the car, and we bounded over the third, then down a small embankment into a field and I slammed against the wheel but I held his neck as we tumbled downhill through weeds and rocks, shaking and falling until we were at the edge of the canyon and that was when I let go of the murderous son of a bitch and he sprang up like a jack-in-the-box, squealed in terror as I yelled in triumph, because for just a moment, Rye, we goddamn flew—

37

Rye was aware of sounds as he ran, his own breathing and crying, the clap of his new shoes on the street, people yelling, crashing metal, then a thunderous *boom!* and still he ran, down Madison Street toward the river gorge, over the railroad tracks, and down an embankment as black smoke began to waft up, and finally, he reached the gorge and peered over the edge.

He'd watched the car speed away, down Madison Street, past buildings, swerving and jerking, the passenger door flapping, and then it had crossed the tracks and then it was just gone.

And now he was looking down at what appeared to be the back half of a Model T, burning on a ledge on the steep hillside forty feet below. The front half of the car had been sheared off or blasted away and had cartwheeled over the gorge, another two hundred feet into the river. Smoking pieces of debris littered the banks and floated in the water, moving slowly downstream toward Peaceful Valley.

Rye stood panting at the edge of the canyon. He looked around. People were rushing to both sides of the gorge. On the bridge, a streetcar had stopped, and passengers were running to the railing to look over the side.

"Did you see that?" a man asked him.

Rye slumped over, his hands on his knees. He vomited in the grass.

Then he slid over the edge and began picking his way down the canyon wall to the burning wreckage, using his hands to hold on to grass and rocks. The hillside was steep, though, the footing loose, and he slipped and tumbled before catching himself on a tree root. He slid on his belly toward the burning car. "Gig!"

He reached the small ledge that had caught part of the car, and

Rye stood shielding his face from the smoke. He was staring at the smoldering rear end of a Model T, the torn backseat, two back fenders, one broken wheel, and the twisted frame of the top. The rest of the car had been shorn completely off and tumbled down the canyon or blasted into the river.

Down there, he could see part of a tire, floating around the bend, toward Peaceful Valley, where they had all met.

"Ryan!"

He looked up. A big man was sliding down the ledge toward him. He braced himself against the canyon wall, leaned over, and offered Rye a hand up.

"Come on," Willard said. "We gotta get you out of here."

Sullivan, 1911

THE POLITICIANS are what I hate, them and the newspapermen. In fact, I maybe hate the newspapermen worse than the politicians, and both I hate worse than the vagrants, which I spent a life knocking around. At least a vagrant has the decency to shit on your lawn because he needs to, not like politicians and newspapermen, who shit on your lawn to make a point.

They come at me all at once that winter, all the lawn shitters in the world. All that fall, I had beat back the Wobblies, five hundred I'd knocked and thrown in jail, and I'd have made room for another thousand if that labor tart Gurley Flynn brung them. I'd make room for every Slav bum and socialist Jew and old Indian who raised a stink in my streets, streets I was paid to protect.

But then Gurley Flynn spends one night in the women's jail and makes a terrible fuss of it, and the church and women's groups huff and protest, and every paper from here to Boston prints this story that we're running a brothel down there, and Christ, no one wants to protect women more than me, that's why I don't allow them to work in the jail, but they twist it around like I'm Chief Pimp, protecting cops. And do my boys make an occasional play for themselves? Sure, some of them are in on the dip. The city council knew it because their pockets were being lined by the same men who owned the cribs and brothels, the same men who owned the mines, the same men who paid my cops so their birdhouses could run straight.

But to put this scandal on me? Me, who was never in on it? Me, who if I had a dollar for every girl who come at me over the years, every dove tried to get off an arrest by opening her legs, I wouldn't need a pension. Me, who never touched a one. But after Gurley Flynn writes this about the women's jail, the mayor says, John, we need to do something about this.

Point being I should have never taken the job, I said to Annie in our living room in the flats near the courthouse, and pretty soon, every time I said that she took to patting my arm and saying, I know, John. Especially since I never even *got* the job I shouldn't of taken! *Acting* police chief!

And that whole winter of 1910, it's one buggering thing after another for the acting chief. First they acquit Gurley Flynn! Acquit her! When the judge should turn her over his knee and throw her in jail until she bleeds gray.

Again the mayor calls me in. John, with her acquitted, we can't ignore this women's jail thing anymore. And I say, Who's ignoring it, Nellie? Not me. I got a hole the size of a fist in me guts over it. And then a patrolman sticks his head in the mayor's office and says, Chief. You'll never guess what happened.

Not two hours after the verdict, a Ford Model T has taken flight right into the river gorge. The mayor and I run outside and peer over the edge, and I will be damned, but there is the butt end of a car burning on the hillside across the gorge. My cop tells me the gas tank must have blown, for the front half of the car was shot off and down the canyon into the river.

Drunks, I assume, or the shite kids who steal automobiles, and if there is any justice, it's there smoldering on the hillside.

But the day's not even done, for one of my detectives finds a bomb in a satchel left outside the station. It's sealed in a carpetbag, left suspicious right at the door, like maybe the bomber lost his nerve and ran off, says this detective, a good man named Hage, poor Waterbury's old pal, and Hage says that when he saw the satchel, he thought it odd on the day of the verdict in the big union case. So rather than open it at the top, which might be wired, he cut into the leather on the side. And what did he find?

Dynamite. Hage asks me if I think it's connected to that car in the river.

Christ, I say, do you think it is? I hadn't thought of it.

And I really wish I was smarter, because there's nothing in the bomb to tell us. Just dynamite and a cap stolen from a mine in Montana, and some metal scraps taken from a tin shop, but that's it. Cold after that.

Until a few weeks later, when a note comes for me. Unsigned. Typed.

The note says, What if a certain prominent mining man in town hired someone to get inside the union, to put them at odds with the police? How far do you think that inside man would go? Would he try to bomb the police station? Would he have another bomb that might blow up a car in the river? Would he even shoot a cop investigating a burglary?

And that's it. The whole note.

God, I wish I was a smarter man, I tell Annie that night.

Why, she asks.

Well for one, I say, to shut up those newspapermen coming at me every day, especially those pot-stirrers at the *Press* who mock my brogue, *Nat on your loife*, they quote me saying, like I'm just off the boat, and who wrote that I run *the rottenest police system in the nation* and must be removed and the whole department reorganized.

You are smart, John, Annie tells me.

But I'm not. And the worst is that I know I'm not. I've got a car in the river and a bomb outside the police station, both on the day of the unionists' trial, and a note saying it's maybe connected to poor Waterbury's death, and I can't figure any of it, Annie.

And she says, Maybe there's nothing to figure, John.

And I say, See, even you're smarter than me.

But here is something I do know. I know when a man's support and protection have given out on him.

For soon, with Gurley Flynn's release and the bad publicity and the prospect of another riot and spring coming and those mining and timber men wanting their floating workers back, the city council surrenders to the IWW and sets all the prisoners free. A commission shuts down the worst job sharks and lets the Wobblies operate again, practically gives them the key to the city.

All because of this women's jail business. And they blame me for it and threaten to charge me with misconduct. Charge a man what gives his life to be a policeman in your town and been doing it since the Great Fire? Charge the last man standing from that class of twelve cops back in '89, a man only wants to keep your streets safe, and you charge *that man* with misconduct?

I had already agreed to hire a policewoman to shut the noise, but I put her on dance halls and parks and theaters, stuff for a proper woman, and then the mayor says, That's not the point, John, the city has taken a beating and we want her in the jail and paid the same as a man, and I said, Nellie, that's where I draw the line, for no one loves a woman more than me, but I'm not going to pay her to pick daisies for the same wage I pay a man who puts his life on the line.

And all this time, the preachers and ladies' clubbers are coming at me in the newspaper: Clean up the city, clean up the city.

What do they think I done my entire life, but I give in on that, too, and I send out my cops to arrest every working girl in town, and rid the streets of vagrants and faro boys and opium dens, and we fill the jail again, just like we did with the unionists, we shut down the brothels and nail up the cribs.

Oh, but I know whose pockets I'm into now.

And I know what it means for me.

So I have no cover at all when this Rose Elliott case comes—a teenage girl raised by this Civil War veteran J. H. Elliott, and he files a complaint that two of my officers, a kid named Hood and that old wart Clegg have had relations with young Rose and took her to get an operation. But when we interview the girl Rose, she says that the stepfather, J.H., is the one had relations, and that he is the father of her six-year-old son which everyone thinks is her little brother. But then Rose changes her tune, says maybe Clegg did what her stepfather did, too, and she names the woman who gave her an operation, an old dove of Clegg's, so I fire Clegg, and still the *Press* hounds me and mocks my speech—*I have nothin' t'say to ye, fer I dasn't believe ye'd print th' trouth*—and that's when the city council officially charges me with misconduct.

I'm done now. I come home to Annie and say, I should never have taken this job, and she says, I know, John, and I say, I'm not what they say, am I?

No, she says, you're not, John. You're a good man, truly.

I wonder, am I, though? And I don't drink, but one night I feel drunk as I leave the house and I walk downtown and past the Spokane Club, and I see the warm lights in there and something breaks in me. I go straight into that rich dining room, four fat millionaires sitting around drinking brandy in front of a roaring fire, and I grab that pork chop Lem Brand and pull him out of the dining room and into the street, and I only mean to question him about the note I got, or to scare him, but Brand is saying, What is the meaning . . . and I will have you brought up . . . and do you know who I am?

Yeah, I say, I got a pretty good idea who you are, and though I just mean to scare the man, instead I give him two hard Irish hammers to his fat face, like I'd have done a bum back in the old days, and he crumbles and I get down in the blood and I say I wish I was a smarter man, Brand, but all I got is these, and I give him another right to remember me, leave him whimpering in the street, and walk home to Annie.

That's it, I tell her, I'm done. I'm not going to be chief, I tell her, and she says, That's fine, John, and the next day, I resign. Go back to being a captain.

I tell the papers I did nothing but stand up straight while others were blowing in the wind, but when the weak look for someone to blame, it'll be the man standing up.

We always lived in the flats north of the river, for even on a chief's salary, the South Hill was beyond us, and I should offer that as proof of my honest heart, for did a policeman ever take a bribe, sure, but as God is my witness, one cop who never took a dime of that city's whore money was me—and look, I'll not ask for credit for doing my job without being shite, but sometimes an honest man has the hardest go of it, especially if he's not perfect, or smart, and God knows I am neither.

I said so to Annie as she left our house to go to the theater, but she said again, You're a good man, John, and I sat in my rocking chair facing the fireplace in our little house, hoping it was true. And that's when the window behind me cracked like a bird hit it and I tried to get up to check, but I had been stung in the back and my chest went tight like five hundred pounds was on me and my first thought was what poor man on this earth gets shot twice?

The bullet had come out my chest and was in my lap. They shot *me?* Christ. Through the back and out the chest, a rifle shot by the hole in the glass and the slug in my lap, and I tried again to get out of the chair to go beat the man to death with his own rifle, but I was going nowhere and they shot *me?*

I carefully set the bullet on the table. Evidence.

I would die if I didn't move, so I forced myself up, stumbled to the telephone, and remembered that two days earlier our line had been cut, but it was fixed now, for it was department policy no captain be without a phone, and the operator came on and I said, Police desk, and Ed Pearson was the sergeant, and I said, Send a wagon, and Ed said where to and I said 1318 West Sinto and Ed said that's your house, John, and I said I know it's my house, Ed, it's where they shot me. And then I asked him to call the theater and tell Annie to meet me at Sacred Heart.

Then I hung up and waited. I turned to the window but it was black outside. Could of been anyone shot me, I had no shortage of enemies, anarchists, unionists, thieves, pimps, Black Hand or Tong, even a cop or two, could have been about Rose Elliott or that fat pork chop Brand. And it didn't matter except I wanted to see the man. Look in the eyes of who done this to my family.

I'm here! I called through the cowardly little hole in my window. Come inside and meet your maker!

But I could tell by my breathing that it was me headed to such a meeting and not him. And I did not want to face God with hatred on my heart, so I forgave my enemies, the thieves, vagrants, and unionists. But I did not forgive the politicians and newspapermen, because they are beneath forgiveness. Lastly, I forgave the man who shot me, and prayed for his soul and mine, sorry we'd been born into such a place.

"It's okay," I said to Annie when she came weeping into my room at the hospital, and to little Kathleen and baby John, too, "It's okay," I said, and with that, my shift was done.

EPILOGUE

Life did not stop, and one had to live.

—Tolstoy, *War and Peace*

Rye, 1964

TIME AND patience are the strongest of all warriors.

Tolstoy wrote that. I used to say it to my boys to get them to do their schoolwork and to practice baseball. I think they thought I made it up, and I never told them otherwise, not because I wanted them to think I'm smarter than I am, but because they wouldn't have known Count Tolstoy from Count Dracula.

My daughter, Betsy, she's the one who got my love of books. She's a high school English teacher and would've seen right through me stealing from Tolstoy. In fact, she keeps trying to convince me that *Anna Karenina* is superior to *War and Peace*, which she calls "needlessly unwieldy." Why does it make a father so proud to hear a phrase like that? The mysteries of parenting.

Bets never needed a saying like *Time and patience* because she drew on her own deep well of ambition. Born deaf in one ear, she got all A's through high school and put herself through teacher's college. She still works as hard as anyone I've ever met—she's a back, as we would've said—even with two little ones at home and a lazy, bottle-tipping husband. She probably would've been the best ballplayer in the family, too, if they'd let her play.

My youngest, Calvin, might have grown into a reader, too, but he died before turning twenty, in the Pacific, at the Battle of Leyte Gulf in 1944, when his light carrier, the USS *Princeton*, was bombed by a Japanese warplane. I don't think he'd ever even shaved before he drowned.

Of the 1,469 men on board the *Princeton*, 108 were killed and the rest rescued, so I guess you could say Calvin was unlucky. But I'm not convinced luck has much to do with war or with life. Two of my three sons fought in the Pacific. One returned and one did not. Does that make me lucky or unlucky?

I will turn seventy-two in a few weeks. I've been having dizzy spells and find myself breathless after walks, or a flight of stairs. My doctor says my heart is giving out, and that I am at the end of things. He has given me nitroglycerin pills to put under my tongue and keeps using phrases like "affairs in order."

But if this is to be my last year, I wouldn't mind it too much. Other than losing my brother in 1910 and my son twenty years ago, I'd have no complaints. I was an orphan and a tramp who made a home here in Spokane. In 1916, I married a shy, pretty girl named Elena, the daughter of my friends Dom and Gemma, and—we found out a few years later—the granddaughter of my old friend Jules. Gemma told Elena the truth in 1920, not long after Dom passed, near the end of the Spanish flu outbreak. Elena said she'd always suspected it, and that her mother told her the world had just become too fragile for such secrets. When Calvin was born a few years later, we gave him Jules for a middle name, although my mother-in-law was adamantly against it. She thought it would bring the boy bad luck.

"It wasn't his real name, anyhow," she said, "and Jules was lost in the world without his real name." Gemma died a few weeks before Calvin was born. As I say, I don't believe in luck, but I do sometimes wonder if she wasn't right about that name.

Elena and I raised our kids on the north side of Spokane. We lived for ten years in a little house that I built in an orchard, then we moved to a bigger house along the river canyon. I worked almost fifty years as a machinist, starting as stock boy for a small shop owned by two brothers. I apprenticed, became a journeyman, and eventually the shop steward for my machinists' local. In '43, the brothers sold their business and I got a job at a government smelter north of town. When the war ended, Henry Kaiser bought our plant and we went from making aluminum for ships and airplanes to making it for Buicks and TV trays. I became a member of the United Steelworkers, and twice was elected grievance officer of my local.

I retired from Kaiser six years ago. Now we live on my pension. Elena and I putter around the garden and wait for our kids to ask us to babysit. We have eight grandchildren, five of them boys and not a decent ballplayer among them. How's that for luck? I can't bowl anymore because of my heart, but on Fridays, I go to Playfair racetrack with my old machinist pal Paul Orlando, and we bet on the last horse to take a piss or the one with the fastest-sounding name. In the afternoons, I read, or rearrange the tools in my garage, or take short walks along the river. I listen to the Dodgers on the radio. I sit on my front porch with the newspaper and a glass of iced tea.

That's what I was doing this afternoon when I opened the *Chronicle* and read that the chairwoman of the Communist Party USA, Elizabeth Gurley Flynn, had died. The story said she kicked around the west as a young labor organizer, was the author of three books and a founding member of the ACLU (along with Helen Keller and Supreme Court Justice Felix Frankfurter). That she became a Communist in '36 and, during World War II, fought for day care services for women workers. That she ran unsuccessfully for Congress and, in '51, was arrested with sixteen other members of the Communist Party and served two years in prison for "advocating the overthrow of the U.S. government." That in the last decade, she fought for civil rights and against McCarthyism, and worked to get her passport restored so she could visit the Soviet Union, where she hoped to write another book. That she was greeted as a hero in Moscow but was diabetic and fell into a coma and died there. That she was seventy-four and had no survivors, her son, Fred, having died in 1940.

And that's it.

A life in two paragraphs.

At my age, you don't cry for the loss of old friends. You make a noise, "Ah," that is an expression of sorrow, but also of contentment that your friend lived a good life. It is, I suppose, the sound, too, of loneliness—here is yet another person I will never see again.

After that come the memories, and these swirl for days afterward.

It is as sharp as a photograph in my mind, the last time I saw her. February 24, 1910. She is climbing in a car. She has just been acquitted of conspiracy. I am following in the crowd but get left behind on the courthouse steps. Then, as she gets into the car, she sees me and gives a half-wave. A half-smile. Then she's gone.

What happened next cemented that day forever in my mind—my brother, Gig, dying with an anarchist spy named Early Reston after their Model T sped away from the courthouse and flew off a cliff into the river gorge.

Their bodies were never recovered, and Gig and Early were never identified as the men who drove off the cliff, but I knew.

An old Pinkerton named Willard, who was working for the mining magnate Lem Brand, dragged me off the riverbank that day. He led me to his car, put me in the passenger seat, and drove me away. "You don't want to talk to the cops about this," he said.

I was wearing the suit I'd bought for Gurley's verdict. It was covered in mud and soot. It took six months to pay for that suit and I never wore it again.

Willard talked gently as he drove me back to the boardinghouse where I lived. They must have had a bomb in the car, he said, the way it exploded like that. Was it possible they had wanted me to deliver a bomb to Lem Brand? Did I know anything about that?

I looked over at him, unable to even comprehend what he was asking.

"No," he said. "Of course not. Do you think your brother got cold feet?"

Then I remembered meeting Gig's eyes right before he started fighting with Early in the car. "I don't think he knew," I said.

Willard parked in front of the house. I was crying again. He lit a cigarette and sat smoking until I stopped.

"Here's what's crazy," he said, "you giving them the money right before all of that."

"But I didn't," I said. I reached in my inside pocket and held out the envelope.

But he wouldn't look at it. "Crazy," he said again. "I'll bet they were fighting over the money. I'll bet that's why they went off the cliff."

Had he not heard me? I held up the envelope again for him to see, but he just kept staring straight ahead, smoking. "No peripheral vision," he said, "remember?"

I barely recall the rest of 1910, except for its darkness, its emptiness. I mourned. I worked at the machine shop. I read Tolstoy and picked through the newspaper. I wondered if the whole world wasn't collapsing. The news was all famine and influenza, murder and war, every day some fresh horror.

The snow that year just kept coming, and on the first of March, a lightning storm caused an avalanche that swept down the Cascades, picked up a Great Northern passenger train, and tossed it like a toy, tumbling cars down a thousand-foot embankment and burying ninety-six people under forty feet of snow. I had been on that run once, carrying Gurley's story to Seattle. Ghostly people on the platforms.

In April, a boy went missing near the river, and when they couldn't find his body, the city decided to dynamite below the falls in Peaceful Valley. They did this every few years to dislodge the tons of construction debris and garbage that collected there, to move it all downstream, and they usually got to clear a few missing persons cases while they were at it.

So, the first Sunday in May, I went downtown to see if my brother was coming up from the riverbed. There was a big crowd, people with picnic baskets and camera tripods, hundreds gathered on the same cliffs where I had watched Gig's car burn. At noon, the explosives went off, a plume of water blasted into the sky, the *boom* came a half-second later, and a great cheer rose as bricks and logs and boards and random bits were vomited to the river surface and flushed downstream.

Later, police identified three bodies in the risen tumult, none of them small enough to be the missing boy and none of them Gig or Early. There was a woman who had apparently committed suicide. And an old drifter who might've just fallen in the river drunk. And finally, there was the bloated, washed-out body of a private detective from Denver named Del Dalveaux, who had gone missing three months earlier, and who the coroner said had died of knife wounds to the chest and throat.

That spring was bone dry, and summer was the hottest on record, and I read in the newspaper about a traveling preacher who portended that the Great Drought of 1910 was the beginning of the end of the world.

It felt like it. Lakes dried up, cattle died, farms went bust, and all summer, trains sparked small brush fires. In August, when the great forests were tinder, a dry typhoon blew down through Canada and fanned a small fire into a conflagration that swept over three states, four mountain ranges, and nine national forests, burning three million acres in two days.

They called it the Devil's Broom, and it killed eighty-seven people and destroyed half of Wallace and parts of forty other towns. Seventy-eight firefighters died, crews giving up fire lines to run for their lives, only to be swallowed by flames. Tens of thousands were evacuated, fleeing in train cars that ran just ahead of the smoke, or waited out the fire in seething railroad tunnels that heated up like woodstoves. Seven towns were burned completely to the ground and lost forever.

On the second day of the blaze, a desperate fire crew retreated into the ragged old work camp of Taft, Montana, where they tried to rally the men in the dark wooden barracks to dig a break and set backfires to save the town. But the men were more interested in draining Taft's booze stores, and as firefighters dug trenches, the residents trudged from saloon to saloon. By the time the last drunk staggered onto the evacuation train, hot embers were raining down on the faded wood buildings. The train wasn't a half mile down the track when the inferno devoured Taft and wiped it from the earth forever.

Not a lot of things that I wish I'd gotten to see in my life, but I'd have paid to see that one.

I don't know when I became convinced that Early Reston was still alive, but over the next year, I began to have nightmares about him. He'd be sitting on Gig's cot or standing outside the house. And every time I read something terrible in the newspapers, I imagined he was out there, setting fires, causing avalanches.

The way his car door had flapped open, I wondered, had I seen a body roll out just before the car went off the cliff? Then, that winter, someone shot big John Sullivan. The old police chief was sitting in his living room, and was shot right through the front window. "This world," Gemma Tursi said at dinner that Sunday. I could do nothing but nod in agreement.

His assassination dominated the news for weeks. The cops rounded up foreign tramps for questioning, and they arrested two labor men, but they let them go. They found a threatening letter from the Black Hand, so they arrested Italians, then they recalled the chief cracking down on the Tongs, so they arrested Chinese. Then a murderer in Seattle confessed, but that same man confessed to shooting President McKinley and being Jack the Ripper. A lawyer was quoted in the *Press* anonymously saying that Sullivan had been killed by a hired assassin because "certain forces" hadn't wanted him testifying before the grand jury investigating police corruption.

Through it all, I couldn't help wondering if it wasn't Early Reston.

One day in 1911, I was working at the machine shop when Willard came in. He wasn't dressed in his usual suit but in a sweater and light jacket. He said he couldn't believe how much older I looked. "Like your brother," he said.

I stepped outside to talk to him. He said he was no longer working for Mr. Brand.

"Why not?" I asked.

"He is—" Willard cleared his throat. "Unwell. He's been under some pressure from the city and divested his holdings here, sold out to various partners. He's going to move east, spend his retirement with his family."

"What will you do?"

"I'm going to British Columbia," he said. "I have a sister up there." He looked around and then leaned in. "Ryan, I was wondering. The money. From that day. I hate to ask, but, well, I'm in kind of a spot and—"

The money. Right. For a year, five thousand dollars had sat in an envelope under my mattress. I hadn't spent a dime of it. Most days I forgot it was there.

"Of course," I said. "You can have it all."

"No!" he said, and his face flushed. "One or two hundred would be fine. Just enough to get me staked up there."

"I don't want it, Willard," I said. "Where that money came from, what happened—I don't want it."

"Listen to me," he said, "it's just money. It's as good or as bad as what you do with it. And whatever you do, Rye, it'll be better than Brand having it."

That night he met me at Mrs. Ricci's house, and after much convincing, he agreed to take five hundred-dollar bills. I took them out of the envelope and handed them over. He folded them, his hands shaking, and put them in his pocket. "You have to promise me you'll do something with the rest of it," he said.

I promised.

He shifted his weight on the porch. "I said that Brand was unwell. He's actually in a sanitarium, babbling like a lunatic. He's convinced Early Reston is still out there and coming for him."

My mouth went dry, and I told him that when Sullivan was killed, I'd had the same thought.

"No," Willard said, "come on. You saw that wreck. Nobody could've survived that." But Willard wouldn't meet my eyes, and I could see even he wasn't entirely convinced.

It was thirteen years later, in 1924, that the police announced they'd finally solved John Sullivan's murder. I was married by then, with three little kids at home. It had been years since I'd even thought of the big police chief.

I gasped when I saw the story in the paper. A woman in Alabama had killed her husband in self-defense, and when the police arrested her, she said that he had been a drifter and outlaw who'd worked out west in the mines and had fallen in with anarchists. He'd told her that he'd killed dozens of people out there, including a police officer somewhere in the west, Spokane or Seattle, she thought.

The man's name was Victor Claude Miller. I stared at his picture. It didn't look like Early Reston. But how could I be sure? By that time, Early wasn't so much a man anyway, but a shadow in my worst dreams.

Not long after Willard left, I sent Mrs. Ricci's son Marco a letter, offering him five hundred dollars for his father's old orchard.

He drove up two days later and we sat at the kitchen table. "You don't have that kind of money," he said.

"I inherited it," I said.

"From who?"

"My uncle Willard." I reached in my pocket and set the five hundred dollars on the table.

He stared at the money. "We'll need a lawyer to draw up papers."

"Oh!" It dawned on me. "I have a lawyer."

Marco looked as shocked by this as he had been by the five hundred dollars.

Two days later, Joe gave me the afternoon off, and I took the streetcar downtown to Mr. Moore's office. He was happy to see me and said he couldn't believe how much older I had gotten in just the year since Gurley's trial.

"How is Elizabeth?" I asked.

"She's fine," he said. "Living in New York with her parents and her sisters, organizing garment workers there, of course."

"And her husband?"

"She told him she wasn't cut out to be a miner's wife." He smiled. "He tried to talk her out of it, but she went back to New York after the trial, filed for divorce, and is raising the baby herself.

"It was a rather bittersweet victory," he said. "She missed seeing the results of it—the anti-speaking ordinance overturned, the police chief fired, the IWW prisoners released, nineteen of the worst employment agencies shut down." He shook his head. "She did all of that. And she wasn't here to see it." But the success in Spokane had inspired other free speech actions, he said, in Fresno and in Los Angeles. He was leaving in two days to consult with the IWW in California.

"And the baby?"

For a moment, Mr. Moore seemed confused. "Oh, yes. A boy. Fred," he added shyly. "She named him Fred." He laughed, and then he wrote something on a slip of paper and handed it to me. It was Gurley Flynn's address.

"I don't have the first idea what I'd write," I said.

"She told me you were the one who got her story out," Mr. Moore said, "that you took it to the *Agitator* in Seattle. I know she was quite moved by that, Ryan. She always believed, as I did, that you were a pawn in the other side's treachery."

I could think of nothing to do but nod.

"How's your brother?" he asked.

My breath left, as it always did when someone asked about Gig. "He's great," I said. "Riding the rails, seeing the world."

Mr. Moore was staring at me. "That's who you look like," he said. "I just realized it. You look like him."

I smiled and cleared my throat. "I don't know if you're still my lawyer," I said, "but I need a couple of things. And I can pay."

I explained about drawing up the paperwork for buying Mrs. Ricci's orchard. Then I put $505 on his desk. "Take your fees out of the five hundred and donate the rest to the IWW's legal fund," I said. "The other five dollars is for my dues. I never paid them."

Mr. Moore just stared at the money. "Where—"

"Inherited it," I said.

My next stop was the Phoenix Hotel. I hadn't seen Ursula since the night I tried to find Gig, and I thought she should at least know what happened to him. A young man at the desk called the hotel manager, Edith, who excused herself to call Ursula. I sat in the lobby waiting.

After a moment, Edith came back. "One thing," she said. "She doesn't go by Ursula anymore. She performs under her real name, Margaret Burns."

"Oh," I said. "She's not doing the cougar show anymore?"

And that's when she came in, as big and lovely as ever, in a blue bustled dress with a feathered hat. "They shut down the variety shows," Ursula said. "Thank God."

"Margaret's doing real theater now," said Edith, "a touring production of George Cohan's *Forty-five Minutes from Broadway*."

"It's a small part," Ursula said.

"It's a star turn!" Edith said.

"Don't listen to her. The producers are merely filling some of the lesser parts with local actors, and I got one of the singing roles."

"Don't listen to *her*," said Edith. "She steals the show."

Ursula put a hand on the other woman's arm. "Edith, can Ryan and I have a moment alone?"

I followed Ursula to Edith's office, and once the door was closed, she gave me the warmest hug, and the smell of her, the press of her bosom, it all made me think of my brother, how much Gig had liked her, and my own boyish fantasies that she and Gig would raise me someday. I fought against crying.

"I'm sorry about what happened to Gig," she said, and before I could ask how she knew, she added, "Willard told me. I was very fond of your brother. I hope you know that. When I heard, I felt responsible. For getting you tangled up with Lem that way. My intentions—" She didn't finish the thought but leaned in, confiding. "I sent an anonymous letter to the police. Nothing came of it, but I had to do something."

I reached in my pocket. I put five hundred dollars on the office desk.

"What's this?" she asked.

"Inheritance," I said.

She looked as if I couldn't be serious.

"Gig would want you to have it," I said.

"Oh, God, no," she said.

"Please," I said.

"Absolutely not." She said that she owned the hotel free and clear now and was doing quite well for herself. I tried several times, but in the end, she was the only one who wouldn't take the money.

She walked me out of the hotel and, on the street, ran a hand across my face, as if memorizing it. She looked at me from both sides. "You look older," she said.

"Like him?"

"Oh, God, no."

I only saw her once more, eight years later, in December 1919. Spokane had become a quiet and conservative place by then. The rushes had ended, timber and mining were in decline. The population had flattened, and temperance and religious forces had succeeded in shutting down the vice in Spokane.

Elena and I had come downtown to see the Christmas windows at the Crescent. Gregory was almost three, Daniel just a baby. Bets and Calvin hadn't been born yet. This was just weeks before Prohibition went into effect, but Spokane had already banned alcohol. I parked in front of Jimmy Durkin's old place, got out, and was reaching in the backseat for little Gregory when I felt a hand touch my shoulder.

It was her, walking with a poodle and a well-dressed older gentleman. "Well, hello there," she said. "It's Margaret Burns."

Before I could say anything, she gestured up at the old Durkin's. It was a dry pool hall and cardhouse now. A sign advertised free coffee and ginger ale.

"Well," she said, "at least Gig didn't live to see *that*." Then she took the dog and the gentleman and strolled off.

"Who was that?" asked Elena.

"That"—I watched her walk down the sidewalk on the gentleman's arm, a fur stole flapping over her shoulder—"was Ursula the Great."

I must've started ten letters to Gurley. But in the end, I never wrote to her. I had only known her a few months, after all, and the more time passed, the less I felt it would make sense, getting a letter from me. Meeting her was like being swept up in a typhoon, then dumped back on the ground. But the storm had long ago passed. My old friend Tolstoy said the closer a man gets to history, the less he seems to have his own free will, the more his life is commanded by the gravity of big events.

I imagine Calvin would've agreed with that as seawater swirled around him. And Gurley, too.

Gurley. How many times as a young man did I roll that name across my tongue. I had never told Elena this, but at one time I believed that I loved her, although that's a strange word for someone like Gurley—love. She seemed too tough for it. Back then, I knew cops and killers, detectives and anarchists, and not one of them had her strength, could have done what she did.

I watch the TV news now and I see the Freedom Riders and Martin Luther King Jr., people protesting at lunch counters and on buses. She would be right alongside them, alone and pregnant, nineteen, and not a doubt in her mind that goodness would eventually prevail.

I wish I could be so sure.

There was always a part of me that felt she was too bold, asking too much, going too far. I was a strong union man my whole life, but I could never go that fast, like she did, like Gig did. I sometimes felt guilty, living my quiet life, paying my union dues and getting small rewards, while true believers like Gurley fought with their lives.

The labor wars continued throughout the teens. In 1916 three hundred Wobblies boarded steamers in Seattle to go support a strike in Everett, but when they got there, two hundred armed men were waiting, and for ten minutes they unloaded on the steamers, 175 bullets tearing into the pilothouse alone. Most of the men on board were unarmed, but a few returned fire, including a private detective who had been planted as a spy inside the union. One steamer nearly capsized from the men running from gunfire, and when it was over, five Wobblies were dead on the ship, and more in the water, their bodies never recovered. Almost thirty were wounded. Two deputized citizens were killed, although it was determined later that they'd been shot in the back by vigilantes on their own side. Twenty citizens were wounded, including the sheriff.

The next year, Gig's old friend Frank Little was organizing for the IWW near Butte when six men broke into his boardinghouse, beat him, tied him to a car, and pulled him down the street, over granite blocks that tore off his kneecaps. They bashed in his head and hung him from a railroad bridge at the end of town. Pinned to his torn pants was a note that read, "First and last warning," with the initials of other union leaders.

What do you make of such times? I feel a similar sense of despair now, watching those southern sheriffs turn firehoses and dogs loose on civil rights protestors. I find myself looking up from the newspaper and saying to Elena, "The world is tearing itself apart."

My wife has her mother's quiet wisdom, her grandfather's great laugh. "Always," she says to me.

By 1917, the IWW had been run completely out of Spokane, and when the union objected to the U.S. entering World War I, the government cracked down, raiding union offices, charging leaders with sedition, and deporting thousands. In those years, I could no more admit being an old Wobbly than I could admit being a German spy.

So I never talked to my kids about the IWW, about the riots, about jail, about any of it. I didn't think it would make sense to them. It would have been like talking about the gold rush or the Civil War.

My oldest son, Greg, is a partner in his father-in-law's car dealership. He tells me he's going to vote for Barry Goldwater for president. He gave me Goldwater's book, *The Conscience of a Conservative*, for Christmas. Last year, he gave me *Atlas Shrugged*. He likes to lecture me about the dangers of unions and the spread of communism.

Elena reminds him that without his dad's union job, he wouldn't have had a roof over his head, but he's one of those men of fragile confidence who needs to always believe that he's made his own way in the world.

Now, as I sit with Elizabeth Gurley Flynn's obituary in my lap, I think I'll tell him all about my past, about his anarchist uncle, about how his father once fancied a girl who grew up to be president of the Communist Party. I don't have any hope of changing Greg's opinion. I just want to see the look on his face. It's another mystery of parenting: how you can love your kids without always liking them.

Maybe it's being close to the end, but I have this desire to pull Greg aside—to pull all my children aside, and my grandchildren—and to whisper something profound, to pass on the great wisdom I've acquired. Something that would open their hearts and create in them an unassailable courage, a generosity of spirit, faith in humanity.

But the only thing I can think of is *Time and patience*.

And *Bet on the last horse to piss*.

I remember something Gurley told me, the night we sat up in the Missoula train station. We had been robbed and nearly killed in Taft. We were as beaten as people could be. And here she was, gearing up to start the fight all over once we got back to Spokane.

"How do you do it?" I asked her. "How do you keep getting up every day and fighting when winning seems impossible?"

She thought about it, and then she said, "Men sometimes say to me: *You might win the battle, Gurley, but you'll never win the war.* But no one wins the war, Ryan. Not really. I mean, we're all going to die, right?

"But to win a battle now and then? What more could you want?"

That day in 1911, after I went to see Fred Moore and Ursula, I decided to keep another five hundred dollars for myself, to use on the house I was going to build. That still left almost three thousand dollars of Lem Brand's money.

I thought about walking into Bradley & Graham's, slapping it on the counter, and saying, "Dress me, Chester!" The thought of it made me laugh.

Instead, I went to a shop that made headstones and memorials. I asked whether a person could get one if there was no body, no grave.

"Of course," the man said. So I picked the simplest one, granite, flush with the earth. It cost forty dollars engraved. Later, I put it in a corner of the orchard in Little Italy. It read: "Gregory T. Dolan, 1886–1910, loving brother and member in good standing of the IWW."

After I picked out the headstone, I walked through the east end of downtown. There were a few floaters out, a man begging, a handful of people outside the Salvation Army, where the regular brass band was playing in the street, including an old toothless man blowing a French horn that looked like it had been in a hailstorm. The army used volunteers for its band, but every once in a while, they'd employ a tramp with musical ability, and that's what the toothless French horn player looked like.

We always made fun of it, called it the Starvation Army. But I thought of how many meals, how many pairs of shoes and shirts, I had gotten there, and it felt right, walking up and sliding almost three thousand dollars into the bucket next to the French horn player's dirty shoe.

He took his lips from the mouthpiece. "God bless."

"You, too," I said.

ACKNOWLEDGMENTS

As Albert Camus once said, "Fiction is the lie through which we tell the truth." And as Jessamyn West said, "Fiction reveals the truth that reality obscures." And as my kids said, "Dad, that sounds made up."

Kids, this is made up. *The Cold Millions* is fiction.

But that doesn't mean there aren't some obscured truths in here, a few relevant philosophical questions rattling around these pages, as well as some "real" historical figures—among them the great labor organizer Elizabeth Gurley Flynn, Spokane police officer Alfred Waterbury, the police chief John Sullivan, IWW organizers John Walsh and Frank Little, the labor lawyer Fred Moore, and others.

In setting a fictionalized story among real historical figures and events, I have endeavored to trace a basic chronology and outline of what happened. Much of what the real people do and say in the book came directly from books or newspaper accounts of the time. What happens to the historical figures in the novel is *generally* what happened to them in life.

The free speech riots of 1909 and 1910 really did occur in Spokane, and five hundred transient workers, socialists, and unionists were jailed, often under brutal conditions. At least three prisoners died upon their release. Police officers were killed before and after—and their killings went unsolved for years. The history involving the tribes, the horse slaughter camp and the hangings at Latah Creek are true, horrific events. Elizabeth Gurley Flynn's campaign to raise money, her arrest, her exposing jail corruption, her trial (in fact, she had two trials, which I have condensed into one)—these all occurred.

But this is a work of fiction. Dates and events have been altered, names have been changed, motives and actions invented. I urge readers to treat even the historical figures as fictional characters. A fictional Gurley Flynn and a fictional John Sullivan set in a fictional Spokane, all seen through a fictional lens.

For those who want to learn more, there are some great books about these people and their time that were useful in my research:

The Rebel Girl: An Autobiography (My First Life 1906–1926) by Elizabeth Gurley Flynn (International Publishers, 1955) and *Elizabeth Gurley Flynn: Modern American Revolutionary* by Lara Vapnak in the Lives of American Women series, edited by Carol Berkin (Westview Press, 2015).

Rebel Voices: An IWW Anthology edited by Joyce L. Kornbluh (CH Kerr Publishing, 1955); *Solidarity Forever: An Oral History of the IWW* by Stewart Bird, Deborah Shaffer, and Dan Georgakas (Lakeview, 1985); *The Wobblies: The Story of the IWW and Syndicalism in the United States* by Patrick Renshaw (Ivan R. Dee Publishing, 1967).

The Big Burn: Teddy Roosevelt and the Fire That Saved America by Timothy Egan (Houghton Mifflin Harcourt, 2009); *Big Trouble* by J. Anthony Lukas (Touchstone Books, 1997); *Joe Hill* by Wallace Stegner (Doubleday Books, 1950); *Bad Land: An American Romance* by Jonathan Raban (Vintage Books, 1996); *Pinkerton's Great Detective: The Amazing Life and Times of James McParland* by Beau Riffenburgh (Viking, 2013); *The Lost Detective: Becoming Dashiell Hammett* by Nathan Ward (Bloomsbury, 2015).

Showtown: Theater and Culture in the Pacific Northwest, 1890–1920 by Holly George (University of Oklahoma Press, 2017); *Selling Sex in the Silver Valley* by Dr. Heather Branstetter (History Press, 2017); *Alice: Memoirs of a Barbary Coast Prostitute*, author unknown, edited by Ivy Anderson and Devon Angus (Heyday Publishing, California Historical Society, 2015).

The terrific Inland Northwest and natural histories of Jack Nisbet, most recently *Ancient Places: People and Landscape in the Emerging Northwest* (Sasquatch Books, 2015); the pictorial history books of

Tony and Suzanne Bamonte, most notably *Spokane: Our Early History* (Tornado Creek Publications, 2012) and *Life Behind the Badge Vol II* (Walsworth Publishing, 2010); *African Americans in Spokane* by Jerrelene Williamson (Arcadia Publishing, 2010); *Vanishing Seattle* by Clark Humphrey (Arcadia Publishing, 2006); *People of the Falls* by David H. Chance (Kettle Falls Historical Center, 1986); and *The Spokane Dictionary*, compiled by Barry F. Carlson and Pauline Flett (Alex Sherwood/Mary Owhi Moses Memorial Trust, 1989).

I'd like to give special thanks to the Salish School of Spokane, the dynamic immersion school committed to preserving and revitalizing the language of the Spokanes and other Inland Northwest tribes by teaching children and adults of all ages. Thanks to Christopher Parkin and LaRae Wiley for help with an especially delicate translation (and a great suggestion for a character's line). Please visit www.salishschoolofspokane.org for information about supporting their work.

Thanks also to Spokane writer and historian Jim Kershner, and to Eastern Washington University professor of history and author Bill Youngs, both of whom should be absolved of blame for any Apple watches or cell phones that appear in this novel. The great Spokane newsman Bill Morlin, either anticipating the research I would need, or just to remind me that he's always two steps ahead, independently wrote pieces about the history of Taft, Montana, for the *New York Times* and the *Spokesman-Review* that I highly recommend.

Much of my research involved hours in the stacks and in front of microfilm at the Spokane Public Library, reading newspapers from that time, including the *Spokesman-Review*, the *Spokane Chronicle*, the *Spokane Press*, and the *Industrial Worker* (and longing for a time when newspapers flourished that way). As stacks are being consolidated and digitized, I want to especially thank the staff in the Ned M. Barnes Northwest Room at the Spokane Public Library for letting me wander. There's nothing like the shelves of an actual physical library when you're unsure of what it is you're seeking. It was in the Northwest Room that I was steered toward a terrific resource,

Jonathan David Knight's 1991 Masters in History Thesis from Washington State University, *The Spokane and Fresno Free-Speech Fights of the Industrial Workers of the World (1909–1911)*. A big thank-you to Mr. Knight.

Thanks to a few writer friends who read pages along the way and made suggestions, among them: Anthony Doerr, Shawn Vestal, Sherman Alexie, Anne Walter, Jim Lynch, Sam Ligon, and Katy Sewall. A special thanks to Katy for her continued help with research, organization, and encouragement.

A great thanks to my editor, Jennifer Barth, for her calm, smart, steady hand, and for pushing me to make the book better, and to my agent Warren Frazier, for his friendship and counsel, and to everyone at Harper and John Hawkins and Associates.

The roots of this novel go back to my grandfather Jess Walter, and his stories of hopping trains as a young man to find itinerant work around the west. And to my father, Bruce, a lifelong union man who passed on his steadfast belief in fairness to my sister, Kristie, my brother, Ralph, and me. And finally, I want to give the biggest *thank-you* to my kids, Alec, Ava, and Brooklyn, and to my wife, Anne, for the profound love, support, and inspiration.

He just wanted a decent book to read ...

Not too much to ask, is it? It was in 1935 when Allen Lane, Managing Director of Bodley Head Publishers, stood on a platform at Exeter railway station looking for something good to read on his journey back to London. His choice was limited to popular magazines and poor-quality paperbacks – the same choice faced every day by the vast majority of readers, few of whom could afford hardbacks. Lane's disappointment and subsequent anger at the range of books generally available led him to found a company – and change the world.

'We believed in the existence in this country of a vast reading public for intelligent books at a low price, and staked everything on it'
Sir Allen Lane, 1902–1970, founder of Penguin Books

The quality paperback had arrived – and not just in bookshops. Lane was adamant that his Penguins should appear in chain stores and tobacconists, and should cost no more than a packet of cigarettes.

Reading habits (and cigarette prices) have changed since 1935, but Penguin still believes in publishing the best books for everybody to enjoy. We still believe that good design costs no more than bad design, and we still believe that quality books published passionately and responsibly make the world a better place.

So wherever you see the little bird – whether it's on a piece of prize-winning literary fiction or a celebrity autobiography, political tour de force or historical masterpiece, a serial-killer thriller, reference book, world classic or a piece of pure escapism – you can bet that it represents the very best that the genre has to offer.

Whatever you like to read – trust Penguin.

read more
www.penguin.co.uk